"I'm not heartless," he informed her.

"I just don't allow emotions to get in the way, and I don't believe in using more words than are absolutely necessary," he added pointedly since he knew that seemed to bother her.

"Well, lucky for you, I do," she told him with what amounted to the beginning of a smile. "I guess that's what'll make us such good partners."

He looked at her, stunned. He viewed them as being like oil and water—never being able to mix. "Is *that* your take on this?" he asked incredulously.

"Yes," she answered cheerfully.

The fact that she appeared to have what one of his brothers would have labeled a killer smile notwithstanding, Ronan just shook his head. "Unbelievable."

"Oh, you'll get to believe it soon enough," she told him.

CAVANAUGH STANDOFF

BY

MARIE FERRARELLA

First Published in Great Britain 2017
By Mills & Boon, an imprint of HarperCollins*Publishers*
1 London Bridge Street, London, SE1 9GF

ISBN: 978-0-263-92891-4

46-0617

Our policy is to use papers that are natural, renewable and recyclable products and made from wood grown in sustainable forests. The logging and manufacturing processes conform to the legal environmental regulations of the country of origin.

Printed and bound in Spain
by CPI, Barcelona

USA TODAY bestselling and RITA® Award-winning author **Marie Ferrarella** has written more than two hundred and fifty books for Mills & Boon, some under the name Marie Nicole. Her romances are beloved by fans worldwide. Visit her website, www.marieferrarella.com.

To
Adelynn Marie Melgar
Welcome to the World
Little One

Prologue

The first kill had been easy.

All it had taken was a sense of detachment—and that had been there, hovering like a dark specter, growing closer and closer for the last two years.

Detachment had been the only way to survive ever since it had happened.

"It." The event that had turned the world completely upside down, draining everyday life of all happiness, of what made life worthwhile. The event that had left nothing but a pile of ashes in its wake.

Placing the gun barrel up against that worthless scum's head and then firing, had brought with it an unexpected, tremendous release of pent-up anger.

And just as unexpectedly, it had caused a sense of purpose to return to the emptiness loosely termed as "life."

The first kill had originated from a chance encounter. After that, a plan had been born. A plan that had required a great deal of careful research, coordination and, above all, meticulous timing. But every risk, every dangerous moment, was ultimately *so* worth it.

And now? Now, finally, the end of the road was within sight.

Five bodies down, four to go. This would take more planning because they were on their guard now. But it didn't matter.

However long it took, they were going to die.

Every single one of them!

The target had already been chosen, his day-to-day movements committed to memory. Just like the others.

If a conscience had been involved, it had long since been numbed into nonexistence.

Four more to go.

The words hummed like an enticing siren song. Four more people to kill and the score would finally be even.

Four more and then maybe, just maybe, life could begin to get back to normal.

And if not—and there was a big possibility that it wouldn't—well, those evil, cold-blooded bastards all had it coming. Their deaths would be no loss to the world because they all dealt in death as if it was of no great consequence. With all of them wiped from the face of the earth, maybe someone else would go on living rather than have their life snuffed out as if they didn't matter.

Maybe the self-righteous defenders of the public safety would even see it as a public service. Because that was what it was.

A public service.

A public that would be a little safer once those people were all dead.

And maybe, just maybe, sleep would finally return, bringing with it some measure of peace.

Peace, after two years.

Finally.

At least, there was a sliver of hope that it would. Something that had been missing all these many long months.

Chapter One

"Heads up, O'Bannon, your serial killer's body count just went up by one."

The declaration came from the Homicide Department's lieutenant, Jacob Carver, as he came out of his office and walked toward the lead detective assigned to the unusual case.

A twenty-three-year-old veteran of the Aurora Police Department, the lieutenant had a Countdown-to-Retirement calendar prominently displayed on his wall. It was the first thing anyone saw entering his office. The second thing they noticed was the pile of travel brochures amassed on his desk, a pile that seemed to increase weekly.

But any hope the lieutenant had of having the time until his retirement go by quietly had evaporated with the advent of multiple murders—executions, actually—that pointed to a serial killer having invading the northern perimeter of their normally peaceful city.

Ronan Cavanaugh O'Bannon frowned. "Are they sure the body is courtesy of our serial killer?" he asked.

If it was the work of the serial killer who was selectively eliminating members of not just one gang but two, that brought the body count up to a frustrating five. Maybe this time the killer had gotten sloppy and left behind something that could be construed as a clue.

"One bullet to the back of the head, execution style, and,

according to the first officer on the scene, the guy's right hand was cut off," Carver recited.

"Yup, sounds like our boy," Detective Sebastian Choi, also assigned to the case, agreed. He shuddered. "Lot of anger there."

"So you still like the theory you came up with?" Carver asked, sounding rather skeptical. He looked from Choi to O'Bannon, to Nick Martinez, Choi's partner and also assigned to the case. "That it's just gang retaliation, with one gang attacking another to even the score?"

"It could still be that," Ronan allowed, the note of certainty missing from his low, deep voice. His frown deepened. "But according to the ME reports on the other four victims, all the killings were done exactly the same way. That points to one killer, not a mixed bag of executioners, the way we first thought."

Carver's gaze was unwavering as he looked at his lead detective. "Is that your gut talking?"

It was hard to miss the sarcasm but Ronan wasn't the type to be intimidated. He was long past something like that. "It's a family thing," was all he said.

The lieutenant sighed, clearly impatient. Everyone knew what it looked like to retire with something of this magnitude left unsolved on his record. It was tantamount to a black mark. He needed this solved. Yesterday. "And that's as far as you've gotten in the investigation?"

"Rome wasn't built in a day, Loo," Ronan replied quietly.

"No," Carver agreed. "But it was demolished and fell apart pretty quickly."

"What's the big deal?" John Deeks, one of the squad room detectives who was eavesdropping, asked. "I mean, as long as these so-called gang members are only doing away with one another, that means there's less of them to turn on the decent residents of their own cities, much less Aurora. Everyone remembers that drive-by shoot-out just within the city limits two years ago. Maybe this'll teach them to keep away."

Ronan turned his chair in Deeks' direction. "Our job is to catch killers regardless of who they kill," he informed the detective coldly.

"Yeah, they don't pay us enough to pass judgment on the lifestyle and character of the victim," Choi spoke up, joining in.

Deeks raised and then dropped his wide, sloping shoulders, retreating. "I'm just saying…"

Ronan leveled a steely gaze at the other man. "Everyone knows exactly what you're saying."

"Hey, back to your corners, everybody," Carver ordered sharply. "I want to see this kind of energy out in the field, not here." He turned his attention to Ronan and got down to the other reason he'd come out of his office rather than summon the detective in to see him. "Since the body count is up to five, I'm thinking maybe you need a little extra help."

Ronan's expression darkened just a shade. He had Choi and Martinez working with him. He didn't want any "extra" help. Nor did he like what was being inferred. That he couldn't do the job.

"We'll get him," he told Carver with the sort of finality that was known to end discussions.

Another man might have backed off, but dark looks and growled responses had no effect on Carver. In general, that was his domain. "I know you will."

Whether that was meant to be patronizing or it was actually an honest statement was anyone's guess, Ronan thought. But an inner voice told him to brace himself.

He watched as Carver turned, glanced over his shoulder to the far end of the squad room and then beckoned. "Carlyle, mind coming over here?" It was not a question but a civilly worded command.

Having been forewarned a few minutes earlier by Carver as to what the lieutenant proposed to have happen, Detective Sierra Carlyle was on her feet as soon as he uttered her name.

Aware that more than one set of eyes was on her, she wove

her way between the desks that littered the squad room until she reached Carver.

Although she didn't make eye contact with Ronan, she was instinctively aware of the fact that he appeared to be glaring at her. Well, she thought, this hadn't been her choice, but now that it had been made, she intended to go along with it to the best of her ability. Her job was to follow a superior's orders whenever possible, not to buck them.

With an acknowledging nod in her direction, Carver turned back to the man he'd selected to head the current investigation.

"Okay, O'Bannon," Carver announced, "as of right now, consider Detective Carlyle part of your team."

Ronan did *not* look pleased. "I don't get a say in this?" he asked, his voice all but rumbling from deep within the caverns of his chest.

"Sure you do," Carver loftily answered the younger man. "You get to say yes." The lieutenant glanced around at the team, now increased by one. "You take that empty desk," he told Sierra, pointing to the one butted up against O'Bannon's. "Any other questions?" When no one said anything in response, Carver nodded, satisfied. "Didn't think so."

Placing the piece of notepaper he was holding with the current crime scene's address on Ronan's desk, he stepped back.

"All right, that's the location of your newest dead body," he told Ronan. "A drunk patron of the Shamrock Inn tripped over the body while apparently trying to duck out the back way to avoid paying his tab." Carver laughed under his breath. "Seeing that body lying there was definitely enough to scare him sober," he commented. He spared one last glance at the now team of four. "Okay. Do me proud. Solve this damn thing before it gets completely out of hand."

"You ask me, it's already out of hand," Choi murmured under his breath the moment the lieutenant left the scene. Turning his attention to the detective who had just been added to their team, the father of three smiled broadly at her. "You can ride with me to the crime scene."

Nick Martinez instantly came to attention. He moved in to flank Sierra's other side. "If you want to arrive there in one piece, Carlyle, you can ride with me," he offered.

Choi appeared annoyed at the inference. "Hey, what's wrong with the way I drive?"

Martinez gave the other man a look that quipped, "Really?" Out loud he said, "Can't go into it now. It would take too long and we've got to get to the crime scene."

Ronan turned from his desk, his dark green eyes washing over the two men he'd been working with for a couple of months now. And then he looked at the woman Carver had added to the mix without so much as a warning—as if the situation wasn't already difficult enough.

"You're coming with me before these two jokers decide to play tug-of-war with you." There wasn't a hint of humor in his voice as he made the pronouncement.

The last thing Sierra wanted to do was appear to take sides in what she perceived to be some sort of unspoken power struggle.

"If you give me the address," she told Ronan, who had already slipped the paper Carver had given him into his pocket, "I can drive there myself."

"Good to know," Ronan answered drily, making no move to take the paper out of his pocket and show her the address.

O'Bannon had just given her what amounted to a non-answer in her book. And now he was walking out of the squad room. Biting back a comment, she forced herself to hurry to keep up. Martinez and Choi were right behind her.

"So do you want me to drive myself over to the scene of the crime or not?" Sierra asked.

"Not," Ronan answered, pressing for the elevator.

The elevator arrived the second he took his index finger off the down button. Ronan walked into the empty car and was quickly followed by the other three members of his team.

"Not very talkative, are you?" Sierra said, moving so that she was standing right next to him.

"Pet rocks have been known to talk more than O'Bannon does," Choi told her. Both he and Martinez were behind her and the lead detective.

Not to be left out, Martinez assured her, "You'll get used to it."

Sierra slanted a look at the man to her right. He seemed oblivious to the conversation around him, although she couldn't see how he didn't hear them.

"I really doubt it," she answered Martinez with sincerity.

The elevator doors parted on the first floor. Ronan spared her a glance just before he got off. He had one word for her.

"Try."

And then he took off again, making her hurry if she wanted to keep up. At about a foot taller than she was, O'Bannon's stride was a good deal wider than hers.

"Or," she suggested, determined to keep pace, "you could try using sentences containing more than just one word."

Ronan made no attempt to answer her. He continued walking toward the rear exit and then made his way through the parking lot until he came to where he had parked his vehicle. Only after he released the door locks did he turn toward the other two detectives who'd kept pace with him. He told them the address he'd been given by Carver.

"Got it," Martinez said, nodding. It was a given that he was driving the other car. "We'll be right behind you."

It was unclear, at least to Sierra, whether the other detective had said that to O'Bannon or to her in an effort to let her know she wouldn't be alone with their wooden leader.

Getting into the passenger side of O'Bannon's car, Sierra buckled up. The second she secured her seat belt, O'Bannon took off.

Doing her best to relax, Sierra waited for him to say something.

But after they had gone two city blocks in complete silence, she realized that this was the way it was going to be, at least until they reached the scene of the murder. While she didn't expect the detective to engage in rambling chatter, this "silent treatment" or whatever it was, was totally unacceptable to her.

"You know, it is all right to talk," she told him, trying to sound cheerful. Unable to "get in his face," she leaned forward and did the best she could by peering at his profile.

Aware that she had assumed a very unusual position, Ronan waited until he had driven through the intersection before he finally responded to her statement.

"Why?"

"Because," she began patiently, "that's what people do, especially when they're thrown together in a situation that was not of their own choosing—like now," she stressed. "They talk."

Accelerating just a little, Ronan drove through the next intersection a shade before the light turned yellow. "I don't."

"Maybe you should," she countered. She saw him turn his head slightly, as if to look at her, and then apparently he changed his mind. She began to feel as if she was dealing with a robot. Nevertheless, Sierra pushed on. "I'm sure you have something to say," she told him, knowing she was setting herself up, but it was better than this feeling of being in exile.

"I'm thinking," he informed her.

"Think out loud," she suggested.

He obviously hadn't expected that. "What?"

"Think out loud," she repeated. "I know you're not thrilled with this but, for better or worse, Carver made us partners for this case and partners use each other for sounding boards. That only works if they talk out loud because, despite what my brothers seem to think, I am not a mind reader." She took a breath and waited. When Ronan still made no response, she told him a bit more forcefully, "So talk to me."

Rather than comment on the case they were undertaking, Ronan contradicted what she'd said earlier. "We're not partners."

Caught off guard, she looked at him in surprise. "What?"

"You said Carver made us partners," he said. "He didn't. He put you on my team. There's a difference," he informed her.

Smiling, she said, "Now, was that so hard?"

Because she wasn't responding to what he'd just told her, Ronan was momentarily confused. "What?"

Sierra spelled it out for him. "Talking. You talked in a full sentence. Several of them, actually. So my point is—was that so hard?"

He didn't answer her question. Instead, Ronan announced, "We're here," as he brought his vehicle to a stop at the curb, parking it several lengths in front of a club named the Shamrock Inn.

The tavern had originally been considered to be in Tesla, the city neighboring Aurora. But somewhere along the line, someone had redrawn Aurora's boundaries, placing the establishment partially over the city limits, leaving it in both jurisdictions.

A cartoon leprechaun was whimsically winking on the sign proclaiming the tavern's name just above the door. What might have once been regarded mildly amusing in the dark of night now just looked sad in the light of day, Sierra thought, walking up to the squat building.

She expected Ronan to go in through the front door but he didn't. Wordlessly, he circled the small tavern with its peeling paint and walked toward the alley behind the Shamrock Inn.

Suppressing a sigh, Sierra stepped up her pace again and quickly followed him.

Once in the alley, she saw that the Crime Scene Investigative Unit had reached the area ahead of them. Three investigators, including the head of the unit, Sean Cavanaugh, Ronan's uncle, were spread out documenting the crime scene. The medical examiner was also there, his attention strictly focused on the victim lying facedown in the alley.

Sean looked up the moment he heard the detectives arrive in the alley. A tall, distinguished-looking man with a genial way about him, he waited until his nephew reached him before saying anything.

"Looks like your killer got another one," he said grimly.

Ronan nodded as he assessed the lifeless victim. Like the others, the man had a single gunshot to the back of the head. Blood partially covered the tattoo at the nape of his neck. And, like the other victims, one of the man's hands had been completely—and cleanly—hacked off.

Ronan looked at his uncle. "How long has he been dead?"

Sean pointed to the back of the tavern where a thin man of about forty or so was leaning against the wall, looking as if he was about to collapse at any moment. The first responding officer on the scene was next to him.

"That white-as-a-sheet-looking patron tripped over our victim at around two in the morning—right around closing time—so the victim's been dead for at least that long. My guess is that he most likely departed this earth an hour before that."

"The victim's hand was cut off," Sierra noted, struggling to separate herself from the horror of the scene. She saw that the appendage had been thrown haphazardly near the Dumpster and looked quizzically at CSI unit leader. "But the killer didn't take it." The act made no sense to her. Why cut off a hand and then just leave it? She would have thought the killer would have wanted it as a souvenir of his crime.

"He never does," Sean told her. Looking at Ronan, he said, "You've got a new member," and then smiled at Sierra. "Welcome to the party—such as it is," he added. "A fresh pair of eyes might see something we don't."

"Yeah." Ronan exhaled the word with a touch of impatience. He didn't notice Sierra making her way to the police officer, nor did he notice her talking to him. He was focused on the victim. Moving in, he squatted down for a closer view of the man. The victim was dressed in what appeared to be designer jeans, undoubtedly boosted from some venue, Ronan guessed, and an ordinary T-shirt, now blood-stained. Like his neck, the back of the dead man's arms had several tattoos, but nothing that struck Ronan as outstanding.

"Another gang member?" he asked his uncle.

"Looks that way," Sean replied cautiously. "Working theory is still that this is a retaliation for the last killing."

Martinez and Choi stood on either side of the body, bracketing the three people already there.

"But Fearless Leader's gut says it isn't, right, Fearless Leader?" Martinez asked, looking at Ronan. The latter returned a laser-like expression that effectively wiped the wide smile from Martinez's face. "Sorry," he murmured, backing off.

"How soon can you get an autopsy done on this one?" Ronan asked.

That was an easy question to answer. "As soon as we get the body back to the morgue. It's not like there're bodies piling up, waiting for the ME to work on them," he added, looking at the medical examiner who was methodically working on the body, preparing it for transport. "Technically, if the killer had waited until Mr. Walker here had done his drinking in his own city, this wouldn't even be our call, but because the Shamrock Inn is partially located just inside our city limits, that makes the homicide ours."

"How do you know his name?" Ronan asked.

"Victim was nice enough to have his wallet on him," Sean answered. "And apparently his killer wanted us to know who his latest victim was, so he left it untouched."

"Just like the others," Choi commented.

Joining the rest of the team, Sierra looked at the gregarious detective. "What do you mean?"

Sean supplied the answer. "None of the other victims lived in Aurora, either."

"Come to Aurora and die," Ronan murmured grimly under his breath as he continued looking at the dead man on the ground.

Chapter Two

"I don't think that'll catch on as a slogan," Sierra commented, overhearing what Ronan had just said to himself.

Ronan glanced up at her as if she had suddenly started babbling nonsense. "*What* won't catch on?"

"You just said 'Come to Aurora and die' and—" Sierra waved her hand at him. She might as well save her breath. "Never mind."

One look at Ronan's impassive expression and she knew that she could talk herself blue in the face and he still wouldn't really understand what she was saying, or why. More importantly, he wouldn't crack a smile. The man was in serious need of a sense of humor, she thought. She firmly believed that, at times, a sense of humor was the only thing that could see a person through the harder times.

Working with O'Bannon was definitely going to be a challenge, she decided. But then, she wasn't being paid to have a good time, Sierra stoically reminded herself. Her job was to keep the residents who lived in Aurora safe any way she could. And right now, working with O'Bannon and his team was the best way she could do that.

Squaring her shoulders, Sierra looked at the lead detective. "All right, what would you like me to do?" she asked since Ronan had gone back to intently studying the victim. When he raised his eyes to look at her, she instinctively knew what Ronan was about to say and voiced it before he could. "Besides going back to the squad room."

Rising to his feet, Ronan addressed the other two detectives who were first on the scene. "You two see what you can find out from the guy with the sickly green complexion—" he nodded toward the man still leaning against the wall "—and also find out who was tending bar last night. Maybe the bartender noticed if our victim was hanging out with someone. It would be nice if we could finally come up with a real witness who saw something we can use."

Determined not to be ignored, Sierra spoke up. "You think the victim was in the bar before he was killed?"

Forced to acknowledge her, Ronan said, "It's a safe bet."

Choi leaned in over the body and took a deep breath. His expression became slightly pained. "Oh, yeah, he still smells like he was soaked in alcohol."

"That could be because the guy who found him threw up when he realized what he'd just tripped over," Sierra pointed out. "And according to the statement that guy gave the officer on the scene," she said, "he'd been in the Shamrock drinking for hours. I just talked to the officer," she added before any of the detectives could ask her how she had found that piece of information out.

Making no comment, Ronan looked at Choi and Martinez. "When you're done, come back to the station."

"Okay," Choi readily agreed. "Is that where you're going to be?"

In response, Ronan first turned toward his uncle. "Let me take a look at that wallet you found," he requested.

Sean handed the plastic-encased wallet to him. It had been placed inside the envelope with its two sides spread open so that the driver's license was visible. Ronan read the address, then handed the secured evidence back to his uncle.

"I'm going to Walker's apartment to see if he lived with anyone who might be able to shed some light on the situation, tell us if Walker was targeted recently by anyone."

"You mean like a note from his friendly neighborhood serial killer saying, 'you're next'?" Sierra asked with a touch of sarcasm.

Ronan shot her an annoyed look. "You think this is a joke?"

"Not at all, but at least I got you to talk to me."

Ronan was already turning away. Sierra began to talk more quickly. "I guess since you didn't give me a separate assignment, you want me to go with you."

He had to admit that her persistence reminded him of his sisters, but he gave no outward indication as he asked, "And what makes you think that?"

"Simple process of elimination," Sierra responded without any hesitation.

He knew he had to utilize her somehow and maybe she could to be useful. "All right, you might as well come along. You might come in handy if there's a next of kin to notify." Ronan began walking back to his car. "I'm not much good at that."

"I'm surprised," Sierra commented.

Reaching the car, Ronan turned to look at her. "If you're going to be sarcastic—"

"No, I'm serious," she told him then went on to explain her rationale. "You're so detached, I just assumed it wouldn't bother you telling a person that someone they'd expected to come home was never going to do that again. It would bother them, of course," she couldn't help adding, "but not you."

Ronan got into his vehicle, buckled up and pulled out in what seemed like one fluid motion, all the while chewing on what this latest addition to his team had just said. Part of him just wanted to let it go. But he couldn't.

"I'm not heartless," he informed her. "I just don't allow emotions to get in the way and I don't believe in using more words than are absolutely necessary," he added pointedly since he knew that seemed to bother her.

"Well, lucky for you, I do," she told him with what

amounted to the beginnings of a smile. "I guess that's what'll make us such good partners."

He looked at her, stunned. He viewed them as being like oil and water—never being able to mix. "Is *that* your take on this?" he asked incredulously.

"Yes," she answered cheerfully.

The fact that she appeared to have what one of his brothers would label a "killer smile" notwithstanding, Ronan just shook his head. "Unbelievable."

"Oh, you'll get to believe it soon enough," she told him. Before he could say anything, Sierra just continued talking to him and got down to the immediate business at hand. "I'm going to need to see your files on the other murders once we're back in the squad room so I can be brought up to date."

He didn't even spare her a look. "Fine."

"Are you always this cheerful?" she asked, "or is there something in particular that's bothering you?"

This time Ronan did slant a quick glance in her direction. The woman sounded as if she was actually asking that, not just being nosy. He'd grown up in a family with talkative sisters and there was a time when the noise of constant chatter hadn't bothered him. But that had been before life had taken the drastic, horrible turn that it had, changing all the ground rules on him.

Forever changing his life.

These days he preferred work and quiet, but for now, it looked like one of those ingredients would be seriously missing from the equation.

Moreover, he had the distinct feeling that if he mentioned to Carlyle that she was talking too much, she'd only get worse despite any so-called "efforts" to rein herself in. So, for now, he fell back on a plausible, albeit vague, excuse.

"I don't like serial killers," he said between clenched teeth.

That wasn't it and she knew it. Her guess was that O'Bannon didn't like being saddled with her, but he was just going to have to make the best of it. She intended to make him glad she was on his team rather than viewing it as some sort of cross he had to bear.

"I don't think anyone does," she said conversationally. "Anyone normal, anyway," she added just before she flashed him another thousand-watt smile. "Lucky thing for you, you're in the business of getting rid of them."

He spared her a look that defied reading, so she put her best guess to it. He was probably labeling her a Pollyanna in his mind, but there was really more to her philosophy than that.

"You have to always find the upside to everything, no matter how bad it might seem to you at the time," she told him. "That's something my dad once told me." And then she dropped the bombshell, thinking it was best if he found this little piece of information out sooner than later. "I think he picked it up from your mom."

For a second Ronan didn't think he'd heard her correctly. But he had keen hearing and he had heard *everything* the loquacious detective he'd been forced to add to his team had said since Carver had called her over to his desk, so he reasoned he hadn't misheard. That raised an immediate question.

"You *know* my mother?" he asked incredulously.

"Yes, I do." Then, before he could ask, she volunteered just how her father knew his mother. "The ambulance company she runs is attached to the firehouse my dad oversees." Which was just another example of what a small world this really was.

Granted he didn't know anything about her background, but then he didn't know any more than he had to about either Martinez or Choi. It was what they brought to the table as detectives that had always mattered to him.

Ronan glanced at her for half a second before looking back on the road. "Your dad's a fireman?" he asked in disbelief.

It was an old, standing joke that firemen and policemen were natural rivals. How did she square being in the police department with her family?

Sierra seemed completely comfortable with her admission. "He is. So are my three brothers. Everyone at the fire station thinks your mother's a great lady—and a hell of an ambulance driver in her day, too," she added.

She wasn't certain if that praise would somehow annoy O'Bannon—or make him proud. She didn't know him well enough yet to make that kind of a call. But she had told him the truth and she didn't see any reason not to say as much. She knew that *she* always liked hearing good things about her family from other people.

"Yeah, I know," Ronan responded, his voice so low it almost sounded as if he was talking to himself rather than answering her.

Low voice or not, it was a start. Maybe, in time, she'd wear him down and actually draw O'Bannon into a normal conversation that didn't require pulling teeth.

Focused on getting O'Bannon to talk to her, she hadn't really been paying attention to the area they were driving through. But when he brought his vehicle to a stop a few minutes later, Sierra looked around for the first time.

They definitely weren't in Aurora anymore.

The buildings on both sides of the streets all had a worn, run-down feel to them. Poverty, desperation and fear almost seemed to waft through the air. This was the kind of area people with any sort of ambition typically strove to leave behind, not come home to night after night.

And yet, for many, there was no other choice.

Eventually the streets won and the area beat people down, stripping them of all their hopes and dreams, as well as their dignity, leaving them with nothing to hold on to.

Ronan glanced at her. "You wanted to come along," he said gruffly.

It was as if he could intuit what was going through her head, Sierra thought, doing her best to banish her reflections.

"I'm not complaining," she told him, getting out on her side.

"Maybe I am," Ronan murmured, hardly audible enough for her to hear.

The address on Walker's license coincided with a five-story brown building that had gone up in the early seventies. Situated in the middle of a block, there was a bakery right next door to a shoe repair shop. A boarded-up dry cleaner's was on the other side.

The building where Walker had lived had a front stoop. Several men, ranging from the ages of around seventeen to their midtwenties, were either sitting or standing in the stoop's general vicinity. There were five of them, just enough so that, immobile, they all but barred access to the entrance.

"Mind getting out of the way?" Ronan asked evenly. His no-nonsense tone told the loiterers that they had no choice in the matter.

Mumbling, the five men moved only enough to create a small, accessible space to the door. Ronan went first, creating the path.

When Sierra started to follow him, one of the men on the stoop shifted just enough to keep her from entering the building.

Ronan never even turned around. "I heard one of you shifting. That had better be to give her more space, not less," he warned.

The immediate shuffling noise that followed told him that the offender had moved out of the detective's way.

"That's a neat trick," Sierra told him, falling into place beside Ronan once she'd crossed the threshold and had gotten inside the building. "Do you have eyes in the back of your head, too?"

"Don't test me," he told her. He expected that to be the end of it.

"Don't tempt me," she countered.

Since it didn't appear as if there was an elevator, Ronan walked to the base of the staircase. "You always have to have the last word?" he asked.

"Not always," she answered. Her cheerful response told him more than her words. "Lead the way, Fearless Leader."

He looked back at her and frowned. "Don't call me that."

"Choi did," she reminded him, using that as her excuse.

"That doesn't make it right."

"Want me to tell him to stop?" she offered, still searching for a way to get on O'Bannon's good side—if there was such a thing.

"I want you to be quiet and stay sharp," he told her, looking around the poorly lit area carefully. The dim lighting on the stairs made it difficult to see beyond a few feet, which in Ronan's mind placed them at a definite disadvantage.

"I can do both," she told him, but for the sake of peace—and pleasing O'Bannon—she deliberately kept quiet as they carefully made their way up the next five flights of stairs.

Coming to the landing, Sierra blew out a breath. She exercised daily and felt she was in decent shape, but climbing all those stairs still took a bit of a toll on her, given that she was trying to keep up with O'Bannon's pace.

"Wow, I'd hate to have to do that after a long day at work," she commented.

"Could be why Walker and his so-called 'friends' didn't work," Ronan said cryptically, adding, "At least not in the traditional sense."

Finding the apartment number he was looking for, Ronan knocked on the door. He gave it the count of ten and was about to knock again when they heard the sound of several locks being opened on the other side. Then someone pulled the apartment door back a crack. There was a chain holding the door in place.

The wary-looking woman on the other side of the door appeared as if she had once been very attractive. But it was obvious she had weathered more than her share of the worst that life had to offer.

Dark brown eyes regarded them both suspiciously, coming to her own conclusions. "If you're selling religion, I tried it but it didn't work."

With that she began to close the door on them but Ronan put his foot in the way, which prevented her from shutting it.

"Hey!" she shouted in protest.

Ronan held up his badge so she could see it. "We're with the police department."

"I tried them, they didn't work, either," the woman informed him. There was a deep chasm of bitterness in her voice.

"Are you related to John Walker?" Sierra's question was an attempt to cut through any further protest the woman might have to offer.

A flicker of despair passed through the woman's eyes. "I'm his mother, why? What's he done this time?" she demanded. There was anger in her voice as well as weariness that went clear down to the bone.

"May we come in?" Sierra asked politely.

But the older woman held her ground.

"No. You have something to say, you tell me from where you're standing. What's he done?" Walker's mother demanded again, looking from Sierra to the man who still had his foot in her doorway.

Despite Ronan's thoughts to the contrary, she had never had to break this sort of news to a deceased's family member before. Sierra could feel a lump forming in her throat as she struggled to push the words out.

It almost felt surreal as she listened to her voice saying, "Ma'am, I'm sorry to have to tell you—"

"Oh, Lord, he's dead, isn't he?" Mrs. Walker cried. Her small, frail body began to shake. She struggled as she removed the chain from the slot where it was anchored. "I told him," she cried with anguished frustration. "I told him that the kind of life he was leading would kill him." The woman sobbed, looking as if she was going to dissolve where she stood.

Once inside the apartment, Sierra tried to put her arms around the woman to keep her from sinking to the floor.

Walker's mother fought her for a moment and then gave up as she broke down, sobbing against her shoulder. And then, after several minutes, Mrs. Walker straightened, seeming to tap into an inbred resilience.

Squaring her bowed shoulders and holding her head high, she looked at Sierra. "How did it happen?"

"Someone shot him. His body was found in the alley behind the Shamrock Inn," Ronan told the woman, reciting the words in almost a clinical fashion.

Mrs. Walker nodded numbly, led the way into her small, cluttered living room and sank onto a sagging sofa that was all but threadbare.

"Tell me everything," she requested in a hoarse whisper.

Chapter Three

Although it made him uncomfortable, Ronan had no choice but to take a seat beside the victim's mother on the sofa.

Sierra, he noted, sat on the woman's other side. Looking at her, he saw nothing but compassion in the detective's eyes.

Maybe he should have dispatched her to do the notification on her own, but there'd been no way of knowing who Walker lived with ahead of time and he couldn't just cavalierly put her life in danger because he was uncomfortable notifying a thug's mother of her son's demise.

Taking a breath, Ronan told the victim's mother, "I'm afraid there isn't much to tell, Mrs. Walker. Your son was found in the alley behind the Shamrock Inn. A single gunshot delivered to the back of his head was the cause of death."

The woman jolted as if she'd been touched by a live wire but, struggling, she managed to regain some of her composure.

"He didn't suffer, did he?" she asked, obviously trying to rein in her emotions.

"Well, it looked—" Ronan began.

Oh, Lord, he is going to be truthful, Sierra realized. Didn't he know that there was a time when the truth wasn't welcome?

"No, it was quick," she assured the older woman, talking quickly and deliberately avoiding eye contact with O'Bannon.

Her goal right now was to make sure Mrs. Walker didn't fall apart. As long as the woman held it together, there was a good chance she would remain coherent and maybe even answer a few more questions for them.

"Was your son having trouble with anyone?" Ronan asked. "Any unusual arguments? Had anyone threatened him lately?"

"Well, this wasn't done by a friend now, was it?" Mrs. Walker snapped sarcastically, then immediately appeared to regret her show of temper as tears filled her eyes. "I'm sorry. This is all such a shock. You spend every day worrying something's going to happen to your kid, but when it does you're just not ready for it."

Sierra placed a comforting hand on the woman's shoulder. Mrs. Walker released a shuddering sigh. For a moment she looked as if she was about to dissolve into tears, but then she managed to rally again.

"We're very sorry for your loss, Mrs. Walker," she told the woman with genuine feeling. "Is there anyone we could call for you?"

The woman laughed softly, although the sound was completely devoid of any humor. She shook her head. "No one who would come if they saw the police around."

It wasn't an accusation but a simple statement of fact. Sniffling, she took out a crumpled tissue out of her pocket and wiped her eyes, then returned the tissue back to her pocket.

"When can I claim his bod—my son?" she asked, choking up.

"The medical examiner has to do an autopsy first, but as soon as your son's body is released, we'll let you know," Sierra assured her. "Until then, here's my card. If you think of anything to add, please call. Or if you just need someone to talk to—" Sierra gave the woman's hand a squeeze as she gave her a business card "—call mc."

Mrs. Walker grimly nodded her head. The card went into

the same pocket as the tissue. She tried to choke out a thank-you, but the words seemed to stick in her mouth.

"Thank you for your time," Ronan said, rising. "We'll let ourselves out."

"WELL, THAT WOMAN'S never going to be the same again," Sierra observed sadly as soon as they walked out of the almost airless little apartment.

"Nobody who loses someone ever really is," Ronan commented drily.

Something in his voice caught her attention and Sierra looked at the tall man walking next to her. But his face was impassive, so if there had been an expression she could have interpreted, it was gone in an instant.

Ronan remained silent as they walked to his car. She decided it was just as well because he was undoubtedly disappointed that nothing new had been learned.

It wasn't until they had pulled away from the curb and were driving back to the precinct that Ronan spoke again. To her surprise it wasn't about the fact that they had learned nothing new about the victim.

"You weren't half-bad in there."

Sierra blinked, stunned as well as puzzled. "I'm sorry, I'm confused," she confessed. "Are you praising the half-full glass or criticizing it because it's half-empty?"

Ronan upbraided himself for having said anything, but since he had, he knew he needed to clarify it or Carlyle would just go on asking questions. He was beginning to realize she was just built that way.

"What I'm saying is that you handled an awkward situation without making it worse."

Sierra suppressed a laugh. "That really is a left-handed compliment, you know."

His eyes on the road, Ronan shrugged. "It's all I've got."

This time she did laugh. There was a decent human being

in there somewhere, he just had to be dug out. She wondered if he was even aware of that fact.

"I really doubt that," she told him.

"And just what is that supposed to mean?"

"Your mother's a really nice, savvy woman," Sierra said, hoping that would put what she said into perspective for him.

"So?"

She leaned back in her seat. "Never mind."

"No, out with it," Ronan ordered, sparing her one quick glance. "You started to say something, so now finish it."

"And if I do, you'll have reason to get rid of me?"

Did she really think he was that petty? What did he care what she thought about him? he asked himself the next second.

But he had pushed this and he wanted it resolved. "We'll talk consequences later. Now, out with it. What are you trying to say?"

Sierra chose her words carefully, aware he would examine each one. "Your mother's a really great, outgoing woman—"

"You already covered that part," Ronan told her impatiently.

She supposed she could sugarcoat this, but she couldn't get herself to lie. So she didn't. "And you act as if you'd been raised by a she-wolf in a cave."

Well, that was certainly straightforward enough, he thought. This woman obviously didn't have any trouble telling the truth. He supposed that was a valuable asset—to both him and the team. Still, they weren't going to get anywhere with this investigation if they kept clashing all the time.

"If you have a problem with the way I do things, Carlyle, you can always transfer out," he told her. There was no emotion in his voice.

That just made her angry. "I don't quit things," she informed him.

"Then I'd say you have a problem."

"I guess I do."

He had no idea where she stood after saying that. And he certainly couldn't just leave it. Easing into a stop at an intersection, he looked at her. "So, what's it going to be? Are you in or are you out?"

She was probably going to regret this, Sierra thought, squaring her shoulders. But she'd told him the truth. She didn't quit things. That left her only one answer. "I'm in—but don't expect me to stop trying to get through that stony exterior," she told him, qualifying her answer.

"What I expect," Ronan stated deliberately, "is that you do your part to solve the crime to get whoever's playing vigilante off the streets."

The word he used caught her attention. "So now you think it's a vigilante?"

He reminded himself that she was brand-new to the team and as such wasn't apprised of pertinent details. He reviewed them in a nutshell. "This is the fifth street thug who's been 'executed' this way. Three from one gang—the War Lords—and two from another—the Terminators. If it's not a vigilante, what's your take on it?"

"Well, off the top of my head," she said, working through the problem as she spoke, "maybe it's the work of a third gang, trying to get rid of the competition."

"Aurora doesn't have a gang. We had a few nerdy types a few years ago who tried to flex their muscles by spray-painting a couple of buildings, but the fact that they'd painted slogans using four- and five-syllable words gave them away. They were tracked down pretty quickly and turned over to their parents. That was the end of Aurora's one and only 'gang,'" he declared. "Anything else?"

Sierra grinned. "Nope. Not at this time."

He caught her expression out of the corner of his eye as he continued to the precinct. "Then why do you look like some damn cat that swallowed a canary?"

"Because that's the most number of words you've said

to me since I became part of your team. I knew you had it in you."

Ronan shook his head, exasperated. He didn't trust himself to say anything in response so the rest of the ride to the precinct was made in silence.

THE MOMENT HE reached the squad room, Ronan walked straight to Martinez and Choi's desks. "You guys learn anything?" he demanded.

Choi spoke first. "In between a bout of dry heaves, Billie, the guy who tripped over our victim, swore he'd never seen him before. I tend to believe him," he said and then explained why before Ronan could ask. "The guy thought he was going to die and most people tend to tell the truth when they think they're going to die."

"And the bartender?" Ronan asked. So far, this wasn't going well, he thought dourly.

"The guy who opened up the tavern wasn't the guy on duty last night. He had that guy come down, but the evening bartender wasn't all that helpful. According to Dave, the guy tending bar last night," Martinez interjected, "it was really crowded and our victim didn't make much of an impression on him. He said he 'thought' he saw our victim downing some tequilas with some sexy little number making eyes at him, but when Dave came back to that side of the bar, our victim and the woman who might or might not have been with him were gone."

"There was no sign of a woman being in the alley," Choi reminded the others.

"Maybe she left before anything happened," Martinez speculated.

"Or maybe she saw what was happening and managed to get away before the killer saw her. That would make her a witness," Sierra said, looking at Ronan to see whether he liked that idea.

Ronan nodded to himself. "Maybe you've got something

there, Carlyle. It's worth exploring." He turned toward Choi and Martinez. "Go back to the bartender. See if he'll sit with our sketch artist and describe this 'sexy little number' so we can pass it around Walker's neighborhood, see if anyone recognizes her," Ronan instructed.

"On our way," Choi said, leaving the squad room with Martinez right behind him.

He'd gone with her theory, Sierra thought, rather surprised Ronan hadn't given her an argument first. She turned toward him, a wide smile on her lips, and asked, "Still annoyed that Carver assigned me to the team?"

Ronan was practically stone-faced. "You waiting for a pat on the head?"

"No, but a 'hey, not a bad idea' might be in order," she countered.

The expression on his face was dark. "Okay. Hey, not a bad idea. Happy?" he asked.

"You're a tough nut to crack, aren't you?"

"They haven't made a nutcracker tough enough for that," he told her as he began to walk to the break room.

"Don't count on it," she called after him.

She saw him stop for a second then resume walking. She got to him, she thought with a satisfied smile. Step one.

WHEN RONAN RETURNED to the squad room half an hour later, he was halfway to his desk when he stopped dead. There was a bulletin board mounted on wheels pushed up against the wall nearest their desks.

He walked straight to Sierra. "Where did that come from?" he asked sharply.

Busy tacking up a few last-minute things she'd jotted down, she didn't turn around as she answered, "The store room."

"What's it doing here?"

"I thought we could do with some visual aids," she told

him. Finished, she turned around to face him. "Might stimulate our thinking."

The woman was taking over, he thought, and he didn't run things that way. "I think my thinking is stimulated enough right now," he warned her. There was a definite edge in his voice. "Where did you get those?" he asked, waving a hand at the board.

There were five photographs tacked on the board, each with a name and time of death listed beneath it.

"I pulled up the list of victims and then scanned their photos, the ones off the DMV records," she explained, adding, "because the others were too gruesome. I put those up along with the date and time of their deaths." She kept talking even though she could see that, so far, her answers were annoying him. Her hope was that if she bombarded him with enough facts, he'd see things her way. "I thought that having them up there like that might get us to see something we're missing."

His eyes met hers, pinning her to the spot. "Who told you to do that?"

"No one. It's call initiative. Isn't that why I'm here?"

He felt as if she'd pushed him to the edge. "Frankly, I don't know why you're here. I'm still trying to figure it out."

"Here's a hint. It's to help with the investigation," she told him.

He could feel his temper rising. "You can 'help' by following orders."

"Which would be okay if there were any orders to follow," she countered. "Look, other homicide detectives find having this kind of board up is helpful." When he continued to glare and said nothing, she blew out a frustrated breath. She wasn't trying to challenge his authority, she was trying to help, but this was still his team to manage. "You want me to take the photos down and take the board back to the storeroom?"

The look of anger on his face abated somewhat. Ronan glanced at the bulletin board again.

"No, leave it up," he told her in a resigned voice. "Just next time check with me before you do anything."

She still couldn't help feeling as if she was being tethered. But if she wanted to work this case—and she really did—she was going to have to abide by his rules.

Inclining her head, Sierra said, "I'm going to the break room for lunch now, is that okay with you?"

Damn, but she was irritating. "If you're trying to get under my skin, Carlyle, you've already done it," he told her.

"Lunch?" she repeated innocently, still waiting for him to tell her it was all right.

He waved his hand at her impatiently. "Go. And if you solve the case over your ham-and-cheese sandwich, let me know first before you run off to cuff anyone."

"It's roast beef," Sierra corrected. "And you'll be the first to know if I solve the case," she promised, elaborately drawing a cross over her heart. The next second she turned on her heel to leave—all but running into a tall, dark, younger, smiling version of Ronan. "Sorry," she mumbled, withdrawing.

"What was that about?" Detective Christian O'Bannon asked, coming up to his older brother. He took one last look over his shoulder at the disappearing woman. "Is she telling you she loves you?"

Ronan's mouth dropped opened. "What the hell are you talking about?"

Chris jerked a thumb in the direction of the departing detective. "She just crossed her heart. I thought she was miming 'I love you.'"

Ronan scowled at him. "Did you come here to make an already bad day worse?"

Chris's face seemed to almost light up. "No, actually I came to ask you to be best man."

"I already am the best man. I always have been," Ronan answered wryly.

"At my wedding, you idiot," Chris said, giving Ronan a friendly shove. "Suzie Q and I are getting married."

That caught Ronan's attention. "For real?"

If possible, the grin on Chris' face widened. "As real as it can get. Priest, flowers, everything."

Ronan shook his head. "Damn, I thought she had more sense than that."

"Show a little respect or you'll be demoted," Chris warned. "The position of flower girl hasn't been filled yet."

"I have a lot of respect for Suzie," Ronan said honestly, referring to the absent detective. "It's you I don't have all that much respect for," he added drolly. "Never have."

"Then that's a yes?" Chris asked, a touch of anxiousness surfacing in his voice. "I know you don't care for all that attention."

Ronan shrugged. "Nobody's going to be looking at me, they'll be looking at Suzie—and the lucky stiff who's marrying her."

Chris wanted to nail things down and he needed a direct answer. "Again, is that a yes?"

Ronan grinned, genuinely happy for his younger brother. "Try and keep me away. Just tell me where and when."

Relieved, Chris answered, "I'll tell you a lot more than that, but this'll do for now."

Ronan shook his head and smiled as he watched his younger brother leave. He envied Christian, he really did. He could remember being that happy. Once.

Chapter Four

"You should do that more often," Sierra said.

Ronan turned, surprised to see her standing near him. He thought she was still in the break room and hadn't even heard her come up.

"Do what?" he demanded.

"Smile." Even as she said it, his expression went back to its normal impassive look. Still, determined to make him come around, she pushed on. "You don't look quite as scary when you smile."

He caught himself almost smiling again and wondered what it was about this woman that had him responding in ways he hadn't for a long time. "You're missing the point," he told her gruffly. "Why wouldn't I want to look scary?"

"Well, you got me there," she answered, tongue in cheek. "If you don't know, I can't explain it to you."

"Good." Ronan turned back to look at the photographs she'd put on the bulletin board, waiting for something to nudge his brain. But nothing came. He glanced at Sierra. The latter had gone back to the desk that had been assigned to her for the duration of this case. "Anything occur to you?" he asked.

"Not yet," she admitted honestly. "But it's still early."

"Yeah," he said with a sigh, turning back to the bulletin board. He frowned a little as he told her, "You know, this isn't a half-bad idea, using the bulletin board."

She made no effort to hide her stunned expression. "Wow, two half compliments in one day. Aren't you afraid that I'll get a big head?"

"Bigger than it already is?" he asked.

She took no offense. She had a hunch he felt he had to say something like that to counter the left-handed compliment he'd just tendered.

"I don't have a big head," she told him. "I just know my capabilities."

Ronan began to say something about the extent of her "so-called" capabilities when he saw her suddenly sit up and look alert. For just a second, the expression in her eyes captivated him. She looked almost ethereal. Definitely beautiful. And that was when he realized that when she held her head a certain way, she reminded him of Wendy.

Startled, he quickly got hold of himself. This wasn't the time to think about Wendy. He wasn't ready to go there now. Maybe he never would be.

The next second he turned to see Martinez and Choi walking back into the squad room. He crossed to them. "Anything?" he asked.

Martinez refrained from letting his disappointment show. "If anyone recognizes her—" Martinez nodded at the sketch put together from the bartender's recollection "—they're not talking. But in their defense, that is a pretty generic-looking sketch. Pretty girl, wavy hair, nothing really outstanding."

"What about the surveillance camera?" she asked.

"The one in the back alley's inoperable," Ronan informed her dismissively. It was the first thing that had been checked by his uncle and the team Sean had taken with him.

"Okay," she allowed, "how about the one inside the tavern?"

"There isn't one. The owner's got one up strictly for show," Ronan told her. "But it doesn't record."

"And the one outside, by the entrance?" she pressed, recalling seeing it as they'd passed the front door to get to the alley.

Ronan didn't answer her. Instead he headed out of the squad room.

Sierra was on her feet immediately, hurrying after him. Moving fast, she managed to catch up to him by the elevator. "You're going down to the CSI lab to take a look at that surveillance video, aren't you?" she asked.

"Don't you have files to go through?" he asked Sierra crisply.

"You know I do, you gave them to me. But they can wait until later," she answered. "I want to see if we can isolate the footage and find our mystery woman. Maybe she can help us solve this thing."

He doubted it. Things didn't just resolve themselves this way. "You realize she could just be someone playing up to anyone who'll buy her a drink," Ronan said just as the elevator arrived.

Sierra got in the second the elevator doors opened, not taking a chance he would leave her behind. "I know. But she could still be a witness."

"She could still be a witness," he admitted grudgingly, echoing what she'd said. And then his frown deepened. "Don't grin so hard, Carlyle. Your face'll crack."

"There's a few years left on my warranty, so I'm safe for now," she said cheerfully.

"Right," he murmured to himself. Just what he needed on his team—to be saddled with a crazy woman. A crazy woman who reminded him of his own loss. "C'mon, then," he ordered as the doors opened in the basement.

Sierra didn't have to be asked twice.

"THERE, THAT'S GOT to be her!" Sierra cried excitedly, pointing to the image on the monitor in the viewing bay. "Rewind it!"

They had been watching the surveillance video from the Shamrock Inn for the last half hour. The footage wasn't exceptionally clear because the camera was at least ten years old and the video being used had been taped over and over countless times to save money. As well, the camera had lost its ability to time stamp so they had been unable to isolate the hours they'd needed, which had forced them to review the entire video recorded over the last ten hours.

Ronan had already hit Pause and then Rewind. When he played the tape forward, he did it in slow motion, allowing them to study the scene.

"She wasn't with anyone when she came in," Sierra observed.

Annoyed, Ronan looked at her over his shoulder. "I've got eyes, Carlyle. I can see."

"Sorry." The apology was automatic. "Just getting excited, that's all."

"Save your energy. It's going to be a long haul," he told her.

He hit Pause again, then got up from the desk he'd been using. He went to find his uncle.

Bringing him back, he indicated the surveillance tape they had been reviewing. "I'm going to need a hard copy of that woman," he told Sean.

"You mean other than the one you already have?" Sean asked, not bothering to hide his amusement.

"What are you talking about?" Ronan asked, puzzled.

Rather than answer his nephew, Sean pointed to the colored print of the woman entering the tavern that Sierra was holding in her hand.

Ronan stared at the print. "Where did you—"

"I got it off the printer," Sierra told him innocently, anticipating his question. And then she smiled, adding, "This isn't my first rodeo."

Sean nodded his approval. "Nice to have good help," Sean told his nephew. "Well, if you don't need anything else..." He looked at Ronan pointedly. It was obvious he had more than his share of work to get back to.

"Not from you at this time," Ronan acknowledged. "Thanks for letting us look through the video."

"We all want the same thing," Sean answered. "To get whoever's doing this off the streets and behind bars." He started to leave. "I'll have the ME send the autopsy report up to you when it's done, but I don't expect that there'll be any surprises."

"Will that include a tox screen?" Sierra asked, suddenly turning around just before entering the hallway behind Ronan.

Homicide's lead detective stopped in his tracks, reluctantly turning around.

"Of course," Sean answered. "Tox screens can include a wide range of tests. Are you looking for something specific?"

She answered his question with a question of her own. "Does that include checking for date-rape drugs?"

That pulled both men up short.

"Not in this case. Why?" Sean asked, crossing back to her. "What are you thinking?"

"Well, it's just an idea..." Sierra began. "But whoever lured Walker away and executed him would have wanted Walker to come along peacefully and not try to fight him off, right?"

Ronan exchanged looks with his uncle. "Makes sense to me," Sean agreed. "I'll get a more specified tox screen done on Walker and let you know what it comes up with," he promised.

They left the lab and she turned to Ronan as they waited for the elevator. "Now aren't you glad I came along?"

"The jury's still out on that," Ronan said wryly.

"Are you reverting back to the strong, silent type again?" she asked. "I've seen you smile, O'Bannon. You can't fool me."

The elevator arrived and they got on. Ronan pushed the button for their floor rather forcefully. "I've got a question for you, Carlyle. Do you *ever* stop talking?"

"On occasion," she replied.

"Do you think that this could be one of those occasions?" he asked. "I think better when there's silence."

She laughed softly. "Considering the squad room we work in, you're pretty much out of luck."

Ronan looked at her pointedly. "I know."

"But, if it helps, I'll stop talking—for now," she said gamely. "I've got some reading to catch up on anyway."

Ronan made no comment, afraid that if he uttered a single word, it would set her off again and she'd launch into yet another long, winding topic. He really did want to savor a few moments of peace before something else came up.

SIERRA SPENT THE rest of the day, as well as the next, reading and rereading the files that had been compiled on the five victims. All of them had belonged to neighborhood gangs and all the killings had been identical: one bullet to the back of the head, then removal of one of the hands. In the first four cases, it was the right one that had been severed.

But the last victim had had his left hand removed, not his right.

"Why just one?" Sierra asked, looking up from the file.

All three men on the team were at their desks, working. Martinez and Choi were currently on phone duty, fielding calls from people who swore they had either just seen the serial killer or had just barely escaped being another one of his victims. Each call had to be taken no matter how baseless it turned out to be, but doing so was tedious, not to mention wearing on the detectives' nerves, as well.

Hearing Sierra's question, Ronan looked up in her direction. "What did you say?"

He knew he would regret asking because he was all but giving her an invitation to start running off at the mouth again and it had been really pretty peaceful for the last few hours. But she'd asked a question and since she'd been dead-on about the surveillance video, he couldn't afford to ignore her just for the sake of his own peace and quiet.

"Why does the killer just cut off one of his victim's hands?" she asked.

Ronan shrugged. "Because it's the victim's dominant hand most likely."

"Okay. And?" She waited for more of an explanation. It wasn't enough to satisfy her and she had a feeling that if they had an answer, it would get them one step closer to finding who was behind the killings.

Ronan frowned. "And what?"

Taking a breath, Sierra worded her question more succinctly. "Why would the killer want to cut off the victim's dominant hand?"

"How the hell should I know?" Ronan asked. Frustrated, he scrubbed his hand over his face. "The guy's a whack job."

"A whack job who knows how to practically surgically remove a hand from its wrist," she said pointedly.

Ronan frowned. "Anyone wielding a meat cleaver with a little momentum could do the same thing."

"I suppose you've got a point," she was forced to admit.

"Why are you focusing on the way the killer cuts off his victim's hands?" Choi asked, finally getting off the phone. "You think the killer's a Jack the Ripper type? Some people thought he was a doctor, the way he vivisected those prostitutes."

"I thought maybe if our killer had some kind of medical background, we might be able to narrow the suspect pool," she explained.

"We have a suspect pool?" Martinez asked, glancing from Sierra to Ronan and then Choi. "You mean you think that somebody other than the members of those two gangs still left standing is behind this?"

She waved away Martinez's facetious question. "Right now, I'm just thinking out loud," Sierra said with a shrug.

"Spit-balling ideas until something winds up sticking, I guess."

Ronan had a thoughtful expression on his face. "And what are your thoughts about why the killer cuts off just one of his victim's hands? The *dominant* hand." His tone underscored the word.

Sierra was surprised he was asking her for input rather than simply telling her *not* to think out loud until she had something worthwhile to share.

"Like you said, it's the victim's dominant hand," Sierra said. She kept coming back to that. It *had* to mean something. "The hand he uses to shoot his gun with."

Ronan's eyes met hers. "You think these killings are payback for something." It wasn't a question so much as an assumption. And it made as much sense right now as any of this did.

"Maybe," she answered, leaving herself a little leeway. "But I can't find a connection between the two gangs, other than they pretty much stayed out of each other's way."

And that was what was frustrating her. There had to be *something*. But what?

"At least for the last couple of years," Choi recalled.

"Until these killings started," Martinez spoke up. "Now, according to what I hear from my friends on the Tesla police force, there've been a number of revenge killings." He pulled up a recent story he'd read earlier on the internet. "See?" He turned his monitor so that it was visible to the others.

Choi scanned the story quickly. "Maybe this *is* all just gang-related in one way or another," he suggested, looking at O'Bannon.

One of the newer lab techs from the CSI unit had just walked into the squad room and crossed to Ronan. He was carrying a large manila envelope.

"Captain Cavanaugh wanted me to bring this to you, Detective," the lab tech said, referring to Sean. "He said you were waiting for it."

"We all are." Accepting the envelope, Ronan began opening it. "Tell him thanks. I really didn't think he'd get it to me so quick."

"He had the lab rush it," the tech said before leaving.

Eager to know if she was right, Sierra was on her feet and rounding her desk to get to Ronan's side.

"You planning on reading this over my shoulder, Carlyle?" Ronan asked, still holding the envelope. The reports were only partially showing.

She offered him a quick, quirky smile. Without saying yes or no to his question, Sierra told him, "I speed-read."

He shook his head. The woman had an answer for everything. "Of course you do."

Removing the papers from the envelope, he found that in addition to the autopsy report, it also contained the extended tox screen Sierra had requested.

He picked up the latter first, knowing it was what really interested Sierra. Now that she had raised the point, so was he.

Before he could scan down to the portion he was looking for, he heard Sierra exclaim behind him, "I was right. Walker was drugged. The tox screen shows that he had a date-rape drug in him when he died."

"Well, that explains why there was no sign of a struggle in the alley," Martinez said. Looking in Sierra's direction, he inclined his head in silent tribute.

Sierra's mind was going a mile a minute. "Can we get a tox screen panel worked up on the other victims?" she asked Ronan eagerly.

"Not likely," he answered. He'd only taken over the case after the third victim had surfaced. "Three of the victims have already been buried. We'd have to get court orders to exhume their bodies."

He saw a flash of frustration in Sierra's eyes. For just a second he was caught up by the way her blue eyes seemed to almost change color, from light to dark, depending on the feelings that were surfacing.

Upbraiding himself for the momentary lapse, he focused on the business at hand. “It can be done, but not as easily as you might think. We’d need a really compelling reason. For now, I can find out if victim number four is still in the morgue. From what I’ve heard, I don’t think anyone has come forward to claim his body yet.”

Glancing at Sierra, he saw her face change. He’d expected her to be elated. Instead she seemed really sad. “What’s with you?” he asked. “I’d thought you’d be happy to hear that.”

“I’m glad we’ve got another body to test,” she said, “but think about how awful that is, to be dead and not have anyone come forward to claim your body.”

“Don’t waste your pity. That’s the kind of life these thugs signed on for,” Martinez told her, trying to make her feel better in his own way.

“I’m just glad we’ve got another body to run a tox screen on without having to get any court orders,” Ronan said.

He expected her to say something cryptic, like “You’re welcome,” but she didn’t.

He suppressed a sigh. Apparently, Carlyle was more complicated than he’d initially given her credit for. That was all he needed. A complicated woman on his team, stirring things up.

Stirring him up.

The thought came and went in a split second. He blocked its return. He didn’t have time for anything but solving the case, he silently insisted.

Chapter Five

"Son of a gun, that new team member of yours was right," Sean told his nephew, calling Ronan once he'd had the opportunity to run the requested tox screen on the serial killer's fourth victim. "Looks like she's two for two."

"Joggers found that fourth victim in the park," Ronan recalled. "The last victim probably ingested Special K in his drink. How did this one get it into his system? We didn't find a flask or anything like that near the body and he wasn't dumped there. There was blood from his wound on the ground, which meant that he had to be killed there."

"Glad you asked. Juan Marley got his the old-fashioned way," Sean told him. "The ME found a very small hole just behind his ear. He's ashamed to say that he missed that the first time around."

"The drug was injected?" Ronan asked.

"That would be my guess," Sean told him. "Your serial killer is very cold-blooded, very methodical. And he's got surgical skills. Those hands that were cut off from the victims, there were no hesitation cuts. Each amputation was clean, precise. This guy knew what he was doing and he apparently wasn't squeamish."

"Yes, that's what we're thinking," Ronan said, playing back what Sierra had said earlier. "Did the killer use Special K again?"

"No, this time it was Rohypnol. Maybe he couldn't get

his hands on his drug of choice," Sean told him. "Tesla's facing a backup of bodies so they've asked to borrow our ME for a couple of days—unless you feel that there's a reason to keep him here."

"As long as you can get him back if this serial killer takes down another victim."

"I've already made that a provision with their chief medical examiner," Sean said.

"Thanks for the info, Uncle Sean."

He laughed drily. "I'd say my pleasure, but it really isn't. Just catch this bastard as soon as you can, Ronan. I know that some people think he's doing a public service, killing thugs and gang members, but that's not our call to make. First and foremost, the victims were all people and it's our job to make sure that everyone's kept safe."

"We're all doing our best, sir," Ronan said just before he terminated the call.

Returning the receiver to its cradle, he saw Sierra watching him. He knew she was waiting for the lab results and was surprised that she didn't immediately jump on him, demanding to know what his uncle had said. He decided to put her out of her misery and tell her the results.

"Well, you're two for two," he told her.

"The tox screen for victim number four was positive for a date-rape drug?" she asked, unable to keep the note of hope out of her voice.

Ronan nodded. "The ME found traces of Rohypnol in the victim's system."

Choi looked up. "Roofies?" he questioned.

"That's the popular name for it," Ronan confirmed. "Maybe he couldn't get his hands on Special K."

"Ketamine is what vets use," Martinez said, getting into the conversation. "My dog Ralph got attacked by this pit bull that got loose in my neighborhood early one morning. Damn dog tore holes in Ralph. I didn't think he was going to make it when I drove him to the vet. Dr. Lai had to knock Ralph out with ketamine before she could sew him up."

"You named your dog Ralph?" Sierra asked.

"I didn't. His last owner did. I got Ralph from a shelter after his owner was reported for abusing him," Martinez answered. "Poor dog shook for, like, two weeks until he got used to me and the girls," he said, referring to his wife and daughters. "Anyway, Dr. Lai told me that Special K knocked Ralph out for four hours."

"How big is Ralph?" Sierra asked.

"He's a ninety-three-pound Labrador," Martinez said proudly.

"All the killer would need would be to knock out his target for half an hour or less," Ronan speculated. "Special K or a roofie would do the trick."

Choi asked what everyone was thinking. "You think our serial killer might be a vet—the kind that deals with animals not battlefields?" he clarified.

"Either that, or someone with access to those kinds of drugs," Sierra suggested.

"The question is," Ronan said, getting up from his desk and crossing over to the bulletin board, "why would a vet—or someone with access to a vet's drugs—" he acknowledged, glancing in Sierra's direction, "be executing gang members?"

When no one answered, Sierra decided to give it a shot.

"Off the top of my head, maybe one or more of these guys ran up a bill with the vet and didn't pay it and things escalated from there. Or maybe they shot up the vet's place of business and this is his way of getting even?" Sierra proposed.

"Sounds plausible enough, except for our initial problem," Ronan pointed out. "These are two different gangs we're talking about. When did they ever do anything in concert?"

Choi sighed. "You really are a killjoy, you know that?" he asked.

Sierra had an idea. "Have you tried exploring social media?" Sierra asked.

He turned toward her, as did Choi and Martinez. "I know I'm going to hate myself for saying this, but would you add a few more words to that? Exactly what do you want us to do with social media?" Ronan asked.

She had a strong feeling that Ronan spent as little time on the computer as possible and had no social accounts. Even her father kept in touch with some members of the family who lived out of state that way.

She made it simple for Ronan, doing her best not to make him feel that she was talking down to him. "These guys are all under thirty. For the most part, that age group posts everything they do on their media pages. They'd certainly brag on the internet if they felt they had something to brag about. Why don't we start looking there?" she suggested to Ronan. "Something's got to give us a clue as to how these deaths are connected because I'm willing to bet my shield that these were *not* random murders."

"You volunteering for the job?" Ronan asked her, seizing on her wording.

"Don't we have techs in the computer lab who do that sort of thing?" she asked him.

Ronan recalled what his brother had said about his last trip to the computer research part of the CSI unit. "Last time I checked, they were backed up until the turn of the century."

Sierra sighed. "Then I guess I'm volunteering to find out if any of these jokers posted online," she said with resignation.

HIS CONSCIENCE GOT the better of him.

He'd done his best to ignore it. After all, it had been Carlyle's suggestion and everyone in the department pulled their own weight, so there was no reason why she shouldn't be the one doing the heavy lifting on this internet search she'd brought up.

But he had assumed that she would approach the job like any normal person, taking breaks and time out for meals. But the woman hadn't budged from her desk since he'd put her on the task.

And that had been hours ago.

Choi and Martinez had left for the night a little while ago, as had a good many of the detectives in the squad room. Even Lieutenant Carver had gone home about half an hour ago.

As for him, he'd walked out as well. But he'd gotten as far as the break room and then forced himself to double back after making an all-important pit stop at the vending machine.

"You know," Ronan said, setting a can of diet soda on Sierra's desk, "when I told you to see what you could find on these guys from anything that they might have posted on social media pages, I didn't mean for you to exhaust all the search engines before you could finally go home."

Reading, Sierra didn't immediately look up. "I know," she answered Ronan. "I just kind of got caught up in it."

He sat on the edge of her desk but she still didn't look up. She was busy trying to make sense of something she was reading.

"There's 'caught up' and there's 'obsessive,'" Ronan pointed out.

She glanced in his direction for half a minute. "Don't worry, I'm not going to turn into one of those people who forgets to shower or change their clothes," she promised. "It's just that each thing I check out just feeds into something else." It astonished her how mindless some people could be, to be proud of hurting people and getting by without doing any work. "These guys were really maniacal, crazy people." Sierra shook her head.

"Well, at least we agree on something."

That caught her attention and she looked up. "I've got a feeling that we'd probably agree on a lot of things, once you stop thinking of me as the enemy."

"I don't think of you as the enemy," he told her, tamping down his temper.

"No? Try being on my side of this thing," she told him. "The lieutenant brought me over to your team and you acted like you'd just been given an infestation of body lice."

"That's getting a little carried away, don't you think?"

She raised her eyes to his. "Am I?"

"Go home, Carlyle. Get some sleep. The internet'll still be here in the morning."

"I know that," she answered. "I just wanted to find something to get us a step closer to getting this guy." She looked up at Ronan as she made her point. "So that you'd see I could be an asset."

He frowned, debating whether or not to let that go or to say what he knew should be said. It was late, he was tired, and maybe that influenced him into deciding to give her her due.

"You came up with the idea that the victims were given drugs to keep them from fighting back. The rest of us hadn't thought of that. That puts a gold star under your name. Now go home and get something to eat," he ordered gruffly.

Arguing was in Sierra's nature, but she refrained. She paused, then nodded. "I guess I am hungry." She looked back at her monitor and something occurred to her. "Just five more minutes and I'll close everything down."

Ronan watched her for a long moment, knowing that if he left, there was no telling how long she would remain at her desk, going from one site to another. She had to be the most stubborn woman he had ever encountered, and that included his mother and sisters—which was saying a lot.

"Carlyle," he said sternly, "go home."

"I will," she promised, the keys clicking beneath her fingers. "In a minute."

Ronan got off her desk. Moving behind it, he bent and flipped a switch on the power strip beneath her desk.

"Now," he ordered, getting up.

Her jaw dropped. "You just shut off my computer," she complained.

He appeared completely unfazed by the accusation in her voice. "I gave you a direct order and you ignored it."

She drew herself up, ready to go a few rounds with this annoying man. "You're lead detective, not my supreme leader," she informed him hotly.

A hint of a smile played along his lips. "I'll pretend you didn't say that."

With that, he turned away and began to walk out of the squad room.

She raised her voice as she called after him. "I know your mother and I'll tell her what a hard time you've been giving me."

Ronan turned then and slowly crossed back to her desk. "Did you just threaten me with my mother?" he asked in disbelief. "What are we, twelve?"

She braced herself. "I'm not. But I'm not sure about you."

"You're tired. I'll pretend you didn't say that. *Now go home.*"

He might be the lead detective and in charge, but she was not about to be intimidated. "Why are you acting like I'm the invading force?"

"Because you're the invading force," he retorted. He'd had no choice in the matter when Carver had brought her over. He had to work with her and he didn't appreciate not being given a choice.

"Hey, you're a Cavanaugh," she reminded him. "*Nobody* invades you," she pointed out. "You guys practically *are* the police department. I'm just trying to do my part. I don't want the credit," she stressed. "You can have the credit for solving this thing."

"This isn't about credit," he informed her, annoyed she thought that way.

"Then what is it about?" she demanded, confused. "Why

do I get the feeling that you don't want to be in the same space with me?"

Denial was on his tongue but he never voiced it. Possibly because she'd stumbled onto something. "Because you remind me of someone," he finally said, struggling to keep from yelling the words at her.

"Who?"

"Someone," was all he trusted himself to say and then, before she could attempt to grill him any further, he stalked out.

"That's not an answer!" she countered.

Grabbing her bag, Sierra quickly headed out of the squad room after him.

But when she got to the hallway, Ronan was nowhere to be seen.

He'd probably caught the elevator. For a second she thought of taking the stairs and ambushing him on the ground floor, but she had a feeling that would just lead to more of the same. He wasn't about to tell her anything. Most likely, he regretted having said as much as he had just now.

The bottom line was that she needed answers and O'Bannon wasn't about to give them to her.

But she thought she knew someone who just might be able to.

Taking the elevator to the ground floor, she hurried to the parking lot and made her way to her car. Once she got into her vehicle, she put her key in the ignition but she didn't start the engine.

Instead she took out her cell phone and placed a call.

Once the call connected, she heard a deep, gravely voice answer. "Carlyle."

"Hi, Dad," she said with more cheer than she was feeling. "It's me. Sierra."

"Sierra?" her father repeated. "Wait, wait, I know that name, just give me a second. Sierra, Sierra—" he repeated as if doing that would unearth some memories, help him recall who she was.

"Very funny, Dad. Okay, I know I haven't called or been by lately, but I've been a little busy," she told him.

"I take it that the police department has been working you hard, chaining you to your desk and all that. Okay, so why is the black sheep of the family suddenly calling me?"

He'd called her that the day she had told him she was applying to the police academy instead of signing up for the fire department like the rest of her family. In time, he'd come to terms with it, but he still wasn't exactly thrilled.

"Dad, I work in the police department, not for some escort service. There's no reason to call me a black sheep."

"Sure there is," the deep voice rumbled in her ear. "You didn't go into the family business the way you were supposed to."

Sierra sighed. "This is why I don't call very often," she told her father.

"Okay, okay, I'll make nice," her father promised. "To what do I owe this unexpected but delightful call?"

"You're laying it on way too thick, Dad, but I'll let that ride for now. I need your help," she said seriously. "I want you to find something out for me."

"You mean like detective work?" he asked, a touch of surprise in his voice. "Isn't that your field of expertise?"

"Yes, but this is more up your alley if you'd only stop trying to make me feel like I failed you and just listen?" she asked.

"I guess I'd better," her father conceded, "or you'll hang up, right?"

She wasn't going to get sucked into that. Instead she asked, "Do you still talk to Maeve O'Bannon?"

"She's a damn fine woman," her father said with feeling. "Why shouldn't I still talk to her? She had the good sense to work alongside the fire department, unlike the rest of her family."

Sierra ignored that, as well, and went straight to the heart of her request. "I want you to ask her something for me."

"All right," Chief Craig Carlyle said. "What do you want me to ask?"

She braced herself for her father's possible reaction. "Could you ask her what her son Ronan's story is?"

"Come again?"

Sierra decided to give her father as much background as she felt he'd need to understand why she was making the request. "I'm working with Ronan and he let it slip that I remind him of someone. I need you to ask Maeve if he ever had a problem with someone who looked like me."

"I've got a suggestion," her father said. "Why don't *you* ask Ronan?"

"It's kind of complicated, Dad."

"Isn't he treating you right?" her father asked.

She knew all she had to do was say that he wasn't and her father would be right there, in Ronan's face. She didn't need him to champion her. All she needed him to do was what she'd asked.

"Please, Dad, just ask Maeve," she repeated.

She heard her father sigh deeply. "Look, Sierra, I always told you what cops were like. If Maeve's son isn't treating you with the respect you deserve, quit," he told her. "You know I can always use you on my team. Your brothers'll show you the ropes and we can make this a whole family affair."

She closed her eyes, searching for strength and the right words. "Dad."

"What?"

"Just ask her for me, okay? Thanks. I'll call again soon."

With that, she ended the call. She loved her father—and her brothers—more than anything, but there were times when talking to the man could make her feel so drained.

And then she smiled to herself. She supposed that could be viewed as a two-way street. She was fairly certain her father probably felt the same way about her.

Chapter Six

"Well, this is a surprise," Andrew Cavanaugh said to his younger brother as he opened his front door. "Come on in, Brian." Closing the door again, he said, "You don't usually stop by in the middle of the week like this." Since the kitchen had become the hub of his activity, the former chief of police led the current chief of detectives to the kitchen. "Things a little slow at the police department these days?"

"Actually," Brian answered, crossing the threshold into the state-of-the-art kitchen, "they're a little more hectic than usual."

As the oldest, Andrew had always been able to read his brother like a book. But this time there was a note he couldn't quite identify in Brian's voice.

"Something wrong?" he asked, stopping by the counter and studying his brother more closely. "Something you couldn't tell me over the phone?"

Brian smiled for a long moment. "Not in the way you think."

Andrew crossed to the industrial-size refrigerator. "Well now you really have me curious. Want a beer? Something harder?" he asked when Brian didn't take him up on the beer.

Brian glanced toward the refrigerator. "You have any of that cake left over that you served at the last gathering?"

Praise, even implied praise, never got old, Andrew thought. He'd been a dedicated chief of police in his time, but the culinary arts had always been his passion. He'd put himself through school that way and it was a love that lingered to the present day.

"No, but I whipped up a new cake if you're interested."

"I'm always interested in cake, you know that," Brian said, taking a seat at the extra-long, custom-made kitchen table. He grinned ruefully. "Lila says if I keep this up, I'm going to have to go on a diet. I thought I'd just remedy the situation by putting another notch on my belt."

"That doesn't mean what it used to, does it?" Andrew's wife, Rose, asked as she came into the kitchen. She smiled warmly at her brother-in-law.

Brian laughed softly. "Not since before Jared was born," he told her, referring to the first of his four adult children, three of whom were police detectives. The fourth, Janelle, was an assistant DA.

"Okay, other than my cake, what's brought you out on a school night like this?" Andrew asked, placing a healthy slice of amaretto cake in front of his brother.

Fork poised over his serving, he looked at Andrew and Rose. "You two aren't having any?" Brian asked. "I feel strange, being the only one eating."

"Like I believe that." Andrew laughed. "But I'll have a small slice to keep you company. Rose?" he asked his wife as he cut himself a slice that was half the size of the one he'd just given his brother.

His wife demurred. "I'm still full from dinner, Andrew. I'll just get myself some tea and leave you two to talk."

"No, don't go," Brian protested. "This includes you, too, Rose."

"Oh?" Taking the kettle from the back burner, she poured hot water into a teacup and then placed a teabag with chai tea into it. Holding the teacup with both hands, Rose took a seat beside her husband. Her attention was focused on her brother-in-law. "What is it?"

"Well, there's good news and there's bad news," Brian began. "Which would you like?" he asked them.

"Might as well get the bad news over with first," Andrew said. Years on the force had taught him to hope for the best but brace for the worst. "This isn't about any of your kids, is it?" he asked, concerned. Aside from Brian's own four, he also had four stepchildren, thanks to his second marriage, and all of them were on the force, as well.

Brian shook his head. "No, it isn't."

"Our kids?" Rose asked, immediately concerned. All five were detectives and she did her best not to worry, but worry had long become part of her everyday life.

"In a way—but not the bad news part," Brian added quickly, wanting to set both of their minds at ease before he went on.

"I seem to remember you being better at making announcements," Andrew told his brother. Finished with his small portion, he got up to get a beer. He brought two bottles to the table.

"Sorry. This kind of thing is never easy to say," Brian admitted, apologizing. "Chief Walter Hudson just died in his sleep. He had a massive heart attack," Brian told them. The man had been a personal friend and the news was hard to deliver.

"The man who took over Andrew's place on the force when he retired?" Rose asked. Distressed, she looked at her husband. "Walter wasn't *that* old."

"No, but he really didn't take care of himself and he let the job get to him," Brian told her. "His doctor had been after him for years to lose at least seventy pounds, but we all know how that is," he said, looking just the slightest bit guilty as he finished his slice of cake.

"He's going to be missed," Andrew commented, shaking his head. It took him a moment to make peace with the news. "I appreciate you coming over to tell me." He had more questions. "When did it happen? Do you know when the funeral is being held?"

"It happened last night. The funeral's scheduled for next Monday. But that really isn't the main reason why I'm here."

"Right, you said you had good news. It's going to have to be really good to balance this out," Andrew commented, taking a long drag from his bottle of beer.

"The police commissioner doesn't want to leave the position vacated any longer than he has to, so he quickly reviewed the list of possible replacements for Walter that he had on file."

"He had a list on file already?" Andrew asked. "The man always believed in overachieving," he reminisced, his tone somewhat marveled. "So, has he picked anybody? You wouldn't be here if he hadn't, right?"

"Right," Brian admitted. "All that's necessary is for the candidate he picked to say yes."

That seemed almost like a trivial thing. "So what's the problem then?" Andrew asked.

"No problem," Brian answered. "I just wanted to tell you who it was before the candidate was officially notified."

"You're being awfully mysterious about this, Brian," Rose observed. And then a leery look entered her eyes. "The commissioner isn't thinking of asking Andrew to step up again, is he? Because Andrew won't take it," Rose said defensively. "Right, honey?" She turning toward her husband for backup. "You've done your time."

Andrew slipped his arm around his wife's shoulders. "Don't worry. Those days are long behind me, Rose. I wouldn't be doing *anyone* any good stepping into those shoes again."

"Not that I agree with you," Brian told his brother, "but no, it's not you." He paused an infinitesimal second then said, "The commissioner wants to offer the position to Shaw."

"My Shaw?" Andrew cried. Surprise quickly gave way to a pleased expression.

"Our Shaw?" Rose asked at the same time, clearly stunned.

"Yes, 'your' Shaw," Brian confirmed. "Think about it," he said, addressing his words more to Rose than his brother. He could see that Andrew was happy about this turn of events.

Rose appeared to be more undecided about it. "He's been on the force for a number of years. He gets along really well with the men and he's got you as an example to follow."

"Shaw is his own person," Andrew pointed out.

"There's that, too," Brian agreed. He was as proud of the appointment as if it had happened to one of his own children. They were an incredibly close family.

"So, when's the commissioner going to be notifying Shaw?" Andrew asked.

"As far as I know," Brian answered, "he'll be calling Shaw into his office tomorrow morning."

"So I can't call him until tomorrow morning." Andrew was more or less confirming that fact rather than asking his brother.

"No, you can't," Brian said firmly.

"What if he calls us for some reason tonight?" Rose asked, a hesitant note in her voice.

Andrew looked at his wife. "Rose, Shaw doesn't check in with us. He hasn't for years. There's no reason to believe that he'll call out of the blue tonight. And if for some reason he does, I'll be the one to talk to him. I'm a lot better at keeping secrets than you are," Andrew told her with affection.

Rose sighed. "Yes, you are," she was forced to admit.

That settled, Andrew turned toward his brother. "Well, this calls for a celebration. What's your preference?"

"Not to run the risk of having the Chief of Ds picked up for a DUI," Brian said honestly. "I've got to be going, anyway. We'll celebrate once this is public knowledge," he promised, getting up from the table. "You'll have a really big excuse to pull out all the stops for the next family gathering."

"Just having family together is enough of an excuse," Andrew told him with all sincerity as he walked Brian to the door. He clapped his brother on the back. "Thanks for coming by and telling me."

"My pleasure," Brian assured him. "And, oh, don't tell

Dad about this until tomorrow. We wouldn't want him exploding, trying to keep the secret," he cautioned.

"Oh, I don't know," Andrew said, thinking back. "As I recall, that old man kept a lot of secrets in his time. But don't worry. I'm not planning on talking to him, either. And neither is Rose," he added, glancing back toward the kitchen.

Brian nodded. Just before he turned to leave, he grinned at his brother. "I guess the family tradition continues."

Andrew couldn't have been more pleased. "It certainly looks that way," he agreed. "Drive safe, now," he called after his brother.

"I'm the chief of detectives. I have to drive safe," Brian told him, waving as he walked to the curb where he had parked his car.

"DON'T GET COMFORTABLE, people," Carver said as he came out of his office the following morning. "Gather in closer because I don't intend to yell this announcement out."

"That's a first," Martinez murmured under his breath.

Choi was next to him. Hearing his partner, Choi stifled a laugh, ducking his head so that the lieutenant wouldn't see him struggling not to grin.

"Everyone here?" Carver asked, glancing around the large room. It was more or less a rhetorical question since most of the squad room looked full. "If you see that anyone's not here, one of you pass this on to them when they do get in."

"Pass what on, Lieutenant?" one of the detectives standing closest to him asked. "Something going down?"

"Chief of Police Hudson died of a heart attack the night before last."

The lieutenant paused as echoes of sympathy and surprise were heard around the room. The chief hadn't been as well liked as Andrew Cavanaugh had been, but he had been well respected.

After a couple of minutes Carver continued with his announcement. "There's going to be an official funeral for

Chief Hudson on Monday at ten in the morning. Everyone who's not on patrol at that time is expected to attend," he told the detectives in his department. "Dress blues everybody." He paused again, as if trying to deal with his emotions.

"The chief was a good man and we'll all miss him." Carver said the words almost mechanically, unable to deal with the loss any other way. And then he clapped his hands together, signaling an end to the announcement. "Okay, everyone back to work."

The detectives began to return to their desks, some slowed by shock, others digesting what this meant to the force as a whole.

"Do they have a replacement yet?" Detective David Reynolds, one of the stragglers asked.

The lieutenant's expression was unreadable. "You volunteering, Reynolds?"

The older man shook his head. "No, no. I was just curious."

"Apply that to your work," Carver advised. "And when they have a replacement for the chief, there'll be another announcement.

"Now, like I said, get back to work, everyone. Clear your cases. That's the best way to honor the chief. Speaking of which," he began, switching direction as he turned toward Ronan, "your team getting any closer to finding that serial killer, O'Bannon?"

Ronan glanced at Sierra. "We're pursuing a few leads," he answered vaguely.

"Well, pursue faster," Carver ordered. "I'd like to have this off the books by the time they swear in the new chief of police."

"Doing our best, Lieutenant," Martinez said, backing Ronan up even though none of them really thought the case would be solved that quickly. The reason behind the killings—if there actually *was* a unifying reason—was not clear yet.

"See that you do," Carver said almost curtly, returning to his office.

Ronan waited until he saw the door to the lieutenant's office close, then headed back to his desk.

"So, *are* we any closer to finding our killer?" Ronan asked the other three detectives once they had gathered around the bulletin board.

Since neither Choi nor Martinez took the opportunity to say anything in response, Sierra spoke up. "I thought maybe I'd go back and talk to the other three victims' next of kin. I'll show them the photo we captured off the surveillance camera of that woman Walker was with. Who knows," she theorized, warming to her subject, "maybe she's working with the killer. You know, setting the victims up one at a time so that her partner can kill them."

"That's kind of a stretch, don't you think?" Choi asked uncertainly.

"Well, I'm open to suggestions, but it's the only thing I can think of," she said honestly. "And talking to the next of kin might bring something else to light that we missed the first time around."

"*You* didn't miss anything," Martinez reminded her, "because you weren't there to question them."

"And she won't be," Ronan said firmly, talking more to Choi and Martinez than to her.

She looked at him in disbelief. "Are you telling me not to go?"

"You catch on quickly." Ronan turned to the detective closest to him. "Martinez, you and Choi go and show this photo to the first four victims' next of kin. And any of the neighbors living in the vicinity. See if anyone recognizes her."

She was getting tired of being treated like a pariah. Every time she thought she had finally become part of the team, Ronan took her down a peg.

"And what am I supposed to do?" she demanded hotly. "Sit here and knit sweaters for all of you?"

"Crocheting is faster," Ronan told her dismissively.

He was *not* going to get rid of her that easily. Catching

him by the shoulder, she tugged and made him turn around to look at her. "Showing the photo around was my idea."

"And I thank you for it," he told her crisply. "Now Martinez and Choi will take it from here."

Sierra refused to back off. "Why?" she challenged. "Because they're men and I'm just a fragile little female?"

"Nobody is ever going to think of you as being fragile, not with that tongue of yours," Ronan informed her.

Her eyes narrowed as she pulled him around to face her again. "I have a gun and I'm trained in two forms of martial arts. No matter what you think, I can protect myself. And if you're that worried about me, then send Choi or Martinez with me, but don't just bench me like I'm a helpless rookie who keeps messing up."

"She's got a point, Fearless Leader," Choi said. "If she hadn't thought of it, we wouldn't have that photo of the girl from the Shamrock."

"Did I ask you for input?" Ronan said in a voice that would have made a true rookie's blood run cold.

But Choi and Martinez had both been with him for a while now and they rolled with the punches.

"No, I thought maybe it was just an oversight," Choi returned. "You know how caught up in things you get."

Ronan blew out a breath. For a minute it looked as if he was going to become really angry. But then he said in an even voice, "Okay, Carlyle, you want to knock on doors that don't want to open for you? Fine, go ahead. But I'm coming with you." He looked over his shoulder. "You two, work up a list of all the vets in that area. See if any of their prescription medications are missing."

Momentarily turning in Sierra's direction, he uttered a guttural command. "Let's go." And then he strode out of the office.

The next second, Sierra hurried after him. She had to quicken her pace to keep up.

Chapter Seven

As Ronan drove to the serial killer's first victim's last-known address, Sierra couldn't look away from what she saw through the windshield.

It was almost like being in a different world.

The streets of Aurora were wide, clean, with an air of brightness about them. As they drove through Tesla, there was a pervading feeling of hopelessness emanating from the crowded, neglected streets. There were people aimlessly hanging around on street corners and half the stores behind them had been abandoned.

How did this kind of thing happen? And why did it go on? Sierra wondered. Didn't the people who lived in these neighborhoods care about their community? About their kids?

"Not exactly like Aurora, is it?" Ronan asked, breaking into her chain of thoughts.

"No," she answered quietly. "Hard to believe that there's only about twenty-five miles separating the two cities."

His laugh was dry, mirthless. "Oh, there's a lot more than that separating them," Ronan said. "Attitudes are different, expectations are different. Kids here aren't sheltered. Parents are busy either holding down two, three jobs—or strung out. Either way, they're not there to look after their kids."

"Maybe they should be," she said, feeling sorry for what she could only imagine many went through, the odds against them before they even began. "How much farther is it?" she asked.

"Want me to turn around and go back?" he offered. The people on some of the corners were watching them as they drove by. It wasn't too difficult to visualize trouble breaking out.

"No, I'm just trying to figure out when this'll be over," she told him. "Are we going to the first victim's neighborhood?"

"We're beginning at the beginning," he told her. When they parked the vehicle in front of a tenement building, she eyed the car dubiously.

"Something wrong?" Ronan asked.

The last group of teens they had passed had made her feel uneasy. They looked as if they felt they had nothing to lose. "I feel like we should be chaining your car to a fire hydrant."

"If anyone wanted to jack the car, they'd find a way to take the hydrant with them, too," he commented, far more familiar with the sort of determination that lived on these streets than she was. "Victim number one lived on the fourth floor of this tenement building." He nodded toward a five-story building that had been built in the early sixties.

Sierra turned and scrutinized the building, trying to imagine the people who lived there. "Alone?"

"File said he had two roommates."

"Male?" Sierra asked as they walked toward the tenement.

Forcing himself to shorten his stride so that she could keep up with him, Ronan shook his head. "One of each."

She was drawing a blank as far as the first file went. "Was the other his girlfriend?"

He pulled open the door for her. The smell of sweat, despair and stale alcohol assaulted them. Sierra noted that Ronan didn't react to the stench.

"Nothing that committed, from what I gathered," he answered.

The elevator was out of order. They took the stairs. When

they arrived on the fourth floor, Ronan found the first victim's—Raul Pena—apartment.

"Stand behind me," he instructed as he raised his hand to knock.

She stood her ground beside him. "Why?"

Why did everything turn into an argument with her? Ronan wondered impatiently. "Because in places like this, they sometimes shoot first before they answer the door."

"If they do, you're just as likely to catch a bullet as I am." She looked at him, annoyed at the heavy-handed way he was trying to protect her. "I didn't just get here from Fantasyland, O'Bannon. I've actually been in tough neighborhoods before."

"Good for you," he snapped, pushing her behind him just before he knocked.

"Don't want any!" a voice gruffly shouted through the door.

"Police!" Ronan announced. "Open the door. We just want to talk."

"Yeah," the male voice on the other side of the door jeered. "And I just want a million dollars."

"It's about Raul," Ronan said.

They heard two locks being flipped before the door was finally eased open a crack. A young male, approximately nineteen or so, looked at them with clear suspicion and distrust on his face.

"He's dead, man," the teen said angrily. "Can't you leave him in peace?"

Sierra spoke up before Ronan could answer. "We're trying to find his killer."

A flicker of interest flashed through the teenager's eyes, growing more so as those eyes washed over her. And then his jaded, distrustful expression returned.

"Yeah, right. Like I believe that. *Nobody* cares about who killed Raul. They're just glad there's one less of us." He raised his chin, which sported only a sparse covering of hair that passed as the beginning of a beard. "But we've got you outnumbered," he boasted.

"Not if your gang keeps being eliminated," Ronan told him flatly. Taking out the photograph lifted from the surveillance video, he held it up in front of the angry teen. "You recognize this woman?"

He barely looked at the photo. "No," he said defiantly. "That your girlfriend?"

"You never saw her with Raul?" Sierra pressed, annoyed by the teen's lack of respect.

"I said no," the teen snapped. Since the photo was still in front of him, he looked at it, longer this time. There was no sign of recognition in his eyes. "Why? Who is she?"

"Someone saw her with the killer's last victim before he was found dead in an alley," Ronan said, putting the photo away.

For the first time the teen smiled. "Oh, yeah. Read about that. John Walker," he said, citing the victim's name. The smile on his lips grew malevolent. "Good to know he's gone. One less jackass making a mess of things in the world."

"You're absolutely sure that you don't recognize her?" Sierra asked, not ready to give up. "Maybe she was with Raul before he was killed?"

"I said no, damn it. Don't you hear good?" the teen asked nastily. "Now, if you got nothing else, I'm busy." He underscored his statement by slamming the door in their faces.

Sierra blew out a breath then looked at Ronan. "Well, that went well."

Ronan turned and walked toward the stairs. He seemed unfazed by what had just transpired. "Never really expected anything else."

"There's always an outside chance," Sierra told him as they slowly made their way down to the ground floor, warily watching each door opening onto the stairwell before they passed it.

After the last confrontation, he couldn't understand how

she could logically think that way. The answer to that, he decided, was that the woman *wasn't* logical. He shook his head at her naïveté.

"Bet when you were a little girl, your mother read you all those stories that ended with 'and they lived happily ever after,' didn't she?"

He was surprised to see a somber expression pass over her face.

"My mother died right after I was born," she answered. "So, no, she didn't read any 'and they lived happily ever after' stories to me."

"Sorry," he told her. "I didn't know."

Sierra shrugged. It wasn't something she talked about. Being raised by her father and three older brothers had made her the rough-and-tumble person she had become.

"That's all right, you didn't know," she said, absolving him of any guilt. "So now what?" she asked as they continued down the stairs. "We go to victim number two's family?"

He shook his head. "I've got a feeling this approach is just a dead end. There's no reason to believe that the woman at the tavern was instrumental in the executions of the other victims—we have no proof she was even instrumental in Walker's execution."

They'd reached the ground-floor lobby. Crossing to the entrance, Sierra pushed open the door. The moment she stepped outside, the sudden sound of gunshots filled the air.

Reacting automatically, Ronan quickly pulled her over, pushing her against the wall as he shielded her with his body, simultaneous pulling out his weapon.

Stunned, Sierra opened her mouth to protest that she wasn't some civilian who needed protecting but, for just a second, she couldn't summon the words. Words that had all been pushed into the shadows by the sudden, exceedingly hot flash that had rippled through her body when it had made such hard contact with his. It felt as if she had been branded.

The earthquake was not one-sided. It hit Ronan with

breath-draining force as he turned, intending to look into her face. With steely resolve, he did his best to block his reaction. "Stay here," he ordered harshly.

The next moment Ronan was gone, playing hide-and-seek with storefronts as he headed in the direction of the gunfire, intent on curbing whoever was doing the shooting.

Sierra spoke up when she finally found her tongue. "The hell I will."

Imitating the pattern Ronan had just executed, she moved stealthily and quickly, managing to catch up to him just as there was another burst of gunfire.

Loud and disconcerting, none of the shooting was directed at them. The volley turned out to be an exchange between two factions of the local gangs, perpetrated by the executions by the serial killer they were still hunting.

Incredibly, considering the number of shots exchanged, there were no casualties. All four shooters involved got away, commandeering two separate vehicles by throwing the drivers to the ground and then driving off.

Sierra looked around. The panic the shoot-out had created had cleared the streets. They were deserted now.

"What the hell was that about?" Sierra cried, still eyeing the street.

"They call it Thursday," Ronan answered and then he shot her an accusing look. "Didn't I tell you to stay put?"

"I don't know, did you?" she asked innocently. "The gunfire was too loud and I couldn't hear anything. I also thought you might need backup," she told him. "You know, being on your six and all."

Ronan looked as if he wanted to say something, but he didn't. It was clearly a solid struggle for him to keep his words to himself.

He turned and marched back to the car. Miraculously, it was untouched. Triggering the locks, he got in on the driver's side. When she followed suit on the passenger side, he told her curtly, "If you're going to go on being on my team, we need to have some ground rules."

She was way ahead of him. "Rule one, you trust me. Rule two, you treat me like a detective not like an administrative assistant. Deal?" she asked.

"Buckle up," he ordered.

She did as he told her. "I'll take that as a yes," she said, underscoring her declaration with a pleased, wide smile. "Look, all I want to do is help. We both want to find this serial killer and stop him. So let me help," she concluded.

"Okay, I'll let you help," he told her grudgingly. "If you don't make me strangle you first."

"Sounds like a deal to me," she told Ronan cheerfully.

"Ready to go back to the precinct?" Asking her was a mere formality. He had already turned the car in that direction.

"Sure," she answered gamely. "*After* we go check out the other three victims' neighborhoods."

He looked at her in disbelief. Hadn't she been paying attention? If he hadn't pulled her back, she would have come very close to being shot as collateral damage. How could that not affect her?

"You're serious," he said incredulously.

"As a heart attack," she responded then flushed. "Oh," she cried, realizing what she'd just said. "Poor choice of words," she admitted, thinking of them in light of what had just happened to the chief of police. "But I *am* serious," she insisted. "Besides, it wouldn't hurt to talk to some of the people in the neighborhood. Maybe we'll find someone who did see something—"

Ronan blew out a breath. "You're a lot more optimistic than I am."

That drew a quiet laugh from her. "That doesn't surprise me," she told him. "So, can we go?"

He wanted to say no, that it was pointless and all they would be doing was going on a wild-goose chase, but without anything else to direct their attention to, he couldn't get himself to flatly refuse. No matter how much he wanted to.

As it turned out, he didn't have to.

Just as he was turning the car to go back into the heart of Tesla, his cell phone rang.

"You going to get that?" Sierra asked as it rang again.

He murmured something under his breath but didn't bother answering her out loud. Instead he pulled over to the side of the road so he could safely take his phone out of his pocket.

Once he had his phone out, he handed it to a surprised Sierra. "You talk, I'll drive." So saying, he got back into the right lane again and continued on his way.

She accepted the phone, but let it ring again. "What if it's personal?" she asked. Sierra had a healthy amount of curiosity, but she didn't believe in simply butting in where she didn't belong. That was just plain rude in her book.

"Everyone I know is a cop. I don't get personal calls," he told her.

"Cops can get personal," she argued as the phone rang again.

"Just answer the damn phone, Carlyle," he ordered.

With a dubious expression, Sierra swiped open his phone. "Detective O'Bannon's phone. He can't talk right now because he's driving, but I'll be happy to take a message."

Her cheerful tone faded as she listened to the caller on the other end. "Yes, sir. I'll tell him. Right away, sir." Sierra exhaled a deep sigh as she terminated the call.

"I've never heard you switch gears like that before. Who was on the phone?" Ronan asked.

"That was the lieutenant. They just found the body of another gang member."

The first thing he thought of was the shoot-out back at the tenement building. "There was a casualty, after all?"

They were on the same wavelength. She understood what he was referring to. "No, not where we just came from. Our serial killer executed another member of the War Lords gang."

The timetable was stepping up. "They're sure it's him?"

"'Bullet in the back of the head. Right hand missing,'" she recited. "It's him."

"Got an address?" he asked.

"The lieutenant said he'd text it to your phone." She paused and hit the app for text messages then read the message. "We might have a problem," she told him.

"Why?"

"The body's not in the city limits. It's in an empty lot just inside of Allegro."

"But it was an execution, right?" he asked her.

"Right," she said grimly.

"And the guy's hand is missing, right?"

"The hand's missing, but it's not a guy."

He came close to swerving out of the lane but managed to regain control of the car. Ronan glanced at her. "Come again?"

"The executed victim was a female gang member." Sierra fell back on old, time-honored clichés. "You know, deadlier than the male, the one who bears the babies and all that sort of thing."

"'Deadlier than the male,'" he repeated. Ronan glanced at her just before he went through an intersection. "You don't have to convince me of that one. Now what's the address?"

She read it off to him. He made sharp right at the next corner and drove toward the outskirts of Aurora and beyond.

"I guess this killer, whoever he is, doesn't discriminate," she said, clearly disturbed that the serial killer had added another victim to his tally.

"He's also escalating," Ronan said.

She thought a moment. "By my count, he's killing two a week."

"Right, but the executions were all spaced apart. Four

days between each execution. This one and the last one were closer together."

Her breath caught in her throat. "That means there's going to be another execution soon."

"That's what it means," he acknowledged in a solemn tone.

She squared her shoulders.

The picture of determination, he thought, looking at her again.

"Unless we stop him," Sierra said.

A hint of a smile curved his mouth. "Like I said. You're an optimist."

Chapter Eight

The moment that Ronan brought the car to a stop behind the gleaming white CSI van, Sierra immediately got out and hurried through the abandoned lot. She headed toward the three CSI investigators who were documenting everything that could be a potential clue. Considering the state of the lot, there were a great many things to go through and photograph.

Sierra hardly saw any of them. Instead her attention was focused on the killer's newest victim. At first glance it was hard to tell if the body was that of a female or if it was in reality just a young boy. Dressed in well-worn jeans, a T-shirt and a tattered denim vest, the victim, lying facedown in the dirt, sported a short, blunt haircut and the bare arms were covered with a network of tattoos.

Sierra squatted beside the body to get a closer, better look. She took special care to avoid the pool of blood that had formed just beneath the victim's neck and shoulders.

"Can I answer any questions for you?" Sean Cavanaugh offered, adding, "The ME hasn't gotten here yet, but he's due any minute."

Rising to her feet just as Ronan joined them, Sierra asked the senior CSI agent, "We're sure the victim's a female?"

In response Sean held up a wallet—now safely sealed in an evidence bag—that had been retrieved from the victim's back pocket.

"That's what her ID says. Shantina Ramirez. She just turned twenty yesterday," he told them. "It's like the killer wants us to know who he's eliminating. Like with the other victims, everything was left intact in the wallet. The killer didn't even bother taking any of the money."

"And we're sure about her gang affiliation?" Ronan asked.

"The tattoo on the right shoulder is the insignia the War Lords all get after they've been initiated into the gang," Sean replied.

"Wait. You said that…Shantina—" it took her a moment to remember the name Sean had used "—turned twenty yesterday, right?"

Sean nodded and sighed as he shook his head. "They're getting younger and younger. I keep thinking what a waste it is to die so young. They haven't even begun to be people yet."

Sierra turned to Ronan just as Choi and Martinez arrived on the scene, crossing the lot to join them. "Maybe she was celebrating somewhere close by last night. Isn't there a bar on the next block?" she asked him.

In response, Ronan turned toward the other two detectives. "Choi, you and Martinez pull Shantina Ramirez's photo from her DMV license and enlarge it. Show it around to the locals here. Maybe someone saw something. And I want all the—"

"Surveillance videos in the area pulled," Martinez said, completing the sentence. "Yeah, we know the drill, boss."

"While you're canvassing the area, show them this photo, too," he told Martinez, handing over the photo he and Sierra had showed to the first victim's roommate.

Sierra looked at the lead detective, clearly surprised.

"Why not?" he said, answering the unspoken question he saw in her eyes. "Might as well cover all the bases while we're at it, right?"

"Right," she agreed, feeling rather good about the fact that at least Ronan was no longer pretending to ignore her suggestions.

"Oh, and when the ME does the autopsy on this one," Ronan told his uncle, "have him run the same tox screen he ran on the last two victims."

Sean smiled as he nodded. "I was going to suggest that myself."

Turning around to face Sierra, Ronan caught the satisfied look on her face. "What did I tell you about grinning so hard, Carlyle?"

"That it'll crack my face," she repeated dutifully and then laughed. "I'll chance it," she told him. "It's just nice to know that you're finally taking my input into account."

They headed back to his vehicle and he did his best to frown, but the truth of it was he was getting accustomed to Carlyle. She wasn't half-bad at her job. But he couldn't just appear to capitulate all at once. He needed to remain in control.

"Don't let it go to your head, Carlyle," Ronan warned. "Even a broken clock is known to be right twice a day."

Sierra just continued to smile in satisfaction. "You can't fool me with all that bluster, O'Bannon. I'm growing on you."

"Oh, heaven forbid," he groaned, then waved at his vehicle. "Just get in the car, Carlyle.

"Where are we going?" she asked as she put her seat belt on.

"Back to the precinct," he told her, pulling away from the curb. "To find out if this latest victim has any next of kin to notify. Plus, I want to get in touch with a couple of my CIs, see if they've heard anything on the street about this serial killer that might prove to be useful."

Sierra regarded him with surprise. "You have criminal informants?"

"Yes, I do." He could feel her staring at him as if he'd just grown an extra head. "Why do you sound so surprised?"

Sierra shrugged. "Oh, I don't know. Maybe because it involves talking, something you don't seem to be overly keen on doing if at all possible."

Ronan knew he should just ignore her but something seemed to goad him into answering. "There's not a whole lot of talking on my end," he told her. "That's why *they're* the ones called informants."

"Oh. Sorry, my mistake," she said, still making no effort to hide the wide smile presently curving the corners of her mouth.

"You know, that little know-it-all smile of yours gets to be pretty annoying really fast," Ronan told her curtly.

She pressed her lips together, doing her best to suppress the smile and only marginally succeeding. There was humor in her clear-water blue eyes as she promised, "Sorry, I'll work on it."

Ronan made a dismissive noise. The sound only had her smile widening despite all her so-called efforts to the contrary.

"Why don't I find that comforting?" Ronan said darkly.

"Want me to make a guess?" she offered brightly.

The last thing he wanted was to listen to her optimistic babble. "No!"

"You're the boss," she told him with a profusion of innocence.

Ronan grunted in response. "At least one of us believes that," he muttered under his breath.

As it turned out, Shantina Ramirez had been a ward of social services by the time she was nine years old and shuffled from one foster home to another for the next nine years. Thrown out of the system when she turned eighteen, she'd been on her own for the last two years.

The address on her driver's license, while seemingly in the general area of Allegro, was bogus.

"So, no next of kin to notify," Sierra concluded.

Ronan didn't look unhappy about that particular turn of events. "Not this time," he told her. "I want you to see what you can find out about the six victims that connects them to one another. Start with the internet."

"What are you going to be doing?" she asked.

"Something else," he told her, walking out of the squad room.

DOING HER BEST to be a team player, Sierra spent the rest of the day combing through the internet, looking for any and all stories she could find involving gang violence in both Tesla and Allegro. She was ultimately hoping to see if any of the six victims' names appeared in the stories.

Every so often, she looked toward the squad room entrance, waiting for Ronan's return. How long did it take to contact confidential informants? she wondered impatiently.

She tried not to let it, but the truth of it was, it drove her crazy that Roan hadn't shared any of what he was up to with her. Not that he was obligated to do so, but the last partner she'd had had never kept her in the dark like this about anything.

She began to think that once this case was solved—and she was determined that it would be—she just might transfer into Major Crimes or any of the other departments. If she remained in Homicide, eventually she would find herself being teamed up with O'Bannon again and that was just asking for more trouble.

IT WAS SIX O'CLOCK. Sierra sighed and combed her hand through her hair. She felt as if she was on the verge of going cross-eyed and decided that she'd spent enough time scrolling for news items on the internet. Ronan hadn't returned to the squad room and she assumed he'd just gone home after his business with the CI or CIs was completed.

Time for her to do the same.

Powering down her computer, she took her messenger bag out of the bottom drawer and slung the bag over her shoulder. She had just pushed in her chair and was ready to leave when the phone on her desk rang.

Looking at it, she fought a strong urge to just ignore the phone and walk out, but her sense of duty had her hesitating. The more she hesitated, the more she weakened.

Maybe it was something to do with the case.

Picking up the receiver, Sierra braced herself as she declared, "Carlyle."

"That's what I thought. I already called you at home and, guess what, you're not there. Don't they let you go home at a decent hour?" the deep, gravelly voice on the other end asked.

Sierra shifted from one foot to the other. She was tempted to remind her father that she had a cell phone that was always on her person, but she let it go. In a lot of ways, her father was still living in the middle of the last century.

"Did you call just to ask me that, Dad? Is this some catch-22 thing?"

"I called to give you an answer, but if you're not interested…" Craig Carlyle deliberately allowed his voice to trail off.

"An answer?" she repeated, confused. Pulling out her chair, she dropped into it, her entire attention focused on the voice on the other end of the line and what he had to say. "Does this mean that you talked to Maeve O'Bannon?"

"That I did. Not a hardship, really," he said, sounding rather cheerful about it. "Salt of the earth, that woman. Loyal as they come. And if you'd ever seen her drive that ambulance—which she still does on occasion when they're short-handed—"

"I'm sorry, are you drawing up her job résumé or did you call to tell me what you found out when you asked her about her son?"

"Always the impatient one," her father said reprovingly.

"May I remind you that I got that impatience from you, Dad?" she said.

"Okay," he granted, switching subjects. "You wanted me to find out anything I could from Maeve about her son."

She'd asked for something specific, but for now, she let that go. She didn't want her father to be distracted. "And did you find out 'anything'?" she pressed.

"Well, of course I did," he said with a trace of annoyance. "He's the oldest and she came to rely on him a great deal when her husband died. Of course, she does have that large family, being born a Cavanaugh and all, but there's nothing like the bond a parent has with their firstborn," he said with conviction.

"Dad, I'm growing old here. Ronan said I reminded him of someone," she prodded. "Was there someone significant in his life that kind of looked like me?"

"I asked her that. Had to work my way up to the subject. You just don't come flat-out and ask that sort of thing without building up to it," he added indignantly.

"I'm sure you did a lot of fine building, Dad, but could we cut to the chase? *Please?*"

"I was just getting to that," he told her.

Sierra had her doubts, but said nothing. She knew how to play the game.

"Ronan was engaged to someone who looked a great deal like you. Maeve showed me a picture of the two of them she had on her phone and, for a minute, I thought it actually *was* you."

"What happened? Did they break up?" Sierra asked. She really couldn't picture Ronan in love or even in a relationship.

"In the most permanent sense possible," her father told her. "Apparently she was caught in some cross fire. Turns out someone was stalking Ronan and the gunman wound up shooting her instead. She died instantly—in his arms. Maeve said he just withdrew into himself after that."

Her father paused, waiting for some sort of response from her. When only silence met his ear, he prodded, "Sierra? Did you hear what I said? Are you still there?"

"Yes, I'm still here, Dad, and I heard what you said," she said quietly. She felt stunned and almost numb. Most of all, she felt exceedingly sorry for Ronan. "Thanks for finding out for me, Dad."

"Maybe you'd better not say anything to Ronan," he advised.

"I don't plan to," she told him. "But this does answer a lot of questions for me. Thanks again, Dad," she said just before hanging up.

Wow, Sierra thought, staring at the receiver she'd just hung up. It took her a moment to digest the news and its import. Her heart had instantly gone out to Ronan. The whole thing had to have been devastating for him. And if she looked as much like his late fiancée as her father had just said, then no wonder Ronan seemed uncomfortable and was having so much trouble being around her.

Short of asking for a transfer or wearing a bag over her head when she came to work, she had no idea how to make this any easier for Ronan.

You can do whatever you can to solve this case and then leave the team, she told herself.

"Anything wrong?"

She nearly jumped when she heard Ronan's voice. Startled, she said, "You're back."

"I work here—at least, I did last time I checked. Why do you look like you've just seen a ghost?" he asked, looking at her suspiciously.

"I just got off the phone with my father."

"The fireman?" he asked.

Uneasy, she fell back on her tool of choice: sarcasm. "My father, the superhero, and I don't talk very much so, yes, that was my father, the fireman."

Annoyance creased his forehead. "Just trying to orient myself with the facts. Did he say something to upset you?"

Yes, he told me all about what you went through. How

do I tell you how sorry I am? And how much I wish I didn't remind you of her.

Shrugging and doing her best to look nonchalant, Sierra asked, "Isn't that a father's job? To make his daughter crazy?"

"Well, not being a daughter and not having a father," he replied, "I couldn't begin to answer that question." He nodded at her computer. Standing on the other side of it, he didn't realize she had already shut it down. "Find out anything useful?"

"Just that the victims were busy little thugs—involved in drugs and petty crimes—but no more than any of the other members of their gangs. Either of the gangs," she corrected herself. "I still couldn't find a reason why they might have been singled out for execution while other members of the gangs weren't."

He regarded what she'd said thoughtfully. "What's to say that our serial killer is finished?"

She hadn't considered that. "You think the executions will continue?"

He didn't answer the question one way or another. "Bloodlust has a way of feeding on itself, if that's the main reason behind it."

"'Bloodlust,'" she repeated. He hadn't mentioned that before. "Is that what your CIs told you?"

He shook his head, feeling pretty drained right about now. "They had no information to give me, but they promised to ask around and see what they could find out." He looked over to where Choi and Martinez usually sat. Both their desks were empty. "Did Choi and Martinez have any luck?"

When the two detectives had returned to the squad room, she'd made a point of asking what they'd found out. She told Ronan what they'd told her.

"The Ramirez girl did party—hard, according to the bartender they talked to at that bar you sent them to. But when they asked around the neighborhood, no one had anything to say to them. Nobody in that area wants to talk to the police," she told him. It was more or less a given in certain neighborhoods, but she still found it exceedingly frustrating.

"And the surveillance camera videos?" he asked.

"Are down in the computer lab. Your uncle promised to get back to us as soon as they could isolate something on them."

He nodded and took in a deep breath. "I'm wiped out. How about you?"

"That pretty well describes it," she agreed.

"How about grabbing a drink at Malone's?" he asked completely out of the blue. "I'm buying."

It took Sierra a moment to recover from the friendly overture. Rising from her desk, she said, "Sure. Best offer I've had all day."

She couldn't help marveling at the change in Ronan's attitude toward her and at the same time wondering if the fact that she looked like his dead fiancée had anything to do with it.

Chapter Nine

It was understood that Ronan and she would drive to Malone's in separate vehicles. After agreeing to go, Sierra wasn't quite sure he would actually show up. After all, for the most part, O'Bannon had behaved as if it was a hardship for him to interact with her during work hours. Why would he want to be around her when they were off the clock?

Still, she gave him the benefit of the doubt. O'Bannon had been the one to tender the invitation, not the other way around, so she felt she needed to give him a chance to show up.

Parking her car as close to the front of the tavern as she could, she turned off the ignition, took a deep breath and got out.

Here goes nothing, she thought and made her way to the entrance. Once inside, there was the old, familiar feeling of having arrived home. She knew that was intentional and by design. Malone's was owned by a retired cop and, on any given evening, three-quarters of the clientele milling around inside were active law-enforcement agents or recently retired members of the department.

As with any good establishment, it wasn't the alcohol that drew them, it was the company. And the knowledge that no matter what they were going through on the job, someone else in the crowd understood and perhaps had even had a similar experience and could offer words that would help navigate whatever it was that a colleague-in-arms needed help with.

Sierra looked around quickly, scanning the area. For a second she thought she spotted him, then realized it was just someone who resembled him. Considering that Ronan had a couple of brothers and a large number of cousins, that was to be expected.

O'Bannon wasn't there.

He'd undoubtedly changed his mind. Sierra shook her head; she hated it when the optimist in her suffered a defeat. She considered going back out, but decided that would look strange to anyone who might be absently watching—after all, she knew some of the people who frequented Malone's—so she went up to the bar.

"Hey, is it Christmas already?" the bartender, a retired patrolman named Wade Preston, asked her.

Sierra was just about to say hello to the man and was thrown off guard by his question. "What?"

Rubbing at an imaginary spot on the counter, the big, burly man drew closer to her. "The last time you were here was for the department's Christmas party last year. You don't show up here very often," he pointed out.

"You can't possibly remember that."

The smile on Wade's broad face widened. "I'm right, aren't I?"

Sierra inclined her head. "You are," she admitted. "How did you remember that?"

"I remember the pretty ones," he answered with a wink. "So, what'll be? Or are you meeting someone here and want to wait?"

"I thought I was," she admitted, "but, no, I don't want to wait. I'll have a screwdriver—heavy on the orange juice," she specified.

Wade laughed. "Usually when I get an order it's the other way around."

"I'm my own designated driver," Sierra told him, "so my alcohol intake has to be at a minimum."

"You got it, Detective," Wade told her. He took two bottles from the shelf behind him and quickly mixed the drink for her. After finishing with a flourish, he placed the tall, frosted glass on the bar in front of her. "There you go, one screwdriver, heavy on the orange juice, as requested."

Sierra took out her wallet and placed a ten on the bar beside her glass.

Picking the bill up, Wade told her, "I'll get your change."

"That's okay, keep it," she said, picking up her drink. She look a long sip, then sighed with satisfaction. There was just the barest hint of vodka detectable, which was all she wanted. "Perfect," she pronounced.

"That's what I like to hear," Wade said with a chuckle. Someone called out his name. "Gotta go. Duty calls. Let me know if you decide you want another," he added just before he went down the bar to attend to another customer.

"You starting without me?"

Turning around, she was surprised to see that O'Bannon had come up behind her.

"To be honest, I thought you'd had a change of heart and I felt rather dumb just coming in and then going out again, so I ordered a drink. My one and only drink of the evening," she added.

Ronan looked at the tall glass. He wasn't into mixed drinks. As far as he was concerned, the mixes got in the way of the taste of alcohol. "What are you having?"

"Nothing exotic. Just a screwdriver. I told him to go heavy on the orange juice," she added in case Ronan wondered why the liquid in the glass looked so terribly orange in color.

Ronan merely nodded. "Wade probably wishes all his customers were like you. The charge is the same, even if he uses less alcohol."

She shrugged. The news didn't faze her. "He's got to make a living," she said philosophically.

"Oh, I think he does rather well here," Ronan said with certainty. Raising his hand, he succeeded in making eye contact with the bartender. "Scotch on the rocks," he called out. Wade gave him the high sign. Turning toward Sierra, he asked, "You want to get a table or stay at the bar?"

"I'm okay either way," she answered. "I'm only staying until I finish my drink, but I intend to nurse it, so it's your call."

"Why don't we get a table, then?" He didn't wait for her reply. Wade had just put his drink on the bar so he picked it up, leaving a bill in its place, and walked away from the bar. Sierra quickly picked up her own drink and followed him. She nodded at several people as she passed them.

Ronan sat at an empty table for two. Sierra took her seat opposite him.

There was noise all around them—it had obviously been a rough day for everyone, she thought—but all Sierra was really aware of was the silence that existed at their table. She had never been good with silence. It usually made her want to fill the space with words. Any sorts of words.

She thought back to the conversation she'd had with her father just before Ronan had gotten back to the squad room. It was, she decided, as good a place as any to start.

"My dad thinks very highly of your mother. Everyone at the firehouse does," she added when Ronan made no comment.

He took a tentative sip of his drink, then put it back on the table. "What made you become a cop?"

The question, coming out of the blue the way it did, surprised her. She wasn't even sure that she had heard him correctly. "What?"

"Everyone in your family's a firefighter." He knew that because he'd done a little digging into her background, telling himself it was only because he needed to know if there was something in her background that might be a liability to the team. "But you broke rank and became a cop. Why?"

She had her hands around the glass but it remained on the table in front of her, its contents untouched. "Is this a job review or something?" she asked him, somewhat confused. He'd made it clear that he wasn't all that interested in extraneous conversation, which was the category his question fell under.

"I'm just curious," he told her with a careless shrug. Pausing for a beat, he threw back his drink. "I mean, there's always been an unofficial rivalry between cops and firefighters, so I'm just wondering why you would opt to break rank and work for the APD? Didn't that get your father and brothers angry?"

"My dad and brothers were upset to begin with," she granted, "but they all came around eventually. My dad had raised all of us to follow our dreams."

"And you dreamed of strapping on a gun and chasing bad guys?" He had two sisters and both were detectives with the police department, but he always felt that Brianna and Shyla were different from the average female, thanks to their family background.

"No, of helping people," Sierra corrected, "and that's what you and I do, really. We *help* people." She emphasized the word. "And to be honest, I think my dad's a little relieved that he doesn't have to worry about me running into burning buildings."

"No," he conceded, adding sarcastically, "just running into a bullet."

She let the remark pass.

"Alcohol doesn't make a difference, does it? You're just as gloomy with it as without it. I obviously seem to bring out the worst in you, so why don't I just call it a night and go?" she suggested, pushing her drink aside and getting to her feet.

Ronan caught her wrist, managing to surprise both of them, he reasoned, judging by the expression on Sierra's face. His eyes met hers.

"Stay put," he ordered and then his voice softened. "You don't bring out the worst in me. This isn't my worst, not by a long shot."

"Oh, Lord, is that a warning?" Sierra asked, pretending to be uneasy.

"Just a statement of fact," Ronan stated, then went on to say, "Look, I might have ridden you a little too hard. If I did, it was just to find out what kind of mettle you're made of."

"And does my 'mettle' pass your test?"

"Well, despite some less-than-warm 'fireside moments,'" he pointed out, "you didn't run to Carver, asking to be taken off my team."

Quitting had never been an answer in her book. "I fight my own battles."

Raising his hand to get Wade's attention, Ronan indicated the need for a refill.

The bartender nodded, then poured another Scotch into a new glass. He handed it off to a waitress who proceeded to bring it over to their table. Ronan traded a bill for the drink.

"Yeah, I got that impression. Sure you don't want anything stronger?" he asked, nodding at the tall, mostly filled glass in front of her.

Looking at the waitress, she shook her head. The woman withdrew, taking Ronan's empty glass with her.

"Not when I'm driving home," Sierra told him.

"I could always call you a cab."

She noticed that he didn't offer to drive her home. Did that mean he intended to consume a lot tonight, or hadn't the thought of taking her home even occurred to him?

Why?

For one second that thought stuck in her head and she was tempted to explore it from all angles, but that way lay only complications and, right now, she had more than she could handle. Having the very somber Ronan take her home, despite his looks and rock-solid body, would only be asking for trouble, and that was one thing she definitely didn't need.

But, obviously, that thought hadn't even occurred to O'Bannon.

"I don't like spending money needlessly," she told him after a beat.

He shrugged, taking a long sip of his new drink. "I'd pay for it."

"Don't like spending other people's money, either," she said.

He laughed, shaking his head as he drained his second drink, waiting for it to hit him. He'd built up a rather large tolerance since Wendy had died. And today marked two years since he'd lost her. The very thought corkscrewed into his soul, tearing holes as it went.

"Well, that makes you a rare woman." Looking at his glass, he was almost surprised to find it was empty. Rather than wave to the bartender again, Ronan stood.

"Leaving already?" she asked.

"What?" Belatedly, her question registered. "No, I'm just going to get another drink."

"Maybe I should drive *you* home," Sierra suggested.

"I can hold my liquor," he informed her gruffly.

"So can that glass." She nodded at the glass he had clutched in his hand. "But I wouldn't trust a glass to drive me home."

"That's because they don't drive," he said flippantly, going to the bar.

Well, at least he wasn't weaving, but if he continued downing drinks the way he was, it wouldn't be long before walking a straight line would be an impossibility.

He was back before she could think of a course of action. Sitting at the table, he took a sip of the Scotch before putting his glass down. "Don't worry about me," he told her.

"I'm not worried about you," she informed him, even though that was exactly what she was worried about. "I'm worried about the other people on the road."

Ronan's face darkened and he looked annoyed. It was unclear whether it was the conversation he was annoyed with, or her, but the man had a habit of getting annoyed so, at this point, she just accepted it as his standard behavior.

She intended to remain until he was ready to go home. There was no way she would let him drive, even if she had to drag him to her car.

He looked at her face and surprised her by laughing. "Put your wings away, Carlyle, I'll be fine."

"I have no doubt," she replied, this time deliberately flashing a wide smile. "But I'm still staying. You invited me to Malone's for a drink."

He nodded at the barely touched screwdriver in front of her. "You said you were only having one."

"Yes, but it's not done." She pointed toward it as if it was exhibit A.

Ronan shook his head. "Never saw anyone nurse one drink for so long."

"We all have our special talents," she remarked. Searching for something to say—she didn't want to turn the conversation toward the serial killer they were pursuing—she thought of what he had just asked her. "So, why did *you* become a cop?"

His eyebrows drew together in a quizzical squiggle. "What?"

"You asked me why I became one," she reminded him. "I thought it would only be fair to ask you the same question."

"Well, yeah," he murmured then paused as if he was trying to form an answer to give her. But when he spoke, it was as if he was addressing another question. "I ask myself the same question," he said in a quiet voice.

She had a feeling she'd accidentally stumbled into a dark area. Her mind worked quickly. Since his fiancée had been killed by a stray bullet when someone had been gunning for him, it wasn't a stretch to think that O'Bannon blamed himself for her death, thinking that if he had just gone into another profession, she might still be alive.

Sierra spoke up, trying to help him out. "Well, the short answer to that is that you want to protect and serve."

He finished his drink and put the glass down hard as he

laughed harshly. "Well, that isn't exactly working out very well lately."

"Most days it does," she insisted. "And if everyone took that stance," she went on firmly, "everyone would win."

He leaned back in his chair and instead of ridiculing her as she expected, he grinned and pointed to something just behind her.

"There, I see them."

She turned to look, but didn't see what he might have been referring to. "See what?"

"Your wings." He took a deep breath and exhaled, trying to get hold of his thoughts, which were beginning to slip in and out of his head. "They're opening up, Carlyle. You'd better go home before you can't get into your car because they've spread out too wide."

Sierra raised her glass to his line of vision. "Still drinking."

He waved his hand at her dismissively. "That's not drinking. That's barely wetting your lips."

By her count, he'd downed three drinks and was about to do the same to a fourth. He gave no sign of stopping. This wasn't good.

"Why don't you let me drive you home now?" she suggested gently.

"I told you, I don't need to be driven home," he said curtly.

She wasn't about to let up. "You don't want to cause a scene and I certainly don't," she informed him forcefully. "Why don't we go now before you do something you're going to regret?"

His thought turned toward what day it was. There was a sadness in his voice as he replied, "It's too late for that."

She took a guess at what he meant. "If you're referring to inviting me out for a drink—"

"I'm not," he said cutting her off. "You don't have anything to do with it." And then he realized that his voice had gotten louder. A couple of people, sitting close by, were looking their way. "Sorry, didn't mean to snap like that."

"Put the glass down, Ronan," she ordered, keeping her voice low but sounding far more authoritative than she ever had around him. "It's time to go."

She looked at him, her eyes meeting his as she put on the same no-nonsense face she reverted to with her brothers when one of them had had too much to drink and needed to be extricated from a bar.

Ronan gazed at the empty glass. Just like his life, he thought morosely.

Something pinched inside him.

He should have never invited Carlyle out for a drink. What had he been thinking? She wasn't a substitute for Wendy.

"Yeah," he mumbled to himself, "maybe it is." Ronan raised his eyes to hers.

She saw the sadness there and it hurt to look at. It had to hurt even more to live with it.

She made up her mind.

Because, despite his protests, Ronan was somewhat unsteady on his feet, she slung his arm over her shoulders and threaded her arm around his waist.

"Are we going to dance?" he asked.

"Shut up, Ronan. You can do this," she told him in what amounted to almost a whisper.

Taking small steps, she managed to guide him to the front door and out of Malone's, relieved that no one had stepped up to help. Because if they had, they would have recognized the kind of shape Ronan was in and she knew that would prove to be embarrassing for him tomorrow.

"One foot in front of the other," she coached. "My car's not far away."

"Where did you park? Washington?" he asked.

"Closer than that," she assured him. She just hoped they'd get to her car before her arms ached too much to keep him upright and moving.

Chapter Ten

"This isn't my car," Ronan said as she leaned him against the passenger side of her vehicle. Sierra watched him to make sure he didn't slide to the ground while she fished out her car keys so she could release the door locks.

"No, it's mine."

Finding her keys, she pressed the key fob and all four locks were released. Very gingerly, she moved Ronan back just enough so that she could open the passenger door for him. But he tilted slightly and she almost fell over with him before she finally managed to pull him upright.

Unaware of the sudden, unexpected meeting he almost had with the ground, Ronan found his face buried in her hair and took a deep, appreciative breath.

"You smell good," he pronounced.

She tried not to dwell on the feelings generated by having Ronan's face against the side of her neck. But it wasn't easy. There were sensations slivering up and down her spine and parts in between.

"Thank you," she said with effort. "That's probably my cologne mixed with the smell of the bar," she said. "Now get into the car, please." Not waiting for him to comply, she all but pushed him onto the passenger seat.

"Um, what are you doing?" he asked, amused and curious as she stuck her head into the car and reached over his torso.

"I'm securing your seat belt, something I'm not sure

you're up to doing right now." Sliding the metal tongue into the slot, Sierra immediately stepped back, creating space between them. "I'd hate to stop short and suddenly have you flying out through the windshield."

Ronan stared at the dashboard in front of him, his face the very picture of concentration, like an elementary-school student trying to work out a tricky math problem.

"Don't your air bags work?" he asked as she got in on her side.

"With my luck, probably not." Buckling her own seat belt, Sierra put the key into the ignition and then turned to Ronan. "Okay, give me your address."

A very coy and utterly sexy smile rose to his lips. This was *not* the Ronan O'Bannon she knew.

"Why?"

She focused on her goal and not on the way her stomach muscles were quickening. "Because I'm taking you home and I need to know where you live."

He looked around his surroundings. "This isn't my car."

She suppressed a sigh. "We've already established that. You've had a little too much to drink," she said, wording it as tactfully as possible, "so I'm taking you home."

His brow furrowed, obviously trying to process what she was saying. "How will my car get there?"

"Tomorrow, I'll pick you up and bring you back here so you can get it." It was getting late and all she wanted to do was to get this over with and get home herself. "Now will you *please* give me your address?"

He closed his eyes for a minute, as if he was trying to remember, but when he opened them again and looked at her, there was a warm smile on his face. "Don't play coy, Wendy, you know my address," he said. "You're there all the time."

Oh, Lord, she was losing him, Sierra thought. "It slipped my mind."

"Yeah, right." He laughed as if they were sharing a private joke. "Okay, I'll play your game," he told her, then recited his address.

"Hold on." Looking both ways to make sure there was no one in her path, Sierra backed out of the space and drove off the parking lot.

The address he had given her belonged to a house located in a residential development that wasn't too far from the precinct.

"I've missed you, Wendy," he told her as if they were in the middle of a conversation.

She had *no* idea what to do with that. So she said the only logical thing she could, assuring herself that he wouldn't remember any of this tomorrow. "I've missed you, too."

She did the speed limit—and a little beyond that—and flew the rest of the way to his house.

Ten minutes later she was pulling up in front of a small, one-story house. Making a judgment call, she parked in his driveway instead of at the curb, which she would have preferred. But in his present state, she wasn't sure Ronan could get out of the car if it was parked close to the curb.

Turning off the ignition, she got out and quickly hurried around to the passenger side. Ronan had already opened the door on his side and had one foot out. But it was as if he was undecided whether or not to bring the second foot out, as well.

"I think you'll have more luck getting out of the car if you unbuckle your seat belt," she advised, pressing her lips together not to laugh.

Ronan looked at her blankly. Rather than repeat herself, she reached over him just as she had before and hit the release button.

"How could I have forgotten that?" Ronan shook his head.

It sounded as if he was asking himself the question rather than asking her, but she still answered, "It happens sometimes," just to make him feel better about himself and the situation.

Leaning in, she eased Ronan around so that he could finally get out. "Put your hand on my shoulder," she coaxed, slipping her arm around his waist again. She tugged but found that she couldn't budge him. "You're supposed to be helping me, Ronan," she told him. "I can't do this alone."

Instead of answering her, or doing as she'd asked, with one sudden move, he pulled her onto his lap.

Sierra was so surprised, the air seemed to just whoosh out of her. And then the next moment he was cupping her cheek with his hand, his lips were against hers and he was kissing her. Her first instinct was to struggle, but his kiss was so gentle, so tender and so completely soul-melting, she found herself surrendering without even realizing what she was doing.

Before she knew it, she was going with the moment and kissing him back.

As the kiss deepened, she felt emotions suddenly popping up and swirling around inside her, taking her for a breathless ride she was totally unprepared for.

Mayday! What are you doing? a voice in her head demanded. *Stop this right now!*

The problem was, she really didn't want to, but she knew it was the right thing to do.

The *only* thing to do.

Ronan wasn't kissing her, he was kissing someone named Wendy. Someone, she knew, who was no longer among the living.

Pulling herself together, Sierra wedged her hands against his chest and pushed, then stumbled onto her feet, putting some much needed space between them. Her heart was hammering so hard, she was surprised it didn't just break through her chest.

She saw that Ronan had a bewildered look on his face and realized that he still, obviously, thought she was someone else. She had to find a way to spare his feelings until he was thinking clearly again—like, in the morning.

"We can't make out in the car like a couple of teenagers, Ronan," she told him, speaking softly. "You don't want the neighbors seeing us like that."

"I don't care who sees, but you're probably right. I don't want you to feel embarrassed." He began to get out of the car but he was unsteady and his knees buckled for a moment.

Afraid he was going to hurt himself, she lunged forward, making a grab for him.

Ronan grabbed onto the car door, managing to steady himself. "I'll be okay in a second," he promised, taking a moment.

Sierra repositioned herself so that she was once again acting like a human crutch. She slipped her arm under his. "Let's get you into the house so you can sleep it off."

"That's not what I want to do," he told her, turning his head so that his face was flush against her cheek and his breath was slipping almost seductively against her skin.

Warm waves rippled through her, swiftly weakening her knees.

Think of something else. Think of something else! Sierra ordered herself.

"You need your sleep, Romeo. Plenty of time for that kind of thing later on," she added, hoping she sounded convincingly gruff.

A few false starts impeded her but she finally managed to get Ronan to his door. Trying not to pant—as a limp weight, he was exceedingly heavy—she said, "Give me your key."

"You telling me you don't think I can open my own door?"

If he was actually asking her the question, Sierra was certain it would have sounded far more hostile or belligerent. But he wasn't asking *her*, he was asking Wendy, and unless she was hallucinating, his voice had taken on a teasing quality.

She almost wished she was Wendy. For a number of reasons.

But she wasn't Wendy and right now her main goal was

to get him into his house and onto something horizontal he could just sack out on.

"Go ahead, unlock your door," she told him.

He jabbed his key toward the door, attempting to go higher, then lower, without coming anywhere close to breaching the keyhole.

"I would," he grumbled, "if this damn lock would just stop moving around so much."

Still supporting him as best she could with her shoulder under his arm, Sierra put her hand out. "Maybe I can get it to stop," she told him, using her best upbeat voice.

"Good luck," he told her, handing over the key. When she unlocked the door and pushed it open, he looked at her with nothing short of awestruck wonder. "How did you do that?"

"Beginner's luck," she said, giving him back his key. "Now let's get you inside."

He groaned a little and swayed as she managed to get him past the threshold.

There was a sofa several feet into the house and she silently blessed the fact that the ordeal of getting him safely inside the house and onto a horizontal surface was almost over.

Exerting a mighty effort, Sierra finally managed to get him to the first piece of furniture in the room and then released her hold on his body. He slumped onto the sofa.

"I don't understand." She was panting. "How did you manage to get like this on only four drinks?" She marveled that his ability to hold his liquor wasn't better than this, even if she had seen him down the drinks rather quickly.

"They were doubles," he answered, his voice all but muffled because he was lying facedown on the sofa cushion.

"Of course they were," she said. Well, that explained it, she thought. "You are going to be one sorry man tomorrow morning—if you wind up making it through the night," she amended.

Ronan didn't answer her.

In fact, he was out like a light. Good. That was the best thing for him right now.

Starting to walk away, Sierra was almost to the front door when she stopped abruptly. She looked over her shoulder at the slumped figure, concerned. If Ronan woke in the middle of the night, nauseous and needing to throw up, he would probably never make it to the bathroom—wherever that was.

She decided to put a pail by the sofa just in case that happened—but first she had to find one. She turned on a light switch on the wall, illuminating the room. Fearing she would wind up waking him, Sierra held her breath as she looked in his direction. But Ronan didn't stir.

Crossing back to the sofa and standing over him, she listened intently. Ronan was sound asleep—and breathing.

Okay, back to looking for a pail.

She wandered through the living room and made her way to the next room, which was the kitchen. She briefly considered dragging the garbage pail over to the sofa, then decided against it. Going on to the next room, she found herself in what she took to be the master bedroom.

His bedroom.

It looked nothing short of chaotic. The double bed's sheets were all bunched up and partially on the floor, as was one pillow. Neatness obviously didn't count in his book, she mused.

She found what she was looking for in his bathroom: a small white garbage pail right next to the sink. Taking it, she passed through his bedroom again on her way to the living room.

That was when she noticed it.

He had a framed photograph on his bureau. Curious, she turned on the light to get a better look. When she did, her breath backed up in her throat.

At first glance she could have been looking at a picture of herself. Closer scrutiny had her seeing the differences, but that first glance—

No wonder Ronan had kissed her. In his present state of

intoxication, he had confused his past with his present and when he'd looked at her, he'd thought he was looking at his fiancée.

"I am sorry," she whispered to Ronan.

Replacing the framed photograph, she shut off the light and took the pail she'd found to the living room. She positioned the pail right beside the sofa where she knew he was bound to see it.

At least, she thought he was bound to see the pail.

But then she reconsidered. Given his present state, he might not.

Torn, she looked back at Ronan, who at least for now was still asleep although he had begun making strange, fitful noises. If he continued that way, he was going to wake himself up. Or maybe make himself sicker. It would be a shame if he wound up throwing up on the sofa. It appeared to be relatively new and was a nice medium gray color. Getting it cleaned would be a real challenge.

But she couldn't just stay there for the rest of the night, babysitting him, Sierra silently argued. He wouldn't be grateful for her sacrifice when he woke in the morning. Other than being hungover, he'd be annoyed that she'd stayed to "watch over him" as if he was some helpless frat boy liable to choke on his own vomit.

The hell with him and his pride. She didn't care what he'd say.

With a sigh, she looked around the living room for somewhere that she could spend the rest of the night.

There was his bedroom, of course, but that defeated the purpose. She wouldn't be able to keep an eye on him from there.

All he had in the living room beyond the coffee table and the sofa was an upholstered chair. Resigned, she dragged the chair over to the sofa so she could sit closer to him.

She sank into it and began her unofficial vigil.

Chapter Eleven

Every single part of Ronan ached and he felt like hell, inside and out. The worst was his head. It throbbed so hard, it felt as if it was on the verge of exploding into tiny pieces at any moment.

He'd forgotten just how miserable a hangover could feel. It wasn't something he welcomed revisiting, especially after having been sober for close to an entire year.

A year. That was the last time he'd felt like this. On the day after the anniversary when he'd lost her.

Lost Wendy.

Damn. He thought he'd gotten better hold of himself than this.

He felt as if the room was on the verge of spinning around, which would only make things worse. He needed to open his eyes. If he opened his eyes and sat up, he was certain the brakes would come back on and the room wouldn't start going around and around like a cheap ride at an amusement park.

Pushing his body into an upright position, Ronan forced himself to concentrate not on his swirling stomach but on getting his eyelids to open.

He felt as if he was prying them apart.

It took concentration and effort and it wasn't easy because once he opened them, he'd officially be back in a world without Wendy in it.

A world that he had been partially sleepwalking through for two years now.

C'mon, O'Bannon, you're made of tougher stuff than that, he upbraided himself. *At bottom, you're a Cavanaugh. Build on it.*

His eyes opened, followed almost immediately by his mouth. For one split second he thought…he thought he saw her.

And then he realized that although he wasn't alone, the woman sitting just opposite him in the upholstered chair—the one he and Wendy had found in that silly little garage sale—wasn't Wendy.

It was Carlyle and it looked like she was dozing.

"What are you doing here?"

The harsh voice broke through the gauze-like haze surrounding her brain, stripping her of the last remnants of pseudo-sleep.

Alerted, Sierra grasped at the armrests and sat as straight as an arrow. Ronan's question echoed in her head. She cleared her throat before answering him.

"Making sure you don't choke to death during the night."

"How's that again?"

Shifting to the edge of the chair, she tried to explain. "I was afraid that you'd throw up and choke on your own—well, you get the idea. But now that you're awake, I'll just go—no, I can't," she realized as her scattered thoughts began to fall into a more coherent whole.

"You can't?" he questioned, just going with the last thing she said. "Why not?"

"Because whenever you're ready and feel up to it," she told him in a patient voice that teachers used with slow learners, "I have to take you to your car."

"My car?" he repeated. Wasn't it in his driveway? He waited for an explanation.

"Yes, it's still in Malone's parking lot."

Why couldn't he remember anything? He began to shake

his head and immediately stopped. He didn't want his head to explode. "Why's it there?"

"Because you were in no condition to drive home," she said simply.

He opened his mouth twice to say something, changing his mind each time. Finally he said, "You don't have to stay here. I can call my—"

His face suddenly turned a greenish shade of pale.

Her brothers had looked exactly the same shade during their college-rebellion days. "There's a pail right by your foot," she prompted, pointing.

Ronan valued his dignity and had he been able to walk out of the room and make it to the bathroom with some semblance of that dignity, he would have. But his stomach didn't care about dignity and gave him absolutely no choice.

With the greatest sense of urgency, he made a grab for the pail and brought it up to his mouth—with less than a second to spare.

When he finally finished purging the swirling contents of his stomach, he put the pail on the far side of the sofa, as far away from either of them as possible.

Looking up, expecting to see a reproving expression on Sierra's face, he realized that instead of looking judgmental or sickened by what she had just witnessed, she was handing him a kitchen towel, slightly dampened on one end.

"You might want to use this," she suggested tactfully.

Ronan passed the damp side of the towel over his face and then dried it with the other end. "Sorry," he murmured.

"For being human?" she quipped, making light of the situation. "Happens to the best of us. I know this recipe that helps with hangovers. It's seen my brothers through some pretty bad bouts when they'd had too much to drink. I would be happy to whip it up for you while you take a shower."

He looked down at himself, taking that to be a hint. "I guess I need one, huh?"

She gave him the most innocent of smiles. "Just a suggestion."

He rose to his feet slower than he was happy about. It was a precaution just in case his legs weren't steady enough to support him. The last thing he wanted was to fall right in front of this woman. Deciding that he could at least manage to walk away on his own two feet, he paused just before he began to head for the bathroom. "What about you?"

She assumed he was asking about her own state of sobriety. "I'm fine," she told him. "I only had that one drink and it was mostly orange juice."

"No, I mean did you get any sleep?" He felt guilty that she'd spent the night watching over him.

"I do well on catnaps," Sierra told him evasively. He began to walk away when she brought his attention to something else. "Oh, and don't forget to take that pail with you. I got it from your bathroom," she told him just before she went into his kitchen.

She heard him groan as he picked up the pail.

HE TOOK AN extra-long time in the shower, letting the water hit him until he felt strong enough to face the rest of the day—and the world.

Though he would have preferred it, he knew he couldn't call in sick. Not when he was just dealing with a hangover and not at death's door. There was too much work to do on the serial killer case and besides, he wasn't really sick, just miserable. And miserable would eventually pass.

Getting out of the shower, Ronan decided to forego shaving and just got dressed. He didn't bother with the hair dryer, either, letting his wet hair dry on its own. It wasn't as if he was trying to impress anyone, just get back to the business of living.

Dressed and probably feeling as good as he was going to feel today, he squared his shoulders and walked out of his bedroom, heading for the kitchen.

Sierra was still there, moving about in his kitchen. He hadn't imagined her. For a few seconds there, he thought he might have. The way he sometimes imagined Wendy.

"What are you doing?" he asked her as he walked into the kitchen.

She turned from the counter, a dish with what looked like two slices of bread in her hand. "Making you something to eat."

His stomach rebelled at the very mention of food, even as he took a seat at the kitchen table. "I can't eat," he told her.

Undaunted, Sierra placed the plate on the table in front of him. "Eat this. My brother Danny used to say that it helped him when he was trying to shake off a hangover."

He looked down at the plate quizzically. "Toast?" he questioned.

"With honey. He swears by it." Turning away for a second, she took a mug from the counter. He noticed it was steaming. She put it next to the plate. "And my brother Joey swears by chamomile tea, so I made you some of that, too."

Ronan stared at the two things she pushed a little closer to him on the table. Where did she get these items? He tried to think.

"I have honey?" he questioned. "And I *know* for a fact I don't have tea."

"You don't have either one," Sierra agreed, "but I do."

He tried to make sense out of what she was telling him. "You carry this stuff around with you?"

"In my purse," she specified. "I carry around a lot of things in case of an emergency," she added. "You never know when you might need something. Now, go ahead, eat the toast and drink the tea even though you don't want to," she instructed. "I promise you'll feel better."

He contemplated the two items in front of him, weakening. "Well, I don't think that I could feel any worse."

"That's the attitude," Sierra told him, cheering him on.

He took a tentative bite of the honey sandwich, waiting

for it to come back up. When it didn't, he took another bite, chewing slowly and amazed that his stomach was cooperating.

"By the way," he said, taking a sip of the tea, "what did you do to my kitchen?"

Watching him closely and holding her breath, hoping he could hold down the toast and honey, she wasn't sure what he was referring to. Sierra looked around then recalled the condition of the kitchen when she'd walked in last night. There were dishes in the sink, things left out on the counter and in an overall general state of disarray.

"Oh, that. I cleaned it up. I had nothing else to do," she explained. "This way, I figured it would be easier for you to find things. You wouldn't have to waste your time looking for them."

"I had a system," he protested with just a touch of indignation as he took another bite of the toast and honey.

It took effort not to laugh at that statement. "Sure you did," she said, humoring him. "The good news—for you—is that you'll probably go back to that system soon enough," she told him. "So, feeling any better?" she asked as he finished off the last bite of the honey sandwich, washing it down with the tea.

Ronan shrugged. "I guess. Now I only feel like death warmed over."

"Progress," she declared, pleased. "It happens in little steps." Standing, she took the empty plate and mug over to the sink. "If you don't feel up to driving in today, I'll drive us in and then take you to Malone's after the shift's over. To Malone's *parking lot*," she stressed because she didn't want him to think she was suggesting he stop at the bar for a drink.

"Stand down, Jiminy Cricket, I'm not about to repeat last night."

"Never said you did," she told him innocently. "I just wanted my meaning to be clear, that's all. Sometimes I have a tendency not to do that," she said with a quick smile.

He watched her rinse off the plate and mug, and it occurred to him she hadn't had anything yet. "Don't you want to eat anything?" he asked.

"Your cupboard is almost bare," she pointed out. "I don't want to rob you of the last of your provisions. Don't worry, I'll get something at work." Drying off the two items, she put the mug and plate away.

"I guess I'm ready to go, then," he told her, getting up from the table. And then he realized that something was missing. "Wait a second." He looked around. "Where's my weapon?"

"Don't worry, you didn't lose it. It's right here." So saying, Sierra opened his dishwasher.

He stared at her as if she'd lost her mind. "You put my gun in the dishwasher?"

"Well, I didn't know where you normally kept it and I wasn't planning on using the dishwasher, so I figured it was as good a place as any to store it."

That raised a question in his mind. "Where do you keep your gun?"

"In the breadbox on the counter."

"Where do you keep your bread?"

She offered him a wide smile. "In the refrigerator."

Strapping on his weapon, Ronan shook his head and laughed. "You're one of a kind, Carlyle."

"Funny, my dad says the same thing," she told him, "usually when he's reading me the riot act."

He could see her being a real pain. But for some reason the thought made him smile. "Does that happen often?"

"Not as often as it used to," she replied. And then she added, "I think he's getting less crusty in his old age."

Ronan laughed. "He probably thinks the same thing about you." He stopped short just before opening the front door and going out. "Hey, what did you slip me in that funny tea?"

"Nothing. Chamomile just looks like that," she assured him.

"No, I'm not talking about the way it looks." He locked the front door, slipping the key into his pocket. "We're talking."

Sierra disarmed the alarm on her car and then got in. "I noticed that."

Ronan got in on the passenger side, closing the door then putting on his seat belt. "I don't do that," he pointed out. "Talk," he added in case she didn't understand what he was referring to.

She patted his shoulder and smiled. "Maybe it's just been building up in you all these years."

He sincerely doubted that. Things felt strange and unsettled in his head. Bits and pieces of last night began coming back to him, not in any sort of order, but enough to make him wonder if he'd been like this last night, talking too much.

He looked at her as she started the car. "Did I say anything last night?"

"You said a lot of things last night," Sierra answered.

He frowned impatiently. "No, I mean to you."

"So did I," she answered brightly. Pulling out, she guided the car out of the development.

"Did I say anything...unusual? Or, um, *do* anything unusual?" he asked, feeling incredibly uncomfortable talking about this—whatever "this" was.

It was just that something felt...off. Something was teasing his brain, whispering just along the very perimeter of his mind but not materializing enough for him to be able to put his finger on it.

"I guess that would depend on your definition of unusual," she told him, keeping her eyes on the road.

He'd dreamed of Wendy last night. Small, fitful, unformed fragments that refused to be pieced together into even a semblance of a whole. He remembered holding her and kissing her, and that everything had felt right for just a tiny, tiny moment.

But that had been just a dream, right? He hadn't actually done that because Wendy was gone. Yes, Carlyle looked a little like her at first glance—maybe even at second—but he knew the difference. There was no way he would make that sort of a mistake.

Would he?

He looked at Sierra's profile, growing progressively more uncomfortable as doubts began to pop up in his mind and haunt him.

"Then I didn't—make a move—on *anyone*?" Ronan emphasized the word.

He just couldn't get himself to say "a move on you." But he knew she'd correct him and tell him if he'd overstepped his boundaries with her.

Without fully realizing it, he held his breath, waiting for Sierra to give him an answer.

"Not that I could see. You sat at that table with me until we left, so if you're worried that you made a move on some unsuspecting woman at the bar, you didn't," she told him.

Ronan sighed, relief flowing through his veins. One concern put to rest.

"That's good to know, because I just wouldn't have wanted anyone to misunderstand and think that I was putting moves on them." The next second his words echoed back to him in his mind. "Damn, I shouldn't be telling you this," he said, upbraiding himself.

She smiled then. "Haven't you heard, O'Bannon? They say that confession is good for the soul."

"I don't have a soul," he grumbled.

"Well, on the outside chance that it might turn up again, confession will be good for it," she said with a laugh.

His answer to that was something unintelligible and she decided it was wiser to just leave it at that and not ask any questions.

On the bright side, if it could be seen as that, she silently noted, it looked like O'Bannon was back to his old surly self.

Chapter Twelve

"So, I don't suppose anyone came forward between last night and this morning with anything that remotely could be mistaken for a lead?"

The question came from Carver. The lieutenant had come out his office and crossed to Ronan's desk the moment the detective walked into the squad room.

"Have a heart, Lieutenant. We just got here," Sierra said, going to her own desk and trying to deflect Carver's attention away from his prime target.

"So, what, she's doing the talking for you now, O'Bannon? When did that happen?" Carver asked. He took a closer look at the lead detective and frowned. "You look a little green, O'Bannon. You sick?"

"He had a touch of food poisoning," Sierra spoke up again. When the lieutenant glared at her, she pretended not to notice as she continued. "We rode up in the elevator together and he told me about the food poisoning when I commented on his pale coloring, same as you, Lieutenant."

Carver made a disparaging noise, as if the lead detective's bout of food poisoning had occurred simply to annoy him. And then he said, "If you're not feeling well, go home, O'Bannon. We can't have you throwing up all over the squad room."

"I've got it under control, Lieutenant," Ronan told him, finally managing to get a word in edgewise.

Carver seemed unconvinced. "Doesn't look that way to me," he commented. "But if you say so, carry on. And *find* something," he demanded. "I'm getting pressure from above on all sides. We're supposed to be a safe city, not a city where some crazy serial killer's running wild, playing judge, jury and executioner."

"We're trying to follow up some possible leads, Lieutenant," Ronan answered.

"Well, follow up faster," the man ordered before turning on his heel and returning to his office.

Ronan turned toward Sierra the second the lieutenant was back in his office. One look at his face told her what was coming.

"I don't need you running interference for me, Carlyle."

"Sorry, I was just doing what I'd want someone to do for me if I wasn't feeling well."

Ronan scowled at her. "I said that I was fine," he snapped.

Exasperated, Sierra threw up her hands. "Fine, have it your way." With that, she began to head out of the squad room again.

"And just where are you going?"

"To get some breakfast if that's all right with you. I told you that this morning," she reminded him.

He'd forgotten. "Yeah, fine. Go." He waved her on her way.

Yes, Sierra thought as she left the squad room, O'Bannon was definitely back. And she should definitely have her head examined.

WHEN SHE RETURNED several minutes later, a container of coffee and a toasted muffin stuffed with all the basic ingredients that made up a filling breakfast—fried egg, ham and cheese—she saw that the other two detectives on the team had come in and were gathered around Ronan's desk.

Was something up?

Sierra quickened her pace, crossing to her desk.

"Morning, guys." She nodded at both Martinez and Choi. "What did I miss?"

"Not much," Martinez told her. "We were just telling O'Bannon here that we showed that photo of the woman from the Shamrock around and a couple of people at the latest victim's party thought they might have recognized her—maybe," the detective noted with a less than triumphant look.

"Was that a hard and fast 'maybe' or a so-so 'maybe'?" Sierra asked, sitting at her desk.

"I think it was more of an 'if I answer this question the way you want, will you go away' maybe," Choi answered. "You ask me, that photo we took off the surveillance video isn't very clear. I think I had an ex-girlfriend who looked like that. And, no, it wasn't her," the detective quickly added.

"You have enough ex-girlfriends to fill up the break room," Martinez said to his partner. "That doesn't mean anything."

"I think you two are getting punchy," Ronan commented. It felt as if they were going around and around with this case. "Why don't we go at it from the angle that someone wants to rid the streets of both of these gangs, and see where that gets us?"

"You mean like a real vigilante?" Choi asked.

"I was thinking more along the lines like there was a new drug gang in Tesla who were looking to get rid of the competition. Both of the known gangs deal in drugs to some extent, maybe someone is looking to go exclusive. Talk to your CIs, any DEA contacts you might have who owe you a favor…see if anyone knows anything."

Martinez sighed as he nodded. "More hamster wheel activities."

Confused, Ronan looked at him. "Come again?"

"You know, like running in a damn wheel, getting nowhere," Martinez explained. It was obvious that was the way both he and his partner felt after coming up empty conducting the other canvasses.

Ever the optimist, Sierra said, "At least we'll be running." All three men looked at her in surprise. "And who knows, the forward momentum might actually wind up getting us someplace."

Ronan turned to the other two detectives. "Can either of you get her to stop?"

"That's above my pay grade, boss," Choi told him, walking away.

"Not me, Fearless Leader. I know better." Martinez winked at Sierra. "Besides, I've got phone calls to make, contacts to reestablish."

"All I'm doing is just trying to spread a little optimism," she told Ronan in her defense.

"You're certainly spreading something," he told her. The next moment, he rose from his desk.

"Did you decide to take Carver up on his order and go home?" she asked. Ronan still looked rather greenish to her.

"No," he retorted. "I'm going to see if I can get some of that damn tea." He gave her a silencing look, indicating he didn't want her making any speculations. "Don't say a word."

Doing her best not to smile, Sierra mimed a zipper being pulled across her lips. She heard Ronan mumble something under his breath as he walked out, but the words were indistinct.

She was getting through to him, Sierra thought in satisfaction.

THE UNIFORM FELT oddly confining, not to mention itchy. She couldn't remember the last time she'd had her dress blues on. It had to have been just prior to her becoming a detective, which, at this point, seemed to her like an eternity ago. She vaguely recalled that the occasion had been for some sort of ceremony, not a funeral the way this was.

Everyone had turned out to pay their respects and say goodbye to the chief of police who had died suddenly last week.

The church was large but it had still been filled to overflowing, not just with the members of the police department, but with city officials as well as an impressive number of state officials.

The eulogies, which ran long, were touching, remembering Walter Hudson, the man, as well as his service to the city he loved.

Sierra was only half listening. Her heart went out to the police chief's widow who seemed to have shrunk into herself. The thin woman looked almost numb and so terribly lost as she'd hung on her son and son-in-law's arms when she had entered the church. No matter how beautiful the ceremony, no words anyone could say would make up for the fact that the woman's husband was gone and nothing was going to bring him back.

Because each department sat together, Ronan was sitting next to Sierra in the pew. The service was almost over when he glanced in her direction and saw that her cheek was damp.

"You're crying," Ronan whispered in surprise.

"No, I'm not," she denied stubbornly. Why was he looking at her? Everything worth seeing was happening at the altar in the front of the church.

"All right, then it's raining on your face," he observed, still whispering. He dug a handkerchief out of his pocket. "Here." He pushed the handkerchief on her. "You don't want to be caught with rain on your face."

Sierra had no choice, so she took the handkerchief, saying nothing as she sniffled. She absolutely hated crying, but there were times when she just couldn't help it. Hearing the eulogies reminded her of other funerals she'd been to, usually for firemen her father and brothers knew who had died while saving someone.

It always seemed so unfair to her, having life taken away when there was still so much for them to do, to enjoy.

A few minutes later, the ceremony was concluded. As they filed out of the pews, she tried to hand the handkerchief back to Ronan, but he shook his head.

"Hang on to it. You never know when it might rain again. We still have to go to the grave site," he reminded her.

She wasn't sure if she was up to that. "I think I'll just skip that and go back to the squad room to work," she told Ronan. "Nobody'll notice if I'm not at the grave site."

"The lieutenant will notice," Ronan assured her. "Not to mention other people. And you're not going to solve this case in the next hour, so suck it up, Carlyle. You're coming to the grave site." It wasn't a request, it was an order.

For a moment she debated her options, but to not go would be in direct defiance of O'Bannon's authority. She decided it would just be easier to go along with what he'd told her to do than to resist and argue with him over it. For one thing, it would draw too much attention, something she wanted, in her present vulnerable state, to avoid.

"All right," she said, giving in. "I'll go to the cemetery," she told him.

He hadn't expected her to give in this quickly. "You okay, Carlyle?"

She kept her eyes focused straight ahead as she made her way out of the church. "It's a funeral. I'm never okay at a funeral."

Her comment touched something inside him.

"Yeah, I know what you mean."

The words had slipped out before he could think better of them, think better of making such a personal admission. He slanted a glance at her. But if Sierra heard, for once she made no comment on what he'd said and for that he was grateful.

"HERE," SIERRA SAID the following morning as she placed what appeared to be a freshly starched and ironed, folded handkerchief on Ronan's desk. "I washed it for you."

In the middle of powering up his computer, Ronan glanced down at the handkerchief he had given her in church yesterday.

"You didn't have to do that." It wasn't as if she'd done more than just wipe away a few tears with it. "It didn't look this good when it was new," he commented, slightly amused as he picked the handkerchief up and tucked it into his back pocket.

Because he'd been nice to her, Sierra supposed she owed him a somewhat of an explanation.

"I didn't mean to break down that way," she told him, her voice a little gruff to hide her discomfort at displaying her vulnerable side. "It's just that the funeral reminded me of just how fragile life is. And the chief's wife looked so absolutely devastated, it just got to me. They'd been together since they were freshmen in high school and I know what she had to be thinking—that she didn't know how she was going to manage to draw a single breath without him being somewhere close by."

He remembered feeling that way once. Ronan deliberately kept a stony exterior as he said, "She'll find out that she can."

"Yes, I know." Again, the image of the chief's widow flashed through her mind. "But the amount of pain she has to be going through right now… I just wish I could help her somehow."

"There *is* no help for something like that," Ronan told her, his voice detached. "All you can do is put one foot in front of the other, go from one end of the day to the other, until it becomes almost automatic."

His eyes met hers and, for a brief instant, Ronan couldn't help wondering if she somehow knew about Wendy, knew about the circumstances surrounding his loss. The next moment, he shrugged it off. He was probably just letting his imagination get away from him. Carlyle was given to running off at the mouth. If she knew about Wendy, she would have said something to him. It wasn't in her nature to keep that sort of information just to herself.

"All right, enough philosophizing things that can't be changed. Where are we with this serial killer case?" he asked, throwing the question open not just to Sierra but to the other two detectives who had just walked in.

"Every one of those victims had people who wanted to see them dead, so we thought, until something else comes up, we'd start checking out their alibis around the times of death," Choi volunteered.

"Great. How many names?" Ronan asked.

"About thirty or so—so far," Martinez clarified.

That was actually less than he'd thought. "Let's divide the names of every one of those possible suspects and see if we can come up with one *genuine* suspect," Ronan told them.

"It bothers me that if it's just one guy with a beef against another member of the gang, then why were all those other victims killed?" Choi commented.

"There's that, but also what about that 'new drug pusher on the block' theory?" Ronan asked, looking at all three detectives.

"Oh, yeah," Choi remembered. "Intel on the street says that there is no new wannabe drug lord trying to make his mark by getting rid of the competition. If there is one, it's news to the DEA," Choi told him. "And they'd be the first to know."

"No argument," Ronan agreed. "Okay, so we go back to questioning gang members. See if someone slips up." He wanted to let Carver see that every effort was being made to track down and capture the serial killer. "Let's start herding War Lords and Terminators, bring them in for questioning," he told the team. "The answer's got to be out there somewhere," he insisted. "Let's find it before this bastard kills someone else," he urged.

"Okay," Sierra said, getting up from her desk. "We've got our marching orders, let's go."

"You sound like you're enjoying this," Ronan observed.

"What I'll enjoy is bringing these executions to an end," she said, taking one list of possible suspect names with her.

"I DON'T KNOW about the rest of you," Choi declared as he powered down his computer late in the day four days later, "but I, for one, have never been so grateful to see Friday put in an appearance in my life. It's going to be really great to get away from this case for a couple of days."

It had been four days filled with one fruitless interview after another. With one dead end after another. And now, with more than a week having passed since the last victim had been found, there were no new leads to follow, no old ones to readdress.

The investigation had apparently come to a grinding standstill.

"Maybe the guy has decided he has enough blood on his hands and just abruptly stopped killing," Martinez suggested.

"Or maybe a rock fell on his head and he's dead," Ronan countered. "That's the more likely scenario. If bloodlust made him kill, there's no reason to think that he'd just walk away from it."

"But what if it wasn't bloodlust? What if it was for a specific reason?" Sierra asked.

"Agatha Christie again?" he asked wearily.

"No." She was sorry she had ever raised the idea, even though there was a part of her that felt there was validity to a hide-in-plain-sight sort of situation. But exactly what was it that was being hidden in plain sight?

"Then what?" Ronan asked.

"That's the part I haven't worked out yet," she confessed.

"Well, keep working on it," he told her, surprising Sierra. "See if you come up with anything. At this point, I'm ready to grasp at any straw," he said honestly.

"I'm with Carlyle," Martinez said. "Unless this is all just basic bloodlust—and if that's the case, where is this guy?—there's got to be something to tie these victims together."

"Isn't this where I came in?" Choi asked.

"Go home. We'll get a fresh start on Monday," Ronan told them.

"Don't have to tell me twice," Martinez said. "What I need now is a cold beer and a hot date."

"You're married," Sierra pointed out.

"Never said I wasn't. The hot date is with my wife," he added with a wide smile. "See you all Monday."

"Wait up, I'll walk out with you," Choi called out.

"As long as you don't want to come on my date, sure," Martinez answered good-naturedly.

Taking out her purse, Sierra looked at Ronan. "You're still sitting at your desk."

"There's that keen eye of yours again," he said cryptically.

"If you found an angle to work, I'll stay and help," she offered.

He didn't even bother looking up. "Go home, Carlyle."

Instead she came around to stand behind him to look at what he was working on. He was reviewing cases dating back two years that had to do with gang members involved in crimes in Tesla and in Allegro.

"Go home, Carlyle," he repeated.

"This is after hours. I don't have to listen to you."

"Yes, you do," he insisted.

"Sorry," she told him, sitting and rebooting her computer. "I know that your lips are moving, but I just can't hear you."

"You're annoying, you know."

She looked up and smiled just for a moment. "I know."

Ronan gave up. And did his best not to smile.

Chapter Thirteen

The silence within the squad room was getting to her. She'd never cared for stone-cold silence. She worked far better with at least some sort of noise in the background.

Glancing up, she saw that Ronan was reading something on the screen. She debated going back to the silence, then decided she had nothing to lose.

"Are you going to the ceremony tomorrow?" Sierra asked.

He didn't bother looking up. It was as if he was just waiting for her to say something. Anything. "I sort of have to," Ronan told her.

Since being paired up with Ronan, she'd taken it upon herself to be more up on the Cavanaugh network than she had previously been.

"Because you're related to him and showing up is a show of support?" she queried.

She couldn't read his expression when he looked up. "Because my mother would have my head if I didn't," he told her honestly. Since she'd asked him about his attendance, he decided to do the same. "Are you going to be there?"

There was no hesitation. "Of course. It's a show of respect for the new chief. I hear he's a very fair, good man."

"Yeah, he is. If you're interested, the former chief of police—his father," Ronan added, "is holding a celebration the day after the swearing-in ceremony. I hear he's pulling out all the stops."

She loved a good party, but she wasn't about to crash one. "I'd have to be invited," she pointed out.

"Well, you kind of are." Even as he said the words, he didn't know why he was saying them, given how he was trying to keep the lines between his work and his private life separate.

"Excuse me?"

"It's an open invitation to the entire police force," he explained impatiently.

That sounded a little overwhelming. "The former chief is hosting a party for the entire department?"

"And their plus ones," Ronan added, wanting to be entirely accurate.

That sort of thing could set someone back quite a bit, she thought. "I don't mean to be crass—"

"There's a first," Ronan observed wryly.

Sierra ignored the remark. "But isn't feeding *that* many people awfully expensive?"

He scrolled over to another article before answering her. "The family chips in to cover costs. Uncle Andrew would throw those gatherings anyway, but nobody wants him to go broke, so we all put some money in, or bring the groceries he needs to create those mind-blowing meals he whips up."

Nodding her head, Sierra pulled out her messenger bag then fished out her wallet, taking several bills out. "So, how much is it?"

Ronan frowned at her. "Put that away, Carlyle. There's no charge for you," he informed her. "You're not family."

She couldn't gauge his attitude from his tone of voice. "I don't know if I'm being insulted or given a pass," she told him. Following his lead, she looked back at her screen then switched to another story and scrolled down, looking for something that might be pertinent.

"Just accept it," he instructed. "So, are you coming?"

"Sure. I need an address, though," she told him. "I don't know where the chief lives."

He started to tell her then stopped. "Tell you what. You drove me in my less than steady state. Let me return the favor. I'll pick you up at noon on Sunday for the party. Makes it easier, actually. When everyone shows up, parking is hell and, like I said, this promises to be a pull-all-the-stops-out party."

His offer surprised her. And pleased her. "Okay, thanks."

She quickly wrote down her address on a piece of paper and then leaned across her desk and handed it to Ronan.

He took it, not bothering to tell her that he already knew where she lived. She might get the wrong idea. At the very least, she'd ask him a dozen questions as to why he knew her address and he didn't want to get into it with her. He didn't like explaining himself, especially when he couldn't even do it *to* himself. He just chalked it up to idle curiosity.

He could feel Sierra looking at him even after he tucked her address away in his pocket. Ordinarily, he could tune something like that out. But there was just something about this woman that didn't allow him to do that.

"Something wrong?" he asked her.

"Are we bonding?"

"What? No. What makes you say that?" His voice went through three entirely different tones, one for each sentence, ending on a confused note.

"Well, we were just having a conversation—"

He'd just lost his place on the link he'd pulled up. Irritated, he told her, "Which you initiated."

"But which you continued," she pointed out. "And now you actually offered to pick me up for a party." That wasn't merely random bonding. That was being a friend, in her book.

"I explained why."

"You explained it to assuage your own concerns," she told him. "I have a different take on it, though."

"I know I'm going to regret this," Ronan said as a preface before asking, "Which is?"

"That we really are bonding," she said happily. "You finally realized that it's better to talk to me than to ignore me."

He sighed audibly, passing a hand over his eyes. "I was right. I regret asking."

Rather than be affronted, Sierra grinned. "Don't worry. I won't tell anyone."

She had lost him. "Tell them what?"

"That you're human. And nice. That under that crusty shell is—"

"Another crusty shell," he pronounced with conviction.

She merely smiled at him. "Have it your way."

He would have said she was patronizing him, except that he didn't think she was capable of that. "I intend to. I—oh, hell, never mind. I'm not getting anywhere."

Sierra cocked her head, looking at him and silently asking him a question. He put his own interpretation to it.

"With this," he all but shouted, waving his hand at his computer screen. "I might as well just call it a night." And with that, he powered down his computer, shutting off his monitor at the same time. He needed to get some air.

"See you at the ceremony tomorrow," she called after Ronan cheerfully.

"Yeah, right," he muttered, barely audible as he walked out.

He swore roundly under his breath as he jabbed his finger at the down button for the elevator. He had no idea what had come over him, or why he'd extended the invitation to her in the first place.

Yeah, you do, the voice in his head countered.

It had to do with the fact that Carlyle reminded him of Wendy. She'd been nice to him, going out of her way to do it. But those were precisely the reasons why he *shouldn't* have anything to do with her beyond what was absolutely necessary because of work.

Because being around her—when he let his guard down—made him remember. And memories eventually brought pain. Pain that couldn't be resolved because Wendy was never coming back.

She couldn't.

If he knew what was good for him, he'd find a way to make Carlyle's life a living hell until she asked to be transferred out of the department altogether or at least off the team.

But that was just the problem. He couldn't get himself to make her life a living hell. The best he could do was behave as if he didn't want her intruding into his life.

He was going to regret this, Ronan predicted. Just as he had earlier.

SIERRA ARRIVED AT the ceremony early to ensure that she got a seat. It was being held in the square behind city hall, which could hold a sizable crowd and was now filled with a sea of folding chairs. She had a feeling that even more people would show up for the new chief of police's swearing-in ceremony than had attended the previous chief's funeral.

Within half an hour, she saw that she was right.

Taking a seat on the end of a row near the middle of all the chairs, she was in a perfect position to observe all the members of the new chief's family—and there were a great many of them—react to the fact that one of their own was being made chief of police.

To a person, they beamed.

Even Ronan, whom she'd spotted early on, sitting with his immediate family, including his mother, looked proud and happier than she had ever seen him.

Seeing him that way made her happy in turn. She was glad to see that he could relax amid his own like this. It showed her a whole different side of him.

She caught herself paying more attention to Ronan than to the ceremony unfolding on the stage in front of the assembled audience. Paying attention to Ronan and smiling. And, at one point, running her finger along her lips and remembering what she was fairly certain Ronan had no memory of.

The moment the ceremony concluded, Sierra quickly slipped out. It was her main reason for taking a seat at the end of a row. She didn't have to wait for the other occupants of the row to file out, which in turn meant she didn't run the risk of having Ronan see her. This was his day, his and his family's, to enjoy.

She thought about his smile a lot throughout the rest of the day.

HE MUST HAVE lost his mind.

It wasn't the first time the thought had crossed Ronan's mind. He'd already accused himself of that three times before he ever got into his car to drive to Carlyle's house to pick her up for his uncle's celebration.

If he could have come up with a plausible excuse that didn't sound as if it had been conceived by an eight-year-old with no spark of creativity to his name, he would have called the detective and begged off.

But nothing came to mind and, besides, he supposed he did owe her. She could have left him to his own devices in Malone's that night he'd wound up drinking too much and just gone home. Granted, it wasn't as if he'd been stranded on a deserted island. Someone would have given him a ride home, or worse coming to worst, he could have hailed a cab.

But she hadn't gone home. She'd played the Girl Scout and not only taken him home but then put on the hair shirt of an early, unsung Christian martyr and stayed with him to make sure he'd make it through the night without some sort of mishap.

Okay, that would have been a long shot, but she'd obviously believed it was possible, which was what ultimately counted in this scenario.

What kind of a person did that, anyway? he asked himself.

A nice person.

That was why he couldn't just bail on her, much as his spirit to survive urged him to.

Besides, once he brought her to the celebration, there was no rule that said he had to stay with her. She wasn't some shy, reclusive shrinking violet who needed to have her hand held. The woman was nothing if not upbeat and outgoing. She would be talking people's ears off in a matter of seconds, taking no notice of the fact that he had stepped back and melded into the crowd.

It wouldn't be too bad.

And on that supposedly encouraging note, Ronan squared his shoulders and reached over to ring her doorbell.

"Be right there," he heard her call out from within the house.

"No rush," he called back, resigning himself to a car ride filled with the woman rattling on and on.

Maybe he'd just put on the radio. As long as she didn't opt to sing along, that would be a good way of keeping her quiet.

At least he hoped so.

The next second, thoughts of radios, quiet and doing penance while trapped in a car with her endless chatter filling the air vanished as Sierra opened her front door. Ronan found he had to struggle not to gape at her like some wet-behind-the-ears adolescent.

"Sierra?" he asked uncertainly, not even aware that he was using her first name, something he rarely did, even in the privacy of his own mind.

"Yes? Is something wrong?" she asked, looking down at the dress she was wearing to make sure she hadn't accidentally gotten something on it.

The dress, with its hem some three inches above her knees, was blue-gray and very formfitting, highlighting curves that Ronan had no idea, until this moment, she actually possessed.

And she seemed different somehow. Softer, more feminine. And there was one more thing.

"Are you taller?" he asked her.

"No, but the heels are," she told him with a grin. "I don't usually wear heels that are this high," she confided.

He looked down at the strappy, light blue sandals that were sexy in their own right.

"No. No, you don't," he agreed. But it wasn't her higher heels that had shanghaied his attention. It was the way the dress she was wearing seemed to almost make love to her body with every step she took. The keyhole neckline with its flirtatious hint of cleavage had caused his mouth to grow dry.

What the hell was wrong with him? he sharply demanded. He was a grown man, not some teenage boy freshly escaped from a monastery.

"I can change my shoes if you'd like," she offered.

He cleared his throat, wishing he could clear his mind just as easily. "No, that's fine. Leave them on. We'd better get going," he told her.

The sooner he got her to the celebration, the sooner he could just lose himself in the crowd. Out of sight, out of mind, he told himself.

"I'm ready," she said. "Just let me get my purse and the present."

"Present?" he repeated. "What present?"

"The one for the new chief of police," she said with a smile. "It's a big deal, being made chief and it must be extra special to him since his father was once the chief before he retired, right?"

Grabbing her purse and the gift she'd wrapped, topping it off with a silvery bow, she returned to the front door. One look at his expression explained why he'd asked his question.

"You didn't get him one, did you?" she ventured.

"No," he answered shortly. He hadn't even thought of it. And it wasn't that he didn't like Shaw. There wasn't a single person around who didn't like Shaw. Giving gifts was just something he didn't think about.

"That's okay, don't worry. I can add your name to the

card. I didn't seal the envelope," she went on. "I just tucked the flap in so adding your name to the card will be easy."

It was like being next to a whirlwind, he thought. "You don't have to—" he began.

She put her own meaning to his protest. He was embarrassed at forgetting.

"No problem. I asked around and found out the new chief's a big Dodgers fan. There's this memorabilia store in the mall and I found a DVD with all the games from the last World Series that they won. I thought he'd get a kick out of it."

Ronan got into his car and waited for her to get in on the passenger side. "You went to all that trouble getting him a gift?" he marveled, not knowing what to make of her.

"Sure. If you're going to give someone a gift, it should be something you know they'll like. Otherwise, why bother, right?"

"Yeah, right." He spared her a look just before pulling out of her driveway and onto the winding road that would get him out of the development.

"You don't even have to sign it," she went on. "I can fake your signature on the card," she offered, taking the card out and resting it on her purse after taking a pen out. "I've seen it often enough."

"You dabble in forgery?"

"No, but your signature's a squiggle. Not exactly a challenge. You really should work on that, you know," she told him, adding his name beneath hers on the card. "Forgers love people whose signature is that easy to imitate."

"And now you're giving me penmanship lessons." He shook his head, keeping his eyes on the road. "I'll see if I can fit them in."

Finished, she tucked the card back into the envelope. "Just a suggestion," she told him.

Ronan blew out a breath and frowned. He was acting like

a jerk and he knew it. But the woman was being just too nice and it was putting him on edge.

She was only trying to help, he argued. "And a good one," he murmured.

He didn't have to look at her to know she was grinning. But he stole a covert glance anyway.

Damn, but he hated being right.

And he wanted to be annoyed at her for so many reasons. But she had a smile that would have given the devil pause—and made him behave, at least for a little while.

Chapter Fourteen

Parking near the former chief's house was just as Ronan had predicted. Tricky. He also expected the woman he'd brought with him to start pointing out spaces where he could try to ease his sedan into. But, to his surprise, Sierra remained quiet, as if she thought that saying anything might distract him from finding a parking space that would accommodate his car.

Maybe Carlyle wasn't as bad as he thought she was. But then again, it wasn't really her talkativeness that was the problem. He realized that now.

It was the fact that she reminded him of Wendy.

Cruising down the next block, he finally found a decent space that could accommodate something larger than a smart car or a motorcycle. Parking his vehicle, they got out.

And then Ronan looked back toward his uncle's house. "Maybe I should have let you out in front of the house. It's kind of a long walk."

"That's all right," she told him. "I'm not afraid of a long walk." To prove it, she began to walk toward the house.

Ronan looked down skeptically at her footwear. "I was thinking about those high heels."

Sierra smiled. Typical male, she thought, amused. "I wasn't. I can run in these things," she told him. "Walking is no problem."

"When have you ever run in those things?" Ronan

scoffed. It was obvious that he thought she was just making that up for some reason.

She never hesitated. "When I was undercover and had to run down a perp."

He looked at Sierra in surprise. "You were undercover?"

"Uh-huh. In my pre-Homicide days," she told him. "I guess you didn't read my file all that closely, did you?" she teased.

Ronan became defensive. "What makes you think I read your file?"

She gave him a knowing look before answering, "Because you're you and you like to know just what you're getting into—although that wasn't exactly worded well." She realized her gaff once the words were out. "But you know what I mean."

Denial crossed his mind, but that would be lying and lies had a habit of catching up to a person. If they were going to have any sort of a decent working relationship, it wasn't a good idea to throw lying into the mix.

"I just skimmed your file," he finally admitted.

"And here we are," she declared, waving her hand at the house and wanting to spare Ronan any further awkwardness since she could see that the topic was obviously making him uncomfortable.

He'd focused completely on the idea of her being undercover—she was obviously more of a risk-taker than he'd thought—so much so that he hadn't realized they'd reached his uncle's house.

"Oh, yeah, so we are." The second the words were out of his mouth, he upbraided himself for sounding so incredibly stilted.

"It's a really nice-looking house," Sierra said as they went up the walk. And then she noticed something that gave her pause. "Is the front door supposed to be open like that?" she asked. Ordinarily, in their line of work, an unlocked door usually meant that there was either someone waiting to get the drop on them on the other side of it or a dead body in the house. "Isn't your uncle afraid that some stranger might walk in?"

"There're probably over fifty cops in there right now," Ronan told her. "I doubt if he's worried about a home invasion. Anyone breaking in is going to be really, really sorry," he commented then grew serious. "Uncle Andrew probably left the door open because he got tired of having to come and answer it. I told you, he invited the whole police department and then some to this celebration."

Pushing the door open with his fingertips, Ronan walked into the house with Sierra right behind him.

The moment she entered, she could almost feel the warmth that seemed to all but radiate from every corner of the house.

It was a house that had seen its share of trouble and coped with it and now resounded with love. The love of family, of friends and of good times, past and present, Sierra thought.

It was a house where the heartsick could come to heal. Without being fully conscious of it, she glanced at Ronan, wondering if he could feel it.

"C'mon," he told her. "Let me introduce you to Uncle Andrew."

Ronan felt it was the least he could do and once it was taken care of, he would be free to mingle with his family, leaving her to mix with and talk to whomever she wanted. He didn't have to worry that she'd feel like an outsider. His family never left anyone to his or her own devices once they were all gathered together.

"I'd like that," Sierra told him.

Hurrying to keep up, she almost grabbed his hand to keep from losing him in the crowd, but at the last moment she caught herself and dropped her hand to her side. She was here as his colleague, not as anything else, and she didn't want him to think that she *thought* anything else—even if, here and there, for a fleeting second, she might have.

"There he is." Ronan pointed to a tall, silver-haired man who looked like an older version of the man she'd seen being sworn in as chief yesterday.

Stopping whatever he was saying to the people with him, Andrew turned just as his nephew approached. A wide, welcoming smile graced his rugged features.

"Ronan, your mother said she thought you were coming. I'm glad you could make it. How have you been?" Andrew asked, grasping his nephew's hand in his and shaking it heartily.

"I've been good," Ronan answered vaguely. And then, because Andrew looked at him knowingly, he added, "Getting better," to forestall any questions.

Andrew wouldn't embarrass him in public, but Ronan knew that if there was an occasion to corner him in private, questions would come. Not because Andrew was curious, but because he genuinely cared. Andrew more than anyone else here knew what it meant to lose someone and feel as if his heart had been carved out of his chest and skewered.

But in Andrew's case, the wife he'd thought had been swept out to sea had turned up, a victim of amnesia but alive.

There was no such resolution for him, Ronan thought, but he appreciated that Andrew cared and was sensitive of his situation.

Andrew's green eyes shifted toward the young woman beside his nephew. "And you brought Detective Carlyle with you." The large hands closed around hers in a warm handshake. "Welcome to my home. This is your first time here, isn't it?" It was a rhetorical question. Andrew was aware of every new face that turned up in his home. "I hope it won't be your last."

Sierra looked at the older man, stunned. "You know who I am?"

"He knows who everyone is, don't you, Dad?" Shaw said, joining them. He nodded toward Ronan and the detective with him. "When I was a kid, I found that knack of his kind of spooky. It's like he memorized the general population of Aurora and could call up a name at will." Turning to Sierra, Shaw put out his hand. "Hi, I'm Shaw Cavanaugh."

"The new chief of police, yes, I know. I was there at the ceremony," Sierra said with a smile. "Oh, this is for you," she said belatedly, handing him the gift she'd brought.

"This really isn't necessary," Shaw objected, appearing pleasant and almost shy at the same time.

"It's nothing big," she told him. "Just something you might want to relax with."

"Now you've got me curious." He tore away the wrapping paper. "The 1988 World Series games," he said, reading the cover. He looked at her. "Thank you," he told her sincerely.

"It's from both of us," Sierra told him, nodding at Ronan.

"Well, thank you," Shaw said again, this time looking at his cousin.

"Yeah, well, it was her idea," Ronan said, not really wanting to take the credit for it, but not wanting to say that she was lying, either. "So how does it feel, being the new chief of police?" he asked.

"Not sure yet." Shaw glanced toward his father. "He left me some very big shoes to fill."

"Not that anyone's measuring," Andrew replied, "but you've got some pretty big shoes of your own, son. We all find our own path." The next moment he waved away the topic. "But all these people didn't come to talk shop today."

"No, they came to eat those great dishes you whip up," Rose Cavanaugh told her husband, coming up behind him and threading her arm through his in a gesture that simply radiated love. "Man won't let me near the kitchen," she told Sierra. "Not that I'm complaining, mind you. He cooks better than I do," she added with a wink.

"Way better." Andrew laughed. He turned toward Ronan and made a suggestion. "Why don't you take Detective Carlyle—"

"Sierra, please," Sierra corrected.

Andrew inclined his head, smiling. "Sierra," he amended, "and introduce her around? I'm sure she doesn't know everyone here."

"You'd better pay attention. There'll be a quiz at the end of the day," Shaw deadpanned.

"Do I get to stay here until I get it right?" Sierra asked, amusement shining in her eyes.

Tickled, Andrew laughed heartily. "I like this one, Ronan."

Sierra instantly became alert. She didn't want anyone thinking their relationship was anything but professional. "Nice meeting you, sir," she said, this time taking Ronan's arm and drawing him away.

"What was that?" Ronan asked her the moment they were out of his uncle's earshot.

Knowing that Ronan was a man who insisted on fighting his own battles, Sierra tried to seem as innocent as possible as she asked, "What was what?"

"Were you just coming to my rescue?" he asked.

She started to say no, then gave it up. "I just thought the situation was getting a little awkward for you."

"Why, because my uncle said he liked you?" he asked. "My uncle is entitled to like anyone he wants to like. As a matter of fact, I think I'd probably be really hard-pressed to find someone my uncle *didn't* like. The man's got a big heart and he's just that kind of a person—unless, of course, you're a criminal and even then, he'd most likely give you the benefit of the doubt if you told him that you were really sorry for what you'd done and wanted to reform."

She looked over her shoulder toward the man they had just left. Andrew was in the middle of another crowd of people gathering around him. "Your uncle seems like a really nice guy," she told him.

"There is no 'seems' about it," Ronan told her with feeling. "He is."

His tone was a little gruff and she didn't want him to think she'd insulted their host. "I never meant to imply anything else," she said sincerely. And then she added, "It's nice."

She had a habit of snatching words out of the blue, confusing him. "What is?" he asked.

She knew he didn't like attention drawn to him, or flattery. But sometimes he just had to suck it up, she decided. "I was talking about you being so protective of your family."

Sierra wondered if the frown that came over his face went clear down to the bone. He switched subjects so fast, a bystander would have gotten whiplash, she thought.

"You have your choice. Do you want something to eat, or names?" he asked. It took her a second to realize that he was letting her choose between eating and introductions.

"Can't I have both?" she asked innocently. "I got the impression from your uncle that the party is going to last a while. If that's the case, we have time to eat and to meet people—for *me* to meet people since you already know them," she amended.

"You can have both," he said, answering her question. "I just meant, which do you want to do first," he clarified.

She didn't get a chance to answer. The next moment his attention was diverted elsewhere.

"Ronan!"

By the time he turned around, the thin, small woman with the sharp green eyes and engaging smile swooped in and threw her arms around him in a fierce embrace.

"You came!" the woman cried happily. "I mean. I told Andrew you'd be here, but I honestly wasn't sure if you would be." Her face split into a wide, wide smile. "But you are."

"Mom," he choked out. "I'm having trouble breathing." For a little woman, she had an incredibly strong grip. "You can let go now."

"Trouble breathing," she laughed, negating his protest. "You're a big, strong man and I'm just a little woman," she said, releasing her son.

Turning to Sierra, she began to introduce herself. "Hi, I'm—oh, my lord," she cried, putting her hand to her chest. Her eyes darted toward her son. "Do you— Yes, you do." She completed the sentence without actually saying the words that had run through her head when she'd first seen Sierra.

Ronan did what he could to cover so that his mother wouldn't voice the fact that she was struck by the resemblance between Sierra and his late fiancée.

"This sometimes incoherent person is my mother, Maeve Cavanaugh O'Bannon. Mom, this is Sierra Carlyle."

"Carlyle?" the woman repeated, obviously turning the name over in her head. "Are you by any chance related to Craig Carlyle?"

Sierra smiled proudly. "In every possible way. He's my dad."

"Of course he is," Maeve said. "I can see it now in the way you hold your head. Your father looks like that when he's being defensive. Good man, your father," she added quickly. "Stubborn, but good."

Sierra laughed. "Yes, that's the way I see him, too."

"So," Maeve said, threading her arm around the younger woman's shoulders, "how did you manage to get my son to come?"

She was quick to redirect the woman's assumption. She wasn't about to be cast in the role of the one who motivated O'Bannon to do things.

"I'm afraid you have that all wrong, Mrs. O'Bannon. Your son brought me. I don't think that anyone can get your son to do anything he doesn't want to do. Least of all, me."

Maeve nodded her head. "Spunky," she pronounced, looking at her son. "Good quality." Then, as if a timer had gone off in her head, Maeve retreated. "Well, I'll leave you two to talk or whatever. I'm just so glad to see you getting out," she told her son, getting up on her tiptoes and pressing a kiss to his cheek. "Your brother's getting married, you know," she told him as if she was under the impression he didn't know.

"I know, Mom," Ronan replied patiently. "He wants me to be best man."

Her eyes lit up. She was the embodiment of sheer happiness. Things were obviously going better than she'd hoped.

"And you are. You are," she cried, hugging her son again. "Well, I've got to go, mingle. You, too, you two," she all but ordered. Turning toward Sierra, she reinforced her directive. "Make him mingle!"

"Yes, ma'am," Sierra replied, suppressing the impulse to salute.

"And that's my mother, the drill sergeant," Ronan told her drily.

"She is a dynamo," Sierra said with an appreciative laugh.

"That she is," he said with a weary sigh. "But she means well, even though I sometimes wish she'd mean a little less well."

Sierra grinned. "I actually understand that. My dad likes to meddle in my life, too. And it took him a long time to get over my joining the police force instead of the fire department."

She looked over toward Ronan's mother, a bemused expression on her face. "I think that parents feel they can lay out our lives for us and everything'll be fine—but they can't and it's hard for them to sit on the sidelines sometimes."

"Tell me about it," Ronan said, rolling his eyes. And then he came back to the immediate present. "Why don't we get something to eat and then I'll play the good nephew and introduce you around? Uncle Andrew has the pre-dinner tables laid out in the backyard."

"Pre-dinner?" she repeated quizzically.

"Dinner is served in the house," he explained. "Basically, I think he wants to have everyone eating all day long. It's a wonder there's not a real weight problem in the force.

"C'mon, I'll show you. And after we get something in our stomachs, I'll give you a crash course in Cavanaughs. Don't worry about learning names. It took me a while, too. Someone once suggested wearing name badges to these things and, to be honest, I'm beginning to think that might not be a half-bad idea. Not everyone has a mind like Uncle Andrew's."

Nodding, she told him, "I'll do my best."

"Yeah, well, we'll see," he murmured, wishing he wasn't reacting to Sierra the way he was.

Chapter Fifteen

The celebration was more than half over before Ronan realized he hadn't done what he had promised himself he would do. He hadn't made good his escape by leaving Sierra with any one of the relatives he had introduced her to during the course of the day. He was still with her.

What's more, he had stayed with Sierra not out of some sense of duty or obligation but just because it had felt right. Not only that, but he was enjoying himself.

He supposed the latter wasn't a surprise to him. After all, he had always liked his family, liked being around them. There wasn't a single member he would have avoided even if he had been given the opportunity. As for Sierra, it was obvious that she was having a really good time. She appeared to be thriving, surrounded by the various branches of his family.

It wasn't hard to see that she liked them and the sentiment seemed definitely mutual.

And being part of that gave him a really good feeling.

By evening's end, after eating, swapping stories and just plain laughing, Ronan found himself at ease for the first time in a long time. That, he concluded, had to be his long overdue wake-up call.

It was time to let go of the past and move on.

Several members of his family had been through circumstances similar to his and they had all eventually regained their foothold in life. There was absolutely no reason, Ronan thought, why he couldn't do the very same thing.

"You're smiling," his mother said with approval as she approached him again. "It does my heart good to see that," she confided with enthusiasm.

Taking one of his hands in hers, Maeve told her son, "You had me very worried there for a while. You had *all* of us worried," she added with significant emphasis. She reached up to lovingly touch his face. "But you're a Cavanaugh and my son. Life wasn't going to keep you down for long." Maeve beamed at him. "You're too much of a fighter."

There was nothing but affection in his voice. "Then why were you worried?"

"Because I'm a mother and it's a mother's job to worry," she told him matter-of-factly, as if the answer was as plain as the nose on his face. "Don't confuse the issue with logic, Ronan."

"Sorry, don't know what I was thinking," he replied, doing his best not to laugh. He kissed the top of her head, then decided to reverse the table on her, playing the parent to her child. "Shouldn't you be going home, Mom? It's past your bedtime."

"Well, listen to the egg telling the chicken what to do," she said, pretending to be annoyed. "I'll have you know that I'll go home whenever I'm ready, thank you very much."

Christian chose that moment to approach his mother. "Ready, Mom?" he asked, nodding toward a cluster of relatives a few feet away, "Suzie's just saying a few last-minute goodbyes."

Ronan arched a quizzical brow at the exchange. "'Ready'?" he repeated, looking at his brother for an explanation.

"Yeah. Suzie and I brought Mom with us to the celebration and we're dropping her off on our way home."

"Oh?" Ronan turned to look at his mother.

She raised her chin proudly and informed her firstborn, "And now I'm ready to go home."

Ronan laughed and shook his head. "See you soon," he promised.

"I will hold you to that, Ronan," Maeve called after him.

He never doubted it. Waving goodbye to his mother, he went in search of Sierra. It occurred to him that this was the first time all evening they had been separated.

Why that should make an impression on him he didn't know, but it did. And even though he'd initially tried not to pay any attention to it, seeing Sierra interacting with his family had warmed him. It amazed him that after all the time he had spent after losing Wendy, almost a shell of his former self, he could actually *feel* something again.

And, on top of that, that those stirrings could actually be connected to a woman who made him crazy.

He joined Sierra just as she was saying goodbye to both the former chief of police and the present one, as well as their wives.

"Thank you for a wonderful time and for inviting me," she said, addressing the last part to Andrew and his wife, Rose.

Andrew flashed his well-known smile at her. "Well, now that you know your way," he told her with a wink, "I expect to see you a lot more often. The door is always open."

She grinned, glancing in the general direction of the front door. "Yes, I noticed that."

"She thought it was an open invitation to home invaders," Ronan told his uncle.

Andrew looked pleased. "Just proves that she has excellent police instincts." Then he laughed. "But any home invader who comes in here would only do so if he had an extremely strong death wish."

Rose elaborated on her husband's statement. "At any given

moment of the day, there're usually at least a few members of the police force here either having something to eat or kicking back and blowing off steam." She turned toward her husband. "I honestly don't know what it's like to have more than a few minutes alone with this man," Rose told them.

Andrew tucked his arm around his wife's shoulders and pulled her closer. "She's exaggerating."

"Well, maybe just a little," Rose agreed affectionately, smiling at Ronan and the young woman who had come with him.

Sierra realized she could linger indefinitely, just saying goodbye. It was really time to go. Now.

"Again, thank you," Sierra said.

"Good night," Ronan told the couple. "It's getting late and we've got to get going." He exchanged glances with Sierra. "I almost forgot that tomorrow's a school day."

Tucked against her husband, Rose called after them, "Come back soon."

"You know, I'm beginning to understand why the world is such a hard, angry place," Sierra said as they walked out of the house.

He eyed her quizzically. "What?"

"Well, it looks like all the available niceness in the world got used up by your family," she deadpanned. "At least, it seems that way."

Ronan laughed, pleased by the compliment. "Yeah, they're a nice bunch I guess."

"If you have to guess," she told him, "I'd say that you've been pretty spoiled. They're an incredible crowd. And they all get along. That isn't as commonplace as you might think."

"Well, they're *not* saints," he told her. "But they're always on their best behavior whenever they come here. Nobody wants to miss out on Uncle Andrew's cooking."

It was late and the streets were rather dark. His car looked as if it was parked farther away than he remembered. "You want to stay here while I get the car and bring it back?"

She looked at him, puzzled. "Why would I want to do that?"

"Well, you've got to be tired," Ronan told her. They'd been there close to eleven hours.

"No more than you," she pointed out.

He indicated her footwear. "Yes, but I'm not in high heels."

He watched her eyes light up in the moonlight as she grinned. "I'd pay to see that."

"Save your money, it's never happening," he assured her. Well, he'd tried to do the right thing but she apparently was determined not to have any of it. "You want to walk? Okay, we'll walk," he told her.

It amazed him that Sierra kept pace with him all the way. "You really are stubborn, aren't you?" he declared as they finally reached his car.

Sierra turned her face toward him. There was a look in her eyes that completely captivated him. So much so that thoughts kept insisting on popping up in his mind, thoughts that promised to mess everything up in his orderly world.

"Oh, you haven't seen anything yet," she promised, getting into the car.

He felt his breath catch in his throat and he couldn't even explain why. Upbraiding himself, he got into the car on the driver's side.

"That sounds like you're putting a curse on me," he quipped.

Maybe she'd come on a little strong. He'd been really nice today and she wanted him to know that she was grateful.

"After the great time I had today, O'Bannon? I wouldn't dream of it. Thanks for inviting me," she said with sincerity.

He avoided looking at her as he started the car. "I didn't invite you," he mumbled. "That was all Uncle Andrew's doing."

She knew better, no matter how much he tried to disguise it. "But if you hadn't passed the invitation along, I wouldn't have been any the wiser." She looked at his profile as he put the car in Drive. His face was rigid. "Why is it so hard for you to accept a simple thank-you?"

"It's not," he retorted.

Had she felt like challenging Ronan, she would have responded with a dry laugh. But she wanted this evening to end on a good note and that meant not saying anything that would accidentally—or on purpose—pull him into any sort of a confrontation. It was very easy to do that. It was harder not to.

She picked the harder of the two.

So all she said was, "Good," and hoped that would be an end to it. Then, to ensure that, Sierra changed the direction of the conversation and said cheerfully, "Your mother's just as nice as my father said she was. And also feisty."

From where he stood, his mother had been rather laid-back. "You could see that?" he questioned, rather mystified.

"Oh, absolutely," she told him. "I can tell by the way she holds herself. Proud, but ready for anything. But then, she'd have to be, raising five kids on her own the way she did."

He hadn't told her that and decided she must have heard it from her father. But one crucial element had been left out of the story.

"Well, she wasn't exactly alone. My uncles were always there for her. Sometimes," he said with a laugh that had a lot of memories behind it, "they were a little *too* much there for her. I can tell you that none of them was happy when she became an ambulance driver less than a year after my father died. They thought it was too much for her, too dangerous." He laughed again, recalling his mother's reaction. "They tended to be overly protective and she'd have none of it."

"Like I said," Sierra told him, "your mother is a really feisty little lady."

He didn't know why it should make such a difference, but her approval of his mother pleased him.

THE CONVERSATION CONTINUED nonstop and, before she realized it, Ronan was pulling into her driveway. That was when she realized she didn't want the conversation—or the evening—to end.

"Could I interest you in a cup of coffee?" she asked, then added, "Or something stronger?"

Serving him something to drink wasn't what she could interest him in. That was why he told himself he should just pass on her offer, mumble a polite good-night and pull out of her driveway like a band of demons was on his tail.

So when he heard himself answering, "Sure," for a second he was certain he was hearing things.

"Great," she responded, getting out of the car and walking up to her door. "So what'll it be, coffee or something stronger?" Sierra asked since he hadn't stated a preference beyond saying "sure."

They were at her door and she was taking out her key. Looking back, Ronan decided that was when he had officially lost his mind because he told her, "Something stronger."

"Okay." Unlocking the door, she turned around to face him.

And that was the exact moment that something inside her melted.

Quickly.

"How strong?" she whispered.

He didn't answer. Instead he framed her face with his hands and brought his lips down to hers.

He tried to tell himself that he did that to scare her away. To make her say a quick "Good night" and shut the door really fast, leaving him standing on her doorstep and her safely inside her house.

He never counted on not succeeding in scaring her away. And he definitely did not count on Sierra kissing him back.

Most of all, he hadn't counted on having that kiss wake something dormant in his memory banks.

He'd done this before.

With her.

Startled, the fragment of a memory eating away at him, Ronan pulled back. "I didn't mean to..." His voice trailed off.

Sierra pushed open the unlocked door and drew him inside, then closed the door behind him. She flipped the light switch on the wall.

She sensed there was something bothering him. "It was getting chilly outside," she told him. "If you want to talk some more, I thought we'd be more comfortable inside than out."

He looked at her for a long moment, trying to summon the memory. "I've kissed you before, haven't I?" he asked.

She thought of lying, of telling him he was imagining things, but if he did eventually put the pieces together, how would she explain lying to him? He'd think that she'd been repulsed by the experience and the exact opposite was true.

"Yes," she answered quietly.

Things were still cloudy, refusing to take shape. But it was getting there. "When?"

She searched his face for a sign he was putting her on. He wasn't.

"You really don't remember?"

"It's coming back in jumbled pieces," he admitted, "But, no, not really."

She told him the events slowly, watching his face to see if something struck a chord. "The night you invited me to Malone's for a drink and then had a little more to drink than I think you realized. I drove you home."

He nodded, remembering the night but not the kiss. "Right, and then you stayed up with me all night."

"Yes."

He shook his head. He was coming up empty. Why wasn't it coming back to him? "I still don't—when did I kiss you?"

"When I tried to get you out of my car. You turned in your seat, but instead of getting out you pulled me onto your lap and then—" she took a breath "—you kissed me."

With the suddenness of a hot Santa Ana wind, it came back to him.

All of it.

His eyes widened at he looked at her. "I called you Wendy," he realized.

Sierra nodded her head. "Yes."

"I'm sorry." The words seemed inadequate but he had no others.

She smiled at him. "There's nothing to apologize for. It was a really good kiss."

How could she say that? He'd forced himself on her and then added insult to injury by calling her by another woman's name.

"You're being too nice about this."

"If you're looking to do penance," she said flippantly, "I could beat you, but it's going to have to be with a flyswatter. My cat-o'-nine-tails is at the cleaner's."

He laughed then, really laughed. Laughed at the absurdity of her suggestion and at the situation in general.

He laughed so hard, purging all the negative feelings he'd been carrying around for so long, that his laughter was contagious. Sierra began to laugh with him.

And somewhere along the line, when the laughter finally faded away, it created a void that needed to be filled by something else.

It was.

This time the kiss was urgent and mutual, pulling them together as if there had never been any choice in the matter.

This time he kissed her not because she reminded him of someone but because she *was* someone.

And Sierra kissed him because she'd been wanting to kiss him since he'd pulled her onto his lap and opened up an entirely new world for her, a world of desires and passions she'd never experienced before.

A world that seductively beckoned to her now.

Chapter Sixteen

It astonished her how he could make her head spin. Up until now, Sierra had thought descriptions like that were only myths.

But here she was, experiencing it.

With every kiss, all she wanted was more. She'd had no idea, until this very moment, just how much she wanted this.

How much she wanted him.

It was a struggle not to tear at Ronan's clothes and her own so that they could be free to explore each other's bodies. But as his kisses deepened, as his mouth began to trail along her cheek, her neck, the hollow of her throat, the urgency within her grew to almost overwhelming proportions and she could barely contain herself.

And then he stopped.

Just as the frenzy promised to overtake her, Ronan stopped and drew back from her.

It took Sierra more than a second to get her bearings in order to keep from uttering a guttural cry of protest and locate the right words.

"What's wrong?" she asked in a hoarse whisper.

Had Ronan suddenly felt a pang of guilt over becoming intimate with her—because that was where this was hopefully leading—since she wasn't Wendy?

"I don't want to force you," he told her, despite the desire she saw in his eyes.

Was that it? Was his sense of honor holding him back? "Last I noticed," she whispered, "you weren't holding a gun to my head."

But he still held back, afraid he was pushing too hard. "How much have you had to drink?"

"Just enough to be sociable, not enough to lose control." She smiled up at him then began unbuttoning the first two buttons of his shirt. "I know *exactly* what I'm doing," she assured him. "But if you're the one having second thoughts…"

That was all the reassurance he needed. "I'm not thinking at all," Ronan told her, bringing his mouth back to hers.

She nodded. "Handsome and stupid, just the way I like 'em," she deadpanned as she threaded her arms around Ronan's neck and allowed herself to get lost in yet another mind-boggling, bone-melting kiss.

Conversation stopped then. They found an entirely different way to communicate. They did it by touch, by feel, by going back to the very basic levels that had always existed between a man and a woman.

As she unbuttoned the rest of his shirt and pushed it back from his broad shoulders and down his arms, she felt the zipper at the back of her dress being tugged, moving ever lower.

Her dress fell away from her body and gracefully floated to the floor, creating a light green cloud at her feet.

Sierra was vaguely aware of stepping out of it and kicking the material away. She was otherwise occupied, undoing his gray slacks by guiding the zipper down and thrilling to the hardness she felt beneath her fingertips, testifying just how much he wanted her.

They found their way to the sectional as articles of clothing continued to leave them until they were both nude, both focused on only one thing.

Having each other.

With the barriers stripped away, Sierra thought she had only moments to wait before the final act began.

But she was wrong.

Ronan had other ideas. He surprised her by making love to every part of her first. By taking, caressing, and familiarizing himself with every single inch of her.

With his hands.

With his tongue.

Her heart was racing as he anointed every part of her, swiftly turning her into a wanton, crazed being feeling explosions erupt throughout her whole body. Her very breath became labored when he forged a moist, hot trail down to her very core.

Sierra clawed at the cushion beneath her as he drove her up and over into a shuddering climax that had her crying out his name in utter surprise and pleasure.

Limp, she fell back against the cushions, too exhausted to say a word, trying very hard to rally a small semblance of strength.

And then she felt his body slide along hers until his eyes were level with hers.

He was directly over her.

Her heart was pounding so hard, she was sure it was going to break her ribs.

It didn't.

Gathering whatever strength she could muster, Sierra pulled his head down and sealed her mouth to his as she arched her body beneath him.

The next moment she felt him enter her. They had become one.

The rest was pure instinct.

They moved in syncopated rhythm, going faster and faster until they reached the final plateau and the wild, exhilarating explosion they were both seeking came, wrapping itself around them as they claimed it.

The euphoria in its wake was exquisite and she would have given anything to have it last.

But even as it rocked their very foundations, it had already begun to fade, decreasing in magnitude and scope until it wasn't there at all anymore.

She waited for the sadness that was so much a part of this act.

It didn't come.

She felt Ronan collapse against her. The next second, he'd pivoted onto his elbows, shifting his body as he slid his weight over to the side.

She expected him to either fall asleep right then and there, or to get up, grab his clothes and vanish into the night.

Ronan did neither.

For the second time that evening, he managed to surprise her. He slipped his arm beneath her and drew her closer to him.

"And that," he murmured teasingly against her hair, "temporarily concludes our exercise portion of the program."

"Temporarily?" Puzzled, amused, Sierra raised herself up on her elbow to look at him. "There's more?" she asked in disbelief.

The smile began in his eyes and filtered across his face. "Just let me get my strength up. Give me five minutes and then we'll see about 'more' if you're interested."

"'Interested'?" she echoed. "I'd be flabbergasted. Aren't you exhausted?" she asked.

He slowly traced his fingertip along her lips, down her chin and along her throat, creating ripples of heat and desire all through her again. Just like the first time. "Are you?"

Just his light, teasing touch had begun to stir everything up again, making her body feel as if it was humming to a tune she could feel in her soul rather than hear in her head.

"Not quite as exhausted as I was a moment ago," she admitted, surprising herself this time. And then she grew very serious as she studied his face. "Are we going to be all right?"

"Explain 'all right,'" he said.

This was awkward for her, but it would be even more awkward to deal with tomorrow. She needed to be prepared, to know where things stood. "Tomorrow morning, when we go back to the precinct and start hunting for that serial killer, is what just happened here going to be a problem for us?"

He worded his answer carefully so that there would be no misunderstanding between them.

"What happened here has nothing to do with the precinct or the hunt for the serial killer, so I don't see how it's going to be a problem—unless *you* feel uncomfortable about what just happened," he told her honestly.

Sierra smiled, her smile lighting up her entire being. "I've never felt so comfortable about something in my life."

Ronan leaned forward and slowly smiled into her eyes. He realized that he was feeling like himself for the first time in two very long years.

"Then there's no problem," he told her just before he lowered his mouth to hers again.

He'd only intended to kiss her a little more, to hold her body against his and find solace in the warmth being generated between them. But he should have known better.

Because one kiss led to another, which led to the next, and each kiss was a little more urgent, a little more intense than the last, until, before Ronan was fully aware of it, they were making love all over again. Languidly this time, like they knew all the steps and were reveling in each one as it came to pass.

Somewhere in the midst of all this, the shroud that had been wound so tightly around Ronan that it made the very act of breathing painfully difficult for him just fell away like so much rotting cloth.

And he was finally free.

SIERRA HAD ALWAYS been a light sleeper so when she felt the mattress shifting ever so slightly near her, she immediately opened her eyes. She found herself looking at Ronan's muscular back. He was doing his best to noiselessly slip out of bed so he could go into the living room and gather up his clothes.

Daylight had pushed itself into her bedroom. It was time to get rolling.

"Making good your escape?" she asked.

She'd caught him off guard, but only for a second. Ronan

turned around to look at her. He should have known she'd wake up.

"You've got ears like a bat."

"As long as the rest of me doesn't look like one," she answered.

Sierra sat up, bringing the sheet up against her. After making love twice on her sectional, they had made their way into her bedroom where he had made love to her one last time. In her opinion, that had been the best out of the three.

"You'll be happy to know that it doesn't," he told her, pausing to brush his lips against hers lightly.

She sighed blissfully, then said, "It's early. We're not due in for another couple of hours. Why don't you go take a shower and I'll make you breakfast?"

"Thanks, but I've got to get home. I'll shower there and get a change of clothes," he told her. "Why don't you go back to sleep for another hour?" he suggested as he began to head for the hallway.

"Said the naked man in her bedroom." She smiled wickedly at him as he turned back to her and she got up on her knees on the mattress. "Like that's going to happen now."

His eyes slid over her, taking in every inch that he had already previously committed to memory. You'd think that after all that activity between them last night he'd be somewhat immune to seeing her like this. Instead, the exact opposite seemed to be true.

"Oh, hell," he said, slipping back into bed and taking her into his arms. "I'll skip the shower."

Sierra deliberately and urgently pressed her body against his, feeling all the dormant fires igniting all over again.

"Good plan."

BECAUSE SHE LIVED closer to the precinct than Ronan, when she arrived and didn't see his car in the lot, she just assumed she'd made it there before him.

Walking into the building, Sierra logically knew that

nothing had actually changed, but somehow, everything just appeared brighter to her. Even sunnier despite the fact that the day was relatively overcast.

She could have sworn she was still tingling. And it was all she could do to keep from humming. If she didn't know any better, she would have said that this was what it was like to fall in love.

She told herself to slow down and get a grip, but she just wasn't listening.

Her good mood, however, took a nosedive within moments of walking into the squad room.

Carver came charging out of his office the moment he saw her. "Don't you turn on your damn cell phone?" he demanded.

This couldn't be good. Taking out her cell, she looked at it. There were no bars. "I guess the battery died." She had a spare, fully charged auxiliary battery in her desk and took it out, connecting it to her phone. "Sorry, Lieutenant. What did I miss?"

He seemed annoyed at her question. "What did you miss? I'll tell you what you missed. There's been another damn homicide, that's what you missed," he growled. "That serial killer your team hasn't managed to catch yet is at it again." He gestured at the empty desks around her. "O'Bannon, Martinez and Choi are already at the crime scene. I got hold of them as soon as I heard," he informed her angrily. "You, however..." He looked at her accusingly.

"Sorry, won't happen again, sir," she promised. "Just give me the address and I'll go. I take it that it's the same MO?" she asked.

He nodded grimly. "A bullet to the back of the head and one hand severed."

She closed her eyes for half a second, absorbing the news. "I was really hoping he'd stop killing gang members," she said.

"He didn't kill a gang member this time," Carver informed her grimly.

She didn't understand and looked at him quizzically. "But that's part of the serial killer's MO. He kills gang members."

"Not this time," Carver barked.

"But you still think it's the same killer?" she questioned.

"Oh, it's the same one, all right," Carver said. There was no arguing with his tone.

She was almost afraid to ask. "If it's not a gang member, who did he kill this time?"

Carver's face clouded over, as dark as any storm cloud hovering over the desert and threatening a flash flood. When he spoke, it sent a cold chill down her spine. "He killed a cop."

She froze. "A cop? Why would the killer suddenly change his choice of victims?" It didn't make any sense to her.

"How the hell should I know? Maybe if you catch him, you can ask him yourself," Carver all but shouted. "All I know is that if we have a cop killer on our hands, there's no telling where this thing ends.

"The CSI unit hasn't left yet," he told her in the next breath. "Why don't you get a ride to the crime scene with them? There's already going to be plenty of cars there."

"Right." She hurried out the door.

"And, Carlyle," he called after her, stopping her for a third time.

She was almost afraid of what he was going to pile on next. "Yes, sir?"

"I want this thing solved yesterday," Carver ordered. "I *know* the new chief doesn't want to start his career with an unsolved serial killer on his record."

"None of us want that, sir," she assured him, then hurried out of the squad room as quickly as possible before he could stop her again.

Sierra bypassed the elevator and took the stairs to the basement, going as fast as possible. She managed to catch Sean Cavanaugh just before he left the lab.

"I don't have time to talk right now, Sierra," he apologized, closing the case he took with him to every crime scene.

"I'm not here to talk. Lieutenant Carver suggested I catch a ride with you to the latest crime scene—if you don't mind?" she added.

Sean smiled. "I know the last part's not from Carver. Sure, you can ride with me." Leaving the lab, he went to the elevator and pressed Up.

"Why aren't you going with the other detectives, if you don't mind my asking?"

"They're already at the crime scene. The lieutenant called them and sent them there. My battery died," she explained.

Sean took the information in stride and even looked amused. "That must have made him unhappy."

"I don't think the lieutenant is capable of being happy. But right now, all I care about is finding out why our serial killer has suddenly stopped hunting gang members and started killing cops."

Sean sighed heavily as he stepped into the elevator car along with her. "With any luck, we'll find the answer to that question soon," Sean told her.

With any luck.

The words echoed in her head. Lately "luck" seemed to be in very short supply when it came to getting the jump on this serial killer. If anything, all the so-called luck appeared to be completely on the killer's side.

She fervently hoped that would change and soon. What they needed was for the killer to make just one mistake, a mistake that would enable them to finally track the killer down.

Chapter Seventeen

"Nobody moved the body," Ronan said the moment he saw his uncle approach. "The ME hasn't gotten here yet. We left him right where he was." Seeing Sierra walking right beside the head of the CSI unit, he nodded at her, doing his best to give no indication to anyone that they had just spent the night together in the closest of circumstances.

"I was really hoping that the lieutenant was wrong," Sierra said.

She approached the police vehicle slowly. It was parked at the curb not too far from an apartment complex. To the casual passerby, it might have appeared that the officer behind the wheel was dozing. Only a closer look would give lie to that first impression. The victim wasn't dozing. He was slumped over the steering wheel, a single gunshot wound to the back of his head. The officer's left hand was missing.

Sierra's breath caught in her throat. "The victim really is a police officer."

"Is the killer branching out or was this some kind of mistake?" Martinez asked aloud what all of them were thinking.

"Or maybe this is a warning, telling us to back off?" Choi suggested. At this point, everything was possible.

Sierra moved slowly around the perimeter of the vehicle, searching for something, *anything*, that could be a clue. When she looked in through the open window on the driver's side, she caught a whiff of something strong.

"Is that bleach?" she asked, turning to Sean for confirmation.

"Certainly smells that way," Sean agreed. He appeared rather grim as he took a closer look at the dead police officer. "Maybe the killer touched the back of the seat when he executed Murphy and he tried to clean up after himself."

"Murphy?" Ronan repeated. "You know who this officer is?"

His uncle nodded grimly. "Officer Jimmy Murphy. He's been on the force ten, eleven years," he recalled. "He was a decent enough cop, but there was nothing about him to make him stand out." There was a sad note in Sean's voice when he added, "He tried taking the sergeant's exam a couple of times, but he never passed it. He was divorced, no kids."

He dealt with this sort of thing often enough, but it was always harder when it involved one of the department's own. "Nobody should end up this way," Sean said more to himself than to the others standing around him.

The look on Ronan's face was dark. "That serial killer's upped the ante if he's after cops now."

"Maybe he's not after cops," Sierra suggested, working something out in her mind.

Ronan turned to look at her. "What are you talking about? He just killed a cop."

"I know, but maybe he was after this particular cop," she stressed. "I can't shake the feeling that there's something we're missing, some kind of pattern we're overlooking. I keep thinking these victims are connected somehow.

"Otherwise," she insisted, "if all this guy wanted to do was kill gang members, there's plenty of opportunities he's passed up, like setting off a bomb in a local gang hangout." She glanced from one detective to another to see if they followed her thinking. "One well-placed homemade bomb would do it. There's some kind of significance to the executions and the cutting off of the dominant hand."

"Okay, I'll buy that, but what?" Ronan asked her.

"Maybe she's right," Choi said. "Maybe it had to do with a case Murphy was involved in."

"Drugs?" Martinez suggested, mentioning the first thing that came to mind because of the gang connection.

"Speaking of drugs..." Sierra said suddenly, turning toward Sean. "Is there a needle mark on the side of the officer's neck like there was with the last victim?"

Still waiting for the ME to arrive, Sean got into the back of the patrol car directly behind the fallen officer. With a small, powerful flashlight in one hand, he closely examined first one side the dead officer's neck and then the other. The side closest to the passenger side had a small telltale hole just below the earlobe.

"And we have a winner," Sean announced heavily. Turning off the flashlight, he backed out of the patrol car. "I'll be sure to do that tox screen for the same paralyzing drugs that we found in the last two victims," he told Ronan and Sierra.

Ronan nodded. "Get back to me as soon as you can," he requested.

Then, going with Sierra's theory, he turned to the three members of his team. He spoke first to Choi and Martinez.

"Find out everything you can about Murphy. Who he hung out with. If he owed anyone any money. He had a partner. Find out who that is and talk to him or her. Find out why he or she wasn't on patrol with him. And see if that partner knows anything that could shed some light on these executions."

He turned to Sierra. "I want you to comb through Murphy's cases, see if anything stands out or if you can find any connection between Murphy and any of our other victims. You might have a decent working theory there."

She didn't hear the veiled compliment. Instead she heard that she was being taken out of the field. "You're putting me on desk duty?" she cried, not at all happy about this new development.

"No, I'm putting your theory to the test and you're better

on the computer than these two lugs. If there was a connection between Murphy and those other victims, something might turn up in his cases. Also, I want you to find out if Murphy was answering a distress call, responding to a 9-1-1 call. It seems a little too convenient that Murphy just happened to be out here at the wrong time."

"You think he was set up?" Choi asked.

"Something like that," Ronan answered.

"He had to have picked up someone," Sierra pointed out. "Someone he didn't think would do him any harm. Other than that strong smell of bleach, there's no sign of any struggle."

Ronan set his mouth grimly. "Murphy never saw this coming."

Sierra nodded. "Whoever this killer is, he's very good. But nobody's perfect and everyone makes a mistake eventually. We just have to hope he makes one before he kills too many more people—or even one more," she corrected herself.

For one dark moment she thought that maybe it *was* time she got out of Homicide. But then she wouldn't be able to stop the bad guys. And in the sum total of things, that was all counted, not how she felt at a crime scene but being able to prevent the *next* crime from happening.

THE STORY ABOUT the serial killer's latest victim spread like wildfire. Police officers in patrol cars were told to patrol the streets in pairs at all times and everyone was told to be vigilant.

Murphy's execution made the afternoon news, both on the internet and on all the local channels, as well as all forms of social media.

Ronan cursed roundly under his breath after reading one such account by a blogger. "So much for keeping a lid on this," he said angrily.

Sierra looked up from her monitor. She'd been wading

through all of Murphy's old cases and, so far, nothing seemed to stand out. She welcomed the break.

"Maybe this is a good thing," she suggested, choosing to see the positive side. "With everyone aware that there's a serial killer out there, at least they'll be more cautious."

Ronan wasn't nearly as optimistic as she was. "You really believe that?"

"I'd like to," she said, although her tone of voice indicated she wasn't a hundred percent sold on the idea.

"Murphy was partnered with Gary Robertson," Choi announced, hanging up the phone after finally tracking down Murphy's commanding officer.

"Was?" Ronan questioned. "But not anymore? Did something happen between them?"

"Apparently," Choi said, crossing to Ronan's desk. "Sergeant Davis, their CO, said it was some kind of personal matter. Robertson requested a different patrol partner. So did Murphy."

"Murphy was alone in the car," Ronan said. "Who was his partner and where was he?"

"That would be Edward Wojohowicz," Choi told him. "And he wasn't with Murphy because he called in sick yesterday."

"That seems rather convenient." Ronan observed. He looked at Sierra. "Why don't we go find out if Officer Wojoho—whatever the hell his name is—was really sick or if he was just setting his partner up."

"You think that he could have?" she asked.

"At this point, I'm open to any and all theories and I'm willing to look at all the angles," Ronan said. "Choi, get me this sick new partner's address."

Choi was already crossing to his desk. "You got it."

TWENTY MINUTES LATER Ronan was knocking on Officer Wojohowicz's garden-apartment door. When there was no immediate response, he knocked again, harder this time.

That got an annoyed response from inside the apartment.

"Keep your pants on, I'm coming!" a disgruntled voice complained. The apartment door opened and a bleary-eyed man wearing faded pajama bottoms and a washed-out gray T-shirt opened the door. "What?" he demanded.

Ronan held up his badge and ID, as did Sierra. "Detectives O'Bannon and Carlyle. We need to talk to you, Officer—" He looked to Sierra to fill in the man's name, which she did.

"Wojohowicz."

The surly looking officer was immediately contrite. "Hey, I wouldn't have sounded so annoyed if I knew it was you, Detectives," he apologized.

Ronan disregarded the apology. "May we come in?" he asked in a tone that told the officer saying no was not an option.

"Sure, sure." Wojohowicz opened the door all the way. "Place is kind of a mess. I wasn't expecting company," the disheveled patrolman told them, backing up. "Is something wrong, Detectives?" he asked, looking from Ronan to the woman at his side. Without waiting for an answer, he began speaking nonstop. "I don't usually call in sick, but I had this sushi yesterday afternoon and I tell you, it just about cleaned out my insides. I had a 102 fever and—"

It was obvious that officer would have gone on talking indefinitely until he ran out of air. Ronan held his hand up, a clear sign that he wanted the officer to stop, which he did. Abruptly.

"Someone shot your partner," Ronan told the officer, carefully watching his reaction.

The officer appeared to have trouble processing the information. Several emotions passed over his pasty face, ending with sheer astonishment.

"Jimmy?" he looked from one detective to the other. "He got shot? Is he all right?"

"No," Ronan answered, still watching the officer's face. "He's not all right. He's dead."

"Dead?" Wojohowicz repeated numbly, collapsing onto a sofa that had seen better years. He looked as if he was having trouble catching his breath. "What happened?"

"He was executed." Ronan said. "One shot to the back of the head. The killer cut off his left hand. Was Officer Murphy left-handed?"

"What? Um, yes. I think so. You mean he was killed the same way like that serial killer's been doing?" Wojohowicz asked, stunned. "No, that can't be right. Murphy never belonged to a street gang," he protested. "Are you sure?" he asked, obviously searching for something that made sense to him. "Why would that serial killer kill Murphy?" And then he came up with his own answer. "Maybe it's a copycat killer, trying to throw you off." He looked from one to the other to see if that made sense to them.

"That is a possibility," Ronan allowed. At this point, almost *anything* was a possibility. "Why'd you call in sick?"

"I told you, I had some really bad sushi. I think I've still got the receipt from the restaurant in my wallet. Do you want to see it?" he offered.

"If you don't mind," Ronan said in a low, steely voice meant to undermine the officer's confidence if he was lying.

"Sure." The officer quickly crossed into the kitchen and went toward a chair where he had a pair of pants slung over the back. Riffling through the pockets, he found his wallet and took it out, then quickly searched through it. A sigh of relief accompanied the discovery of the receipt.

"Here. See?" Crossing back to the two detectives, he handed his "proof" to Ronan. "I had that for lunch yesterday," he said, indicating the first thing on the itemized receipt. "Two hours later, I was throwing up my insides. I'd steer clear of the Royal Gardens if I were you," he told them, referring to the restaurant by name. Then, when neither one of them said anything, he looked at them nervously. "Am I in some kind of trouble?"

"No, no trouble," Sierra told the officer. "Why don't you tell us about your partner? What was he like to ride with?"

Wojohowicz seemed conflicted. "Well, the guy's dead, so I don't want to say anything bad about him."

"But?" Sierra coaxed.

"Well, he was a good cop," the officer began, "but I could tell something was eating away at him. He didn't talk about it, but I could tell. The guy clearly had his demons."

"Any idea what these 'demons' were?" Ronan asked, doing his best not to sound impatient.

Wojohowicz chewed on his lower lip, thinking. "If I was gonna make a guess, I'd say it might have had something to do with his old partner, Robertson. Something happened between them. I think that might have been the reason they decided to go their separate ways."

"If you had to guess," Sierra prompted, picking up on the officer's language, "would you say it was some sort of a deal that went bad, or maybe they argued and had a falling out over a woman?"

The officer's expression remained confused.

"I don't know," he repeated. "But I do think that's why Jimmy's wife left him, so maybe it *was* over a woman. I'm sorry—" Wojohowicz suddenly paled. "I think I've got to throw up again." He threw the words over his shoulder while hurrying to the bathroom.

"We'll just see ourselves out," Ronan called out to the officer. The bathroom door slammed shut and the sound of retching was heard. "Let's go," he said to Sierra as he led the way out of the apartment.

"Do you believe him?" she asked Ronan once they were outside the ground-floor apartment.

Ronan shrugged, crossing the lot to his parked vehicle. "Place smelled like vomit, so I'm inclined to think he was telling the truth."

"Maybe we should talk to Murphy's ex-partner?" Sierra suggested.

"My thoughts exactly," Ronan agreed.

They got back into his car and he started it up. "What do you think this case is really about?" he asked her as he drove out of the apartment complex.

She thought for a moment, doing a little free association in her head. "Well, considering the mounting dead bodies, I'd say that this serial killer is very, very angry. Until Officer Murphy turned up dead, I would have said that whatever the killer was angry about had to do with something he'd suffered at the hands of a gang—"

"Two gangs," Ronan reminded her.

She nodded. "Two gangs," she amended. "And that broadens the playing field. But since Murphy was killed in the exact same way, this doesn't just involved gangs. There's got to be something else. It's not just someone trying to get back at members of a gang for something that happened to him at their hands."

Ronan nodded. She had more or less put into words what he'd been thinking. And they were clearly missing some of the pieces of the puzzle. "Maybe Murphy's ex-partner can shed some light on this."

"If he wants to," she said.

He spared her a quick look. "What's that supposed to mean?"

"Well, if there really is something that we're missing, whatever it is might incriminate Robertson if it comes to light." She was speculating.

"If there *is* something," Ronan told her, "then fear is going to be our best weapon."

"Fear?" she questioned.

"Absolutely. There is a serial killer out there, killing people. Let's say he's doing it for a reason, a reason that involved Murphy and might very well involve Robertson. That means that Robertson's days might be numbered. We can offer Robertson protection—all he has to do is tell us why someone would want to execute a bunch of gang members and his old partner."

"What if he doesn't know?"

"Let's just suppose that he does," he countered.

She nodded. "Worth exploring," she said as they came to a stop at a red light.

Ronan smiled at her for the first time all day. She could see he was, at least momentarily, thinking of exploring something entirely different. "Yes, definitely worth exploring."

Her stomach tightened, sending butterflies flying inside her.

The traffic light changed and the moment was gone.

For now.

Chapter Eighteen

"Okay, Uncle Sean, what can you tell us about the serial killer's latest victim?" Ronan asked as he and Sierra walked into the CSI lab.

"Your timing's very good," Sean told him. "The ME just did the preliminary autopsy and I finished running the tox screen."

He pulled together several sheets of paper with the information. "Officer Murphy was shot in the back of the head with the same gun that all the other gang members were—a 9 mm Smith & Wesson. The tox screen came back positive for the same date-rape drug we determined was used on the last two victims. And, as you saw, his left hand was severed, not just hacked off. We're dealing with someone who has some sort of medical background in addition to access to medical drugs. In short," Sean concluded, "I've got nothing new for you. Sorry."

"Nothing to be sorry about," Ronan told him. "At least we know it's the same person responsible for all these murders. Thanks for putting a rush on it," he said to his uncle.

"No problem. So what's your next move?" Sean asked.

"We're going to find Murphy's old partner and see if he has any insight on why Murphy was executed," Ronan answered.

"Keep me posted," Sean called after them.

"Will do," Sierra promised, then hurried after Ronan.

SINCE THEY'D STARTED riding together, Officer Gary Robertson and his new partner, a first-year rookie named Jerry Allen, had a ritual they followed every Wednesday. They stopped at a popular Mexican food restaurant—Jose's—for lunch. The food was rated as good and the prices were low.

Jose's was where Ronan and Sierra tracked the two officers down.

Or rather, they tracked down Officer Allen. Robertson was nowhere in sight. "What's wrong with this picture?" Ronan asked as they approached the table where the lone officer was sitting.

"We're one officer short," Sierra commented. "He's got to be around here somewhere, right?"

Aided with a photograph of Robertson, Ronan looked around the outdoor dining area, but only saw Allen. "Let's find out where his partner is," he said to Sierra.

Approaching Allen's table he saw that there were two servings on it. "Officer Allen?"

The slightly heavyset rookie was busy devouring his second chicken enchilada and didn't look up. "I'm on my lunch break. Who wants to know?" he asked in a less than friendly voice.

"Detectives O'Bannon and Carlyle," Ronan snapped, reacting to the officer's tone. "Where's your partner, rookie?"

Officer Allen shot up from his chair immediately, his expression showing he clearly regretted the attitude he'd copped. He answered like a new Marine trainee. "He's in the men's room, sir. Says beer goes right through him, sir."

Ronan looked directly into the rookie's eyes. "Drinking on the job, Allen?"

"Yes, sir. I mean no, sir. I mean Robertson was, I wasn't," he answered, stumbling over his own tongue. "This is ginger ale, sir. See?" He held up his glass so that they could verify what he'd just told them.

Sierra saw no reason to make the rookie suffer. "We're not interested in what you're drinking, Officer Allen," she told him, trying to calm Allen down. "We just need to talk to your partner."

"He's in the men's room," Allen repeated, pointing toward the interior of the restaurant. "Come to think of it, he's taking a really long time in there." He started to turn to go into the restaurant. "Maybe I should go get him."

Ronan put his hand on the rookie's shoulder, holding him in place. "Finish your lunch, Allen. Detective Carlyle and I will go get Robertson."

"You don't want me to come with you?" Allen asked, disappointed.

The rookie's question struck Ronan as rather odd. "What for?"

Allen looked at a loss for an answer, then blurted out hopefully, "Backup?"

"That's what I have Detective Carlyle for," O'Bannon answered in what amounted to a deadpan response.

They walked into the restaurant, which was doing a healthy amount of business. Lively Mexican music was being piped in, adding to the atmosphere as well as the noise level.

"So, I've made the grade as your backup, eh?" she asked, not bothering to suppress her smile.

"In more ways than one," he answered.

She decided to leave that response alone for the time being and looked around the restaurant instead. "Nice place," Sierra commented.

"Yeah," he agreed. "I used to come here when I was a patrolman. They've done a bit of upgrading since then," he observed. He looked to the far end of the restaurant and saw what he was looking for. "But looks like the men's room is in the same place."

"I'll just wait out here for you," she told him once they had reached the men's room.

There was a ladies' room right next to it. A woman came out of it, quickly passing Sierra. The latter was too busy looking at the men's room door to notice her and had to shift to get out of the woman's way.

"Sorry," she murmured, not looking at the woman. The woman made no response, she just kept walking.

"This'll just take a minute," Ronan promised, pushing the men's room door opened. Less than a beat later, he called out, "Carlyle, come in here."

"You need help dragging him out?" she asked, wondering what was going on.

"Not exactly," Ronan answered.

Crossing the threshold, she stopped in midstep, stunned. Less than five feet away there was a man in a police uniform lying facedown on the colorfully tiled floor, a pool of blood gathering beneath his upper torso. It was darkening the tile. The officer was missing his right hand.

Sierra looked at Ronan. "Robertson?" she asked.

"Right on the first guess," he answered.

"The killer had to have stalked Robertson to know that he'd find him here."

Ronan nodded, crouching beside the body. He checked for any signs of life even though he already knew what he'd find. "I think our killer stalked all of them. Bastard's patient," he remarked.

"And very damn cold-blooded," she added. "This is a crowded restaurant," she said. "Anyone could have walked in on him at any time."

"It's a trade-off," Ronan decided. "The noise and music were a perfect cover. Nobody would have heard the gunshot."

"My guess is that he's using a silencer. Why take a chance?" she asked.

Sighing, Ronan took out his cell phone and hit three keys on the keyboard. "This is Detective O'Bannon." He recited his shield number. "I've got an officer down. Send backup," he ordered. "No, don't send a bus. This guy's way past that. Send the coroner and the crime scene investigators. We've got another dead officer on our hands. Officer Gary Robertson." He heard the shocked silence on the other end and gave the dispatcher a moment before he recited the restaurant's address.

Terminating the call, Ronan cursed under his breath as he rose again.

He looked down at the body. "The blood's fresh. This just happened. We must have just missed him."

Sierra looked at him. "That means the killer might still be here. He's trying to blend in with the customers."

He realized she was right. How had that managed to escape him? Ronan snapped into action.

"We need to seal all the exits. Stay with the body," he instructed, moving passed her and out the men's room door.

Sierra crouched beside the body. Myriad emotions undulated through her. The greatest of them all was sadness.

"What the hell did you and your ex-partner get yourselves into?" she questioned, shaking her head. With a sigh, she rose to her feet.

Flashing his badge and ID at the bartender, Ronan announced, "I'm shutting this place down temporarily. No one goes out, no one comes in."

Shocked, the buff bartender protested, "You can't do that."

"The dead body in your men's room says I can," Ronan countered.

"Dead body?" the bartender echoed. "What dead body?" And then, not waiting for an answer, he cursed for a full minute before ending with, "Oh, damn."

"That's one way to put it," Ronan replied crisply.

Obviously alarmed, Allen came hurrying over to Ronan at the bar. "What's wrong? Where's Robertson?" the rookie asked.

"Meeting his maker right about now would be my guess," Ronan answered. When the rookie stared at him blankly, Ronan elaborated, "Robertson's dead. Someone shot him in the men's room."

The rookie's eyes seemed to double in size. "Now?"

"No, yesterday," Ronan retorted. "Yes, now." Realizing that the bartender hadn't moved an inch and wasn't carrying out his instructions, Ronan held up his badge and announced in a loud voice, "Can I have your attention, please? I'm Detective O'Bannon and I'm afraid I'm going to have to ask you to be patient for a while. My partner and I need you to remain in your seats until we've had a chance to question you, collect your names and your contact information."

A chorus of unhappy voices rose to question—or challenge—his instructions.

"What happened?"

"Why?"

"I've got to get back to work. You can't keep me here like some prisoner."

Ronan held his hand up for silence. When the questions finally died down, he told the patrons, "The sooner we get this done, the sooner you'll be able to leave." He turned toward Allen. "I need you to go and relieve Detective Carlyle. She's in the men's room with the body. I want you to take her place."

Allen looked clearly shaken. "Officer Robertson's body?" he asked nervously.

"That's the only one we've currently got," Ronan said sternly.

Perspiration appeared along the officer's upper lip. "Okay," he answered in a shaken voice.

"Don't worry, the coroner's on his way. You won't have to stand guard for long," Ronan promised. He had one more thing to take care of before he began questioning the patrons.

Turning to the bartender, he told the man, "I want all of the videos from your surveillance cameras that were taken today."

He saw Sierra coming into the main room. "Hold it a second," he told the bartender. He beckoned Sierra over to him. "Carlyle, go with the bartender and help him collect the surveillance videos." He wasn't about to take a chance on any of the videos "going missing." At this point, he wasn't sure just who to trust. For all he knew, he could have already passed or talked to whoever had killed Murphy's old partner.

Sierra nodded. "Understood." She turned toward the bartender. "Lead the way," she told him.

As Sierra and the bartender walked to the back office to get the videos, Ronan began collecting names and phone numbers from the disgruntled restaurant patrons.

IT WAS SEVERAL hours before they were finally able to return to the squad room. As expected, no one at the restaurant had seen anything.

In their defense, one of the patrons had said, "Well, you don't come for quesadillas and expect to see someone get shot."

Ronan sank his chair, feeling drained. Scrubbing his hands over his face, he complained, "This is turning into a real nightmare."

"Yes, except you eventually wake up from a nightmare," she said. "This has all the signs of going on indefinitely."

She was well aware that some crimes were never solved and wound up being filed away in a room reserved for "cold cases." While she fervently hoped that no more bodies turned up courtesy of their serial killer, she refused to allow this case to go that route.

Sitting in front of her computer, Sierra stared at the monitor for a few moments, trying to come up with a fresh course of action.

She could think of only one thing. "I'm going to try just feeding all the victims' names into the search engines, see what I can come up with," she told Ronan. "Maybe somewhere in there I can find just how these people all connect with each other—and Murphy and Robertson."

"There might not be a connection," Martinez said as he walked into the squad room. He and Choi had joined Ronan in taking statements and placating angry restaurant customers. "Could just be this killer's way of messing with our minds."

"I know, but I've got this thing about order," she told the other detective. "I like feeling that there are reasons behind everything."

"You want a reason?" Choi asked. "The reason is that this guy's a crazy, bloodthirsty bastard," he said angrily.

"O'Bannon," she turned toward him. "What's your thought on this?"

He shrugged. "See if you can find some kind of a connection," he told her. "Who knows, maybe you'll get lucky." He looked at the other two detectives. "I want you two to find Murphy's ex-wife and bring her in. Maybe she has some idea what's going on. Right now, I'm open to listening to anyone," he said.

"You got it, boss," Martinez said. The detectives were gone within minutes.

Taking a pad from his desk, Ronan walked up to the bulletin board and began writing something down. From where she sat, it looked to Sierra as if he was copying the victims' names. Finished, he headed for the doorway.

"Where are you going?" Sierra asked.

"I'm going to bring this list down to my cousin, Valri, in the computer lab, see if she can find that connection we're looking for. She's an absolute wizard and if anyone can find it, she can."

Sierra pretended to be hurt. "Don't have any faith in me, eh?"

He doubled back for a moment. "On the contrary, I have every faith in you. You're the one who came up with this idea. It's just that two sets of eyes are better than one and she might have some tricks up her sleeve that you don't." He smiled at her. "No insult to your intelligence intended."

Sierra inclined her head. "None taken. My skin's a lot thicker than you think."

Ronan leaned in closer and whispered into her ear, "Not

that I recall, but maybe I need to reacquaint myself with you after we leave here tonight."

If she didn't have an incentive before, she did now. Sierra smiled at him as Ronan straightened.

"You're on," she told him.

THE DOOR TO the computer lab was open. Ronan knocked on it anyway, then stuck his head in. Valri's desk was the first one near the door.

"Valri?" he asked, looking at the petite blonde working intently.

Valri Cavanaugh paused and looked up as he entered the room. "Uh-oh, beware of O'Bannons bearing gifts."

Ronan realized she was referring to the paper in his hand. "This isn't a gift," he told his cousin. "This is an updated list of our serial killer's victims. I need you to cross-reference them on those fancy databases you're always pulling up."

Valri's desk was already overflowing with other work. The woman was fast, but she was still human, a fact that seemed to elude a lot of her cousins.

"I know I'm going to regret asking this, but what are you looking for?"

"Any connection you can find between these people—and I mean *anything*." Ronan emphasized the word.

Her eyes narrowed as she skimmed the list. "Is this right?" she asked, appearing distressed. "Are the last two victims on this list police officers?"

Ronan nodded grimly. "They're the latest victims." "The second victim's name isn't common knowledge yet. But you see why this is so urgent, right?"

Pressing her lips together, Valri sighed, not at the request, but because of the last two names on the list. Whenever police officers were killed, it was like losing family.

"I'll see what I can do," she promised.

He leaned over the desk to brush a kiss on her cheek. "Knew I could depend on you. And just so you don't feel put-upon, I've got one of my detectives going through search engines, too."

"Tell them they have my sympathies," Valri said. Her fingers were already flying across the keyboard, inputting the name of the serial killer's first victim into the database she had accessed.

"I'll leave you to your work," he said, withdrawing from the lab.

Valri hardly heard him.

Chapter Nineteen

The minute Ronan and Sierra walked into the squad room, Martinez crossed over to them and said, "Officer Murphy's ex-wife is waiting for you in Interrogation Room One."

"And FYI," Choi added, joining them, "she's not very happy about being brought in."

Ronan nodded. "Thanks." About to head for Interrogation Room One, he looked at Sierra. "You want to sit in on this?" he asked.

He wasn't asking her just to be polite. She was beginning to get good at reading between the lines. "You mean run interference, don't you?" she asked, amused.

Ronan shrugged. "Six of one, half a dozen of the other," he allowed.

Sierra fell into step beside him as they went down the hall. "And after we finish with her, I want to show you something I found on the internet that might be interesting."

"What is it?"

She waved away his question. "It'll keep. The internet isn't going anywhere. Let's find out what Murphy's widow knows—or doesn't know," she amended as they walked up to the interrogation room.

Anne Murphy was a trim, petite brunette who worked in the admissions office of a local university, where Martinez and Choi found her.

The moment Ronan entered the room, he could see that

the late officer's ex-wife resented being brought in like this. Her brown eyes were blazing.

"You've got a hell of a nerve sending your goons to the admission's office to drag me out of the building and bring me here. What's this all about?" Anne Murphy demanded hotly, rising from her chair.

Ronan gestured for her to remain seated. "We just want to ask you some questions."

"Ever hear of a telephone?" she asked sarcastically, remaining on her feet. She gave every indication that she was about to storm out of the room.

Sierra shifted, blocking the woman's exit. "Ever hear of obstructing justice?" Sierra countered pleasantly. "Please take your seat, Mrs. Murphy."

Scowling, the woman grudgingly sat again. She made it very evident that she was doing so under protest. "So ask me whatever it is you want to ask," she snapped. "I don't have all day to waste."

Ronan glanced at Sierra. He inclined his head, indicating he wanted her to take the lead.

Appraising the hostile woman thoughtfully, Sierra deliberated, then asked, "Why did you divorce your husband, Mrs. Murphy?"

For a second the other woman seemed stunned at the question. And then she answered. "Because he was a brooding ass. Can I go now?"

"Not yet," Sierra said pleasantly. "Was he always like that?"

"No," Anne Murphy answered angrily, clearly resenting being questioned like this. "When I married him, he was a lot of fun." Sadness entered her voice. "But then he changed."

Sierra glanced at Ronan, but it was obvious that he wanted her to continue. "Do you have any idea why he changed?"

"I don't know," Anne retorted, frustrated. "Because of something on the job, I guess." Her anger returned. "Look, Jimmy didn't share what was going on with me. He just shut down."

Sierra leaned in across the table, her eyes on the woman's. "Do you remember when this happened?"

Anne blew out an annoyed breath. "I don't keep a diary," she retorted.

Undaunted, Sierra kept going. "Mrs. Murphy, your husband was executed. So was his old partner—"

"Gary?" she asked, the color draining from her perfectly made-up face. For the first time since they had entered the room, the woman they were questioning looked subdued. "Gary Robertson's dead?" she asked in disbelief. She looked from one detective to the other. "I didn't hear anything on the news—"

"It just happened," Sierra told her. "We're still trying to get to the bottom of all this." Keeping her voice on an even keel, she continued the questioning session. "You divorced your husband—"

"*Ex*-husband," Anne emphasized.

"Your ex-husband," Sierra amended easily, "around the same time that Officer Robertson requested a different partner, and Detective O'Bannon and I were wondering if something happened in that time period to bring all this about."

Anne shifted in her seat impatiently. She clearly wanted to be somewhere else. "Like I said, it was something that happened on the job. Look, I was the last person he'd talk to and I finally got tired of being treated like a piece of furniture, so I left him," she said as if it was a declaration of independence. "Talk to his CO. His CO would know more about it than I do. Now, can I go?" Anne asked again. "We're dealing with a flood of entrance applications at the university right now and I really don't have time to be here," she stressed.

They weren't about to get any more out of her right now, Ronan thought, rising from his chair. "You're free to go, Mrs. Murphy. We'll be in contact if we need anything else."

"I shiver with anticipation," the woman told him sarcastically just before she hurried out of the interrogation room.

Sierra frowned, looking at the departing woman's back.

"I think I can take a guess why their marriage went south," she said.

"Yeah, me, too," Ronan agreed. Turning back to Sierra, he said, "Let's see if we can get a few minutes of the CO's time."

Leaving the interrogation room, Sierra was more than happy to go with him to see the dead officers' commanding officer. "I've got a feeling that he's going to say something to confirm my suspicions."

Ronan stopped abruptly. He'd forgotten that she'd wanted to tell him something. "And what are those suspicions?"

"I found a two-year-old story on the internet. Murphy and Robertson tried to take down some gang members who were shooting it out. Two different gangs were involved."

Pausing by the elevator, she watched Ronan press the down button.

"Neighbors called 9-1-1," she continued. "Robertson and Murphy were in the area so they arrived first. Trying to stop the shootings, they wound up caught in the cross fire and started shooting themselves. According to the one witness that came forward, it was over practically before it started. Several of the shooters were wounded but no one was killed except for a cabdriver. Poor guy had three bullets in him. One of the bullets apparently came from Murphy's gun."

"Do you think that was deliberate?" Ronan asked her, getting into the elevator car.

"I'm think Murphy was just fighting for his life, like Robertson, and that civilian got caught in the cross fire." She looked at Ronan. "That might have been the beginning of Murphy's descent into depression," she proposed.

THE TWO DEAD officers' grim-faced commanding officer, Sergeant Gene Davis, confirmed Sierra's suspicions.

"Murphy had to surrender his weapon and was put on desk duty until he was cleared—which he was—but he took the whole thing really hard." Davis shook his head, remembering. "He felt that everyone was against him. I heard him complaining that he was only doing his job, trying to break up that shooting, and he was really bummed out that the department didn't back him up. We did," Davis protested. "But these were the rules. They both had to surrender their weapons because they were fired, but it took longer with Murphy because the autopsy found that one of his bullets hit the cabdriver. In the end, the department ruled in their favor."

"What about the dead cabdriver?" Sierra asked.

Davis shrugged. "He was unfortunate collateral damage. Poor guy was in the wrong place at the wrong time."

"Does anyone know how this whole thing happened in the first place?" Ronan asked the sergeant.

"Like most of these things," Davis said. "It blew out of proportion over some imagined slight," he recalled. "Tempers got hot, people started shooting. The gang members were all arrested, but before it got to trial, they were let go on some legal technicality. Something about their rights not being read to them at the time." Davis grew angry just remembering the circumstances.

"How did Murphy take it?" Sierra asked.

"Not well. He and Robertson fought because Robertson just wanted to let it slide. Robertson finally asked for another partner. That's about when Murphy's wife left him." Davis shook his head. "I honestly thought that Murphy was going to quit the force, but he surprised me and hung in there. Said, good or bad, being a cop was all he had, *especially* after his wife left him."

"One more thing, Sergeant, and we'll be out of your hair," Ronan promised. "Do you have a list of the gang members arrested in this shoot-out?"

Davis nodded. "I can track it down and have it sent to you."

"While you're at it, Sergeant," Sierra said, speaking up,

"could you add the name of that taxi driver who was killed to the list?"

"Sure thing," Davis said obligingly. "Damn shame what happened to those two," he murmured as the two detectives left his area.

"Wasn't exactly a party for the cabdriver, either," Sierra commented under her breath.

"What are you thinking?" Ronan asked as they walked back to the elevator.

"I'm not sure yet," she admitted. "First I want to see the names of the gang members who were in that shoot-out Murphy and Robertson were trying to stop. If they do match the victims, then we might be onto something."

"You're being very mysterious about this," he commented.

"No, I'm being cautious. Isn't that what you want?" she asked.

He winked at her as they rode the elevator back up to their floor. "Not always."

WHEN THEY GOT back to the squad room, Valri had left a message for Ronan on his landline that she had found a few lines in an online story about a "massacre that wasn't."

They went to the computer lab.

"Your two dead officers were involved in a shoot-out involving members of two rival gangs who were trying to kill each other," Valri told them, reiterating what they had just found out from Davis. "A couple of the gang members were mentioned by name and both of them were recent guests of our morgue," she noted. "Does that help?"

Ronan had no intention of telling her that Sierra had come across the same story. Instead he acted as if this was news to him and said, "I owe you."

"Yeah, I know," Valri replied with a broad grin.

"Would you print that article for me?" he requested.

"Way ahead of you." Valri held up the single sheet of paper that contained the brief piece.

"Thanks," he told her, taking the paper from her.

Scanning the brief article as they rode back to the squad room, Sierra noted, "There's no mention made of the cab-driver."

"Collateral damage, remember?" Ronan reminded her.

"That 'damage' was a person," Sierra protested.

"I know. I don't like it any more than you do," he said grimly.

WHEN THEY RETURNED to the squad room, Ronan found that Davis had forwarded the list of gang members, as well as the name of the only fatality in the shoot-out, to his computer.

Eager to know if she was right, Sierra began reading over his shoulder. "Well?" she pressed.

He pulled over the list of the serial killer's victims he'd copied from the bulletin board and compared the names to the list on his computer. He looked at her over his shoulder.

"Every single one of the gang members arrested at the shoot-out was executed by our serial killer."

She'd had a feeling. Going back to her desk, she sat in front of her computer. "Okay, so now we know that that shoot-out is at the root of whatever's going on. It's obvious that someone's out for revenge. Davis sent you the name of the taxi driver, right?"

Ronan looked down the list. "Yeah, he's on the bottom."

"Okay, what is it?" she asked.

"'Darren Campbell,'" he read, then looked across his desk at Sierra. He could see by the look on her face that something had occurred to her. "What are you thinking, Carlyle?"

"Dark thoughts," was all she said as she typed the dead man's name into the general search engine.

It took a little searching, but she found what she was looking for. "Got it," she declared.

"Got what?" Ronan asked. Not waiting for an answer, he got up and crossed to her desk to look over *her* shoulder.

"Darren Campbell's obituary," she told him. Looking at the screen, she read the bottom of the short obituary out loud. "'He was survived by a wife, a son and a daughter.'"

"Okay. So are a lot of people," Ronan said. "Are you thinking that maybe the guy's son decided to take the law into his own hands and *he* killed all those people, included our two cops?"

She had to admit that was in her head, but she didn't want it to seem as if she was jumping to any conclusions. So she said, "I'm thinking that maybe we should go and talk to Darren Campbell's family and see if that leads to something."

It felt as if they were spinning their wheels, but they certainly weren't going to get anywhere by standing still, Ronan thought. Out loud he told her, "Can't hurt, I guess."

LIKE THE GANG members who had been executed, Darren Campbell's family lived outside of Aurora, in a modest little one-story attached home located in Tesla.

The house looked as if it could stand to have more than a little work done on it. Despite that, there was a For Sale sign erected in the tiny front yard, near the front door.

"Looks like things aren't going very well for the Campbells," Ronan commented as they walked past the sign to get to the front door.

"Maybe they just want to get away from all the bad memories," Sierra suggested as he rang the doorbell.

A tall, young woman of about twenty-five or so came to the door just as he was about to ring the doorbell again. With one hand on the door, ready to close it quickly, she asked, "Yes?"

"Detectives O'Bannon and Carlyle," Ronan said, flashing his ID and badge. Sierra did the same. "We'd like to speak to Mrs. Darren Campbell. Is she in?" he asked politely.

The laugh was dry and mirthless. "She's in, but I'm afraid

you can't speak to her. I'm her daughter, Olivia. Is there something I help you with?" she asked, still holding the door ajar.

Sierra decided to press the issue. "Is she busy?" she asked in a friendly voice, trying to put the young woman at ease.

"She's not very much of anything these days." Olivia Campbell looked at them for a long moment and then said, "Come with me."

They followed the lanky young woman into the living room. There was a hospital bed in the center of the room, a tired older woman lying in it. The television was on, filling the room with low-level noise. The person in the hospital bed wasn't watching it. She was staring into space, appearing to be unaware of her daughter or the two strangers who had walked into the room with her.

There was weary compassion in Olivia's eyes as she gestured toward her mother. "She's been like that since my dad was killed."

"And you take care of her?" Sierra asked kindly.

Olivia squared her shoulders, as if bracing against an onslaught of pity. "When I'm not working," she answered crisply.

"Who looks after her when you're working?" Ronan asked. Remembering the obituary, he asked, "Your brother?"

A look bordering on anger entered the young woman's face. She laughed caustically in response to his question. "Hank? Yeah, right. That'll be the day. Hank took off shortly after our dad was killed and he saw what it did to our mother. His last words were, 'Not my problem.' He's not exactly the steadfast, dependable type," she said dismissively. And then her face softened slightly as she looked back at her mother. "I have a woman staying with my mother whenever I'm out."

Olivia glanced at her watch. "Imelda's due any minute now. I really hope she's on time," she said, talking more to herself than to either one of the two people standing in front of her. "They hate it when I'm late for work."

Ronan took the opportunity to ask her, "Where *do* you work?"

"At Tesla Memorial," Olivia said. "I'm a physician's assistant and I volunteered for the night shift at the ER so that I can look after my mother the rest of the time." The doorbell rang and a look of relief crossed her face. "There she is, just in time."

Without another word to the two detectives, Olivia Campbell hurried to the front door and threw it open. "Imelda, hi." She picked up her purse from the small table next to the door. "Mother's had her medications, but I can't get her to eat anything. See if you have better luck than I did."

A petite older woman with salt-and-pepper hair walked in. She nodded at the information. "I will make her eat, Miss Olivia. Do not worry about your mother."

"Well, that's it," Olivia said, looking at the two detectives she'd allowed into her house. Her stance clearly indicated that she wanted them to leave. "I've got to go. Is there anything else I can answer for you?" she asked impatiently.

"No, thank you. You've got enough to deal with," Sierra replied. "We'll be going now," she said, looking at Ronan. Her message was clear.

They followed Olivia out. The door closed behind them. Sierra heard locks being closed.

Ronan shook his head. "That young woman's got a lot on her plate."

"Certainly makes you grateful for your own life," Sierra agreed. Getting into Ronan's vehicle, she watched as Olivia Campbell's car drove away.

He glanced at Sierra. "It certainly does," he murmured and then said as he pulled away from the curb, "We need to locate her brother."

"That's what I'm thinking," Sierra agreed.

She was also thinking something else, but for now, since it was probably far-fetched, she decided to keep it to herself.

Chapter Twenty

Lacking any other leads, Hank Campbell, the dead cabdriver's son, became their newest person of interest by default.

He was nowhere to be found in the immediate area, or in any of the neighboring counties when the search parameters were extended.

Ronan pushed back from his desk, frustrated. "You can't tell me that in this day and age, a person can just disappear out of sight like that. He's got to be somewhere."

"You'd think that, wouldn't you?" Sierra said, agreeing with him. She'd gone through every site she could think of and hadn't been able to find the man. "But his last posting on his social media page was two years ago and, according to his DMV license, his last-known address was the family house."

They hadn't searched the house when they'd questioned Olivia. Maybe they should have, Ronan thought now. "So maybe Hank does live there and his sister lied because she was covering for him. Maybe she knows what he's done, or at least has her suspicions."

"Maybe." Sierra liked to think that she was open to any suggestion. "But I don't think so. If you ask me, she was giving off a lot of anger when we mentioned her brother's name."

He'd come to respect her intuition. "And you bought that?"

She inclined her head. "I think I did. That kind of anger seems like it would be hard to fake."

Ronan wavered. "Maybe the woman's just a good actress."

She didn't want to get into an argument over this. "Maybe," Sierra agreed.

He saw through her. "But you don't think so," Ronan stated.

There was one way to resolve this, she thought. "We could have someone sit outside the house for a few days, see if Hank Campbell turns up," Sierra suggested.

It seemed as good a solution as any. Ronan looked over at Choi's desk. "How do you feel about a stakeout?"

Choi was less than enthusiastic, but he went along with it. "Love cold coffee, stale sandwiches and getting a backache from sitting in my car way too long," the detective said.

Ronan overlooked the detective's sarcasm. "Good. You can take the first shift." He looked at Choi's partner. "Martinez will take the second. Pull Campbell's picture off his DMV license so you know who you're watching for," he told the two detectives.

Dispatching half his team, Ronan turned his attention to Sierra. "I want you to call the credit bureau, get a list of Hank Campbell's credit cards and find out if he's used any of them lately—and where."

"What are you going to be doing?" Sierra asked.

Ronan rose from his desk. "I'm going back to the CSI lab to find out if they managed to get any fingerprints from any of the serial killer's crime scenes that—no pun intended—point to anyone."

"You know..." Sierra said just as he began to leave the room.

Ronan stopped and turned to hear her out.

"If these executions *are* all about that shoot-out, the killing spree just might be over. From all indications, everyone who was involved in that shooting—six gang members and two police officers—is dead. That means no more killings," she concluded.

"Unless the killer's developed a taste for it—or decided that someone else needs to be punished," Choi interjected just as he left for his stakeout assignment.

"There's a thought," Sierra murmured under her breath.

Something in her voice caught Ronan's attention. "Anything you want to say?" he asked.

She thought he'd left right behind Choi. His question surprised her. "Me? Why?"

"You have this expression on your face, like something's not sitting quite right. Would you like to share with the class?" Ronan asked.

She debated saying anything. And then, because he'd asked, she decided she might as well say it out loud. "I keep thinking I've seen the cabdriver's daughter somewhere."

He waited to see if there was more. "Any idea where?"

Sierra shook her head. "No. But it'll come to me." *Most likely when I least expect it*, she added silently.

"I'm sure it will," Ronan replied, humoring her as he left the squad room.

"YOU READY TO call it a night?" Ronan asked Sierra.

It was almost seven and they had been at it for hours. The lab had found no useful prints or anything else for that matter at any of the crime scenes, including the last two involving the police officers. The surveillance videos from the Mexican restaurant where Robinson had been murdered had yet to be reviewed. But there were only so many hours in a day and they had all but exhausted theirs.

"I don't know about you," Ronan continued, "but I feel like I've just been running in place for hours and going nowhere."

"At least you're running," Sierra told him. "I feel like I was sucked up by the treadmill an hour ago and, at this point, I'm flatter than a thin sheet of paper."

He laughed, shaking his head. "Nobody is *ever* going to compare you to a thin sheet of paper," he told her meaningfully. Then, in a slightly louder voice, he said, "Close up and let's go home."

She was more than ready but asked teasingly, "Is that an order?"

"If it has to be."

She broke into a wreath of smiles. "I hear and obey." She shut off her computer, more than happy to see the screen grow dark.

"Yeah, sure. Like I believe that." He laughed. He saw her raise her chin. "Don't give me that innocent look. I'm not an idiot. The word 'obey' is not in your vocabulary. If you're going along with what I just said, it's because you want to."

She liked the fact that he understood her. It made things easier. "Po*ta*to, po*tah*toe."

He grinned. "Exactly."

She'd been rather oblivious to her surroundings as she searched for some sign of Hank Campbell. She felt as if she had just come up for air as she looked around. The two desks near her were empty. "No word from Choi or Martinez?"

Ronan shook his head. Neither detective had called in. At this point, he assumed Martinez had taken Choi's place in the stakeout.

"All quiet on the western front," he told her. He waited until she got her purse and stood. "You in the mood for Chinese?" he asked, referring to dinner.

The idea of sitting in a restaurant seemed particularly overwhelming. "Only if it's to go."

"To go, it is."

There was no discussion, but after they had picked up dinner at the Cantonese Express, Ronan drove them to her house.

As he pulled up in her driveway, she pretended to look put out. "Am I being taken for granted already?"

Ronan played along. Without cracking a smile, he said, "I can leave."

"Don't you dare," Sierra warned. "I still have my gun on me."

He nodded. "Convincing argument. I guess I'm not leaving," he said, getting out of the car on his side. He took the takeout with him.

"That really smells good," Sierra commented. "I didn't realize I was this hungry."

He nodded, knowing how she felt. "Time to focus on something other than just work."

THEY WERE ONLY able to get halfway through the multicarton meal before other appetites took over. He supposed he'd started it by nibbling on the spring roll she had just picked up.

Electricity telegraphed through them as his lips touched her fingers. He pulled her onto his lap, ready to feast on something else. But when he went to kiss her, she put her fingertips to his lips and asked, "Aren't you afraid that your lobster Cantonese will get cold?"

"Better the lobster Cantonese than you," Ronan answered, lightly licking her fingers between each word he uttered.

That did it for her. A shiver of anticipation shimmied all through her.

"Never happen," she breathed.

It was all the encouragement he needed.

Rising, he swept Sierra into his arms and carried her to her bedroom where he quickly proceeded to separate her from her clothing.

Not to be outdone, Sierra undressed him just as swiftly. Within moments of entering the bedroom, they were exploring already familiar areas as if they were entirely new.

She knew what to expect and yet the anticipation that echoed through her body was glorious, leaving her breathless and wanting.

With the memory of the other night vividly echoing in her

brain, she was a far more active participant this time than she had been before, wanting to pleasure Ronan as much as he had pleasured her.

It was almost like a tennis match. Each stroke, each caress, was mirrored, received and echoed. She was determined to make him feel as wildly exhilarated as she did.

Just before he was about to culminate the moment the way she had been aching for him to do, she drew her last remnants of strength together and surprised him by flipping their positions. Suddenly she was over him and he was beneath her, stunned but quite pleased.

He laughed and the sound warmed her as he framed the face that loomed above his.

"I love the way your hair hangs down like that, making you look wild. My wild woman," he murmured, bringing her face to his. The moment dissolved in hot, wanton kisses that fed on one another.

Something distant stirred in her brain but before Sierra could lock onto it, it was gone, burned away in the overpowering heat he created within her.

She surrendered to the moment and to him as they made love, wildly and passionately, as if there was never going to be a next time.

EXHAUSTED—THE PERFORMANCE had had an encore—she collapsed against him, unable to speak, trying her best to catch her breath. Her heart was hammering like a hummingbird convention within her chest. She felt his heart pounding beneath her palm as she kept it against his chest.

They fell asleep that way.

SHE WOKE WITH a start, then settled back when she saw that Ronan was still there. And awake.

"Morning," she murmured.

"It certainly is," he agreed. Lying beside her, he was lightly trailing his fingertips along her soft skin, silently indicating that she was his and he was hers, even when they weren't lost in the throes of lovemaking, although the latter situation was growing closer to becoming a reality again.

She heard him chuckle. "What's so funny?"

"Hunting a serial killer seems to invigorate you," he teased.

"Hunting a serial killer has nothing to do with it," she protested. Sierra shifted, leaning her chin against his chest as she looked up into his face. "You have a lethal mouth and I haven't learned how to stay out of reach."

"Do you want to?" he asked, running his hand through her hair.

"Hell, no," she said with such feeling she made him laugh. She felt his laughter rumble against her. Felt a fresh wave of excitement begin all over again, linking together with the night before.

"I might have a lethal mouth, but everything about you is lethal," he told her. "Every time you let that hair of yours down like that, looking like some fantasy come to life, it's all I can do to keep my hands off you. I think I'm going to make a rule that you have to keep your hair up when you're on the job."

She didn't bother hiding her amusement. "And that'll do it?"

"No, but it'll help. What?" he asked when he saw her expression suddenly change. The amusement had fled, replaced by a look of sudden awareness.

She raised herself up so that her eyes met his. "Say that again."

He had no idea what had set her off. "Say what again? That it'll help?"

"No." She sat up suddenly as the thought that had drifted through her head last night returned and started to gel. "What you said about my hair."

"That you're going to have to keep it up?" he asked, completely lost why she would want to hear that again. "Sierra, what are you getting at?" he asked. "Where is this going?"

Sierra scrambled to her knees. "That's why she looked so familiar to me," she said excitedly.

"What's why *who* looked so familiar to you? Who are we talking about, Sierra?" he asked, still in the dark.

How could he not be following this? "Campbell's daughter!" she cried.

Maybe it would be best if they started at the beginning, he decided. "What about her?"

Convinced that she was on to something, Sierra struggled to rein in her excitement. "When she answered the door, Olivia had her hair pulled back and she looked almost like some old, severe schoolmarm."

So far, he didn't understand why she seemed so wired. "So? She was going to work. A lot of places require that their employees keep their hair back, out of the way, on the job."

"I know, I know. But picture her with her hair loose," she told him.

"Okay," he answered obligingly. He continued looking at her.

She shook her head. She could tell by his expression that he wasn't seeing the woman the way she was. "No, *really* picture her. Wait—" she told him, getting out of bed quickly and hurrying into the living room.

"Not that I don't love watching you run around naked, but what's gotten into you?" he asked.

He heard Sierra rummaging for something in the next room. His curiosity properly aroused, he got out of bed and went into the living room.

When he walked in on her, Sierra had found what she'd been looking for. Holding her cell phone in her hand, she began scrolling through various photographs until she found the one she wanted to show him.

"There it is!" she dcclared. "I knew I hadn't erased it."

Holding her phone up so that Ronan could see, she said, "Here, look at this."

Ronan took the phone from her and looked at the photograph. He recognized it as the one Valri had enlarged for them.

Glancing up at Sierra, he said, "That's the woman someone saw at the Shamrock that night the fifth victim was killed."

She nodded. "Right. She was the one the bartender identified as being with the gang member before he was found in the alley. Look closer," she urged. "Look beyond the profusion of hair. Doesn't she remind you of someone?"

He looked again then began to shrug. "Just another pretty girl who'll probably get old before her time— Wait a minute," he said, taking a closer look. When he raised his eyes to Sierra's, she was smiling at him like someone who felt she'd finally gotten her point across. "Is that—" he started to ask.

"It is."

To make sure they were on the same page, he still asked. "Is that Darren Campbell's daughter?"

"The same. We didn't recognize her before. She looked so different when we questioned her. But I'm willing to bet anything you want that it's her."

"Okay, so she was at the same bar the victim was in. You can't be thinking—"

She cut him short. Ronan was way too nice, she realized. "Yes, I can. Think about it," she persisted. "She's a physician's assistant. That means she has surgical training. She dresses up—just a pretty girl out for a good time, right? Who's going to suspect her? Or have their guard up around her?

"Picture this..." Sierra continued, her voice growing more enthusiastic. "She tells the victim she wants to go someplace private. The guy thinks he's going to get lucky and the minute he turns his back on her, bang, he's dead."

"It makes sense," Ronan said. "Macabre, but it still makes sense." He had one question left. "Why cut off his hand?"

"His *dominant* hand," Sierra clarified emphatically. "The hand that had a gun in it during the shoot-out that claimed her father's life and turned her mother into a manic-depressant."

He was convinced. "I think we need to have another talk with Olivia Campbell," he said, already beginning to get dressed.

Chapter Twenty-One

Ronan heard his cell phone ringing just as he was looking around for his shoes. Finding the cell first, he swiped it open.

"O'Bannon," he said as he continued looking for his shoes.

He heard Sean's voice on the other end of the line. "Ronan, I think I found something that you and your team might be interested in taking a look at."

After finding his shoes, he slipped them on. "Uncle Sean? Where are you?" Ronan asked. It was too early for the man to be calling from the lab, wasn't it?

"At the lab," Sean answered. "I came in early to see if I could catch up. Your serial killer's been keeping my unit busy. I finally got a chance to go through the surveillance videos."

And his uncle had obviously found something important enough to call him this early. Ronan glanced at his watch. It wasn't even seven o'clock yet. He did a quick calculation. "I'll be right there. Give me twenty-five minutes," he promised.

"Twenty-five minutes?" Sean repeated. "I thought you lived farther away from the precinct than that."

"Long story. 'Bye," Ronan said, terminating the connection.

"What's up?" Sierra asked, coming into the living room to join him. She was dressed and, from all appearances, ready to go.

"That was my uncle," Ronan told her, tucking in his shirt before turning around.

"I need more of a hint than that," she told him. "It's not like you have only one uncle."

"Sean, the one heading up the CSI unit. He said he finally found the time to view the surveillance videos from Officer Robertson's murder and he thinks he might have found something."

From the way Ronan spoke, she could tell that was going to take precedence over their previously decided course of action. "I guess that puts confronting Olivia Campbell on hold," she surmised.

"Temporarily," Ronan amended. "I think that avenue still bears exploring," he agreed, finally turning to look at Sierra. "You got dressed."

"Yes, I've been doing it ever since I was four. Before that, my dad had to help. You look surprised."

"I left you naked." And that had only been a few minutes ago.

"And now I'm dressed," she concluded. "Interrogating a suspect naked was never my style," she quipped. Sierra held out a travel mug filled with coffee. She had one for herself, as well. "What's your point?"

A little dazed, Ronan took the travel mug she'd handed him. "I just didn't know a woman could get dressed that fast," he admitted.

She laughed, patting his face. "When are you going to learn, O'Bannon? I'm full of surprises."

She'd get no argument from him on that. But remarkable woman or not, how had she managed to get dressed *and* make coffee in that short amount of time? "When did you make coffee?" he asked.

"I didn't. The coffeemaker did. I just poured it out," Sierra teased. "We can pick up breakfast on our way in, but I thought we really needed the coffee to kick-start us."

He smiled at her as they left the house, recalling what she'd looked like, searching for her cell phone a few minutes ago. "You already took care of that part for me," he told her.

She immediately knew what he was referring to. "I can't wait until this serial killer's behind bars so we can get back to what's really important," she told him, her eyes sweeping over him significantly.

"Amen to that," he agreed, ushering her to his car with his free hand.

"OKAY, UNCLE SEAN, we're here," Ronan called out as he and Sierra walked into the CSI lab.

It was between shifts and the day shift hadn't come in yet—all except for Sean who was all the way over at the far end of the lab where the video bays were located.

Stepping forward so they could see him, Sean waved them over. "I think you might want to see this."

He waited until they were almost there and then stepped back into the bay.

"What, no popcorn?" Ronan asked as they reached the bay. Sean had the video in question freeze-framed on the first viewing monitor.

"I think that this time, you'll want to skip the popcorn," Sean said and then nodded at the woman next to his nephew. "Good morning, Sierra. I see he decided to drag you out of bed to see this."

Sierra smiled. She didn't like lying, but she didn't think Ronan would be comfortable with his uncle knowing they had spent the night together. "Something like that," she told him.

"Well, I think you're both going to think it's worth it. Remember, we were looking for whoever killed Robertson," he reminded them as if they might have thought he'd made a different sort of discovery. Beckoning them closer to the machine used to review the various surveillance videos, he pointed to the screen. "Here's Robertson going into the men's room. No one's gone in ahead of him since the restaurant opened at eleven. I went through this video carefully to make sure no one was lying in wait for him.

"All right, here's Robertson going in. And now here's you and Detective Carlyle," he continued, "walking into the men's room fifteen minutes later. Robertson's already dead. The only people seen coming or going in the vicinity of the men's room are the two of you, my unit and that young woman coming out of the ladies' room."

She was the one he had currently frozen on the monitor.

Sierra looked at the woman intently. The young woman had bumped into her and kept walking after Sierra apologized. Intent on finding Robertson, she hadn't paid any attention to the woman.

She did now.

"Can you zoom in on her?" she asked Sean.

"I can make her look like Big Foot's mother if you need me to," Sean answered, magnifying that one section of the video.

"She has her head down," Ronan complained. "We can't really make out her features."

"She's wearing her hair just like the woman that was seen with the victim at the Shamrock," Sierra said. "Look at her. She's about the right height, the right age," she pointed out.

"All circumstantial," Ronan countered. And circumstantial didn't stand up in court, he thought.

"Yes, but she doesn't know that," Sierra noted, thinking maybe they could still use it to frighten a confession out of the woman.

"'She'?" Sean repeated. He looked from his nephew to Sierra. "You have someone in mind?"

"Oh, yes," she told Sean with enthusiasm. "We definitely have someone in mind. Can you make us a print of that?" she asked, nodding at the frozen screen he'd enlarged.

"Sure." It was a piece of cake.

"And a copy of that section of video? If you could transfer that to my tablet—" she requested hopefully.

Sean nodded. "Consider it done."

Ronan followed her line of thinking. "We're going to use that to confront the suspect," he told his uncle.

Sean nodded. "Just give me a few minutes," he requested. "And your tablet," he told Sierra.

"I'll be right back," she promised, hurrying out of the lab.

TWENTY-FIVE MINUTES later after calling Choi and Martinez about what they had found, they were back in Ronan's car. Armed with a copy of the surveillance video that showed the woman emerging out of the ladies' room transferred onto her tablet, plus a still of the woman, they were ready to confront Olivia Campbell.

"Think she's back from the hospital?" he asked Sierra as he started his car.

"She said she worked the night shift, so, yes, my guess is that she's back at home. Not to mention that I've double-checked the list of people who were involved in the shoot-out that killed her father and from what I can see, there's no one left to kill. She's eliminated everyone who was there."

Ronan thought over what she'd just said. There was one possibility left. "Unless she's turning her wrath on her brother for deserting their mother in her time of need."

"She's going to have to find him first," Sierra pointed out. "I exhausted every search engine and I couldn't find any trace of Hank Campbell anywhere, remember?"

It wasn't unheard of for a person to shed their identity and get a new one. But that required planning and resources. There was a simpler reason that the late cabdriver's son was nowhere to be found.

"Maybe that's because he isn't anywhere," Ronan told her.

"What are you saying? That he's dead?"

That was exactly what he was thinking. "Maybe Olivia got into it with him, trying to shame him into doing his part taking care of their mother. He told her he wasn't about to sacrifice his life taking care of a zombie. She lost her temper and, I don't know, threw something at him, or maybe even shot him. He could have been her first victim," Ronan concluded then looked at her. "What do you think?"

Considering the kind of person they thought they were dealing with, it was entirely plausible to her. "I think you might be on to something."

That made two of them, he thought grimly.

OLIVIA CAMPBELL APPEARED far from happy to see the two detectives on her doorstep again. As before, she kept the door slightly ajar when she opened it. But this time she kept it that way and stood with her body blocking access into her house, being, in effect, a human doorstop.

"I already talked to you two," Olivia told them sharply.

"We have more questions," Ronan told her.

"Well, I don't have more answers," Olivia snapped. "Look, I just got off the night shift and I'm really tired. Come back later. Better yet, don't come back at all," she told them, starting to push the door closed.

Ronan was quicker than she was and forced it open. Olivia stumbled backward. "Hey!" she protested.

"You need to talk to us, Ms. Campbell," he informed her in a no-nonsense voice.

Olivia looked like a woman tottering on the verge of a breakdown. "If you people put half this effort into putting away those animals who killed my father instead of harassing me," she shouted, "maybe my mother would still be a human being instead of a freaking statue."

"Maybe you should come down to the precinct with us," Sierra said in a low, stern voice.

"I'm not going anywhere with you," Olivia cried. Turning on her heel, she flew back into the living room. They immediately followed her, not quite sure what to anticipate or what the woman was capable of in the presence of her mother.

They found Olivia pressing the remote on the hospital bed, raising the upper section. It looked as if she was trying to modify her mother's position. Her mother still lay completely immobile. Instead of staring unblinkingly at the ceiling, she seemed to be looking straight ahead now.

Maybe she was just trying to make her mother comfortable, Sierra thought, softening a little. "Why don't you call back the woman who watches your mother and then we'll go—"

"No!" Olivia cried, pulling a weapon from the space that had opened up beneath the mattress and the hospital bed's springs.

She aimed the handgun at them.

"You don't want to do that," Sierra told her in an incredibly calm voice, trying to get Olivia to focus on her.

"No, I don't," Olivia snapped, a note of hysteria reverberating in her voice. "But you two just won't leave me alone. Why do you keep hounding me? Why couldn't you just do your jobs? Why did you make *me* do it?"

In an odd sort of way, Sierra could understand the other woman's frustration, although she couldn't condone what she'd done afterward. "Sometimes the law winds up protecting the guilty."

"It *always* protects the guilty," Olivia retorted, shifting the barrel of her handgun from Sierra to Ronan and then back again. "You wouldn't do the right thing. You made me do it. I'm tired," she complained, her voice quavering. "I'm really, really tired." Her face became a mask of hopelessness and there was a wild look in her eyes. "There's nothing left for me."

Sierra read between the lines. The woman was going to kill herself. "You have your mother," she pointed out with feeling.

Mention of her mother made Olivia look even more wild-eyed. She gestured angrily at her mother with her free hand.

"Look at her! She's not my mother, she's a vegetable!" The desperation just seemed to grow. "The rest of my life, I'm going to have to take care of her. What kind of a life *is* that?" she demanded.

"We could find your brother," Ronan suggested, ever so slowly inching his way closer to her.

Olivia laughed to herself. It was a dry, humorless laugh that was more hopeless than anything else. "You're not going to find him. Ever," she declared with finality—and just a little bit of pride. "Don't you understand? I've evened the score but now there's nothing left for me. Nothing," she stressed despondently. Her hand shook as she turned the gun on herself.

"Put it down, Olivia. Please, put it down," Sierra pleaded. "Don't take the easy way out."

That infuriated the woman, just as Sierra hoped it would. "Easy way? You think this is the *easy* way?" she demanded hotly, her eyes blazing.

The distraction was all that Ronan needed. Flying forward, he caught her, one hand going around her waist while he grabbed the hand holding the weapon with the other. He pushed her hand upward so that the muzzle was now aimed at the ceiling, the same ceiling her mother had been staring at for the last two years.

Sierra immediately jumped in to grab the woman's hand, as well. With Ronan holding Olivia, she managed to wrestle the handgun away from Olivia.

Once separated from her weapon, Olivia dissolved into angry, despairing tears and sank to the floor, crying hysterically.

Sierra looked down at the handgun. It was a 9 mm Smith & Wesson. "I think we've found our murder weapon," she told Ronan.

"And our serial killer," he added with a surety she wasn't used to hearing in his voice.

Sierra nodded. It was over. The nightmare was over. All that was left was to get answers to a myriad of outstanding questions.

A deep sigh escaped her as she looked at the sobbing woman in their custody. "So why don't I feel good about this?" she asked quietly.

The look in Ronan's eyes told her he understood.

Chapter Twenty-Two

Taking out her handcuffs, Sierra bent over Olivia to apply the steel restraints to the woman's wrists.

It all happened so fast, Sierra was caught completely off guard.

One moment their prisoner was a sobbing, broken heap on the floor. The next, uttering a guttural shriek, Olivia twisted around and lunged at her, holding a long, thin, blue knitting needle in her hand like a weapon.

In the kitchen, looking to see if the phone number for the aide who took care of Olivia's mother was posted on the refrigerator door, Ronan was alerted by the shriek and immediately sprinted back into the living room.

"Sierra?" he cried, confused and looking at his partner who was in turn pinning down their prisoner with her knee to the woman's neck. "Is everything all right?"

"It is now," she told him, panting. It had been touch and go for a moment, but she'd managed to overpower Olivia and wrestle the woman to the floor. Still trying to get her breath, she said to Ronan, "You put the cuffs on her. I'm afraid if I move, she'll get loose again."

"Gladly," he told Sierra, taking the cuffs from her.

It was only after he'd handcuffed the woman and yanked her to her feet that he actually looked at Sierra and saw it. There was blood all along the left shoulder of her shirt. It was coming from the hole created by the knitting needle that was, appallingly, still stuck in the fleshy part of her shoulder.

"You're bleeding," he informed her, stunned. Like a man standing in the middle of a puzzle, he struggled to put the pieces together. "What the hell happened in here?"

Sierra tried to shrug and found that she couldn't, not without feeling a shooting pain going from her shoulder through the rest of her.

She pushed on through the pain. "All I can guess is that when she crumbled to the floor, she must have found a knitting needle next to her mother's bed. When I tried to pull her to her feet, she lunged at me, trying to stab me with it."

"She *did* stab you," he corrected angrily. "And it's still sticking out of your shoulder. You need to go to the hospital to have that removed and your wound taken care of."

But to his horror, Sierra was already pulling the knitting needle out of her shoulder and covering the wound with a handkerchief.

"What I need to do is go to the medicine cabinet and get a Band-Aid for it," she corrected. "And you need to call for backup so that they can take her to the precinct to be booked," she told him. "And don't take your eyes off her until someone gets here. She just might try to take a chunk out of your ear," Sierra warned as she made her way to the rear of the house, looking for a bathroom.

She found the bathroom, but not before she found Olivia's room. What she saw there had her stopping short. One wall was covered with newspaper clippings and pictures, all dealing with the street gang members who'd eventually found their way into a drawer at the morgue. In addition, one side of that wall was devoted to the two police officers who had also met their end, thanks to the handcuffed woman in the other room.

"Wow," Sierra murmured under her breath as she scanned the various articles and pictures. The woman had really been obsessed with killing these people.

Starting to feel a little light-headed because of the blood loss, Sierra went into the bathroom and opened the medicine cabinet. Just as she'd suspected, there was everything within the small cabinet that she needed to clean, disinfect and bandage her wound.

She was just about finished and shrugging back into her blouse when she heard the wail of approaching sirens in the distance.

"Sierra, what's taking you so long?" Ronan called out, concerned that maybe she'd passed out.

"Just getting this thing cleaned up," she answered, then added, "And getting an education. You need to get the CSI unit down here," she told him, crossing back into the living room.

She saw that not only had he handcuffed Olivia's hands behind her back, he also had one of her wrists cuffed to the refrigerator handle.

"After what she pulled on you, I'm not taking any chances," Ronan said.

"I'm not blaming you. I just hope you have the keys to those cuffs. Otherwise, they're going to have to load that refrigerator onto a truck along with her."

"Worse comes to worst, we can take the door off its hinges," he deadpanned. "She can drag the door along in her wake."

"Funny man," Olivia jeered, then spat at his shoes. "Real funny. Maybe that's why you people can't get anything done. You're just a bunch of comedians."

Ronan looked completely unruffled, but Sierra could tell he was holding his temper in check.

"We got you, didn't we?" he said in a calm, laid-back voice that only succeeded in infuriating the other woman further.

A string of curses emerged from Olivia's mouth. She wound up screaming at both of them.

Ronan turned to Sierra. "What's that old rhyme about sticks and stones?" he asked her.

"And knitting needles," she quipped. "Don't forget knitting needles."

He obliged. "Yeah, those, too. But 'words'll never hurt me' I think is the rest of it."

Instead of a patrol officer, because of their proximity, Martinez and Choi were the first on the scene. They walked into the house and saw the woman handcuffed to the refrigerator.

"So it really was her," Choi commented. "It's always the quiet ones you have to watch out for."

"Glad I didn't bet on the brother," Martinez said as he flanked Olivia's other side.

Ronan uncuffed her from the refrigerator handle.

"My brother?" Olivia echoed, scoffing at the very idea that he could have done what she had done. "That wimp? He couldn't even defend himself against a girl," she jeered with an unmistakable air of superiority.

Martinez looked at Ronan, but it was Sierra who spoke up. "We think she killed her brother, too."

Olivia tossed her head defiantly. "He didn't deserve to live. He was running out on our mother, leaving me to deal with everything. All he could think of was himself, the useless SOB," she cried angrily.

He'd had enough of the woman for now. "Just get her down to the precinct and book her," Ronan instructed the two detectives.

"And be careful," Sierra cautioned. "She's a lot more dangerous than you think."

That was when Choi saw the blood on her shoulder. "What the hell happened to you, Carlyle?" he asked.

"Our serial killer found a new use for a knitting needle," Ronan said, crossing over to take a closer look at Sierra's shoulder. "You're bleeding through the bandage," he told her, adding in a grave voice, "You need that looked at."

"So look at it," she quipped.

"We'll see you at the station," Martinez said, herding the prisoner out along with his partner.

Ronan's attention was focused on his stubborn partner. "By a professional."

"You're a professional," she countered innocently.

"Damn it, Carlyle, you know what I mean. A doctor. You need a doctor."

"And you can play doctor," she told him. Before he could say anything in response, she said, "But first you need to see this."

"See what?" he asked, finding himself following her to the rear of the house.

"The reason I told you to call the CSI unit. Pronto," she added.

He began to tell her that she wasn't going to distract him from forcing her to go to the ER, but the words never made it to his tongue. Having walked into the bedroom behind her, he was stunned speechless as he looked at the far wall. The newspaper clippings and photographs amounted to a huge collage devoted to all the people involved in Darren Campbell's untimely death.

Ronan emitted a low whistle. "She's been at this for a while."

Sierra nodded, looking at the clippings again, this time a little more slowly as she scanned a few of the more recent articles.

"That she has. She's got a notebook there," she told Ronan, pointing to a small, beaten up notebook on a side desk. "It's divided up into sections—one for each gang member as well as the two police officers. It outlines their habits. She was stalking them, Ronan," she told him. "And, if I don't miss my guess, I'd say that's ketamine in that vial on the desk. I don't think the assistant DA is going to have any trouble getting a conviction here."

There was one way around that. "Unless her lawyer goes for an insanity plea," he pointed out.

"Either way, she's going to be locked up for a very long time." It was hard being in the presence of so much evil. She pressed her lips together and glanced toward the living room. "You know, the real victim here is that poor woman in the other room. She's lost her husband, most likely her son if Olivia actually did kill him, too, and now her daughter."

Ronan nodded, a grim expression washing over his face. "Let me see if I can find that aide's phone number," he told her, although he wasn't having much luck so far. "And then I'm taking you to the hospital."

"Unless it's to interview Olivia's coworkers to see just what kind of hours she did keep and if she was missing when the evening executions took place, I'm not interested," she told him with finality.

"Okay, let's go with that. We're interviewing her coworkers."

"You're just saying that to get me to the hospital," she accused.

"Over my shoulder, fireman style if I have to."

"Fireman style?" she echoed. "You can't just toss out terms like that," she told him. "You forget, I come from a firefighting family."

"Good, then you know what to expect," he said.

Ronan was about to carry out his threat, temporarily forgetting about the old woman in the living room, when he heard a commotion outside.

Sean and his team had arrived.

"Looks like the cavalry's here," Ronan announced. "And you are out of excuses. You're having that looked at by a doctor," he informed her in a no-nonsense voice. "Just think you can only catch half the bad guys if you have only one arm."

"I don't want to go to the hospital," she fired back. "All I want to do is file this report and then celebrate at Malone's at the end of the day."

"And you'll do all that," Ronan promised, turning her toward the doorway. "Once you get that shoulder checked out." He saw Sean walk into the living room. "Back me up, Uncle Sean. She's resisting going to the ER."

Sean took one look at the blood on her shoulder and said, "Go. Gangrene is not something you want to fool around with." And then he looked at the woman elevated in the hospital bed, seemingly completely oblivious to everything that was going on around her. "What about her?" he asked his nephew as the rest of his crew went to work.

"Her daughter—our serial killer," he added, "usually takes care of her. She has an aide spelling her, but so far I haven't been able to find the phone number for her."

"Don't worry about it. I'll call social services. They'll have someone out here before we're finished. Now take her to the ER," he told Ronan, nodding at Sierra.

She blew out an exasperated breath. "I said I'm all right."

"Not yet, but you will be," Sean told her. "Now go," he ordered. "I'm not going to be the one making excuses to your father about why his daughter wound up with gangrene."

That had her looking at the older man in surprise. This was the first she'd heard of this. "You know my father?" she asked.

"That, I do," Sean asserted. "It's a small world," he added before repeating his order to his nephew, "Now take her to the ER."

Because she felt herself growing steadily weaker, Sierra surrendered and allowed Ronan to drive her to the hospital.

"SEE? I *TOLD* you I'd be all right," she told him nearly five hours later.

"Yeah, that's what you said. But some things a man wants to verify for himself," he informed her as they walked into her house. Turning on the light, he closed the door behind them. "And I wasn't about to take any chances that you were going to wind up suffering some kind of awful consequences just because I walked out of the room and you wound up getting stabbed."

"Oh, so this was all about assuaging your guilt?" she teased.

"No," he told her, turning her around so that she faced him. It had been one hell of a day and he was just relieved that it was over—and that she was all right. "This is about making sure that you stayed as perfect as you were."

"'Perfect,'" she repeated incredulously as she stared at him. "Me." He had to be setting her up for something, she thought.

But he looked entirely innocent as he said, "You see anyone else standing here?"

"No, but—"

"Not that you're going to be standing here for long," he interjected.

She couldn't read him right now and that bothered her. "Oh?"

"No," he told her. "I think you should lie down. In bed." He paused and then added, "With me."

Now it was beginning to sound like him. "Anything else?" she asked.

"Oh, a great deal 'else,'" he admitted. "But due to your condition, we're going to have to take it slow." He was kissing her between each word, between each expressed sentiment.

She could hardly catch her breath. "Hey, slow down," she told him. "Those pills they gave me at the hospital are making me dizzy."

"News flash," he quipped, a very wicked smile curving his lips. "It's not the pills that are making you dizzy."

She looked at him with wide eyes. "Oh?"

"It's me," he said, still punctuating each word with a kiss, deeper ones now.

With a contented sigh, she smiled up at him. "Maybe it is."

"And maybe you should stop talking and save your strength for something far more important," Ronan suggested.

"Maybe I should," she agreed as she wound her arms around his neck.

The next moment he sealed his lips to hers while carrying her to her bedroom.

There was no need for any conversation after that for a long, long time.

Epilogue

"You know, I've never seen so many good-looking people in one spot before," Sierra commented, looking around at all the people, a good many of them Cavanaughs, attending Christian and Susannah's wedding.

After spending several grueling weeks, first hunting for the serial killer and then helping to put together an ironclad case against Olivia, it felt wonderful to just focus on enjoying herself with the man who had stolen her heart.

Ronan slid in next to her, joining her at one of the small tables that had been set up throughout the grounds behind Andrew Cavanaugh's house.

"Sure you have," Ronan said. "You were at Uncle Andrew's last party, the one he held for Shaw when he became the new chief of police."

"Not the same thing," Sierra protested. "Everyone was dressed in casual clothes then. Now all the men are decked out in tuxedos and the women look like they've stepped out of the pages of a high-end fashion magazine—not to mention that the bride is an absolute knockout." She looked at the newly wedded Susannah Quinn O'Bannon.

"Is she?" Ronan asked innocently, never taking his eyes off Sierra. "I hadn't noticed."

"Hadn't noticed? You've been less than ten feet away from her throughout the entire ceremony, Mr. Best Man." Sierra laughed.

He was working up his nerve to ask her something and Sierra wasn't cooperating. "Sorry, I guess my vision's been obstructed. How did that old classic song go? I only have eyes for you."

She looked at him. Ronan was acting rather strangely ever since they'd gotten back from the church. "Since when do you know the lyrics of old classic songs?"

A smile slowly curved his mouth as he went on looking at her. "Since this uppity little know-it-all with the fantastic mouth came into my life and upended just about everything in it, bringing nothing but total chaos in her wake."

Her eyes narrowed slightly as she concentrated. "I'm sorry, is there a compliment in there somewhere?" Sierra asked.

He laughed softly to himself. It had taken him a long time to get here. A long time to shed the shadows of the past and allow himself to move forward. Now that he had, he needed to tell her, to make her understand. "There's a compliment everywhere you move."

"Just how much have you had to drink?" she asked. She glanced over to where the bride and groom were sitting. "And don't you have to get back to the bridal party?"

He answered her questions in order. "Not much and I've done my duty for my brother. Aisle-marching, guest-seating and picture-taking. The rest of the evening belongs to me—and I want to spend it with the most beautiful woman here."

Okay, something was definitely going on here. "Are you all right?" she asked, peering into Ronan's face. "Seriously, you don't seem like yourself."

"You mean I don't seem grumpy?" he guessed.

She debated rejecting the word he'd used, then decided he would probably value honesty. "Well, I would have put it a little more diplomatically, but, okay, yes. Grumpy."

"Maybe everything we've been through these last few weeks, plus the wedding, has opened my eyes and put me in a different frame of mind." Bccause it had, he added silently.

Sierra looked at him uncertainly. "What kind of frame of mind?"

Rather than having prerecorded music, Andrew had hired a band to play at the reception. A slow tune was just beginning.

"Do you dance?" Ronan asked, rising and putting his hand out to her.

She regarded the hand he offered. "Do you?"

The smile on his lips had slipped into his eyes. "I wouldn't be asking if I didn't."

"You're just full of surprises, aren't you?" she observed, getting to her feet. She put her hand in his. "Yes, I dance."

"Good," he said.

So saying, still holding her hand, he led her to the area that had been designated as a temporary dance floor.

It was a slow number and as Ronan took her into his arms, everything felt just beautifully right—which made her nervous. It felt too perfect in her opinion. Too perfect usually meant that something was going to go wrong. Soon. She tried to steel herself off.

For now, she resorted to small talk. "Your brother looks very happy," she commented.

"Not half as happy as my mother," Ronan told her, glancing in his mother's direction. The smile on the woman's face could have guided ships safely to shore through an impenetrable fog. "He's the first one of us to get married. I heard my mother commenting that she didn't think she was *ever* going to live to see the day that one of her kids got married."

"She shouldn't have talked like that. Your mother's still a young woman," Sierra protested. "Who knows, she might surprise everyone by getting married herself."

Ronan looked at her, mildly surprised. "You know something you're not telling me?"

"No." Sierra laughed. "Just that there's no set age for marriage. People get married at all different ages these days and your mother's a vibrant, vital woman, that's all."

It was the opening he'd been searching for. He was never going to have a better chance to broach the subject than this.

"How do you feel about marriage?"

"Me?" Why was he asking her that? Was he setting her up to let her know that marriage was something he wasn't interested in now? Sierra tried her best to sound nonchalant. "I think it's a good thing, but there's got to be love there in order for it to work."

"Well, we agree on that," he told her, holding her a little closer as they continued to dance to a timeless love song. He needed to stop circling the pool and just jump in, he told himself. "You want me to go first?" he asked, whispering the question into her ear.

She drew her head back to look at him, completely confused. "I might, if I knew what you were talking about."

Again he whispered the words into her ear. "Saying I love you."

This time Sierra stopped dancing. It felt as if her limbs had suddenly gone numb. "Is this some kind of a game?" she asked, doing her best to steel herself for inevitable disappointment. "Or a dare?"

"No to both," he denied with feeling.

Because she didn't want to attract any undue attention and the music was still playing, Sierra forced herself to resume dancing.

He'd started this, he needed to see it through, Ronan told himself. She obviously didn't understand what he was saying to her. "I think I figured it out when you had that knitting needle sticking out of your shoulder. You were beautiful, you were brave and you weren't afraid of anything. I've never met anyone quite like you before."

"I think that goes two ways," Sierra said with a sigh. "Maybe you just have a thing about knitting needles," she joked.

"No," he insisted, "I have a thing about you. And I have to get this out before I lose my nerve," he told Sierra.

The music had stopped, but she continued dancing with

him, focusing only on what he was saying and not the fact that there was no actual music, only what was playing in her head.

"Say what?" Sierra asked, trying not to sound breathless.

"Will you marry me?" He saw her jaw drop and talked quickly. "You don't have to give me an answer yet. You can take your time. Hell, I don't care how long you take as long as the answer's the right one when you finally say it."

Stunned, she could only stare at him. He hadn't struck her as the kind of man who would *want* to get married. At least not for a very long time to come. And she was all right with that, as long as, when he finally decided to settled down, it was with her.

"Hey, you two," his brother Lukkas called out to them with a laugh, "the music's stopped."

But Sierra held up her hand to tell the man who was going to be her future brother-in-law to back off. "Not yet," she told Lukkas, never taking her eyes off Ronan. Mentally taking a deep breath, she said, "Okay."

"Okay?" Ronan asked, not sure exactly what she was agreeing to. He wanted to be very, very sure before he allowed himself to become excited.

"Okay, I love you and okay—" She pressed her lips together. "I'll marry you."

A part of Ronan was still somewhat feeling leery. "Really?"

"Really," she said, everything inside her feeling as if it was singing.

The band began to play again, but despite the fact that she and Ronan were still on the dance floor, they didn't start dancing.

They were too busy sealing their mutual promise with a long, everlasting kiss.

* * * * *

"You're a great guy, but I'd prefer to keep things between us professional," Kayla said.

"So no more kisses?"

"No more." She had to hold back a sigh. The kiss really had been great, but kissing Dylan again would only lead to more kissing and hugging and caressing and… She shoved the thoughts away and sat up straighter. They were almost to the turnoff for her house.

He switched on his blinker to make the left turn. Behind them, headlights glowed in the distance. Kayla squinted and shielded her eyes from the glare in the side mirror. What was the guy behind them doing with his brights up? And he was driving awfully fast, wasn't he?

Dylan took his foot off the brake, prepared to make the turn. But before he could act, the car behind them slammed into them, clipping the back bumper and sending the cruiser spinning off the road and into the ditch. The air bags exploded, pressing Kayla back against the seat. Then she heard another sound—the metallic popping of bullets striking metal as someone fired into their vehicle.

"You're right. But I'd prefer to keep things between us professional," Kayla said.

"So no more kisses?"

"No more." She had to hold back a sigh. The kiss really had been great, but kissing Dylan again would only lead to more kissing and hugging and caressing and... She shoved the thoughts away and sat up straighter. They were almost to the turnoff for her house.

He switched on his blinker to make the left turn. Behind them, headlights glowed in the distance. Kayla squinted and shielded her eyes from the glare in the side mirror. What was the guy behind them doing with his brights up? And he was driving awfully fast, wasn't he?

Dylan took his foot off the brake, prepared to make the turn. But before he could act, the car behind them slammed into theirs, clipping the back bumper and sending the cruiser spinning off the road and into the ditch. The air bags exploded, pressing Kayla back against the seat. Then she heard another sound—the metallic popping of bullets striking metal as someone fired into their vehicle.

MURDER IN BLACK CANYON

BY

CINDI MYERS

First Published in Great Britain 2017
By Mills & Boon, an imprint of HarperCollins*Publishers*
1 London Bridge Street, London, SE1 9GF

ISBN: 978-0-263-92891-4

46-0617

Our policy is to use papers that are natural, renewable and recyclable products and made from wood grown in sustainable forests. The logging and manufacturing processes conform to the legal environmental regulations of the country of origin.

Printed and bound in Spain
by CPI, Barcelona

Cindi Myers is the author of more than fifty novels. When she's not crafting new romance plots, she enjoys skiing, gardening, cooking, crafting and daydreaming. A lover of small-town life, she lives with her husband and two spoiled dogs in the Colorado mountains.

For Coco—Female PI Extraordinaire

Chapter One

As jobs went, this one paid more than most, Kayla reminded herself as she parked her battered Subaru at the mouth of the canyon a few miles from the Gunnison River. A private investigator in the small town of Montrose, Colorado, couldn't be overly picky if she wanted to keep putting food on the table and paying rent, though interceding in family squabbles had to be right up there with photographing philanderers on her list of least-favorite jobs.

Still, this assignment gave her an excuse to get out into the beautiful backcountry near Black Canyon of the Gunnison National Park called Dead Horse Canyon. She retrieved a small day pack from the backseat of the car and slipped it on, then added a ball cap to shade her face from the intense summer sun. A faint dirt trail marked the way into the canyon, through a windswept landscape of dark green piñon and juniper, and the earth tones of sand and gravel and scattered boulders.

A bird called from somewhere in the canyon ahead, the high, trilling call echoing off the rock and sending a shiver up Kayla's spine. Maybe she should have brought a weapon with her, but she didn't like to carry the handgun, even though she was licensed to do so. Her work as a private investigator seldom brought her into contact with anyone really threatening. She spent most of her time surveilling cheating spouses, doing background checks for businesses and serving the occasional subpoena. Talking to a twenty-four-year-old woman who had decided to camp out in the desert with a bunch of wandering hippies hadn't struck Kayla as particularly threatening.

But that was before she had visited this place, so isolated and desolate, far from any kind of help or authority. Someone holed up out here could probably get away with almost anything and not be caught. The thought unnerved her more than she liked to admit.

Shaking her head, she hit the button to lock her car and pocketed her keys. The hard part of the job was over—she had tracked down Andi Matheson, wayward adult daughter of Senator Peter Matheson. Now all she had to do was deliver the senator's message to the young woman. Whether Andi decided to mend fences with her father was none of Kayla's business.

Her boots crunched on fine gravel as she set out walking on the well-defined path. Clearly, a lot of feet had trod this trail recently. The group that referred to themselves as simply "the Family" had a permit to camp on this stretch of public land outside the national park boundaries. They had the area to themselves. No one else wanted to be so far away from things like electricity, running water and paved roads. Her investigation hadn't turned up much information about the group—only some blog posts by the leader, a young man whose real name was Daniel Metwater, but who went by the title of Prophet. He preached a touchy-feely brand of peace, love and living off the land that reminded Kayla of stuff she'd seen in movies about sixties-era flower children. Misguided and irresponsible, maybe, but probably harmless.

"Halt. You're not authorized to enter this area."

Heart in her throat, Kayla stared at the large man who blocked the path ahead. He had seemingly appeared out of nowhere, but he must have been waiting in the cluster of car-sized boulders to the left of the path. He wore baggy camouflage trousers and a green-and-black camouflage-patterned T-shirt stretched over broad shoulders. His full beard and long brown hair made him look like a cross between a biker and an old-testament patriarch. He wasn't armed, unless you counted the bulging muscles of his biceps, and what might have been a knife in the sheath on his belt. She forced herself to stand tall and look him in the eye. "This is public land," she said. "Anyone can hike here."

"We have permission to camp here," Camo-man said. "You'll need to walk around our camp. We don't welcome gawkers."

What are you hiding that you don't want me to see? Kayla thought, every sense sharpened. "I'm not here to gawk," she said. "I came to visit one of your—" What exactly did she call Andi—a disciple? A member? "A woman who's with you," she decided. "Andi Matheson."

"No one is here by that name." The man's eyes

revealed as much as a mannequin's, blank as an unplugged television screen.

"I have information that she is. Or she was until as recently as yesterday, when I saw her with some other members of your group in Montrose." The three women, including Andi, had been leaving a coin operated Laundromat when Kayla had spotted them, but they had ignored her cries to wait and driven off. She had been on foot and unable to follow them.

"We do not have anyone here by that name," the man repeated.

So maybe she had changed her name and went by Moon Flower or something equally charming and silly. "I don't know what she's calling herself this week, but she's here and I want to talk to her," Kayla said. "Or satisfy myself that she isn't here." She spread her hands wide in a universal gesture of harmlessness. "All I want to do is talk to her. Then I'll leave, I promise. What you do out here is your business—though I'm pretty sure blocking access to public land, whether you have a permit or not, is illegal. It might even get your permit revoked." She gave him a hard look to go with her soft words, letting him know she was perfectly willing to make trouble if she needed to.

He hesitated a moment, then nodded. "I'll need to search you for weapons. We don't allow instruments of destruction into our haven of peace."

She was impressed he could deliver such a line with a straight face. "So that knife on your belt doesn't count?"

He put a hand to the sheath at his side. "This is a ceremonial piece, not a weapon."

Uh-huh. And she had a "ceremonial" Smith & Wesson back at her home office. But no point arguing with him. "I'm not armed," she said. "And you'll just have to take my word for it, because I'm not in the habit of allowing strange men to grope me, and if you lay a hand on me I promise I *will* file assault charges." Not to mention she knew a few self-defense moves that would put him in the dirt on his butt.

A little more life came into the man's face at her words, but instead of arguing with her, he turned and walked down the trail. She followed him, curious as to what kind of compound the group had managed to erect in the wilderness.

The man turned into what looked like a dry wash, circled a dense line of trees and emerged in a clearing where a motley collection of travel trailers, RVs, pickup trucks, cars, tents, tarps and other makeshift shelters spread out over about an acre. To Kayla, it looked like a cross between the Girl Scout Jamboree she had attended as a child and the homeless encampments she had seen in Denver.

No one paid any attention to her arrival. A dozen or more men and women, and half as many children, wandered among the vehicles and shelters, tending campfires, carrying babies and talking. One man sat cross-legged in front of a van, playing a wooden flute, while two others kicked a soccer ball back and forth.

Kayla spotted Andi with a group of other women by a campfire. She looked just like the picture the senator had given her—straight blond hair to the middle of her back, heart-shaped face, upturned nose and brilliant blue eyes. She wore a long gauze skirt and a tank top, her slim arms tanned golden from the sun, and she was smiling. Not the picture of the troubled young woman the senator had painted. Rather, she looked like a model in an advertisement for a line of breezy summer fashions, or for a particularly refreshing wine.

Kayla started across the compound toward the young woman. Camo-man stepped forward as if to intercept her, but her hard stare stopped him. "Andi?" she called. "Andi Matheson?"

The young woman turned toward Kayla, her smile never faltering. "I'm sorry, but I don't go by that name anymore," she said. "I'm Asteria now."

Asteria? Kayla congratulated herself on not wincing. "My name's Kayla," she said.

"Do I know you?" Andi/Asteria wrinkled her perfect forehead a fraction of an inch.

"No. Your father asked me to check on you." Kayla stopped in front of the woman and scrutinized her more closely, already mentally composing her report to the senator. No bruises. Clear eyes and skin. No weight loss. If anything, she looked a little plumper than in the photos the senator had provided. In fact… her gaze settled on the rounded bump at the waistband of the skirt. "You're pregnant," she blurted.

Andi rubbed one hand across her belly. "My father didn't tell you? I'm not surprised, but he did know. It's one of the reasons I left. I didn't want to raise my child in his corrupt world."

Interesting that the senator had left out this little detail about his daughter. "He was concerned enough about you to hire me to find you and ask you to get in touch with him," Kayla said.

Andi's smile was gone now. "He just wants to try to talk me into getting rid of the baby." She turned to the two women with her. "My father can't understand the happiness and contentment I've found here with the Prophet and the Family. He's too mired in his materialistic, power-hungry world to see the truth."

Dressed similarly to Andi, the other two women stared at Kayla with open hostility. So much for peace and love, Kayla thought.

Andi turned back to Kayla. "How did you find me? I didn't tell anyone in my old life where I was going."

"I talked to your friend Tessa Madigan. She told me about attending a speech Daniel Metwater gave in Denver, and how taken you were with him and his followers. From there it wasn't that difficult to confirm you had joined the group."

"I only want to be left alone," Andi said. "I'm not harming anyone here."

Kayla looked around the compound, aware that pretty much everyone else there had stopped what they were doing to focus on the little exchange around the campfire. Even the flute player had lowered his instrument. Camo-man, however, had disappeared, perhaps slunk back to guard duty on the trail. "This isn't exactly a garden spot." She turned back to Andi. "What about the Family attracted you so much?" Senator Matheson was a wealthy man, and his only daughter had been a big part of his lavish lifestyle until a few months ago. Kayla had found dozens of pictures online of Andi and her father at celebrity parties and charity benefits, always dressed in designer gowns and dripping with jewels.

"The Family is a real family," Andi said. "We truly care for one another. The Prophet reminds us all to focus on the things in life that are really important and fulfilling and meaningful. Satisfaction isn't to be found in material wealth, but in living in harmony with nature and focusing on our spiritual well-being."

"You can't live on air and spiritual thoughts," Kayla said. "How do you all support yourselves?"

"We don't need a lot of money," Andi said. "The Prophet provides for us."

Camping on public land was free and they didn't have any utility bills, but they weren't living on wild game and desert plants, either—not judging by the smell of onions and celery emanating from a pot over the fire. "You're telling me your Prophet is footing the bill to feed and clothe all of you?"

"I am blessed to be able to share my worldly goods with my followers."

The voice that spoke was deep, smooth as chocolate and commanding as any Shakespearean actor. Kayla turned slowly and studied the man striding toward them. Sunlight haloed his figure like a spotlight, burnishing his muscular, bare chest and glinting on his loose, white linen trousers. He had brown curly hair glinting with gold, dark brows, lively eyes, a straight nose and sensuous lips. Kayla swore one of the women behind her sighed, and though she had been fully prepared to dislike this so-called "prophet" on sight, she wasn't immune to his masculine charms.

The man was flat-out gorgeous and potentially

lethally sexy. No wonder some women followed him around like puppies. “Daniel Metwater, I presume?” Kayla asked.

“I prefer the humble title of Prophet.”

Since when was a prophet humble? But Kayla decided not to argue the point. “I’m Kayla Larimer.” She offered her hand.

He took it, then bent and pressed his mouth to her palm—a warm, and decidedly unnerving, gesture. Some women might even think it was sexy, but Kayla thought the move too calculated and more than a little creepy. She jerked her hand away and her anger rose. “What’s the idea of stationing a guard to challenge visitors to your camp?” she asked. “After all, you are on public land. Land anyone is free to roam.”

“We’ve had trouble with curiosity seekers and a few people who want to harass us,” Metwater said. “We have a right to protect ourselves.”

“That defense won’t get you very far in court if anything goes south,” she said.

The smile finally faded. “Our policy is to leave other people alone and we ask that they show us the same courtesy.”

One of the few sensible pieces of advice that Kayla’s mother had ever given her was to keep her mouth shut, but Kayla found the temptation to poke at this particularly charming snake to be too much. “If you really are having trouble with people harassing you, you should ask for help from local law enforcement,” she said.

“We prefer to solve our own problems, without help from outsiders.”

The Mafia probably thought that way, too, but that didn't make them innocent bystanders who never caused a stink, did it?

"I'm not here to stir up trouble," she said. "Andi's father asked me to stop by and make sure she was all right."

"As you can see, Asteria is fine."

Kayla turned back to the young woman, who was gazing at Metwater, all limpid-eyed and adoring. "I assume you have a doctor in town?" she asked. "That you're getting good prenatal care."

"I'm being well cared for," she said, her eyes still locked to Metwater's.

"Asteria is an adult and has a right to live as she chooses," Metwater said. "No one who comes to us is held against his or her will."

Nothing Kayla saw contradicted that, but she just didn't understand the attraction. The place, and this man, gave her the creeps. "Your father would love to hear from you," she told Andi. "And if you need anything, call me." She held out one of her business cards. When the young woman didn't reach for it, Andi shoved it into her hand. "Goodbye," she said, and turned to walk away.

She passed Metwater without looking at him, though the goose bumps that stood out on her skin made her pretty sure he was giving her the evil eye—or a pacifist prophet's version of one. She had made it all the way to the edge of the encampment when raised voices froze her in her tracks. The hue and cry rose not from the camp behind her, but from the trail ahead.

Camo-man appeared around the corner, red-faced

and breathless. Behind him came two other men, dragging something heavy between them. Kayla took a few steps toward them and stared in horror at the object on a litter fashioned from a tarp and cut branches. Part of the face was gone, and she was pretty sure all the black stuff with the sticky sheen was blood—but she knew the body of a man when she saw one.

A dead man. And she didn't think he had been dead for very long.

Chapter Two

After ten years away, Lieutenant Dylan Holt had come home. When he had left his family ranch outside Montrose to pursue a career on Colorado's Front Range with the Colorado State Patrol, he had embraced life in the big city, sure he would never look back. Funny how a few years away could change a person's perspective. He hadn't realized how much he had missed the wide-open spaces and more deliberate pace of rural life until he had had the chance to transfer back to his hometown.

It didn't hurt that he was transferring to a multiagency task force focused on preventing and solving crimes on public lands promised to be the kind of interesting and varied work he had longed for. "For our newer team members, plan on spending a lot of time behind the wheel or even hiking into the backcountry," FBI Captain Graham Ellison, the leader of the Ranger Brigade, addressed the conference room full of officers. "Despite any impression you might have gotten from the media, the majority of our work is routine and boring. You're much more likely to bust a poacher or deal with illegal campers than to encounter a terrorist."

"Don't tell Congress that. They'll take away our increased funding." This quip came from an athletic younger guy with tattooed forearms, Randall Knightbridge. He was one of the Brigade veterans who had been part of a raid that brought down a terrorism organization that had been operating in the area. The case had been very high profile and had resulted in a grant from Homeland Security that allowed the group to expand—and to hire Dylan and two other new recruits, Walt Riley and Ethan Reynolds.

Next to Randall sat Lieutenant Michael Dance, with the Bureau of Land Management, and DEA Agent Marco Cruz. Behind them, Deputy Lance Carpenter from the Montrose Police Department, Simon Woolridge, a computer specialist with Immigration and Customs Enforcement, and Carmen Redhorse, with the Colorado Bureau of Investigation, listened attentively. The veterans had welcomed the rookies to the team with a minimum of good-natured ribbing.

"We do have a couple of areas of special concern," Captain Ellison continued. He picked up a pointer and indicated a spot on a map of the Rangers' territory—the more than thirty thousand acres of Black Canyon of the Gunnison National Park, plus more than 106,000 acres in adjacent Curecanti National Recreation Area and Gunnison Gorge National Conservation Area. "We've got a group camping in Dead Horse Canyon, some sort of back-to-the-land group. Not affiliated with any organized movement that we can identify. They have a legal permit and may be harmless, but let's keep an eye on them."

One of the other new hires, Ethan Reynolds, stuck up his hand. Ellison acknowledged him. "Agent Reynolds has some special training in cults, militia groups and terrorist cells," the captain said. "What can you tell us about this bunch?"

"They call themselves the Family and their leader is Daniel Metwater, son of a man who made a pile in manufacturing plastic bags. He calls himself the Prophet, though he doesn't identify with any organized religion. There are a lot of women and children out at that camp, so it wouldn't hurt to keep an eye open for signs of abuse or neglect. But so far, they've lived up to their reputation as peace-loving isolationists."

"Right." Ellison eyed the rest of them. "We don't have any reason to harass these people, but keep your eyes and ears open. On to other areas of concern…"

The captain continued with a discussion of off-road vehicles trespassing in a roadless area, reports of poaching activity in another area and suspicion of hazardous chemical dumping in a remote watershed.

"Randall, you and Walt check out the chemical dump," the captain ordered. "Carmen, take Ethan with you to look into the roadless violation. Dylan, you go with—"

The door burst open, letting in a gust of hot wind that stirred the papers on the table. "I want to report a body," a woman said.

She was dressed like a hiker, in jeans and boots, a day pack on her back. Her shoulder-length brown hair was in a windblown tangle about her head and her eyes were wide with horror, her face chalk-white. "A dead man," she continued, her voice quavering, but her expression determined. "I think he was shot.

Part of his face was gone and there was a lot of blood and—"

"Why don't you sit over here and tell us about it." Carmen Redhorse, the only female on the Ranger team, stepped forward and took the woman's hand. "Let's start with your name."

"Kayla Larimer." The woman accepted the glass of water Carmen pushed into her hands and drained half of it. When she lowered the glass, some of the terror had gone out of her eyes. Hazel eyes, Dylan noted. Gold and green, like some exotic cat's.

"All right, Kayla," Carmen said. "Where did you see this body?"

"I can show you. It's in a canyon on Bureau of Land Management, or BLM, land. The Family is camping there."

"Your family is camping there?"

"Not my family." She gave an impatient shake of her head. "That hippie group or whatever you want to call them."

"The peace-loving isolationists," Dylan said.

Kayla looked at him. She wasn't desperate or hysterical or any of the other emotions he might have expected. She looked—angry. At the injustice of the man's death? At being forced to witness the scene? He felt a definite *zing* of attraction. He had always liked puzzles and figuring things out. He wanted to figure out this not-so-typical woman.

"Are you a member of the Family?" Ethan asked.

"No!" The disdain in her tone dropped the temperature in the room a couple degrees. She slid a hand into the pocket of her jeans and pulled out a business card. "I'm a private detective."

"What were you doing in Dead Horse Canyon?" Graham Ellison asked.

She took another drink of water, then set the glass aside. "A client of mine has a daughter who cut off contact with him. He hired me to find her, and I located her living with the group. Then he asked me to check on her and make sure she was okay, and to ask her to get in touch with him."

"He had to hire a PI for that?" Dylan asked.

That hot, angry gaze again. "He hired me to find her, first. He didn't know where she was. After I located her, he thought she might listen to me if I approached her initially."

"Most parents wouldn't be too thrilled about their kid running off to join a group some people might see as a cult," Ethan said.

"Exactly." Kayla nodded. "Anyway, I found the young woman, gave her the message from her father and was leaving when three men rushed into the camp, shouting. Two of them were dragging a body behind them. The body of a man. He was covered in blood and..." Her lips trembled, but she pressed them together, her nostrils flaring as she inhaled. "Part of his head was gone."

"What were they shouting?" Graham asked.

"They said they were walking out in the desert and saw him lying there."

"Saw him lying where?" Carmen asked.

Kayla shook her head. "I don't know. And before you ask, I don't know why they thought they needed to bring him back to the camp. I told the leader—some guy who calls himself the Prophet—that his men shouldn't have touched the body, and that they needed to call the police, but he ignored me and ordered the men to take the dead man back to where they had found him, then report to him for a cleansing ritual."

"He refused to report the incident?" Graham's voice was calm, but his expression was one of outrage.

"He said they didn't have cell phones. Maybe they don't believe in them."

"Phones don't work in that area, anyway." Simon Woolridge, the team's tech expert, spoke for the first time. "They don't work on most of the public land around here. No towers."

"That's why I didn't call you, either," Kayla said. "By the time I got a signal on my phone, I was almost here."

"Did anyone say anything about who the dead man might be?" Graham asked. "Did you recognize him?"

"No. Everyone looked as horrified as I did."

"Did the men do as the Prophet asked and take the body away?" Dylan asked.

"I don't know. I left before they did anything. No one tried to stop me. I wanted to get away from there and I headed straight here."

"What time was this?" Graham asked.

"I don't know. But it's a long drive. So…maybe an hour ago?"

"More like an hour and a half," Carmen said. "Dead Horse Canyon is pretty remote."

"Lieutenant Holt, I want you and Simon to check this out," Captain Ellison said. "Ms. Larimer, you ride with Lieutenant Holt and show him exactly where you were."

"We know where Dead Horse Canyon is," Simon protested.

"The canyon is seven miles long," the captain said. "She can show you the location more quickly."

Silently, Kayla followed Dylan to his Cruiser. He opened the passenger door for her and she slid in without looking at him. He caught the scent of her floral shampoo as she moved past him, and he noticed the three tiny silver hoops she wore in each ear. By the time he made it around to the driver's side, she was buckled in and staring out the windshield.

"You holding up okay?" he asked.

"I'm fine." Her clipped tone didn't invite sympathy or further conversation, so he started the Cruiser and followed Simon out of the parking lot. They followed the paved road through the national park for the first five miles, past a series of pull-offs that provided overlooks into the Black Canyon, a half-mile-deep gorge that was the reason for the park's existence. Every stop was crowded with RVs, vans and passenger cars full of tourists who had come to enjoy the wild beauty of the high desert of western Colorado.

"How long have you been a private detective?" he asked.

She was silent so long he thought she had decided not to talk to him, but when he glanced her way she said, "Two years."

"Do you have a law enforcement background?" A lot of PIs he knew started out with police or sheriff's departments before hanging their shingle to do investigations, but Kayla hardly looked old enough to have had many years on the force under her belt.

"No."

"How did you get into the work?"

She let out a sigh and half turned to face him. “Why do you care?”

“I’m making conversation. Why are you so hostile?”

She ducked her head and massaged the bridge of her nose. “Sorry. I think I’ve just had an overdose of arrogant, good-looking men today.”

She thought he was good-looking? He filed the information away for future reference. “I’m not trying to be arrogant,” he said. “Cops are trained to get the facts of a situation as quickly as possible. That can come across as brusque sometimes.”

She nodded. “I get that. It’s just been a tough day. A tough week, really.” She glanced at him, her expression a little less guarded. “I thought I was applying for a secretarial position when I answered the ad for the job,” she said. “My boss got sick and trained me to take over the business. When he died from cancer last year, he left the business to me.”

“And you like it enough to keep at it.”

Another sigh. “Yeah, I like it. Most of the time. I mean, it beats a job in a cube farm. I like it when I can help people, even if it’s just finding a lost pet or helping a woman locate her deadbeat ex so that she can collect child support. But you see the ugly side of people a lot.”

“What you saw today wasn’t very pretty.”

“No.”

She fell silent again, and he was sure she was back at the camp, picturing that bloody body again. He wanted to pull her away from the image, to keep her focused on him. “Who are the handsome, arrogant men who rubbed you the wrong way?” he asked.

"Daniel Metwater, for one."

"The Prophet of this so-called Family?"

"Yeah. Have you met him?"

Dylan slowed for the turn onto a faintly marked dirt track that veered away from the canyon and the park. "No. What's he like?"

"He talks a good game of peace and love and spirituality, or at least, that's what he writes in his blog. But it all sounds like a con game to me, especially considering he preaches about the futility of cell phones and technology, yet he has a website he updates often when he's away from the camp. Maybe I'm too cynical, but I wanted to shake all those women who were making cow eyes at him and tell them he didn't really care about any of them. He's the kind of guy who looks out for himself and his image first."

"What makes you think that?"

He halfway expected her to slap him down again. Instead, she relaxed back into the seat. "My dad was a charming swindler like Metwater—good-looking, silver-tongued and scary intelligent. His game was as a traveling preacher. I spent most of my childhood moving from town to town while he conned people out of whatever they would give him." She ran a hand through her hair, pushing it back from her face. "I guess that experience has come in handy in my work. I can usually spot a grifter as soon as he opens his mouth. Daniel Metwater may be preaching peace, love and communing with nature, but I think he's hiding something."

"Do you think he killed the guy you saw?"

"I don't know. It depends on when the guy died, I think. Metwater was standing with me for a good while before his followers dragged the body into camp. He was wearing white linen trousers and there wasn't a speck of blood or dirt on him, so he didn't strike me as a man who had just come from a murder."

"So you think the man was murdered."

"I think he had been shot. Whether the wound was self-inflicted or not is up to you people to determine." She shuddered. "I'm going to spend my time trying to live down the sight of him. The only dead people I've seen before were peacefully in their coffins, carefully made up and dressed in their Sunday best."

"Violence leaves an ugly mark on everything."

"Yeah, well, I guess you could say reality does that, too."

She turned away, staring out the side window, as unreachable as if she had walked into another room and closed the door. Dylan focused on the landscape around him—the low growth of piñon and scrub oak, and formations of red and gray rock that rose up against an achingly blue sky. He had grown up surrounded by this scenery. The country here didn't look desolate and hostile to him, as it did to some, but free and unspoiled.

Simon's brake lights glowed and he stuck his arm out the open driver's-side window, gesturing toward a gravel wash to their left. He stopped and the passenger window slid down as Dylan pulled alongside him. "That's the south entrance to Dead Horse Canyon," Simon said. "Where do we go from here?"

"Turn in here," Kayla said. "There's a trailhead about a quarter mile farther on. I parked there, but apparently the campers have been driving right into the camp."

"I'll follow you," Simon said, and waited for Dylan to pull ahead of him.

As camping spots went, this one lacked water, much shade or access, Dylan thought, as the FJ Cruiser bumped over the washboard gravel road into the canyon. But it did offer concealment and a good defensive position. No one would be able to approach without the campers knowing about it.

As if to prove his point, a bearded man in camouflage pants and shirt stepped into the road and signaled for them to stop. Dylan braked and waited for the man to approach the driver's side of the Cruiser. "You can't drive back here," the man said, his eyes darting nervously to the Ranger Brigade emblem on the side of the Cruiser. The words *Law Enforcement* were clearly visible.

"We're here to talk to Daniel Metwater," Dylan said. "Officers Woolridge and Holt."

"I'm not supposed to let anyone drive into the camp," the man said. He was sweating now, jittery as an addict in need of a fix.

"What's your name?" Dylan asked.

"Kiram."

Dylan waited for more, but Kiram had pressed his lips tightly together. "Well, Kiram, we're here on official business and you don't have the authority to stop us. We don't want trouble, but you need to step out of the way."

Kiram ducked his head and peered into the car. "Hey, what are you doing back here?" he asked Kayla.

"I brought them to see your dead body," she said, giving Kiram a chilly stare.

Dylan let off the brake and the Cruiser eased forward. Kiram jumped back. The two vehicles proceeded at a crawl up the wash, around the knot of trees and into the side canyon the Family had chosen as their home in the wilderness.

Dylan shut off the engine, but remained in the car, assessing the situation. The motley cluster of campers, tents and vehicles shimmered like a mirage in the midday heat. A child's ball rolled a few feet, stirred by the wind, which made the only sound in the area.

"The place looks deserted," Kayla said. "Do you think they left?"

"Not without all their stuff. Do you notice anything missing?"

She studied the scene for a moment, then shook her head. "Only the people."

"Stay in the vehicle." With one hand hovering near his weapon, Dylan eased open his door, ready to dive for cover if anyone fired on them. But the camp remained silent and still.

"Daniel Metwater!" he called. "We need to ask you a few questions."

No answer came but the echo of his own words. Simon joined Dylan beside his car. "What do you think?" Dylan asked.

"They could have all headed for the hills, or they could be lying low inside these tents and trailers," Simon said.

"Come out by the time I count to ten or we'll start taking this place apart," Dylan shouted. "One!"

At the count of five, the door to the largest RV, a thirty-foot bus with solar panels on the roof, eased open. A slim but muscular man, naked except for a pair of white loose trousers, moved onto the steps. "I wasn't aware we had company," he said. "We adhere to the custom of an afternoon siesta."

"Are you Daniel Metwater?" Dylan asked.

Sharp eyes scrutinized the three of them. "Yes," he said at last.

"Call your people out here," Simon said. "We have some questions about an incident that happened here this afternoon."

Metwater shifted his gaze past the two cops. Dylan turned to see Kayla standing beside the car. "You had no cause to bring these people here," Metwater said to her.

"We're here because we understand you found a dead body this morning," Dylan said. "Why didn't you report it to the police?"

"We don't have cell phones, and since nothing we could do or say could bring the man back to life, I made the decision to report the incident the next time I was in town." Metwater spoke as if he was talking about a minor mechanical problem, not a dead man.

"Where is the body?" Simon asked.

"I ordered the men who brought him here to take him back where they found him," Metwater said. "They never should have defiled our home with such violence."

"We'll need to talk to these men."

"They are undergoing a purification ritual at the moment."

"Bring them out here." Simon wasn't a big man, but he could put a lot of menace and command in his voice. "Now."

Metwater said something over his shoulder to someone inside the RV. A woman with long dark hair slipped past him and hurried away. "She'll bring the men to you," Metwater said, and turned as if to go back inside.

"Wait," Dylan said. "Who was the man?"

"I don't know. I'd never seen him before in my life. But I believe he's one of yours."

"What do you mean, one of ours?" Dylan asked.

Metwater's lips quirked up in a smirk. "I checked his pockets for identification. He's a cop."

Chapter Three

Kayla watched Dylan as Metwater dropped his bombshell. His was a face full of strong lines and planes, not classically handsome, but honest—the face of a man who didn't have any patience with lies or weakness. Anger quickly replaced the brief flash of confusion in his eyes as he absorbed this new wrinkle in the case. The dead man wasn't a stranger anymore—he was a fellow lawman. "Take me to him," he ordered.

"The men who found him will—" Metwater began.

"No. *You* take me." Dylan's fists clenched at his sides, and Kayla tensed, expecting him to punch the smirk off the Prophet's face. But he remained still, only one muscle in his jaw twitching.

Instead of answering, Metwater looked away, toward a flurry of movement to their right. Kiram and another burly man escorted two other men to them. "These are the two who found the body," Metwater said. "They can answer your questions."

Dylan pulled a small notebook and pen from his shirt pocket and shifted his focus to the new arrivals. Kayla thought they looked young, scarcely out of their teens, with wispy beards and thin bodies. Dylan pointed to the taller of the two, who stared back from behind black-framed glasses. “What’s your name?”

“Abelard,” the young man whispered.

“Your real name,” Dylan said.

Abelard blinked. “That is my real name. Abelard Phillips.”

“His mom was a literature professor,” the other young man said. “You know, Abelard and Heloise—supposed to be a classic love story or something.”

Abelard nodded. “Most people call me Abe.”

Dylan wrote down the name, then turned to the second man. “Who are you?”

He swallowed, his Adam’s apple bobbing. “Zach. Zach Crenshaw.”

“I want the two of you to show me this body you found this morning.”

Their heads moved in unison, like bobblehead dolls. Metwater started to turn back to his trailer, but Simon took his arm. “You’re coming, too.”

Kayla trailed along after them, sure that if Dylan remembered she was here he would order her to wait at the camp. But curiosity won out over her squeamishness about seeing the body again—that, and a reluctance to spend any time alone with the rest of the “family.”

Single file, the six of them followed a narrow path out of camp, out of the canyon and into the open scrubland beyond, following drag marks in the dirt Kayla was sure had been made by the makeshift travois Abe and Zach had used to transport the body. She estimated they had walked about a mile when Abe halted and gestured toward a grouping of large boulders. "He's behind those rocks over there," he said. "We put him back just like the Prophet told us to."

"And you're sure that's where you found him?" Simon asked.

Zach nodded. "You can tell because of all the blood."

"Show me," Dylan said.

The two young men led the way around the boulders. Kayla hung back, but she still had a view of the dead man's feet, wearing new-looking hiking boots, the soles barely scuffed. Had he bought them especially for his visit to the Black Canyon area?

Dylan and Simon stood back, surveying the scene, the wind stirring the branches of the piñons nearby the only sound. The sour-sweet stench of death stung her nostrils, but she forced herself to remain still, to wait for whatever came next. "Was he lying like this when you found him?" Dylan asked. "On his back?"

"Yeah," Zach said.

"Why did you move him?" Simon asked. "Were you trying to hide something? Did you realize you were tampering with evidence?"

"We weren't trying to hide anything!" Abe protested. "We just came around the rocks and almost stepped on him. There was blood everywhere and it was awful. Like something out of a movie or something. Too horrible to be real."

"Once we realized it was a man, we couldn't just leave him there," Zach said. "There were already buzzards circling. And I thought I heard him groan, like maybe he was still alive. We thought if we got him back to camp, someone could go for help, or take him to the hospital or something."

"We couldn't just leave him," Abe echoed.

"All right." Dylan put a hand on Abe's arm. "Tell me exactly what happened. Start at the beginning. What were you doing out here?"

"We were hunting rabbits," Abe said. "We thought we saw one run over here so we headed this way to check it out."

"What were you hunting with?" Simon asked. "Where is your weapon now?"

The two young men exchanged glances, then Zach walked over to the grouping of piñons. He reached into the tangle of branches and pulled out a couple crude bows and a handful of homemade arrows. "The Prophet only allows us to buy meat for one meal a week, so we thought if we could catch some rabbits the women could make them into stew or something," he said.

"And maybe they'd be impressed that we were providing for the Family," Abe added. He looked even more forlorn. "We weren't having any luck, though."

"Why were you hunting with bows and arrows?" Simon asked. "Why not guns?"

"The Prophet doesn't allow firearms," Zach said.

"We're a nonviolent people." Metwater spoke for the first time since they had left camp. "Guns only cause trouble."

"They certainly caused trouble for this man." Dylan looked at Metwater. "You said you checked his identification?"

"The wallet is inside his jacket," Metwater said. "Front left side."

Dylan knelt, out of Kayla's view. When he stood again, he held a slim brown wallet. He read from the

ID. "Special Agent Frank Asher, FBI." He fixed Metwater with an icy glare. "What was the FBI doing snooping around your camp, Mr. Metwater? And what did he do that got him killed?"

As expected, the Family's Prophet claimed to have no knowledge of Agent Frank Asher or what had happened to him. None of the three men had heard any gunshots or vehicles or seen anything unusual in the hour leading up to the discovery of the body. They were like the three bronze monkeys Dylan's dad had on a shelf in his home office—see no evil, hear no evil, speak no evil. Dylan and Simon would bring them all in for questioning, but he doubted the interviews would yield anything useful.

With no cell phone coverage in the area, Dylan was forced to leave Simon with the body and the Family members while he drove to an area with coverage.

"I'm coming with you," Kayla said, falling into step beside him as he strode back toward the camp.

He'd been so intent on his job that for a while he had forgotten about her. She was one more complication he didn't need right now. "Why didn't you stay in the car like I told you?" he asked.

"This place gives me the creeps. I'm not staying anywhere alone around these people." She rubbed her hands up and down her arms. "Do you think one of them killed that FBI agent?"

"I don't know what to think. I need the medical examiner's report on when he died, and what kind of weapon killed him." He glanced toward the motley collection of RVs and tents. "I'm not buying that all of these people are unarmed."

"The agent will have a vehicle around here someplace close," Kayla said. "Those boots he was wearing weren't worn enough for him to have walked very far, and I didn't see a pack anywhere near him."

Dylan stopped and considered her more closely. She had regained her color and no longer looked fragile and shaken. "I'll get someone to look for the car right away. Maybe something in there will tell us why he was out here. That was a good observation," he added. "Did you see anything else?"

"I think the two kids are telling the truth." She glanced back in the direction they had come. "When they said that about not wanting to leave him for the buzzards—I believed them."

"Maybe." He had learned not to trust anyone when it came to crime, but his instincts made him want to focus on Metwater more than the two kids. "Them moving the body makes our investigation tougher. They may have destroyed a lot of evidence."

"For a man who sees himself as a leader, Metwater is a cold fish," she said. "He seemed more annoyed by the inconvenience than anything else."

"He's going to be a lot more inconvenienced before this is over. I'm going to get a warrant to take this camp apart. If the murder weapon is here, we'll find it."

"If it was ever here, they had plenty of time to get rid of it before we got here," she said. "It could be stashed in a cave or buried in an old mine or broken into a million pieces on the rocks."

"Maybe," he conceded. "But we might find something else incriminating."

They walked through the camp, which was as

empty and silent as a ghost town, but he sensed people watching him from the windows of trailers and open flaps of tents. "Who did you come here to see?" he asked Kayla. "I know you said a client's daughter, but who?"

"I don't see how that relates to your case." The frost was back in her voice.

"You're the one who reported the body. You were the only non-Family member present when it was discovered. Some people might think that was an interesting coincidence."

She turned on him, cheeks flushed. "You don't think I killed that man!"

"My job is to rule out everyone. Do you own a gun?"

"I have a Smith & Wesson 40 back at my office. I have a permit for it."

"But you didn't have it with you today? Why not?"

"I don't like to carry a gun. I didn't think this was a particularly dangerous situation."

"Who did you come to see?" he asked again. "I can subpoena your files to find out. Save us both some hassle and just tell me."

She hesitated, a deep crease between her brows as she weighed her options. "I came to see Andi Matheson. She calls herself Asteria now. But she doesn't have anything to do with your case."

"You said her father hired you. Who is he?"

She glared at him.

"I'll bet I can find the answer in five minutes or less online."

She continued to glare at him, and the intensity of her gaze sent a thrill of awareness through him. Oh, he liked her, all right. Maybe a little too much, considering her involvement in this case.

"Her father is Senator Peter Matheson," she said. "I imagine you've heard of him."

Dylan had heard of the senator, all right. Until recently, he had been in the news primarily for his campaign to disband the Ranger Brigade. He had claimed the task force of federal agents was intrusive, expensive and ineffective. He had succeeded in having the group defunded, only to wind up looking like a fool when the Rangers had brought down a major terrorist group that had been operating in the area. Congress had responded by expanding the group, and Matheson had mostly kept a low profile ever since.

And now the senator was mixed up with Metwater and his bunch of wanderers. Dylan scanned the silent camp. "How did you track her down here? You said her father didn't know where she was."

"I talked to her friends. Her best friend told me she and Andi had attended a presentation given by Daniel Metwater and Andi had been very attracted to him, and to the ideas he preached. I did some more digging and verified that she had indeed joined up with Metwater and his group."

Dylan nodded. Textbook solid detective work. "Let's have a word with Ms. Matheson. Maybe she knows something she's not telling about all this."

"I really don't think—" Kayla began.

But Dylan had already moved to the nearest camper, a battered aqua-and-silver trailer wedged beneath a clump of stunted evergreens. He pounded on the door, shaking the whole structure. "Police! Open up!" he called.

A woman with a deeply tanned face and bleached hair eased open the door and peered out at them. “I’m looking for Andi Matheson,” Dylan said.

The woman shook her head. “I don’t know anyone by that name,” she said, and started to close the door.

“What about Asteria?” Kayla asked. “Where does she live?”

“Over there.” The woman pointed to a large white tent next to the Prophet’s trailer.

The tent was the kind used by hunting outfitters as a mess tent or gathering area, with a tall frame and roll-up canvas sides. One of the sides was open to let in the hot breeze. Dylan moved around to the opening and peered in. A blonde woman sat cross-legged on a rug on the floor, eyes closed, hands outstretched.

“Ms. Matheson?” Dylan asked. “Asteria?”

She opened her eyes, which were a deep blue. “I was meditating,” she said.

“Sorry to interrupt, but I have to ask you a few questions.” He took a step toward her. “I’m Lieutenant Dylan Holt, with the Ranger Brigade task force. I wanted to ask you about the body that was brought to your camp earlier today.”

Andi looked away. “I didn’t see anything. I didn’t want to look. It was horrible.”

Kayla moved up beside Dylan, her voice gentle. “We don’t want to upset you, Andi,” she said. “We just have a few questions and then we’ll leave you alone.”

“All right.” She motioned toward the rug across from her. “You might as well sit down.”

The room was furnished with a cot and several folding camp chairs, but Dylan lowered himself to the rug. The coolness of the earth seeped up through the rug's pile. Kayla sat beside him. "Tell me what you saw this morning," he said.

Andi shrugged. "I didn't see much. There was shouting, and Abe and Zach came in, dragging something on a tarp. I thought they had killed an animal at first—there was so much blood. Then I saw it was a man and I looked away. I ran back here and hid." She rubbed her hand across her stomach. "I didn't want to see any more."

"Do you know a man named Frank Asher?" he asked. "He works for the FBI."

"Frank?" She stared at him, eyes wide. "What about Frank?"

"Did you know him?" Dylan asked.

"No!" She shook her head, hands clutching her skirt. "No," she repeated in a whisper, even as tears ran down her face.

"I think you did know him," Dylan said. "Frank Asher is the man who was killed—the body Zach and Abe found this morning."

Andi covered her mouth with her hand. "I told him not to come here," she said, the words muffled. "I told him not to come and now look what happened." She collapsed onto the rug and began to sob, the mournful wailing filling the tent and making Dylan's chest hurt.

Chapter Four

Kayla knelt beside Andi, alarmed by the speed at which the beautiful, defiant young woman had dissolved into this wailing heap of grief. "I'm so sorry," she said, rubbing Andi's back. "Please sit up and try to calm down." She looked back over her shoulder at Dylan, who looked as if he wanted to be anyplace but here at this moment. "Would you get her some water?" She pointed toward a large jug that sat on a stand at the back of the tent.

He retrieved the water and brought it to her. "What was your relationship to Frank Asher?" he asked. "When was the last time you were in contact with him?"

The questions brought a fresh wave of sobs. Kayla glared at him. Did he have to act like such a cop right now, firing official-sounding questions at this obviously distraught woman? "You're not helping," she said.

Frowning, he backed away.

"Drink this." Kayla put the cup of water into Andi's hands. "Take a deep breath. You've had a shock."

"What's going on in here? What are you doing to her?"

The outraged questions came from one of the women Kayla had seen with Andi earlier—a slight figure with a mane of brown curly hair and a slightly crooked nose. She rushed over and inserted herself between Andi and Kayla. "Asteria, honey, what have they done to you?"

"What's your name?" Dylan joined them again.

The brown-haired woman glared at him. "Who are you, and why are you upsetting my friend?"

"Lieutenant Holt." Dylan showed his badge. "I'm investigating the death of the man whose body was brought into the camp earlier today. What's your name?"

"Starfall."

Kayla thought Dylan was about to demand she tell him her real name, but he apparently thought better of it. "Were you here when Abe and Zach brought him in?" he asked.

Starfall wrinkled her nose. "They should have known better than to pull a stunt like that. It was awful."

"What do you mean, 'a stunt like that'?" Dylan asked.

"The man was dead. I mean, half his head was gone. We couldn't do anything for him. They should have left him where they found him and not involved us in whatever happened to him."

Andi began keening again, rocking back and forth. Starfall wrapped her arms around her friend. "You need to go," she said. "You've upset her enough."

"Do you know a man named Frank Asher?" Dylan asked.

"No. Now go. You have no right to harass us this way."

Kayla touched Dylan's arm. "Give her a chance to calm down a little," she said softly. "You can question her later."

He nodded and led the way out of the tent.

The camp was just as deserted as it had been before. "Looks like nobody wants to take a chance on running into a cop," Dylan observed.

"Or maybe they really are taking a siesta." She pulled the front of her shirt away from her chest, hoping for a cool breeze. "It's baking out here."

He glanced back at her. "You should wear a hat." He touched the brim of the fawn-colored Stetson that was part of his uniform.

They left the camp, back on the trail to the parking area. "What are you going to do next?" Kayla asked.

"There's so much that feels wrong here it's hard to know where to start." He gave her a hard look. "What's Andi Matheson's relationship to Frank Asher?"

"How should I know?"

"Her father hired you to find her. You must have looked into her background, talked to her friends and people who knew her."

"I did, but none of them ever mentioned a Frank Asher." No one had mentioned any men in Andi's life, outside of her father and a few very casual acquaintances. None of the photos and articles Kayla had viewed online linked Andi with a man. At the time, Kayla had thought it was a little unusual that a woman as attractive and seemingly outgoing as Andi didn't have a boyfriend, or at least an ex-boyfriend.

"Maybe he wasn't a friend of hers then," Dylan said. "Maybe her father knew him. It's not unreasonable to think a senator would know an FBI agent. Maybe you weren't the only person the senator had tailing his daughter. Maybe he sent the Fed after her, too."

"Or maybe Asher is the father of Andi's baby."

Dylan stopped so abruptly she almost plowed into him. "She has a baby?"

"She's pregnant. Didn't you notice?" Kayla gestured toward her own stomach.

He flushed. "I thought maybe she was just a little too fond of cheeseburgers or beer or something." He patted his own flat belly.

She stared at him. "I can't believe you said that."

"What did you expect? I'm a cop and a rancher—two professions known for plain speaking." He started walking again, long strides covering ground quickly so that she had to trot to catch up with him.

"You're a rancher?" she asked.

"My family has a ranch near here. In Ouray County." He pulled out his keys and hit the button to unlock the FJ Cruiser.

That explained a lot—from the way he seemed so at home in this rugged landscape, to the swagger in his walk that was more cowboy than cop.

He climbed in and started the engine even before she had her door closed. "If Asher is the father of Andi's baby, it would explain why she was so torn up over the news of his death," he said as he put the vehicle in gear and guided it onto the washboard road. "But why would she have told him to stay away from the camp?"

"I thought she joined the Family to get away from her father and his lifestyle," Kayla said. "But maybe she was trying to get away from Asher. Maybe he was the one who wanted her to get rid of the baby. Or maybe he was abusive."

"Would she carry on like that over a man who had abused her?"

"I don't know. Love can make people do crazy things, I guess." After all, her own mother had followed Kayla's father across the United States and back, sticking with him even when he cheated on her and lied to her.

"Are you speaking from personal experience?"

The question jolted her. "Why would you even ask something like that?"

"I'm just curious." He kept his gaze focused on the road, but she sensed most of his attention was fixed on her. "Something in the way you said that made me think you don't have too high an opinion of love."

She hugged her arms across her chest. This was *not* a conversation she wanted to be having. "I'm no expert on the subject. Are you?"

"Far from it. I've managed to avoid falling in love—serious love—so far."

"You make it sound like an accomplishment."

"I don't know. Some people might consider it a failing. My job doesn't really leave a lot of room for close relationships."

"Yet you have time to help run your family's ranch."

"Family is important to me. Which is why I don't get why Andi Matheson wanted to leave hers to live out in the wilderness with a bunch of people she hardly knows."

"Not everyone has a family they care to be close to—and yes, I say that from personal experience."

"Right—your con-artist dad. What about your mom? Brothers and sisters?"

"My mom is dead. I didn't have any siblings."

"I'm sorry to hear that."

"I don't want your pity."

He glanced at her, surprising warmth in his brown eyes. "Sympathy and pity aren't the same things."

She turned away, conversation over. She didn't like not being in control of a conversation. One of the advantages of being a private investigator was that she usually got to ask all the questions. Situations like this one always made her feel like a freak. She didn't do relationships. Not close ones. She couldn't relate to people like Dylan, with his warm family feelings and determination to figure her out.

He apparently got the message and stopped talking. She focused on breathing deeply and getting her emotions under control. They passed through a brown sea of sagebrush and rock, beneath an achingly blue sky, unbroken by a single cloud. She would never get used to how vast the emptiness was out here. The wilderness made her feel small, lost even when she knew where she was.

He stopped the Cruiser and shifted into Park. "Why are you stopping?" she asked.

"I've got a phone signal." He dragged his finger across the screen on his phone. "I'm going to call in to headquarters."

He gave whoever answered the particulars of the

situation at the camp and asked them to send crime scene techs and a medical examiner, along with more Rangers to interview people at the camp. "Simon is waiting," Dylan said. "I'm going to see if I can locate Asher's vehicle."

He ended the call and pocketed the phone, then put the Cruiser in gear once more. Neither of them said anything for several minutes as they bumped over increasingly rugged terrain. Finally, Dylan spoke. "I apologize if my questions were out of line," he said. "It's another cop thing. I want to know everything about people I'm with. I didn't mean to upset you."

His words touched her, and made her feel a little vulnerable. In her experience, people rarely apologized. "I didn't mean to snap," she said. "I'm just—on edge. Seeing that body, and then Andi falling apart like that—I guess it hit me harder than I realized."

"You're a very empathetic person," he said. "You feel other people's pain. You absorb their emotions. It probably makes you a good investigator, but it's tough."

"I guess so." She didn't really think of herself that way. If anything, she would have said she was too cynical most of the time.

He braked and pointed ahead of them. "What's that, up there?"

She caught the glint of sunlight off metal. "Maybe it's a car."

Dylan shut off the engine. "We'll walk from here."

He led the way toward the white sedan, which was partially hidden behind a clump of scrub oak. A small sticker on the bumper identified it as a rental car. When they were approximately ten feet away, Dylan held out his arm. "Stay here while I check it out," he ordered.

She waited while he approached the car. He peered in the front driver's-side window, which had been left open a few inches. Then he pulled a pair of latex gloves from his pocket and put them on. He opened the driver's-side door, which wasn't locked, and peered into the car. Then he withdrew his head and looked back toward Kayla. "You can come up here if you promise not to touch anything."

She joined him beside the car. He had leaned in and was looking through a handful of papers on the front passenger seat. "There's a couple of maps here and a Montrose visitor's guide," he said.

"The parking pass on the dash is from a motel in Montrose," she said. "That's probably where he was staying."

Dylan examined the pass, then pulled out his notebook and began making notes. "I don't see anything out of the ordinary, do you?" he asked.

The only other thing in the car was a half-empty water bottle in the cup holder between the seats. "It doesn't look like he planned to be out here long," she said. "There are no snacks or lunch, no pack or change of clothes."

"So he either figured on a quick trip or he headed out here on impulse, not taking the time to prepare." Dylan opened the glove box, which was empty except for registration papers and the vehicle service manual. He flipped down both visors. The passenger side revealed nothing, but next to the mirror on the driver's side was a photograph.

Or rather, half a photograph. A tear was evident on

the left side of the picture, a color snapshot of a man in jeans and a button-down shirt. Daniel Metwater's smiling face stared out at them.

"Maybe Andi wasn't the person Agent Asher came here to see," Dylan said.

Chapter Five

Dylan retrieved an evidence envelope from his Cruiser and sealed the photograph of Metwater in it. He took a few pictures of the vehicle and wrote down the plate number and the GPS location. "Let's go," he told Kayla as he pocketed his notebook. "I'll take you back to your car. You'll need to give us a statement about what happened at the camp this morning, then you can go. I'll probably have more questions for you later." He wanted to dig deeper into what she knew about Andi Matheson and the Family. And he wanted to see her again. Her mix of cold distance and warm empathy intrigued him.

"Do you do this kind of thing often?" he asked.

"What kind of thing?"

"Finding missing persons. Tracking down wayward children."

"Andi wasn't a lot of trouble to find. She just didn't want to talk to her father. Senator Matheson thought I might be able to get through to her."

"Seems an uncomfortable position to be in—caught in the middle of a family quarrel."

He wondered if she looked at everyone so intently, as if trying to decipher the hidden meaning behind every word he said. He wanted to protest that he didn't have an ulterior motive in talking with her, but that wasn't exactly true. He was trying to figure out what made her tick. Maybe she was doing the same to him.

"A lot of my work involves dealing with people in one kind of pain or another," she said. "Whether it's a divorce or estranged families, or investigating some kind of fraud. Isn't it the same for cops?"

"Yeah." Too much pain sometimes. "You learn pretty quickly to distance yourself."

"My father made his living by preying on people's emotions. He was an expert at making people afraid of something and then offering himself as the way out of their trouble—for a price. I think seeing him in action made me wary of letting others get too close." Her eyes met his, dark and searching.

"Is that a warning?" he asked.

"Take it however you like."

Neither of them said anything on the rest of the drive back to Ranger headquarters. Carmen met them at the door to the offices. "A crime scene team is on its way out to meet Simon," she said.

"I found the victim's car, parked not too far away." Dylan read off the plate number and location.

"I'll call it in," Carmen said. "Some of the team might still be in cell phone range."

"I'll call them," he said. "I'd like you to take Kayla's statement."

"All right." Carmen sent him a questioning look. He knew she wondered why he didn't take Kayla's statement himself. He wasn't ready to admit that the dynamic between him and the pretty private detective was too charged. He couldn't be as objective about her as he liked and that bothered him. He wasn't one to let a woman get under his skin. "I'll be in touch later," he told Kayla, and turned away.

KAYLA WATCHED DYLAN leave the room, annoyed that his dismissal of her bothered her so much. So much for the detachment she'd bragged about. This cowboy cop, with his probing questions and dogged pursuit of information, drew her in.

"There's an empty office back here we can use." Officer Redhorse led the way to a room crowded with two desks and a filing cabinet. She sat behind one desk and indicated that Kayla should sit across from her. "Have you been a private investigator long?" Carmen asked.

"A couple of years."

Carmen opened up a file on the computer, then set a recorder between them. "Why don't you tell me everything that happened, from the time you arrived at the Family's camp this morning," she said. "I'll ask questions if I need you to clarify anything for me."

Kayla nodded, and took a moment to organize her thoughts. Then she told her story, about approaching the camp, and the two men bringing in the body. Carmen asked a couple questions, then typed for a few minutes more. "I'll print this out and you can read it over and sign it," she said, and swiveled away from the computer. "What happened when you and Dylan went back out there?" she asked.

"Are you going to compare my story to his?" Kayla asked.

"I'm curious to get your take on things," she replied. "Women sometimes notice things men don't—emotions and details men don't always pick up on."

"I don't think Lieutenant Holt misses much," Kayla said.

"He's new here, so I don't know him well," Carmen said. "Though he must be good at his job or he wouldn't have been assigned to the task force."

"He told me his family has a ranch in the area."

"The Holt Cattle Company. It's a big spread south of town. Knowing the country and the people here could be an advantage in this kind of work. Are you from the area?"

Kayla nodded. "But not knowing everyone can be an advantage, too. You don't come into a job with any preconceived notions."

"So what's your impression of the lieutenant?"

Kayla stiffened. "Why are you asking me?"

"I thought I sensed a few sparks between the two of you—though maybe not the good kind. Did you two have some kind of disagreement?"

"No disagreement." The two of them had worked well together, even though he sometimes made her feel prickly and on edge—too aware of him as a man who read her a little too well for comfort.

Carmen stood. "I'll get your statement off the printer and you can read through it."

When she was alone in the room, Kayla sagged back against the chair. Only a little longer and she would be free to leave. She wanted to do some investigating of her own, to try to make sense of what had happened this afternoon.

"I WANT A warrant to search Asher's hotel room," Dylan told Captain Ellison. The two stood outside Graham's office, Dylan having filled him in on his findings at the camp. "That might give us a clue what he was doing out there."

Graham nodded. "What about this PI? Kayla Larimer? Does she have any connection to Asher?"

"I don't think so. I'll talk to Senator Matheson to verify her story, but I think she was doing what she said—delivering a message to the senator's daughter."

"Did you learn anything else from her while you were at the camp?" Graham asked.

He had learned a lot—mainly that Kayla Larimer wasn't the type of woman to get close to anyone very easily. "She's good at her job, I think," he said. "Observant. She pointed out right away that Asher had to have a car nearby, after noting that his boots were new, the soles barely scuffed. And she was good with the women at the camp. She thinks Andi Matheson was so distraught over Asher's death because they had a close relationship. He may even be the father of her baby."

"What do you think?" Graham asked.

"Maybe. But Andi might have been distraught because of what she'd seen when the body was dragged into camp. It was enough to upset anyone. And the picture I found in Asher's car was of Metwater, not Andi. Asher may have had something on the Prophet that got him into trouble."

"I've got a call in to the Bureau, asking if Asher was here working on a case," Graham said. "Meanwhile, maybe his hotel room will turn up something."

"Are you going to Agent Asher's hotel?" Kayla asked.

Dylan turned to find the private detective, followed by Carmen, emerging from an office at the back of the building. "I want to go with you to the hotel," Kayla said, joining him and the captain.

"This is a police matter," he said. "You don't have any business being there. You know that."

She opened her mouth as if to argue, but apparently changed her mind. "Fine. Obviously, you don't have a need for me any longer, so I'll say goodbye." She nodded to Carmen and the captain, but didn't look at Dylan.

The snub irritated him. "I might have more questions for you later," he said.

"Maybe I'll have answers." She left, closing the door a little more forcefully than necessary behind her.

"I don't think she likes you too much," Graham observed.

"Oh, I don't know about that," Carmen said.

"What's that supposed to mean?" Dylan snapped.

"If she really didn't care what you thought, she wouldn't react so strongly." Carmen shrugged.

Dylan turned to Graham, and was surprised to find the captain grinning at him. "What are you smiling about?"

"My wife acted as if she hated my guts the first time we met," he said. "Carmen may be on to something."

Dylan turned away. "I'm going to file for that warrant." And he would do his best to forget all about

Kayla Larimer. The last thing he needed was a woman who wanted to play mind games.

KAYLA SCARCELY NOTICED her surroundings as she drove toward town after leaving Ranger headquarters. She had to find a way to see what was in Frank Asher's hotel room. Lieutenant Holt might believe she had no right to get involved in this case, but he had made her a part of it when he took her back to the camp. She couldn't drop the matter now, with so many unanswered questions. And it wasn't such a stretch to see the FBI agent's death as linked to the assignment she had taken on for Senator Matheson. Agent Asher's murder had definitely upset Andi, and Kayla needed to know why.

Even if she had never met Dylan Holt and overheard him discussing searching Asher's hotel room, visiting the hotel would have been the next logical step in her own investigation. She didn't have the authority of a law enforcement agency behind her, but part of being a good private investigator was using other means to gain information. She might be able to charm a hotel clerk into letting her see the room, or to persuade a maid to open the door for her.

She wouldn't interfere with the Rangers' work. But she'd find a way to make Dylan share his information with her. She could even prove useful to him—another set of eyes and ears with a different perspective on the case.

She flipped on her blinker to turn onto the highway and headed toward the Mesa Inn—the name on the parking pass in Asher's car. She found a parking place in a side lot that provided a good view of the hotel's front entrance and settled in to wait.

She didn't have to wait long. Less than half an hour passed before two Ranger Cruisers parked under the hotel's front portico. Dylan and Carmen climbed out of the first one, while two officers she didn't recognize exited the second vehicle. As soon as the four were inside, Kayla left her car and headed toward the hotel's side entrance.

As she had hoped, it opened into a hallway that wound around past the hotel's restaurant and gift shop, to the front lobby. A large rack of brochures shielded Kayla from the Rangers' view, but allowed her to spy on them as they spoke first to the front desk clerk, then to a woman in a suit who was probably the manager. She wasn't close enough to hear their conversation, but after a few minutes the manager handed over a key card and the four officers headed for the elevator.

Kayla put aside the brochure for a Jeep rental company she had been pretending to study and walked quickly to the elevator. She hit the call button. The car the agents had entered stopped on the fifth floor before descending again. Smiling to herself, Kayla found the entrance for the stairs and began to climb.

On the fifth floor, she eased open the door to the hallway a scant inch and listened. The rumble of men's voices reached her. She was sure one of them was Dylan's. Risking a glance, she opened the door wider, in time to see the four officers enter a room in the middle of the hall. Kayla stepped into the hall and checked the number on the room—535.

Now what? She couldn't just barge in—that was a

good way to get arrested. And she didn't want to interfere, but she wanted information.

A loud squeak made her flinch. She turned to see a maid pushing a cleaning cart down the hall. Kayla moved toward her. "Excuse me," she said. "I wonder if you could answer a few questions about the man who was renting room 535." She opened her wallet and the maid, who looked like a student from the nearby university, stared at the badge. It clearly identified Kayla as a private investigator, not a cop, but most people didn't bother to read the fine print.

"Why do you want to know about him?" the woman—her name tag identified her as Mindy—asked.

"He's part of a case I'm working on."

Mindy bit her lower lip. "I don't know if I'm allowed to talk to anyone about the guests."

"Any information you provide could be very helpful," Kayla said.

Mindy pulled a cell phone from the pocket of her uniform top. "I'd better check with my manager."

Kayla held her breath while Mindy put through the call. If the worst happened, she could make a break for the stairs, or bluff her way out of this. But when Mindy explained there was a woman cop who wanted to question her, the manager apparently told her to cooperate. Good thing Carmen was along on this job. The manager probably assumed Kayla was her. "What do you want to know?" Mindy asked, as she slipped the phone back into her pocket.

"Did you see the man who rented that room? Did you speak to him?"

"I saw him," Mindy said. "But we didn't talk or

anything. I saw him when he left the room yesterday morning."

"How did he act when you saw him? What kind of a mood was he in?"

Mindy shrugged. "I only saw him for a few seconds. He just looked, you know, ordinary."

"Did you clean his room? Did you notice anything unusual about it?"

"No. I mean, it's not like I spend that much time in the rooms. I clean them and get out."

"So nothing about this guy stood out for you?"

Mindy rearranged the bottles of cleaning solution in the tray at the top of her cart. "Not really." She avoided looking at Kayla.

"What is it, Mindy? Anything you remember—even a little detail—might be helpful."

"It's nothing, really."

"Even if you don't think it's important, it could be."

"Promise you won't tell my boss? We're not supposed to spy on the clients, you know? I could get in a lot of trouble."

"I won't tell." Kayla would probably never even see the manager.

"I was cleaning the room next door yesterday." She nodded to room 533. "And I overheard the guy in 535. I think he must have been on the telephone, because I only heard one side of the conversation."

"What was he talking about?" Kayla asked.

"I don't know. I couldn't make out the words or anything, but he sounded angry or upset. He was shouting, you know?"

Kayla nodded. "That's very helpful. Could you make out any words at all?"

"Well…I think he said something like 'You can't do this' or something like that."

"Anything else?"

"No. I felt bad about eavesdropping that way, so I turned on the vacuum and went back to work. Did he do something bad?"

"No, he didn't. Thank you. You've been very helpful."

Mindy resumed pushing her cart down the hallway. She had scarcely passed 535 when the door opened and Dylan stepped out. He spotted Kayla before she could duck out of the way. "What are you doing here?" he demanded.

Chapter Six

"Hello, Lieutenant." Kayla gave him a cool look. "I've been waiting for you."

He moved closer, crowding her a little, frankly trying to intimidate her. "What are you doing here?" he asked again, his voice low, but not hiding his anger.

"I'm conducting my own investigation," she said. "I've been talking to the maid and she gave me some interesting information about Agent Asher." Her eyes met his and his heart beat a little faster. She wasn't the prettiest woman he had ever met, but those eyes, so changeable and expressive…

He mentally shook himself. "You shouldn't be here. You're not part of the investigation." Not entirely true. But she wasn't an official part of his team.

"I am. I won't get in the way, but I need to see."

"To see what?"

"I need to see what kind of man he was. To figure out his relationship with Andi. Her father is going to want to know."

"I could charge you with interfering with our investigation."

"I'm not interfering. Senator Matheson hired me because he's concerned about his daughter's safety.

It's possible Agent Asher was a threat to that safety, or that he knew of a threat." She raised her chin, defiant.

He took a step closer and lowered his voice. "You're not going to back down, are you?"

"Did you really think I would?"

No. Part of him—the part that wasn't a cop—would have been disappointed if she had. "I could put you in cuffs and escort you out of here."

"Oh, you'd like that, wouldn't you?" Her voice took on a throaty purr, sending a jolt of pure lust through him.

He struggled to regain control of the situation, and of himself. "I can't let you into Asher's room," he said.

"I know, but you can tell me what you find in there."

"No, I can't."

"Tell me if you find anything to do with Andi and I'll tell you what I learned from the maid."

"I can interview the maid myself."

"Come by my place when you're done here and we can talk."

He shook his head. "No."

"I'll feed you dinner."

"I'm not going to tell you anything."

"I'll still feed you."

Spending an evening alone with Kayla wouldn't be the smartest move he had ever made. She was a witness in his case and a big distraction he didn't need.

She was also the most intriguing woman he had met in a long while. "All right."

The door to Asher's room opened again and Ethan and Carmen emerged, carrying stacks of evidence bags. Ethan glanced at Kayla. "What's she doing here?"

Dylan ignored the question. "Did you get everything?" he asked.

"I think we're done here," Ethan said.

"I'll meet you downstairs," Dylan said. "I want to take one more look."

Ethan looked at Kayla again, then shrugged and headed toward the elevator.

Kayla followed Dylan to the door of the room. "You can't come in," he said.

"I know."

She was smiling when he closed the door in her face. He tried to figure out what the smile meant. Did she think she had got the better of him? They were supposed to be on the same side here—both interested in solving a murder and upholding the law. But he didn't trust her. If her father was a con artist, maybe she had learned a few tricks from him.

KAYLA LEANED AGAINST the wall, arms crossed over her chest. Why had she invited Dylan to dinner at her place? It wasn't as if her cooking was going to work as a bribe. Maybe he thought she intended to seduce information out of him. The idea sent heat curling through her belly. She had walked a little too close to the edge with that remark about the handcuffs, but she hadn't been able to resist. Seeing the cowboy cop angry had been intimidating, but also a big turn-on. There was something about him that got to her, and she wasn't sure if she liked it or not.

Which was probably why she had issued her invitation. She needed to figure out where things were going with them and what it meant. The fact that he had agreed to come by her place probably meant he was curious, too.

The elevator doors opened and Kayla straightened. Two men dressed in jeans and denim work shirts, one carrying a tool bag, emerged. They slowed when they spotted her, and exchanged a look she couldn't read, but the younger one, with brown eyes and olive skin, nodded at her as they passed. They walked to the end of the hall and passed through the door marked Stairs.

Kayla went back to watching the door to Asher's room. What was taking Dylan so long? The other cop had said they were finished, but Dylan must have found something else. Something to do with Andi? She couldn't shake the idea that Asher and the young woman were connected somehow.

She pulled out her phone. If someone came along, she'd look like she was waiting for a friend, or had stopped to make a call. She pulled up an internet browser and typed in Asher's and Andi's names, curious to see what might pop up. She watched the spinning icon as the site loaded, then let out a screech as the phone was wrenched from her fingers.

A hand clamped over her mouth, while strong arms crushed her in a painful grip. She kicked out at her captor, but a second man moved in front of her and cuffed her on the side of the head. She stared at the workman who had passed her earlier—the one with the olive skin and brown eyes.

He glared at her, then grabbed hold of her feet and held them tightly, preventing her from kicking. Together, the two men dragged her down the hall toward the stairwell.

DYLAN STOOD BY the window in the hotel room and surveyed the stripped bed and open drawers. The team had taken the clothes from the closet and a laptop computer from the safe, as well as the sheets and personal items to analyze for any evidence. If Asher had entertained anyone in the room before going to the Family's camp, they would find evidence of that. Dylan hoped the files would reveal the agent's purpose for being in Colorado.

Kayla thought the FBI agent was here because of Andi Matheson, but Dylan saw Daniel Metwater as the key to this case. Asher had Metwater's picture in his car, and the so-called Prophet had been entirely too cool about the sudden appearance of the dead man in his camp.

Dylan moved toward the door. He couldn't waste any more time pondering this. He had to get back to headquarters and start sorting through evidence. He expected to find Kayla waiting for him in the hallway. She had acted as if she intended to stay around, but maybe he had misread her. They had agreed to meet tonight, and he could get her address from the statement she had given Carmen. Still, it bothered him that she hadn't said goodbye.

He started toward the elevator, but a flash of light near the floor caught his eye. He stopped and scooped up a phone. The screen showed a browser open to a search for Frank Asher and Andi Matheson. An icicle of fear stabbed Dylan. This was Kayla's phone. He was sure he had seen her with it earlier.

He glanced up and down the hallway, which was empty and silent. Kayla wouldn't have carelessly dropped her phone. And she wouldn't have left without having a last word with him. Something had happened to force her to leave in a rush—without her phone.

He tucked the device into his pocket and called the front desk from his own cell phone. "This is Lieutenant Holt," he said. "Did a young woman with shoulder-length brown hair, about five-six, dressed in jeans and a button-down shirt, come through the lobby within the last five minutes?"

"No, sir," the clerk said. "No one has been in the lobby since your officers came through here."

"Thanks." He hung up the phone and returned to the hall. If Kayla hadn't passed through the lobby, she must have taken the stairs. He spotted the exit sign at the end of the hallway and sprinted toward it.

When he pushed open the door he caught the faint floral scent that lingered in the air—Kayla. Adrenaline pumping, he pounded down the steps. Below, he heard the sound of a door opening and closing.

He sped up, propelling himself down the stairs, bracing both hands on the railing and vaulting toward the ground floor. If he was wrong, he was going to look pretty foolish, barreling after her like this, but after a decade as a cop, he didn't think he was jumping to the wrong conclusion. Kayla was in trouble, and he couldn't afford to waste a minute. The ground-floor exit opened onto a concrete pad that faced a parking lot. A row of Dumpsters sat at the edge of the lot.

He spotted his quarry right away—two men dressed in denim pants and shirts, carrying Kayla between them. He started toward them just as one of them—the one carrying Kayla's feet—raised a gun and fired. The bullet pinged off metal and Dylan dived for cover behind the nearest Dumpster, the smell of old garbage washing over him in a foul blanket.

He drew his weapon and peered out from between two garbage receptacles. Kayla's kidnappers had positioned her in front of them now, using her as a shield. He couldn't risk a shot. He drew out his phone and dialed 911. "Two men have kidnapped a woman from the hotel by the airport," he said. "There's a state patrol officer there but he needs help." Then he hung up and immediately hit the button for his office. "I'm at the Mesa Inn in Montrose. Two men have kidnapped Kayla Larimer. Send everybody you can spare."

Only half a dozen cars were parked in this back lot. The kidnappers angled toward a dun-colored van, the kind that might have been used by a plumber. A few more yards and they would have Kayla in that van. He couldn't let them get away.

Ignoring the questions from the admin on the other end of the line, he stuffed the phone in his pocket and took aim at the van. The shot was painfully loud, echoing off the metal Dumpsters, but satisfaction surged through him as he watched the windshield of the vehicle explode into a million shards of glass.

The two men with Kayla froze. They shouted curses, though whether at Dylan or at each other, he didn't care. Kayla took advantage of their inattention to kick and flail. The larger of the two, who had hold of her shoulders, punched her savagely in the face. Dylan forced himself to look away, and fired another shot at the van, aiming for the front grille, hoping to hit the engine and disable the vehicle.

His ears were still ringing from the gunfire when the wail of a fast-approaching siren reached him. This brought a renewed wave of curses from the two men. The one holding Kayla's feet had dropped her and was firing at Dylan from behind a parked car, while the first man struggled to hold on to the woman.

Dylan squeezed off a barrage of shots that sent the shooter diving behind the car's bumper. Seeing his chance, he rushed forward and took cover behind another vehicle. He had the shooter in his sights now, and took careful aim.

The shooter's scream when he was hit sent his partner into a panic. The man shoved Kayla away from him, sending her sprawling on the pavement. Then he dived into the van. As a trio of police cars sped into the lot, he took off, tires screeching, heading in the opposite direction.

One of the black-and-whites took off after the van, while the other two skidded to a halt near Kayla and the downed man. Dylan pulled out his badge and stood, holding his gun at his side and his badge up. "I'm Lieutenant Dylan Holt with Colorado State Patrol," he called.

"What happened, Lieutenant Holt?" A trim, graying man who identified himself as Sergeant Connor moved toward Dylan while a second officer helped Kayla to sit. Two other officers knelt beside the shooter, who lay still on the pavement.

Dylan ignored his questioner and knelt beside Kayla. "Are you okay?" he asked.

She was bleeding from her lip, and a purpling bruise was swelling on the side of her face, but she nodded. "I'm okay." She touched a finger to the corner of her mouth and winced. "Or I will be."

"What happened?" Sergeant Connor asked again.

"I was waiting for Dylan—Lieutenant Holt—in the hotel hallway and those two men grabbed me from behind and dragged me down the stairs and out here." Kayla looked at Dylan intently. "Who were they?" she asked. "What did they want with me?"

He shook his head. "I have no idea."

Her gaze shifted to the man on the pavement. "Is he…?"

"He's dead," Sergeant Connor said, and took a step to one side to block Kayla's view of the body.

A Ranger Brigade Cruiser joined the other vehicles in the lot. Graham Ellison climbed out as Ethan Reynolds came running from the lobby. They silently assessed the situation, then strode over to join the others. "Graham Ellison. I'm the captain of the public lands task force." He offered his hand to Sergeant Connor.

"I've heard about you guys. The Ranger Brigade." Connor shook his hand. "We've got an ambulance on the way for the young lady."

"I don't need an ambulance." Kayla struggled to her feet. Dylan reached out to steady her as she swayed. "I'm just a little banged up," she protested, but didn't push him away. "I'll be fine."

"When you're able, we'll need you to come in and make a statement," Connor said.

"I'll tell you what little I know," she said. "But it all happened so fast I can't provide a lot of details."

"Did you recognize either of the men who grabbed you?" Dylan asked.

"No."

Connor's radio crackled and he turned away from them to answer it. But the rest of them clearly heard the message. “We have the suspect in custody,” a man’s voice said.

“We’ll want to question him as soon as possible,” Graham said. “He may be connected with a murder we’re investigating.”

Connor studied Dylan. “Tell me about this investigation,” he said. “How does a crime on public lands connect to an attempted kidnapping in Montrose city limits?”

“There may be no connection,” Dylan said. “But why would someone try to kidnap Kayla outside a room where the murder victim was staying?”

“Who was the murder victim?” Connor asked.

“A federal agent,” Graham said. “Frank Asher. Did you know him?”

Connor shook his head. “Never heard of him. What was he doing in Montrose?”

“That’s what we’re trying to find out,” Graham said. He turned to Kayla. “Let the EMTs check you out, then we’ll get someone to take you home.”

“I have my car here,” she said. “I can drive myself.”

“Someone can drop it by your place later,” Graham said. “Until we know more about these men and why they grabbed you, we’re going to keep a close eye on you.”

She bristled. That was really the only way to describe it. She drew herself up straight and her hair all but stood on end. “I can look after myself.”

“Nevertheless, we’ll be checking in regularly,” Graham said. “And if you spot anything out of the ordinary, call us.”

“Or call *us*,” Connor said.

The ambulance turned into the lot and stopped

alongside them. Dylan left Kayla in the care of the EMTs and joined Graham and Ethan as they walked toward the hotel. "What was she doing here?" Graham asked.

"She followed me," Dylan said. "She thinks Asher is connected with Andi Matheson and she wanted to find out how."

"What did you tell her?" Graham asked.

"I told her she had no business being here and if she didn't leave I could have her arrested for interfering in our investigation."

"I take it she didn't leave," Ethan said.

"I left her in the hallway while I went back into the room." No way was he going to reveal he had agreed to have dinner with her. "When I came out, she was gone, but I found her phone where she had dropped it on the floor. I checked the stairs and saw those two dragging her away."

"How did they know you and Kayla were here at the hotel?" Graham asked.

"They could have followed us. Or maybe the desk clerk tipped them off."

"Or maybe it was bad timing," Ethan said. "They showed up to get something from Asher's room, saw Kayla waiting there and decided they had to get rid of her."

"It's a big risk to take," Dylan said.

"Maybe what they were after was that important," Graham said.

"We got everything from the room, so if there was something there, we'll find it," Dylan said.

"He wasn't on a case," Graham said. "His supervisors said he took two weeks' vacation, starting three days ago. They swear whatever he was doing down here was his personal business."

"Personal business that got him killed," Ethan said.

And almost got Kayla killed, Dylan thought. The idea chilled him.

"Agent Ellison!"

The trio turned to see Sergeant Connor hurrying toward them. "Something just came in I thought you'd want to know about," he said when he reached them. "We ran the plates on the vehicle the shooter was driving and it's registered to Senator Pete Matheson."

"Was it stolen?" Dylan asked.

"That's what we wondered," Connor said. "But when we ran a search for stolen vehicle reports, what we came up with instead was a missing person's report."

"Who's missing?" Graham asked.

"Senator Matheson. No one has seen or heard from him since Friday."

Chapter Seven

Kayla persuaded the Montrose police deputy who drove her home that she didn't want or need a bodyguard. She suggested—and the officer's supervisor agreed—that an occasional drive-by to verify all was peaceful in her neighborhood would be sufficient. She would lock herself in the house and keep both her gun and her phone close at hand.

When she was alone at last, she tried to do as the EMTs had recommended and rest, but every time she closed her eyes her mind replayed the morning's events, from the appearance of Agent Asher's body to Andi's anguished tears to those moments of terror when her kidnappers had held her and bullets whined past.

And Dylan—he disturbed her rest, as well. The man intrigued and aggravated her in equal parts. She told herself she wanted to know what he could tell her only so that she could help Andi and the senator, but deep down she knew she wanted to see Dylan again because she wanted the thrill she felt in his presence—a physical craving coupled with the sense that here was a man who might be worth opening up to.

Unable to sleep, she gave up and went to her computer and once more typed Andi's and Agent Asher's names into the search engine. She found plenty of articles about Andi, mostly mentions of her attendance at various society parties or fund-raisers, with and without her father. But the only mention she found of Asher was a talk he once gave to a neighborhood watch group in Denver. The Fed definitely kept a low profile.

The chime of her doorbell interrupted her thoughts. She started to the door, but froze as she caught a glimpse of herself in the mirror over the small table in the foyer. An ugly purple bruise spread across her left cheek and a black half-moon showed beneath her left eye. She put a hand to the bruising and winced. Apparently, she looked even worse than she felt.

The doorbell rang again. Sighing, she checked the peephole and spotted Dylan Holt rocking back and forth on his heels, staring back at her. She pulled away from the peephole. She didn't really want to see Dylan right now. Not looking like this. Not with her feelings so confused. What did you say to a man who had saved your life? She really wasn't good at this sort of thing. Not that it had ever come up before, but still…

The bell chimed again.

She undid the locks and pulled open the door. "If you came to check up on me, I'm fine," she said.

"I came for dinner." He pushed past her, a shopping bag in one hand.

She'd forgotten all about their dinner date, which felt as if it had been made in an alternate reality, before she'd been manhandled, dragged across a parking lot and shot at—or, at least, shot around. "I'll have to take a rain check," she said. "I don't exactly feel like cooking."

"You don't have to cook." He set the shopping bag on her dining table and began taking out cardboard to-go containers. "I hope you like Chinese."

The aroma of sesame chicken made her mouth water, and she realized she was hungry. Starving. She hurried to the cabinet and pulled out plates. Neither of them said anything else until they were seated across from each other at her small kitchen table with full plates. After a few bites of chicken and rice she paused and grinned at him. "Thanks," she said. "You may have just saved my life. Again."

His expression sobered. "I didn't come here just to feed you."

She put down her fork. "Did you find out anything about the men who attacked me?"

"The truck they were driving was registered to Senator Matheson."

"You mean it was stolen?"

"We don't know. When was the last time you spoke to Senator Matheson?" he asked.

"Friday afternoon. I told him I planned to visit the Family's camp and hoped to speak with Andi."

"How did he take the news?"

"He was pleased. He wanted me to try to persuade her to leave with me and return to his home. I told him all I could do was give her the message, but he seemed optimistic. He told me to call him as soon as I returned from talking with her, to let him know how she's doing."

"Did you call him?"

"Not yet. So much has been going on I haven't had time."

"Would you mind calling him now?"

"Why? What's going on?"

"Call him and then I'll tell you." Dylan softened his expression. "Please."

"All right." She reached into her pocket, then froze. "I can't find my phone."

He pulled the phone from his own pocket. "You must have dropped it when those two thugs grabbed you," he said.

"Thanks." That showed how rattled she had been—she hadn't even realized her phone was missing. She scrolled through her contacts and found the number for Senator Matheson. The phone buzzed a couple times, then a message came on that informed her the mailbox of the person she was trying to reach was full.

"That's odd," she said after she had ended the call. "He's usually good about checking his messages. But his mailbox is full."

"Is that his office number or a private line?" Dylan asked.

"It's his private cell phone, I think. Dylan, what is going on?"

"The senator's administrative assistant reported him missing this morning. He left his office Friday afternoon and was scheduled to attend a Senate hearing on finance today. No has seen him since then. You may be the last person who spoke with him. I expect it will be on the news any minute now."

"I haven't had the TV on. And I was doing research online, so I didn't notice the headlines. So what's the connection between the guys who attacked me and

Senator Matheson? Did they steal the truck and kidnap him? And then they came to Asher's hotel to look for something?"

"To look for what?"

"I don't know—something incriminating? Something that linked them to both Asher and the senator?"

"You're linked to Asher and the senator. The senator hired you to track down his daughter at the camp and while you were there, Asher's body was found."

"So you think, what—that they followed me to the hotel? Why?"

"Maybe they think you saw something you shouldn't have."

"I didn't see anything."

"Then why did they kidnap you? Did they say anything to you?"

"They didn't say a word."

He scowled and bit down hard on a fried wonton. "I can't know you're safe until I figure out why those men grabbed you," he said.

"You don't have to worry about me." His concern unsettled her. "Besides, they're in custody, aren't they? I mean, the one who lived is." She wasn't likely to forget the sight of the man sprawled on the pavement—the second body she had seen that day. "I don't have anything to worry about."

"He's in the hospital," Dylan said. "With a police guard posted at his door. We haven't had a chance to question him yet. What if the attack wasn't their idea? What if someone hired them? He could hire someone else." He looked around the room. "Do you have a security system?"

"No. I don't need a security system."

"Maybe you shouldn't stay here tonight. At least until we get to the bottom of this."

"Lieutenant, I'll be fine. I have good locks, and a weapon if I need to use it. And I can always dial 911. The police station is only a few blocks away."

"I still don't like it." He attacked another wonton. "I'd think you'd be afraid to stay here alone after what happened to you today."

"I was fine until you came along with all these dire predictions of peril. Honestly, you're blowing everything out of proportion."

"Am I? You could have died today. I don't like the idea of someone trying again."

"I don't like that idea, either, but it's not going to do anyone any good for me to run around wringing my hands and fretting about it. I think I'm as safe here in my own home as I would be anywhere else. And I still think the attack on me was random—I was in the wrong place at the wrong time. Those two wanted me out of the way so they could get into the hotel room. They were even dressed like workmen."

"What did you find out when you talked to the maid?" Dylan asked.

"Not much," she admitted. "She said she overheard Asher on the phone with someone. He was arguing, but she didn't know what the argument was about."

"Maybe Asher was arguing with his killer."

"Maybe." She spooned more fried rice onto her plate. "What did your search of Asher's room turn up?"

He hesitated.

"Just tell me if you found anything to link him to Andi," she said.

"We don't know yet. He has files on his computer, but they're all encrypted. We've got people working on it." He dipped an egg roll in plum sauce and took a bite.

"Check his phone, too."

He swallowed. "Thanks. I hadn't thought of that."

She fought the urge to stick her tongue out at him. But perhaps they hadn't descended into such juvenile sparring yet. "I'm going to keep digging," she said.

"What did you learn about Andi and Asher?"

"How did you know I was researching them?"

"I saw the web page on your phone browser. Did you learn anything?"

She shook her head. "Asher has definitely kept a low profile, but maybe that's usual for a federal agent. All the mentions I found about Andi had to do with her father, or some society do she attended. She's certainly living a very different kind of life now."

"I'm going back out to the camp tomorrow to talk to Andi," he said. "I need to tell her about her father and find out if she's heard anything, and I intend to ask her about Asher."

"Let me go with you."

"No."

"She'll talk to me. You just frighten her."

"You make me sound like some kind of bully."

"Let's just say you can be pretty intimidating when you want to be."

"Do I intimidate you?" His eyes met hers and she felt that jolt of attraction again. She wasn't afraid of him, only of where these wild feelings she had for him might take her.

She wet her suddenly dry lips. "I don't know, Lieutenant—do *I* intimidate *you*?"

"*Intimidate* isn't the word I'd use." He leaned across the table toward her and cupped his hand along the side of her injured cheek, not touching her, but close enough that she could feel the heat of him. "You're a puzzle I want to figure out," he said.

She wanted to lean into him, to press her lips to his and learn if he would respond with the same boldness with which he questioned a suspect or faced down danger. But once she crossed that barrier with him, there wouldn't be any going back. Neither of them was the type to back down from a challenge.

The loud strains of Fergie sounded from her phone, making her jump. Dylan sat back, arms crossed on his chest. She avoided his gaze, checking the phone's screen instead. Not a number she recognized, but it could always be a new client—someone wanting her to spy on a cheating spouse or track down a long-lost relative. "Larimer Investigations," she answered.

"Is this Kayla Larimer?" a woman's voice asked.

"Yes."

"I have a message for you from Andi Matheson."

Kayla sat up straighter. "What is it?"

"She needs to talk to you. Can you meet her at the parking area for the Dead Horse Canyon Trail tomorrow afternoon at one?"

"What is this about?" Kayla asked. "Who is this?"

"I'm just a friend. I promised to call and give you this message. Can you meet her?"

"Yes, of course. But—"

The line went dead before she could ask any more

questions. Kayla looked up and met Dylan's eyes. "Andi wants to meet me in the morning," she said.

"I'll go with you," he said.

"She said she wanted to talk to me—not you."

"I'll go with you." His expression was grim. "I don't trust these people. I'm not going to let you go alone."

DYLAN PICKED UP Kayla from her house the next afternoon. He had been tempted to insist on staying with her overnight—on her couch, though he wouldn't have turned her down if she had invited him into her bed. He didn't trust whoever was responsible for the attack on her not to make another try. But in the end he had decided alienating her by pushing to get his way wasn't worth the trouble. He had made her show him her gun and her locks, and he was satisfied both were adequate. Then he had touched base with the Montrose PD and impressed upon them the need to make a few extra passes by her house during the night.

He showed up a half hour early the next afternoon, since he didn't entirely trust her not to slip off by herself. While he admired independence in a woman, she seemed to want to take it too far. He still got chills when he thought about how close she had come to dying yesterday.

She met him in her driveway, her purse slung over one shoulder, a steaming mug in her hand. "I could have driven myself," she said.

Did he know her or what? "Good afternoon to you, too." He opened the passenger door for her. "Look at it this way—you're saving gas and wear and tear on your car."

She slid into the seat and reached for the seat belt. "Just remember, Andi wants to talk to *me*."

"I have to give her the news about her father and try to find out if she's been in contact with him since he disappeared." The FBI had handed that job off to the Rangers.

"So the senator is still missing?" she asked.

"Yes. Apparently, there's no sign of a struggle at his home or office, and no one has seen or heard from him since he left work Thursday." Dylan put the Cruiser in gear and backed out of her driveway.

"What about the man who attacked me? You said the van he was driving belonged to Senator Matheson? Does he know anything?"

"The senator used the van as a campaign vehicle when he ran for reelection two years ago, and some of his staff workers have used it occasionally since then," Dylan said. "We still haven't been able to interview the suspect, but our research hasn't turned up a connection." He glanced at her. "So we're agreed that I'll talk to Andi?"

"Fine. But let me talk to her first. I don't want you scaring her off before I find out what she wants."

"I thought we established last night that I'm not that scary."

She flushed. Was she remembering that moment when he had almost kissed her? His fingertips tingled at the memory, remembering the heat of her against his skin, and the almost overwhelming need he had had to touch her.

"You don't frighten me," she said. "But Andi may be another story."

He pulled to the stop sign at the end of her street.

"Fine. You take the lead, but then I get to ask my questions."

"I think we've already established that you're good at questions." The amused glint in her eyes took the sting out of her words.

"That's right," he said. "When I was a kid my dad threatened to gag me with my own bandanna when we were out working and I'd pester him with too many questions."

He turned onto the highway and she settled back into the seat and sipped from her mug. "Do you like ranching?" she asked after a moment.

"I like being out-of-doors. I like working with the animals. But it can be frustrating. There's so much you can't control, from weather to cattle prices. And sometimes it's just a lot of hard work. I had to go away for a while to appreciate it."

"Where did you go?"

"To Denver. I was in law enforcement there for ten years after college. But I missed all this." He indicated the sweep of land out the windshield. "And my dad had some health problems and needed more help. When the opening for this job came up, I was glad to take it."

She didn't say anything and he wondered what she was thinking. From what little she had said about her past, he gathered she had never had a place she felt rooted to—a real home. She had come to Montrose almost by chance and had no ties here other than her job.

"This work must be different from what you did in the city," she said. "This isn't exactly a high-crime area."

"More goes on here than you might think," he said.

"But a lot of it goes on behind the scene—drugs, theft of artifacts, smuggling. And a lot of people see public lands as a good place to hide out."

"People like Daniel Metwater."

"Yeah. How much do you know about him?"

"Not a lot," she said. "He started calling himself a prophet and recruiting followers a little over a year ago. I take it he comes from money."

"His father was an industrialist named Oscar Metwater. When he died, Daniel and his twin brother, David, inherited the family fortune. David was killed a few months later in what was likely a mob hit. He had a gambling habit and had embezzled money from the family firm and apparently borrowed from the wrong people."

"In one of his official bios Daniel says something about his brother—about how his death made him see the futility of the life he had been leading and made him seek a better way."

"I guess some people would see having a slew of followers turn over all their possessions to you and do your bidding as a better way of life," Dylan said. "And from what I saw, the majority of those followers are beautiful young women."

"While some religions teach the importance of caring for the poor and afflicted, I'm guessing Daniel Metwater isn't one of them," she said.

"What about your father?" he asked. "Was he like Metwater?"

"Oh, he could quote scripture about widows and orphans when he thought it would encourage people to put more in the collection plate," she said. "But the only person he was really interested in looking out for was himself. Metwater strikes me as the same." She shifted toward Dylan. "Do you know why Agent Asher had Metwater's picture in his car?"

"We haven't come up with anything yet. The computer forensics may take a while. Or we might find out something from Andi."

She fell silent and Dylan didn't try to engage her further. Maybe he shouldn't have brought up her father. Clearly, it wasn't a pleasant topic for her.

After a dusty ride on a rugged dirt track, they reached the parking area for the trail, marked only by a bullet-riddled brown sign. The Ranger Cruiser was the only vehicle in sight. Dylan pulled into the lot and shut off the engine, and silence closed around them. He scanned the outcropping of rocks and clumps of scrubby piñons and sagebrush for any signs of life. "This would be a good place for an ambush," he said.

His plan was to wait in the Cruiser until someone approached, but before he could say so, Kayla opened her door and got out. Almost immediately, Andi emerged from behind a large boulder, her long hair blown sideways in a gust of hot wind. She wore the same prairie skirt and tank top she had had on yesterday, a blue cotton shawl around her shoulders.

She eyed Dylan warily as he climbed out of the vehicle and came to stand behind Kayla. "What is he doing here?" Andi asked. "I wanted you to come alone."

"The person who called me didn't say anything about that," Kayla said. "I thought it would be a good idea for him to come along for protection. You can't blame me for being nervous, after what happened to Frank Asher."

At the mention of Asher, Andi's lips trembled, but she brought her emotions under control. "Can I trust him?" she asked.

"Trust me with what?" Dylan said, ignoring the annoyed look from Kayla.

"Can I trust you to keep my confidences?" Andi asked. She wrapped her hands in the ends of the shawl. "I don't want certain people knowing about what I'm going to tell you."

"What people?" Kayla asked.

Andi shook her head and began walking away from them, toward the road. Kayla and Dylan fell into step alongside her, gravel crunching under their feet. "Do you mean Daniel Metwater?" Kayla asked. "Is that why you wanted to meet us away from the camp—so the Prophet wouldn't know you were meeting me?"

"Everyone in the camp is busy preparing for the ceremony this evening," Andi said.

"What kind of ceremony?" Kayla asked.

"We have a new member joining the Family. That's why I couldn't call you myself yesterday. I had to stay and help with the preparations. The woman who called was one of the ones chosen to go into town to buy food for tonight's celebration."

She fell silent again, and Dylan fought the urge to fire more questions at her. Maybe Kayla was right and he needed to let her take the lead here, at least until Andi was more comfortable with him. She was calmer today, though an air of sadness clung to her. The skirt she wore was faded, with a tear in the hem at the back, and the pink polish on her toes was chipped. As the daughter of a prominent senator, she was probably used to designer fashions and spa treatments. Was she growing disillusioned with life in the wilderness with the so-called prophet?

"How are you doing?" Kayla asked when they had walked another hundred yards or so. "You were pretty upset when I saw you yesterday."

"It was the shock of learning about Frank's death." She swept a lock of hair out of her eyes and tucked it behind one ear.

"You knew him, then," Kayla said.

"Oh, yes." She drew in a deep breath. "We were lovers. He's the father of my baby."

So Kayla had been right, Dylan thought.

"Was he coming here to see you?" Kayla asked.

"I don't know." Andi pulled the shawl more tightly around her shoulders. "I told him not to come—that I had nothing to say to him. We ceased being close months ago, before I even learned I was pregnant."

"Why did you break up?" Kayla asked.

She looked away, lips pressed tightly together.

"You probably think the answer to that question is none of our business," Dylan said. "But if there's the slightest chance that the reason the two of you split up could have anything to do with his death, we need to know."

She shook her head, still not looking at them. "I'm sure it doesn't have anything to do with his death."

"We're in a better position to determine that," Dylan said.

"Frank was my father's friend before he was mine, and in the end, he had the same mindset. He was of that world. Isn't that enough?"

"So Frank Asher and your father knew each other?" Dylan asked. He kept his eyes on Andi, though he was aware of Kayla's frown. She wasn't pleased he was asking so many questions, but that was his job.

"Frank worked for my father," Andi said. "That's how we met."

"I thought he was an FBI agent," Kayla said.

"He took a year's leave from the Bureau to work as my father's private security agent. But when my father found out we were lovers, he and Frank argued and Frank went back to work for the Bureau." Andi turned and began walking again.

"When was the last time you saw Frank?" Kayla asked.

"Last week. He must have found out I was here and he stopped me in town and said we had to talk. I was with some of the other women and I told him I had nothing to say to him. He said he would come to the camp to talk to me. I told him not to, but he didn't listen. Men don't, do they? Not when it's a woman talking."

She didn't look at Dylan when she said the words, but he felt their impact.

"Do you know anything about what happened to him?" Kayla asked, her voice gentle.

Andi shook her head. "I was so shocked when you told me it was him." She hugged her arms across her chest. "That's why I wanted to talk to you today. I knew you would wonder why I was so upset over his death. Even though I haven't loved him for a while, at one time he meant something to me, so I grieve. And it saddens me to think my child will never know its father."

Kayla put a hand on Andi's shoulder. "I'm sorry for your loss. I'm sure it was a great shock."

Andi straightened. "Of course, the Prophet will be the child's father, as he is father to all of us."

"Is that how you see him?" Dylan asked. "As a father? You and he are close to the same age."

Andi glanced back at him. "Well, perhaps not a father. But he is our leader. Our guide." She brought the shawl up to cover her head. "We should go back now. I've said what I needed to say."

She led the way ahead, then faltered, stumbling. Dylan reached out to steady her, then froze as a man stepped from the brush alongside the road. Sunlight glinted off the lenses of his mirrored sunglasses, and off the pistol in his hand.

"If you want to know more about me, Lieutenant, you ought to talk to me," Daniel Metwater said.

Chapter Eight

Kayla stood very still, more fascinated than fearful, as Daniel Metwater strode toward them. Though not a large man, he exuded power, a kind of magnetic vitality radiating from him. He moved with a swagger, a gleam in his eyes that told her he was confident of the admiration of all who observed him. As much as she loathed his attitude, she could admit to being compelled by him. She understood why so many young women fell under his charismatic spell. The promise of being the focus of such raw energy and sex appeal could be intoxicating.

When he was a few feet away, he tucked the gun into a holster on his right hip. "Are you all right, Asteria?" he asked.

She nodded, her gaze focused on the ground.

Metwater turned his attention to Kayla and Dylan. "If you want to talk to me or one of my followers, it isn't necessary to sneak around outside the camp," he said. "We have nothing to hide."

"What are you doing with that gun?" Dylan asked. "I thought you preached nonviolence."

"As the unfortunate events of yesterday prove, the wilderness is not as safe a place as it would seem," he said. "And before you ask, we've had hordes of officers swarming over the camp searching for weapons. They have already examined this particular gun and determined it isn't the same caliber as the one that killed Agent Asher. And they haven't found any other guns among my followers."

"Why do you need a gun if you don't allow your followers to be armed?" Dylan asked.

"It is my job to protect my people."

"Have you been threatened in any way?" Dylan asked. "Have there been other incidents you haven't reported to the police?"

"No." He took Andi's arm and pulled her toward him. "Come back to camp now," he said. "You must be tired. You need to rest."

Kayla's skin crawled as she watched any hint of the young woman's personality vanish in Metwater's shadow. "Andi, you don't have to go with him if you don't want," she said.

"No, it's fine," Andi said. "My place is with him. With the Family."

Metwater fixed his gaze on Kayla, an intense scrutiny that made her feel naked and exposed. "You fear us because you don't understand us," he said. "You don't understand the security and refuge I offer my followers. We are having a special ceremony this evening to welcome a new Family member. I'm inviting you both to attend. It will help you to understand us better."

"All right, we'll be there." Dylan took Kayla's arm and squeezed it, cutting off her protest. She had no desire to spend any more time than necessary with Metwater and his followers, but if Dylan thought attending the ceremony would help in the investigation, she was willing to play along.

"Come along, Asteria." Metwater prepared to lead Andi away.

"Ms. Matheson, when was the last time you spoke to your father?" Dylan asked.

Andi stumbled. Only Metwater's grasp on her arm kept her from falling. She looked over her shoulder at Dylan. "My father?"

"Yes. When was the last time you were in contact with him?"

"Months ago," she said. "We haven't spoken since I joined the Family."

"You haven't heard from him recently, in the past few days?"

"She told you she hasn't," Metwater said. "We're leaving now. We'll see you both this evening. Come at dusk and someone will be waiting to escort you to the ceremony."

"Andi, have you heard from your father in the past few days?" Dylan asked again.

She shook her head. "No."

"I'm sorry to have to tell you he's missing."

Andi's expression didn't change. "I don't know anything about that." Then she turned and, holding Metwater's hand, walked away.

Kayla frowned after her. Dylan nudged her. "Let's get out of here."

Neither of them spoke as they made their way back to Dylan's Cruiser, but once they were inside the vehicle, he turned to her. "Does it strike you as cold that Andi didn't react to news of her father's disappearance? She certainly cried buckets over Frank Asher."

Kayla nodded. "Something was off about her reaction—maybe because Metwater was there."

"But we're talking about her father. Her only living parent."

"I wouldn't necessarily have much of a reaction if you told me my father was missing," she said. Her father had been missing from her life—or at least, the fatherly part of him had—for as long as she could remember. "I don't think that makes me a horrible person."

"No, it doesn't." He started the Cruiser and pulled out of the parking area, his face grim. Kayla turned away, staring at the stark landscape. She didn't think of her father much these days, or of any of her family, really. She was sure they seldom thought of her. Since she had refused to work with them in their con games, she had ceased to be useful to them.

Dylan guided the vehicle over the rutted BLM road to the highway, but instead of turning toward Ranger headquarters or town, he took another road that led south. "Where are you going?" Kayla asked.

"We have a few hours to kill before we have to be back at the camp for their ceremony," he said. "Do you have somewhere you need to be?"

She always had work to do, but it was nothing that wouldn't wait. "No."

"Then there's someone I want you to meet."

THE BLEAKNESS IN Kayla's voice when she spoke of her father made Dylan want to punch something. All his life he had known he could count on his family to be there for him. He knew they loved him as surely as he knew the sun would rise tomorrow, and if he needed anything at all, his parents and siblings would move heaven and earth to help him. Kayla didn't have that kind of reassurance, and knowing that made him sick at heart.

"Where are we going?" she asked again, when he turned onto the narrow county road that formed one boundary of his family's ranch.

"I'm taking you home," he said.

"To your home?"

"Yeah. This is my family's ranch." He gestured to his left, and the rolling pastureland dotted with Angus heifers and calves. They rounded a curve in the road and the main house came into view—a two-story log cabin with a green metal roof. A deep porch stretched across the front of the house, and assorted log-sided sheds and other outbuildings dotted the land around it.

Kayla sat up straighter, her back pressed against the seat as if she was trying to put as much distance as possible between herself and the house. "I don't think we should barge in like this without calling first," she said.

"This is my home. I don't have to call before I show up." He guided the Cruiser under the iron archway that proclaimed Holt Cattle Company, and over the cattle guard, to the parking area under a trio of tall spruce.

"You live here?" She stared at the house.

He laughed. "I live in a smaller cabin on another part of the property. But I grew up here. My parents live here."

They exited the car and a pair of Border collies shot across the yard to greet them. Kayla bent to run her hands over their wriggling bodies. "Oh, aren't you a pretty pair!"

"Their names are Lucy and Desi," Dylan said.

"They're beautiful." She grinned as both dogs fought for her attention.

"I see you've met our vicious guard dogs!"

They looked up from the dogs as Dylan's parents approached. As was his habit now, Dylan found himself assessing the older couple. Dad was thinner than he had been before his heart attack three months ago, and he had a little more gray in his reddish-blond hair, but he looked good. So much better than he had when Dylan had first seen him in the hospital.

The ordeal had aged his mom, too, added a few more lines to her face, but she, too, looked stronger than she had when Dylan first came home. "Mom, Dad, I'd like you to meet Kayla Larimer. Kayla, this is my mom and dad, Nancy and Bud Holt."

Kayla straightened. "It's nice to meet you," she said.

"Good to meet you." Bud offered his hand.

"So nice of Dylan to bring you to see us," his mom added. Dylan could read the unasked question in her eyes. He wasn't one for bringing women around to meet the family.

"I wanted Kayla to see the ranch," he said, an answer he knew wouldn't really satisfy his mother, but she was too polite to demand more information in Kayla's hearing.

"Well, come on in." Bud took Kayla's arm and escorted her toward the house. "Are you from around here?" he asked.

"I live in Montrose. I'm a private detective. Dylan and I are working a case together."

"Are you now?" His dad's sharp, assessing gaze

made Dylan feel like the kid who had been caught sneaking out of the house his freshman year of high school.

"Where are you from originally?" Nancy asked.

"Oh, my family moved around a lot when I was growing up," Kayla said. "I love your dogs." She gestured toward the two pups, which had run ahead. "I've always heard how intelligent Border collies are."

"Oh, they're smart, all right," Bud said. "Smart enough to get into all kinds of trouble if you don't keep them busy."

The four of them mounted the porch. At the top of the steps, Kayla turned to look out across the yard, and at the snow-capped mountains beyond. "What a gorgeous view," she said.

"Yes. I never get tired of the view," Bud said. "This country has a way of growing on people, I think. Pulling them back when they try to leave."

This last comment was for Dylan's benefit, he knew. "I missed all of this while I was in Denver," he said. "I'm glad to be back."

"And we're glad to have you back," his mother said. "Now come, sit down." She gestured toward the grouping of chairs on the porch. "Can I get you something to drink?"

"No, thank you." Kayla perched on the edge of one of the oak rockers lined up against the front wall of the house. Dylan took the chair next to her, while his parents chose the adjacent swing that hung from the porch beams.

"What kind of case are you working on?" Bud asked. "Or can't you say?"

"We're investigating some goings-on that might

be related to a group that's been camping in the Curecanti Wilderness Area," Dylan said. "Followers of a man who calls himself the Prophet."

Bud nodded. "I heard a little about them. Sam Wilson ran into a bunch of the women at the farmers' market last Friday. They bought a lot of his produce. He said they seemed nice. Are they causing trouble?"

"We're not sure. Let's just say some things have aroused our suspicions."

Bud rested his arm along the back of the swing and gave it a gentle nudge with the toe of his boot. "There's always a few of these types who take to the wilderness," he said. "Back-to-the-landers or survivalists or religious zealots looking for a better way. Most of them peter out after a while when people find out how tough it really is to live without modern conveniences like indoor plumbing, refrigeration and heat."

"There was a group that passed through here in the seventies," Nancy said. "The rainbow people, or something like that. A bunch of hippies who said they were all for peace and love, but all they really did was sponge off anyone they could, do drugs and leave a mess behind. Bart Tillaman had to take his front-end loader out to the campsite after they left and haul off two or three Dumpsters full of garbage."

"We won't let things go that far," Dylan said. "That's why we're keeping an eye on them."

"And you're helping the Rangers with their investigations?" Nancy asked Kayla.

She looked up from petting the dogs, who had settled on either side of her. "A client hired me to find his daughter," she said. "She's living with this group."

"Those poor parents." Nancy shook her head. "I

can't imagine having one of my children run off like that, having to hire a private investigator to track them down."

"You don't have to worry about that," Dylan said.

"No. Especially now that all three of you are living on the ranch." She smiled at Kayla. "Do your parents live near here?"

"I don't have any close family anymore," Kayla said. She shot Dylan a warning look. As if she had to warn him not to air her private business for his parents.

"I'm sorry to hear that," Nancy said. "But a small town can be a good place to be when you're alone in the world. Stay here long enough and people will be treating you like family."

"Which is another way of saying they'll want to know all your business," Dylan said, but he winked to let his mom know he was only teasing—sort of.

"Speaking of family business..." Bud put his hands on his knees and leaned toward Dylan. "I hope you plan on being at the Cattleman's Club meeting next week."

"I don't know, Dad. Work is taking a lot of my time." The monthly meetings of representatives from all the local ranches had never struck him as very productive.

"The board is really trying to get some of the younger members of local ranching families involved," Bud said. "And you could learn a lot about the way the cattle business works in this part of the state."

"All right. I'll be there if I can." One of the reasons he had returned to the ranch was to take on more of the responsibility of running cattle operations, to ease the burden on his parents. And he knew his dad got a kick out of showing off his son, the cop.

"Private investigation must be interesting work," Nancy said, once more including Kayla in the conversation. "I would think a woman would have an advantage in that field."

"Why do you say that?" Bud asked. "Because women are nosier than men?"

Nancy gave her husband a scolding look. "No. Because criminals would be less likely to suspect a woman—especially one who is so young and pretty."

Kayla shifted, clearly uncomfortable. "I've always enjoyed solving puzzles," she said. "And I like working alone and being my own boss."

"I'd love to hear more about it," Nancy said. She turned to Dylan. "I hope you're planning to stay for dinner."

"Oh, I don't know—" Kayla began.

"We don't have to be back at the camp until dusk," Dylan interrupted. "Might as well not go on an empty stomach."

"We'll grill steaks," Bud said. "Some of our own beef."

"And a salad from the garden," Nancy said.

"Right. The doctor says I've got to eat my vegetables." Bud grinned. "Say you'll stay."

Kayla nodded, and even managed a small smile of her own. "All right."

Nancy stood, and the others rose also. "While I'm cooking, Dylan can give you a tour of the ranch," she said.

Chapter Nine

Kayla eyed the horse, swallowing her trepidation. The animal was considerably taller than her, with a lot more teeth. "I've never ridden a horse before," she said.

"Sunset is an easy mount." Dylan moved alongside her, so close she could feel the heat of him, which sent a corresponding warmth through her. "I'll be right with you, so you don't have anything to worry about."

"Couldn't we drive? Or take an ATV?" She looked longingly toward a trio of all-terrain vehicles parked outside the barn.

"Horseback is the best way to see the place," he said. "Besides, my horse, Bravo, needs exercise. It's been a few days since I rode him. We won't go far, I promise."

The horse snorted and tossed his head. "I don't think he agrees with you," she said. She took a step back, which sent her stumbling into Dylan. His arms encircled her, steadying her. The hard planes and bunched muscles that defined him as so very male stirred something deep in her female core and she stared up at him, lips parted, breathing grown shallow, bracing herself against the flood of longing that weakened her knees.

His eyes locked onto hers, then darkened, and his arms tightened around her. He bent his head, hesitating a fraction of a second with his mouth near hers. Impatient, she slid her hand to the back of his neck and pulled him down.

His mouth was warm and agile, caressing her lips and sending liquid heat through her. He angled his head to deepen the kiss, the brim of his Stetson brushing the top of her hair, the faint afternoon shadow of his beard a pleasant friction against her skin.

When at last he raised his head, she blinked up at him, trying to clear away the fog of lust. "Wh-why did you do that?" she stammered.

"Because you wanted me to. And because I wanted to." He patted the horse's neck. "It stopped you from being afraid of Sunset, didn't it?"

Wishing to deny both the accusation that she had wanted him to kiss her and that she had been afraid of the horse, but knowing she wasn't that accomplished a liar, she turned away him and stuck her foot in the stirrup. "Let's get go—"

Before she could complete the sentence, he had moved to boost her onto the horse, the feel of his hand against the seat of her jeans staying with her even when she was settled in the saddle. He handed her the reins. "Don't jerk on them," he said. "Mostly, Sunset will follow Bravo. You just relax and enjoy the scenery."

That scenery included Dylan on horseback as he rode ahead of her down a trail that led away from the house. He sat relaxed in the saddle, tall and broad-shouldered, his Stetson cocked just-so on his head. What had possessed her to kiss the man like that?

The move was unprofessional and impulsive and probably a lot of other things that in no way described her.

For the next half hour she followed him down the trail. He pointed out various outbuildings and pastures, and talked about some of the livestock and the history of the ranch. "My great-grandfather bought the land during the Depression, when it cost next to nothing. He worked for years adding to it and building it up to make it what it is today." Kayla heard the pride in Dylan's voice and felt a stab of jealousy. What would it be like to feel so connected to a place? To the land?

He stopped at the top of a hill that afforded a vista of a sweeping river valley. "Our place extends to the base of those hills over there," he said, pointing.

"It's beautiful." Unlike the almost barren terrain near the national park, this valley was green, and dotted with small herds of cattle that grazed in the knee-high grass. She glanced at Dylan. He was looking out across the landscape, fine lines spreading at the corners of his eyes as he squinted in the brightness, his lips curved in a half smile. "Did you enjoy growing up here?" she asked.

"I did. I liked to ride and shoot and fish, and being outdoors." He shifted, the saddle creaking as he half turned toward her. "But when I got to be a teenager, I grew restless. I was interested in a career in law enforcement and I didn't see much chance for advancement here. It's a pretty small police department, and there wasn't anything like the Ranger Brigade back then."

"So you went to Denver."

"Yes. And I liked it. The city is a good place to be if you're a single, twentysomething guy. And it was good for my career."

"But you came back."

"My folks needed me. And it was time. As much as I enjoyed Denver, it wasn't the kind of place I could picture myself raising a family."

"You really think about things like that—raising a family?"

"Don't you?"

She shook her head. "No." The idea unsettled her a little. She was happy being responsible for herself, but she didn't need to be responsible for anyone else.

"Maybe that's why Andi Matheson hooked up with Metwater's group," Dylan said. "Maybe she thought that kind of makeshift family would be a good place to raise a kid."

"It sounds like a terrible idea." Kayla's own childhood had been defined by constantly moving around with an ever-shifting group of her father's followers. "What I can't figure is what Daniel Metwater gets out of it."

"A power trip? A bunch of devoted, beautiful women? Or maybe he's looking for a family of his own." Dylan turned his horse and led the way back down the hill. At the bottom the trail widened, so they could ride side by side.

True to Dylan's word, Sunset was an easygoing mount that was content to follow Dylan's horse's lead. Kayla was able to relax and focus away from her own fears and annoyances to the case. "From what I've read, he comes from money," she said. "Why give that up to live in the desert?"

"He thinks he's a prophet. It's his calling."

"Or he's running away from something."

"Or that." Dylan glanced at her. "Anything in particular make you think so?"

"When my father ran into trouble and needed to leave a place, he would always announce that he had had a vision—God leading him to take his message to new, more fertile fields."

Dylan nodded. "You've given me an idea."

"What's that?"

"I'm going to dig a little deeper into Metwater's background. Maybe I'll find something there that will help in this investigation. Some secret he's not keen to have revealed."

THE SUN WAS sinking behind the distant hills when Dylan and Kayla finally left the ranch. Dinner had been a leisurely affair on the back deck of his parents' home—steaks grilled outdoors, served with roasted corn and an enormous salad of fresh greens and tomatoes from his mother's garden.

Kayla had seemed to enjoy herself and Dylan had enjoyed watching her. His lips still warmed at the memory of that impulsive kiss. Maybe not the most professional move he had ever pulled, but he'd been thinking about kissing her practically since they met. When she had pulled his mouth down to hers he hadn't been about to resist. He had enjoyed the kiss very much, and he enjoyed knowing that he'd been able to breach her reserve. She had made it clear she didn't trust anyone—and maybe she had good reason for that, given what little he knew of her upbringing. But that kiss told him that maybe she was beginning to have more faith in him, at least a bit.

He braked to avoid a deer that darted across the road in the graying light. "It's going to be dark by the time we get to the camp," Kayla said.

"Probably." He switched on the Cruiser's headlights. "Maybe they'll think we skipped out on their invitation. I don't mind catching them off guard."

She crossed her arms over her chest. "Nothing about this feels right. Why do you think Metwater invited us to this ceremony?"

"He said it was to help us understand the Family more."

"I don't believe him."

"I'm not sure I do, either, but I want to know what he's up to. Why don't you believe him?"

"Because people like him aren't altruistic. I doubt he cares if we understand him and his group or not. He thrives on manipulating people. I can't help but think he's trying to manipulate *us*."

"We're not going to let him do that, are we?"

"Nobody manipulates me."

When he glanced over, she had her gaze fixed on him. Dylan wondered if her words were a not-so-subtle warning. He could have protested that he wasn't the manipulative type, but better she learn that fact for herself.

Light from an almost full moon bathed the wilderness landscape in silver, highlighting the rocky hoodoos and cliffs, and sending long shadows across the sparse grass. A coyote trotted down the road ahead, turning to regard them with golden eyes before darting into the underbrush. “I can’t believe anyone would want to live out here,” Kayla said. “It’s so…desolate.”

“It would be a tough place to live,” Dylan agreed. “But it’s a good place to hide.” He found the parking area and pulled in and shut off the engine. Silence closed around them like a muffling blanket, the only sound the faint ticking of the cooling motor. Though the moon provided plenty of illumination, Dylan tucked a mini Maglite into his pocket just in case. They climbed out of the Cruiser and looked around.

“Metwater said he would have someone waiting for us, but I don’t see anyone,” Kayla said.

“Maybe he thinks we’re not going to show.” Dylan touched her arm. “Come on. Let’s slip in quietly and see what they’re up to.”

They moved up the path toward the camp, placing their footsteps carefully, trying not to disturb the night’s silence. As they rounded the outcropping of rock that guarded the entrance to the camp, they heard a low murmuring. Dylan stopped to listen and Kayla moved up beside him. “What’s that?” he whispered.

“Sounds like some kind of chanting or something,” she said.

He nodded, and led the way around the outcropping. No guards watched over the entrance to the camp—apparently everyone was gathered around the bonfire in the center of the circle of trailers and tents. The faces of everyone—men, women and children—were fixed on the leaping flames, and voices rose in unison. “In unity is power. Power is unity.”

Power to do what? “Doesn’t sound like a peaceful manifesto to me,” Dylan muttered. “And there’s a burn ban on. Want to bet they don't have a permit for that fire?"

Kayla shushed him as Daniel Metwater stepped from the crowd and stood in front of the blaze, his profile to Dylan and Kayla. The crowd fell silent as he waited. He was naked except for a loincloth, his body gleaming in the firelight as if it had been oiled. He was thin but muscular, and wore the expression of a man who was confident he was right.

Two women moved from the crowd to join him. They were dressed only in loincloths also, their breasts painted with red and black concentric circles, their eyes ringed in black, lips outlined in red. Dylan didn't recognize either of them, but they fit the profile of twentysomething beauties predominant among Metwater's followers.

A drum began a slow, steady beat, gradually increasing in tempo. Metwater extended his arms and the women took his hands. The three began a slow, hypnotic dance, swaying and writhing around each other. Beside him, Kayla shifted. "Do you think he invited us to watch an orgy?" she asked.

"Maybe he wanted us to join in."

She sent him a sour look and he bit back a grin. Then he had a sudden image of her dressed in only a loincloth and he had to look away. He forced his mind back to the business at hand. "Let's wait a bit more and see what happens before we announce ourselves," he said.

The drums stopped and the two women took seats on either side of the circle. Metwater held up his hands to silence the crowd. "Tonight marks a very special night." His voice carried easily in the still night air, with the rounded tones and precise diction of an experienced orator. Those gathered around the fire listened raptly, eyes glowing, some with lips slightly parted.

"We gather under the light of the full moon to welcome a new member to our family." He continued with a flowery speech about the sacredness of family, the importance of connection and generally how superior they all were for having made the decision to join up with the Prophet. "Ours is a sacred bond of mind, body and spirit," he proclaimed. "We are united mentally, physically and in our souls. It is a union of our most sacred natures, and of our blood."

At this last, he pulled a large dagger from a sheath at his side and sliced the blade across his own palm. Kayla gasped, and Dylan put out a hand to restrain her.

Metwater turned away from them, toward the far side of the circle. "We begin, as always, with the sacrifice," he said.

Two men—Dylan thought he recognized Abe and Zach beneath the black-and-white greasepaint that streaked their faces—escorted a young woman to the center of the circle. She wore a long white robe, and her dark hair fell almost to her waist. Her face was ivory white in the moonlight, the flames reflecting in her glassy eyes.

Metwater kissed each of her cheeks in turn, then motioned for her to kneel. He held the dagger over his head, the blade still wet with his own blood, firelight glinting off the steel. "Persephone, you have agreed to sacrifice what is necessary to make our family whole," he intoned. Then he brought the blade down to rest at her throat.

Dylan didn't have to see any more. He drew his weapon and charged forward, Kayla at his heels. "Stop!" he shouted. "Drop the knife and step back with your hands up."

Chapter Ten

Kayla's heart pounded in rhythm with her racing feet as she followed Dylan toward the macabre scene around the fire. Daniel Metwater, blood dripping from the palm of one hand as he gripped the dagger with the other, turned toward them as the girl slumped to the ground beside him. The crowd of followers around the blaze stared, but none made a move as Dylan stopped and trained his gun on Metwater. "Drop the knife," he ordered.

Metwater opened his hand and let the knife fall. Kayla moved to the young woman and checked her pulse, which was strong. She moaned a little and stirred, and Kayla helped her sit up. "It's okay," she soothed. "You're okay."

"Put that gun away now, Officer!" Metwater's face glowed red in the firelight. "I invited you here tonight to witness the ceremony, not to disrupt it."

Dylan didn't waver. "Put your hands behind your back and turn around," he said. "You're under arrest."

"On what charge?" Metwater continued to glare at Dylan.

"For the attempted murder of that young woman." He nodded toward the woman who sat beside Kayla.

Metwater's laughter was loud and raucous. Others in the crowd joined him in the mocking mirth. Anger tightened Kayla's throat, and she read the same rage in Dylan's eyes. Keeping his gaze fixed on Metwater, Dylan addressed the young woman. "Ma'am, are you all right?"

"I'm fine." Now that she had recovered consciousness, Persephone—or whatever her real name was—seemed fine, a little pale maybe, but perfectly calm.

"Of course she's fine," Metwater said. "This was a ceremony, not a murder. Haven't you heard of symbolism, Lieutenant?" He moved to the young woman's side and helped her to her feet. Kayla could smell the sweat and blood on him, odors that made him seem even more primitive and wild. "Persephone and I were acting out the symbolic death of her old self. In the next phase, you would have seen her reborn into her new life with the Family."

Kayla became aware of others in the crowd moving closer. Out of the corner of her eyes, she spotted the two men who had served as Persephone's escorts moving around to flank her.

"Tell your guards to move back," Dylan said.

Metwater flicked his gaze toward the men. "Put away your gun. Your threat of violence has tainted our sacred proceedings."

Dylan holstered his weapon. Kayla joined him, anxious to put more distance between herself and Metwater. "You're one to talk of violence," she told him. "Considering you're bleeding all over the place."

Metwater studied his bleeding palm. "Every member of the Family has some of my blood mixed in their veins," he said. "Symbolizing that I am the father and protector of all."

Kayla wrinkled her nose, but said nothing.

"The ceremony is over." Dylan raised his voice to be heard by the crowd. "Go on back to your camps."

"The ceremony isn't over until I say it's over." Metwater handed Persephone off to one of the half-naked women he had danced with and started toward Dylan.

Kayla stiffened, and wished she'd brought her gun with her. If Dylan needed backup, she wasn't going to be of much use.

"Don't argue with me, Metwater," Dylan said. "I could still take you in for questioning."

"Questioning about what?"

"The murder of Special Agent Frank Asher, for one," Dylan said.

"I told you, I had nothing to do with Agent Asher's death."

"You and your followers are the only ones around," Dylan said. "Asher came here, probably to talk to Andi Matheson, possibly to try to talk her into leaving your group. Maybe you shot him in order to prevent that. Or maybe Asher had uncovered your secret, and you couldn't risk him exposing you."

"What secret? I don't have a secret." But fear flashed in Metwater's dark eyes, though the rest of his expression remained stony.

"Don't you?" Dylan turned to the young woman. "What's your real name?" he asked.

"P-Priscilla," she said. "Priscilla Ortega."

"How old are you, Priscilla?"

"I'm nineteen."

"Enough questions." Metwater stepped between

them. "Persephone has done nothing wrong." He motioned for the dancer to take the younger woman away and she did so. "You need to leave now also, Officer." He glanced at Kayla. "You may stay if you like, Miss Larimer."

Kayla didn't try to hide her disgust at the invitation. "I'm not one of your brainwashed devotees," she said.

"I'm going to remind you again that you're on public land," Dylan said.

Metwater folded his arms across his muscular chest and met Dylan's stern gaze. "This is our home, Officer. And you're not welcome here." With that, he turned his back on Dylan and stalked toward his trailer.

"Somebody put out this fire," Dylan called after him. "There's a burn ban on for the county."

Metwater raised one hand to indicate he had heard.

"I'm going to find out your secret," Dylan called. "And when I do, I'm going to tell all your followers the kind of man you really are."

Metwater stumbled, then caught himself and kept walking. But Kayla knew Dylan's words had gotten to the man. Daniel Metwater was definitely guilty of something. Whether his crime was murder or something else, Kayla intended to help expose him sooner rather than later.

KAYLA SHIVERED AND wrapped her arms around her shoulders, then leaned forward to punch up the blower on the heater in Dylan's Cruiser as they left the wilderness area and turned onto the paved highway leading back to Montrose. "I can't get that girl's face out of my mind," she said. "When Metwater held that knife to her throat, she was absolutely terrified. She believed he was going to kill her, no matter what he told us."

Dylan said nothing, but continued to stare out the windshield, both hands gripping the steering wheel, his body tense. "Well?" she prompted. "What do you think? Do you think he was really going to slit her throat?"

"I've been thinking about what you said earlier," he said.

"What I said?" She blinked. "What did I say?"

"That Metwater is trying to manipulate us."

"Of course he is. That's how people like him operate—how they keep control of any group of people or situation. He— Oh?" Dylan's meaning hit her. "Are you saying he staged that whole business with the knife and the so-called sacrifice for our benefit? That he wanted us to see it?"

"I don't know. But replaying everything in my mind, I think he knew we were standing there from the moment we arrived. And he must have ordered his bodyguards not to make a move, or they would have been on us like a shot."

"But why? So we would think he was capable of murder?" She shook her head. "That's twisted even for a guy who calls himself a prophet."

"Maybe he wanted us to look like a couple of idiots in front of his followers," Dylan said. "Or maybe it's sleight of hand—get us to focus on the perceived human sacrifice so we don't notice something else that's going on."

"So, what else is going on?" She turned down the heater, warmer at last as anger replaced some of her earlier shock. "I can't believe he didn't have something to do with Frank Asher's murder, but he's got a whole camp full of followers who will no doubt swear he was with all of them the morning Frank was shot."

"He could have ordered the hit."

"He could have. But good luck proving that."

"I'm going to do some more digging into his background and see what I come up with."

"Will you let me know what you find?" She leaned toward him, cutting off the objection she was sure he was about to make. "I'm in this with you right up to my ears," she said. "You can't cut me off now. And until Senator Matheson tells me otherwise, I'm still concerned about Andi. I have to figure out how involved she is in all of this."

"When I checked in with headquarters earlier, there was still no sign of the senator," Dylan said.

"How could a man in the public eye like the senator just disappear?" she asked. "Do the police think he was kidnapped—or killed?"

"There weren't any signs of foul play," Dylan said. "Maybe he just decided to take a break from public life. There isn't a law against that."

"Except that Senator Matheson thrives on being in the public eye. I read an article that listed him as one of the most media-savvy politicians."

"So maybe this is some kind of publicity stunt—disappear for a while to get people talking, then show up again."

"And say what—'surprise, I fooled you'?"

"He could say he'd been on a secret fact-finding mission or something. For all we know, he's in Mexico or the Caribbean right now, relaxing on the beach while we waste resources searching for him. Metwater isn't the only manipulator we're dealing with here, I think."

"Maybe." But something about that scenario bothered her. She searched for the words to voice her impressions of the senator. "He was waiting for me to give him my report about Andi. When he hired me, he seemed very anxious to know that she was all right. If he did plan to disappear as some kind of publicity stunt or ploy for attention, it doesn't make sense that he would do so before he heard back from me."

"Was he really concerned, or was he only pretending for your benefit?" Dylan asked.

"I think his worry was genuine." But how could she be sure? She shifted in her seat. "I haven't had that much personal experience with genuine parental devotion, but I'm pretty good at spotting fake emotions. All his pomposity and bombast softened when Senator Matheson spoke about his daughter. He talked a lot about how he had tried all his life to protect her and do what was best for her. How if only she would come back to him, he could give her everything she needed and deserved."

"That kind of love can be smothering to some people—especially a person Andi's age, who is trying to exert her independence."

Kayla nodded. "He said it would be enough to know she was safe, but I had the feeling that once I located her, he would try everything in his power to persuade her to return to him. Which is another reason I can't believe he would voluntarily disappear before he was sure of her safety."

"That investigation is out of our hands," Dylan said. "We have to worry about things closer to home. I'm going to do more digging into Frank Asher's and Daniel Metwater's backgrounds tomorrow."

"Hmm." She'd be doing the same, but there was no point telling him and hearing a lecture about not interfering in police business.

"If you find out anything interesting about either of them, I hope you'll share it with me," Dylan said.

She felt her face heat, and was grateful he couldn't see the flush in the darkness. "I might. If you'll do the same with me."

"Even twelve hours ago I probably would have said no, but I'm beginning to think the two of us make a great team and we'll accomplish more working together than at cross purposes."

This admission surprised her. "What changed your mind?"

"You did great back at the camp just now—and earlier today when we spoke with Andi and Metwater. You've got a cool head and good instincts, and I trust you to watch my back."

She fought back the surge of emotion that tightened her throat. Dylan didn't strike her as the type of person to throw around words like that casually. "Thank you," she managed to squeeze out.

"I hope you'll come to trust me," he said.

She rubbed a hand up and down her thigh. "I'm used to working alone." Depending on other people was too risky.

"I think the two of us make a good team," he said again. He cleared his throat. "I'd like to see more of you."

"I'll stay in touch. I want to know what you find out about Metwater and the rest."

"I meant after this case is resolved. I liked kissing you this afternoon. I'd like to do it again."

Her breath caught and her heart pounded, the memory of his lips on hers and his arms around her leaving her with the same warm, weak-kneed sensation that had overwhelmed her in the barn. "That was a mistake," she said.

"Why do you say that? I got the impression you enjoyed it, too," he said.

Yes, she had enjoyed kissing Dylan. More than she had enjoyed anything in a long while. But letting him get that close to her would only bring trouble. "I don't do relationships," she said. "I'm not good at them." No matter how promising things started, other people always let you down. Maybe that was part of being human, but she couldn't risk any more betrayals. Other people might be good at forgiving, but she wasn't.

"I think you underestimate yourself," he said. "Or maybe you underestimate me. I'm willing to take things slow."

She shook her head, then realized he might not be able to see her. "No. You're a great guy, but I prefer to keep things between us professional."

"So no more kisses?"

"No more." She had to hold back a sigh. The kiss really had been great, but kissing Dylan again would only lead to more kissing and hugging and caressing and… She shoved the thoughts away and sat up straighter. They were almost to the turnoff for her house. She wouldn't have to see Dylan again for a couple of days at least, and that time would allow her emotions to cool off and settle. When he had time to think about it, he would see the sense in keeping his distance from her, as well.

He switched on his blinker to make the left turn, waiting for an approaching car to pass. Behind them, headlights glowed in the distance. Kayla squinted and shielded her eyes from the glare in the side mirror. What was the guy behind them doing with his brights up? And he was driving awfully fast, wasn't he?

The car approaching in the opposite lane passed and Dylan took his foot off the brake, prepared to make the turn. But before he could act, the car behind them slammed into them, clipping the back bumper and sending the Cruiser spinning off the road and into the ditch. The air bags exploded, pressing Kayla back against the seat. Then she heard another sound—the metallic pop of bullets striking metal as someone fired into their vehicle.

Chapter Eleven

Dylan woke to flashing lights and the distant wail of a siren. Pain stabbed at his skull and he realized he was tilted at an odd angle. He blinked, trying to get his bearings. Something about asking Kayla to kiss him. Or telling her he wanted to kiss her… No, that wasn't it.

"Dylan? Dylan, are you okay?" Kayla's voice, strained with anxiety, cut through the fog in his head.

"I'm okay." He tried to shift his body and realized he was sandwiched between the expanded air bag and the back of his seat. "What happened?"

"A car, or maybe a truck, plowed into us from behind. I think they did it deliberately. And I thought I heard gunshots. Are you sure you're okay?"

He felt his head. No blood there, though he must have hit it against the side of the car when they crashed. "I'm fine. What about you? Are you all right?"

"A little banged up, but nothing broken. My door is wedged into the ditch, so I can't open it."

He felt at his side for his phone and dragged it out of its holster. "I'll call for help."

"I think someone's coming. I hear a siren."

The sound was getting closer, but the flashing lights were his own. He must have bumped the control during the crash.

Moments later, two emergency vehicles arrived, followed by a third. Red-and-blue lights strobed across the darkness, and moments later the beam of a flashlight played across Dylan's face. He winced and shielded his eyes from the light as someone yanked open his door.

"Don't try to move," the responding officer said. "Not until the paramedic has checked you out."

"I think I just have a bump on the head." Dylan shoved his phone back into its holster. There would be time enough later to call the captain.

"You part of the Ranger Brigade?" the officer asked, glancing at the logo on the side of the Cruiser.

"Yes. Lieutenant Dylan Holt with the Colorado State Patrol."

A paramedic, young with a dark goatee, joined the officer, directing his flashlight beam over Dylan and Kayla. "How are you doing, miss?" he asked.

"I'm okay," she said. "Just a little shaken up, and I can't get out of the car."

"We'll help you in just a minute." The paramedic turned to Dylan. "Any pain or obvious injuries?"

"Just my head." He touched the knot on his forehead. "Nothing broken."

"You climb out then, and we'll see about getting to your passenger."

Dylan climbed out of the car, the officer and a second paramedic helping. They led him to an ambulance, where he submitted to an examination.

"What happened?" the officer, a middle-aged African American whose badge identified him as Officer Lejeune, asked.

Dylan took a moment to organize his thoughts, though most of his initial fog had cleared. "I was stopped, waiting to make a left turn, when a vehicle plowed into me from behind," he said. He kept his gaze on the Cruiser, where the first paramedic and another officer were helping Kayla climb out. "The other vehicle clipped my back bumper and we spun out of control. I hit my head and must have been out for a minute. Maybe a little longer."

"So whoever hit you fled the scene?" Officer Lejeune asked.

"I guess so." He thought about what Kayla had said—about hearing shots fired. If that was true, why hadn't whoever had targeted them stayed around to finish the job?

"Another driver called it in," Lejeune said. "She said the other vehicle was speeding and plowed right into you, then sped away."

"Did she mention any gunshots?" Dylan asked.

Lejeune and the paramedic exchanged glances. "Gunshots?"

"Someone was firing at us. I'm sure that's what I heard." Kayla limped toward them, moving ahead of the men supporting her.

Dylan shoved aside the paramedic, who was trying to apply an ice pack to the knot on his head, and hurried to her. "You're hurt," he said.

"I just banged my knee. I'll be fine." But she didn't push him away and leaned into him when he put his arm around her.

"I'll take a look at the car," Lejeune said, and strode off.

Dylan escorted Kayla to the ambulance and sat beside her as the paramedic bent to examine her knee. "Did you get a good look at the vehicle that hit us?" he asked.

"No. The brights were on—though I had the impression it was big. Maybe a pickup truck or a big SUV?" She shook her head. "It happened so fast."

The two police officers returned. "We found what could be bullet holes in the driver's-side door," Lejeune said. "Small caliber."

"You're lucky whoever ran you down didn't have a bigger gun or wasn't a better shot," the second officer, Raybourn, said.

"Whoever it was, I don't think they were trying to kill us," Dylan said. "They wanted to scare us."

"They scared me," Kayla admitted. "But they also made me mad. I never have liked bullies."

"You think this has to do with a case you're investigating?" Lejeune asked.

"Maybe." Dylan pulled out his phone again. "I'm going to get someone from my team to check out the Cruiser, see what we can find."

He stepped away to make his call while the paramedics finished checking Kayla. His stomach churned as he stared at the car on its side in the ditch, the back end smashed.

Graham answered on the fourth ring. "Hello, Lieutenant," he said, as calm and alert as if the call had come at midday, instead of after ten at night.

"Kayla Larimer and I were on our way back to town from Daniel Metwater's camp and someone ran us off the road," Dylan said. "They took a couple of shots at us, too."

"Are you all right?" Graham asked, his voice sharper. "Is Kayla all right?"

"We're a little banged up, but okay. I'd like a team to come check out the Cruiser and the area, see if we can come up with any clues."

"We'll send someone. Did you get a look at who did this?"

"No. A woman called in the accident, but it doesn't sound like she got a good look, either, though we'll want to talk to her."

"Do you think it was one of Metwater's followers?"

"Maybe." The hit-and-run was the kind of impulsive lashing out he might expect from the mostly young members of the group, but Metwater himself didn't strike him as that sloppy.

"What were you doing at his camp?" Graham asked.

"He invited us, actually, to observe some kind of ceremony." Dylan rubbed his throbbing head. "I'll give you my report later. Right now, I need to see about getting Kayla home. Then I'll wait here with the Cruiser."

"I'll have someone out there as soon as I can. If we find anything that links this to Metwater's group, you can be sure we'll be hauling them all in for questioning."

Dylan ended the call and stowed the phone, then walked back to Kayla. "I'll find someone to give you a ride home," he said. "I need to wait here."

"Officer Raybourn has already offered me a ride." She rested her hand on Dylan's arm. "Are you sure you're okay? That knot on your head looks like it hurts."

He gingerly touched the swelling. "I'll be okay. My dad always did say I had a hard head."

"I liked your parents," she said. "I forgot to thank you for taking me to meet them. I really enjoyed it."

"I enjoyed it, too." He rested his palm on her shoulder, giving her the chance to pull away, but hoping she wouldn't. "You're welcome to visit anytime."

"Hmm." She looked down, but didn't shift away or remove her hand from his arm. "I'm glad you weren't seriously hurt," she said. "When I first called your name and you didn't answer…" She let her voice trail away.

"I know. I'm glad you're not hurt, too." He brought his hand up to cup the side of her face, then bent and kissed her—just a gentle brush of his lips across hers. She let out a sigh and leaned into him, returning the kiss for a brief moment before pulling away.

"I'm not sure how to handle you," she said. "I'd better go." She turned away and hurried toward where Raybourn and Lejeune waited.

"You're doing a fine job so far," Dylan said softly.

EVERYTHING ACHED WHEN Kayla woke the next morning. She dragged herself into a hot shower, then chased two ibuprofen with a cup of strong tea. She was still sore, but felt able to get to work. She headed to the spare room that served as her home office and flipped through the mail that had accumulated in the last few days. She had been so busy dealing with Senator Matheson and Andi that she hadn't gotten around to reading it.

An envelope from the Colorado Private Investigators Society caught her attention and she slit it open, then unfolded the single sheet of heavy cream-colored paper inside.

Dear Ms. Larimer,

We are pleased to inform you that you have been selected as this year's Western Slope Private Investigator of the Year. You will be one of the honorees at the Colorado Western Region Honors Banquet in Grand Junction on August 23.

Please RSVP to the email address below and indicate if you will be bringing a guest.

Congratulations on your honor,
Madeline Zimeski, President

Kayla stared at the letter, annoyed. She hadn't even known there was a Western Slope Private Investigator of the Year. Who had nominated her? And she had to attend a banquet. Did this mean she'd have to buy a fancy dress? And shoes?

She put the letter aside and forced herself to work on a background check for a legal firm she did small jobs for, then started on a report on some surveillance she'd done on a straying husband the week before. But her mind kept straying back to Andi Matheson, the missing senator and enigmatic Daniel Metwater.

The image of him, almost naked and gleaming in the firelight, blood dripping from his hands as he held the dagger to that young woman's throat, would stay with her for a long time, she imagined. Being around him put her on edge, maybe because he reminded her too much of her own father—handsome and charismatic, good at reading people and promising them what they wanted, or exploiting their weaknesses.

What weakness had he exploited in Andi? Maybe he had painted a picture of the Family as a safe refuge in which she could raise her baby. On his side, he had a recruit with money. At twenty-four, Andi had her own funds. Had she signed them over to Metwater? Or maybe the Prophet merely liked having a senator's daughter in his retinue. Could Metwater be linked to the senator's disappearance?

She jotted these questions into a notebook she kept open on her desk, then pulled out her phone. Time to do a little more digging.

"Hello?" The young woman on the other end of the line sounded sleepy.

"Tessa? It's Kayla Larimer—the private detective who was trying to find Andi Matheson."

"Oh, uh, hi." Tessa sounded more awake, but wary. "Did you find her?"

"I did. You were right in thinking she'd hooked up with that spiritual group you mentioned—the Family."

"The one with that hot guy, right?" Tessa snorted. "I knew it. That night we met I could tell he was really into her. That was the problem with going anywhere with Andi. All the men ended up looking at her. I might as well have been invisible."

"The hot guy is Daniel Metwater, the leader of the group. He calls himself the Prophet."

Tessa yawned. "I remember now. He talked a lot about personal freedom and connecting with nature and building a true family—Andi ate it all up. I figured he just wanted to get into her pants."

"So Daniel Metwater didn't impress you?" Kayla asked.

"He was really hot, but he knew it. I mean, he had all these women fawning over him and he acted like that was just the way it should be. And all his talk about family and connection and everything didn't do anything for me. I already have a family, and the whole reason people build houses is to keep nature at a distance, right?"

Kayla smiled. She supposed that was one way to look at it. "Why do you think Andi was so interested in what he had to say?" she asked. "She had a family, too, and what looked like a pretty nice life."

"She had a nice life, but lately she and her dad were on the outs."

"Do you know why she and her father weren't getting along?"

"Oh, the usual—he still treated her like a child, always trying to tell her what to do and how to act and how to live her life. She hated that. But that wasn't really anything new. The senator was always a little…I'd call it overprotective. I think she even liked it sometimes, how she could crook her little finger and Daddy would come running. I saw on the news about her dad disappearing. Even though they weren't getting along, I'll bet Andi's pretty upset about that."

She hadn't appeared to be, but Kayla didn't bother going into that. "You said Andi and her dad not getting along wasn't anything new, so what was different this time? What made her want to break ties with her father altogether?"

"I'm really not sure. I think it might have had something to do with the guy she was seeing last year."

Kayla sat up straighter. "Who was that?"

"I never met him. Andi said he was an older man, and he worked for her father. It was all very mysterious. I told her I bet he was married, since he never wanted to be seen in public with her. She said it was because her father wouldn't approve, but it turned out I was right."

"You mean the man *was* married?" Kayla asked. No one had mentioned Agent Asher having a wife.

"Kayla told me he had a wife and three kids right here in Denver. She was furious when she found out—but not half as furious as her father. He fired the guy and lit into Andi. She decided she didn't want to have anything to do with either one of them. I think that's one reason this Daniel guy's spiel about getting away from it all and starting over appealed to her. Did she tell you she was pregnant?"

"Yes, she told me."

"So you can't blame her for wanting a better life for her baby—something more peaceful. Is she doing okay with Daniel and his group?"

"She's healthy and she seems content." No sense going into the news of Frank Asher's death.

"I'm glad. If you see her again, tell her I said hi. And thanks for letting me know you found her."

"Sure." That wasn't the reason she had called, but it was okay with her if Tessa thought so.

They said their goodbyes and Kayla ended the call.

So Andi hadn't told her and Dylan the whole story about her relationship with Frank Asher. He wasn't just her former lover and the father of her child, but a man who had betrayed her, in a big way. Had he hurt her enough to make her want to hurt him in return?

She stared at her phone, then scrolled to Dylan's number. He answered right away. "Hey," he said. "How are you feeling this morning?"

"Like I've been run over by a truck. How about you?"

"The same. And you're right about it being a truck, or at least we're pretty sure." Wind noise and the muffled rumble of traffic told her he was outside. She pictured him standing on the side of the road by the damaged Cruiser—or maybe back at Ranger Brigade headquarters in the park. "We found some paint scrapes on the Cruiser and they match up to the height of a pickup—probably with one of those heavy-duty brush guards on the front."

"Any idea who was driving?"

"Not yet. But we're going to keep digging. Have you given your statement to the Montrose Police yet?"

"It's on my list for this morning. I told Officers Raybourn and Lejeune I'd stop by."

"It would be good if you could swing by here and give us a formal statement, too. Just in case this turns out to be connected to Metwater and the Family."

"Sure. I could do that." She fought the urge to ask if he would be there. She wanted to see him again, but didn't want to appear too eager. "I've found something else for you to dig into," she said instead.

"Oh? Hang on a minute. Let me get where I can

hear you better." She waited while he walked somewhere. She heard a door open and close, then everything was quieter. "Okay, what's up?"

"I talked to Tessa Madigan this morning—Andi's friend who told me about their meeting with Metwater and the Family."

"I remember. You said a friend of hers told you about Andi's interest in Metwater."

"Right. I asked her why Andi wanted to join the group—what had made her so upset she would leave her comfortable life behind. Tessa said she thought it had something to do with the man she had been dating before."

"Frank Asher?"

"Tessa didn't know his name. She said the relationship was very secretive. Turns out there was a good reason for that."

"And are you going to tell me the reason or make me play a game of twenty questions?"

"Patience, Lieutenant. Tessa said the reason Andi and this guy split was because Andi found out he had a wife and three kids in Denver."

Dylan let out a low whistle. "I guess that made her furious. But if that man was Asher, was she angry enough to shoot him and leave him lying in the desert?"

"I have a hard time believing it, considering how big a shock the news seemed to be to her."

"Maybe she's a good actress," Dylan said.

"Or maybe there's another woman you should consider."

He was silent for a moment, then said, "The wife."

"If I found out my husband and the father of our

three children was sneaking around with another woman I might want to put an end to the relationship," Kayla said.

"And maybe a permanent end to him," Dylan agreed.

Chapter Twelve

Dylan stepped out to where the techs were finishing their examination of his Cruiser, which they had towed to headquarters from the scene of the accident. Simon walked over to meet him. "We got some chips of the paint," he said, and held out an evidence bag with three black contact-lens-sized fragments. "But they're going to be tough to match without a suspect vehicle."

"I'm thinking we should drive out to Metwater's camp and look for a black truck with a brush guard on the front," Dylan said.

"We will," Simon said. "But before we do, I have something else to show you."

Dylan fell into step with him as they crossed the parking lot toward Ranger Brigade headquarters. Graham met them at the door. "I was finally able to pry some more information from the FBI about Special Agent Asher and what he might have been doing here," he said.

"I thought he took personal time to come here," Dylan said.

"He did, but apparently before that he was looking into David Metwater's mob connections," Graham said.

"The twin brother, right?" Simon said.

"Right. Maybe the picture in Asher's car wasn't of Daniel Metwater, but of David."

"So you think Asher came here to talk to Metwater about his dead brother?" Dylan asked.

"Or his investigation of David turned up some dirt on Daniel." Simon strode across the room and snatched a folder off the corner of his desk. "I've been digging into the files on Asher's laptop," he said. "Pulling off as much as I can before the Feds take it away."

"Anything that will help us?" Dylan asked.

Simon flipped through the papers in the file folder. "Mostly they're notes about the Metwater brothers—everything from bank account information to some surveillance footage of either Daniel or David. I haven't figured out what it all means yet, but I will."

"So Asher may have been coming to the camp to talk to Daniel about his brother, or because he had learned something about Daniel himself, or was just generally snooping around," Dylan said. "Or he wanted to see Andi. He told her when he saw her in town that he had to talk to her."

"Maybe Asher wanted to warn her about Metwater," Graham said. "Maybe he thought she was in danger."

"Turned out Asher was the one in danger." Simon closed the folder. "Metwater may have decided to shut him up."

"Where do the two guys who attacked Kayla outside Asher's hotel room come in?" Dylan asked.

"We don't know," Graham said. "The guy who lived—Bob Casetti—is still in the hospital. He's apparently lawyered up and not talking."

Simon grunted. "When do we get to talk to him?"

"As soon as his doctor gives the okay. Meanwhile, Montrose PD is keeping a guard on his room."

"Does this Casetti have a record?" Dylan asked.

"He's been in and out of prison since he was eighteen, with sealed juvenile records before that. But mostly property crimes and drugs. No kidnapping or rape or even assault. This definitely breaks the pattern for him."

"So we ought to be able to put some pressure on him and make him talk," Simon said.

"Do you think the attack on me and Kayla last night was connected to Casetti and his dead pal kidnapping Kayla at the hotel?" Dylan asked. Getting roughed up twice in two days was too much for coincidence. "Maybe it wasn't me who was the target last night at all, but Kayla."

"It's possible," Graham said.

"Then it's not safe for her to be alone." Pushing back the icy fear that threatened to overtake him, Dylan pulled his phone from his pocket. "I'll call and tell her I'm on my way to pick her up. We've got a vehicle I can borrow, right?"

Graham put a steadying hand on Dylan's arm. "I'll send Carmen to get her and bring her here. She can give us a statement about what happened last night, and you can take over evening guard duty if you want. But right now I want you and Simon out at the camp looking for the truck that ran you off the road."

“They’ve probably ditched it in the desert by now,” Simon said.

“Maybe, but maybe not.” Graham squeezed Dylan’s shoulder, then released him. “Keep digging. If we can find a motive for Metwater to want Asher dead, we can bring him in for questioning. And let’s take a closer look at Andi Matheson, too. Maybe she did meet with Asher and the conversation didn’t go well.”

“Did you know that Frank Asher was married?” Dylan asked.

“Why is that important?” Simon asked. “The FBI is taking care of notifying his next of kin.”

“It’s important because, apparently, Asher is the father of Andi Matheson’s unborn child,” Dylan said. “When Andi found out he was married, she broke off the relationship.”

“So she might have been angry enough to shoot him when he came around to see her,” Graham said.

“Maybe,” Dylan said. “Though we have a lot of witnesses who place her in the camp at the time he was probably shot. And she seemed genuinely shocked when she found out he had been killed.”

“We should take a closer look at her alibi,” Graham said.

“We will,” Dylan agreed. “But I want to question Asher’s widow, too. I’d like to drive over to Denver tomorrow and find out if she—or someone she might have hired—decided to take a trip to the park about the time her late husband was killed.”

“Do it.” Graham shook his head. “Usually with a murder you have trouble coming up with one likely suspect. Frank Asher had any number of people who might have good reasons for wanting him dead.”

"ARE YOU AS sick as I am of making the drive out here?" Simon asked as he steered his Cruiser onto the rough BLM two-track.

"Yeah." Dylan slumped in his seat and tugged the brim of his hat lower to block the midday sun glaring off the rocks that lined the road. "And I hate being out of phone range if anything happens." Before leaving Ranger headquarters, he'd called Kayla to tell her to stay put, but she had cut off his explanation, telling him she didn't have time to talk, as she was just arriving at the Montrose Police Station. Rather than argue with her, he'd called a buddy at the PD and asked them to keep Kayla there until Carmen could show up to escort her to Ranger Headquarters.

"The captain mentioned something about you and that detective driving out here last night," Simon said as they jounced along the road. "What was she doing with you?"

"Andi had asked to see Kayla yesterday afternoon, and I went with her to tell Andi that her father was missing. When Metwater discovered us, he invited us to the induction ceremony later that night."

"Why involve a civilian?" Simon asked.

"Andi knows Kayla and they seem to have established a rapport. And she knows how to handle herself. She doesn't interfere."

"She's still a civilian."

"A civilian who is helping with our investigation."

"That's one way to look at it, I guess."

They passed the rest of the drive in silence. Dylan stared out the window of the Cruiser, nursing his anger and annoyance, not to mention a headache from where he had hit his head in the crash last night. By the time Simon parked outside the camp, Dylan was more than ready to lash out at someone for all the trouble he'd been through.

"What do you think? Look around, or talk to Metwater first?" Simon asked.

"Look around." Dylan led the way down the trail into the canyon. Kiram wasn't on guard duty today. The skinny youth who was took one look at the two grim-faced officers and melted back into the rocks.

"He probably went to tell Metwater we're here," Simon said.

"Saves us the trouble," Dylan said.

The camp was quiet, the heat shimmering off the rocks oppressive. The few people Dylan spotted were lying in hammocks in the shade or lounging in tents or makeshift brush-covered shelters. The two officers walked the length of the camp to the narrowest part of the canyon, where a few rattier tents and a lean-to made of old wooden produce crates were crowded among a collection of dilapidated cars and trucks. The intense sun had faded most of the paper labels on the flattened crates, but Dylan could still make out images of plump red tomatoes and green peppers.

A clank of metal on metal drew them around a tarp-covered shed to where two men dressed only in dirty khaki shorts leaned under the open hood of a black pickup truck with a heavy brush guard attached to the front bumper.

"Something wrong with the truck?" Dylan asked.

Zach Crenshaw jerked his head up, eyes wide, mouth open. Across from him, Abe Phillips held up the wrench. "What do you want with us, man?" he asked, his voice a nasal whine that set Dylan's teeth on edge.

"I want to know why you tried to run me down last night." Dylan took a step closer, backing the young man up against the truck and blocking his escape.

"We don't know what you're talking about." Zach had shut his mouth and regained some of his color. He motioned to the truck. "We were just trying to get this old thing running again."

"It was running fine last night when it forced my Cruiser off the road," Dylan said.

"This truck hasn't moved from this spot in a month!" Abe declared. "It doesn't even run. See for yourself." He beckoned them closer and Dylan looked under the hood at a tangle of wires and hoses, and what looked like handfuls of straw and other debris. "A pack rat built a nest in here." Abe pulled out a wad of dried grass. "Ate the wiring harness and made a mess. I haven't had a chance to get it fixed."

"Is that so?" Simon pulled out a multitool and began scraping at the brush guard, a welded pipe cage around the front grill that seemed to have more rust than paint.

"Hey, what are you doing?" Zach asked.

"I'm collecting a sample of this paint to match with the chips we took from Lieutenant Holt's Cruiser after someone ran him off the road night before last."

"It wasn't me," Abe said. "I told you, this truck hasn't moved."

"Then you don't have anything to worry about." Simon slipped the paint chips into an evidence bag and sealed it, while Dylan walked around the vehicle and took photographs from every angle.

"Why do you people always want to hassle us?" Zach asked. "We aren't doing anything but trying to live in peace."

"I wouldn't say you're doing a very good job of that so far," Dylan said. He stowed the camera. "Did Metwater put you up to going after us last night, or was that your own idea?"

Zach swore and turned away. Abe flushed. "I told you, it wasn't us," he said. "The truck's been out of commission for weeks. I'm trying to get it running again so I can go into town."

"And do what?" Dylan asked.

"I don't know. Buy a burger and a beer. See a movie." He looked around. "Anything's better than being stuck here in the desert all the time."

"I thought this place was the Family's version of paradise," Dylan said. He kicked the front tire of the truck. "Funny that there's what looks like fresh mud and gravel in the treads of these tires, if it's just been sitting here for weeks." He sent Abe a warning look, then turned away.

"Where are you going?" Zach asked.

"To talk to Metwater."

"Don't worry, we'll be back," Simon said.

The two officers made their way toward Metwater's trailer. "So, is that the truck?" Simon asked.

"It fits the profile," Dylan said. "Though the engine did look pretty shot."

"Anyone could yank out a bunch of wires and throw in some grass and trash," Simon said.

"Even a paint match isn't going to prove anything," Dylan said. "Not if they stick to their story."

"They'll cave," Simon said. "Pointing out that fresh

gravel was a nice touch. We'll lean on them some more after we talk to Metwater and we'll be hauling them back to headquarters before you know it."

"I'd rather have Metwater in handcuffs than his two flunkies," Dylan said.

"Get them into an interview room and maybe they'll spill something incriminating." They mounted the steps to Metwater's trailer and Simon knocked. No answer. He knocked again. "Metwater, this is the police. Open up!"

Silence. And no sound of movement within. Dylan moved to the tent next door. "Andi! Andi, it's Dylan Holt. Could I talk to you a minute?"

The tent flap lifted, but instead of Andi, Starfall stood in the opening. "Andi isn't here," she said.

"Where is she?"

"She said she was going for a walk." She scowled at them. "Why can't you leave her alone? She hasn't done anything to hurt anyone."

"Are you sure about that?" Simon asked.

Starfall only scowled harder.

"Do you know where Daniel Metwater is?" Dylan asked. "Did he go walking with Andi?"

"The Prophet left early this morning," she said. "If you want to talk to him, you'll have to wait until he gets back."

"Where did he go?" Simon asked.

"He speaks at gatherings around the country. I don't know where he went this time. It's not my business to know."

"When will he return?" Dylan asked.

"I don't know. It could be this evening or tomorrow or a week from now."

"Maybe he skipped out on you," Simon said.

Her eyes widened. "The Prophet would never desert us," she said.

Dylan could tell Simon was prepared to argue the point, but he cut in. "Do you know anything about Zach and Abe taking their truck out last night after the ceremony?"

She took a step back. "I don't know anything."

"You didn't see them?" Simon asked. "They ran Lieutenant Holt and the woman he was with off the road. Trashed a government vehicle and injured a law officer and a civilian. They could have been killed. If your Prophet thinks this is a good way to get us to leave him alone, he's not even half as smart as he looks."

"I don't know what you're talking about." Starfall let the tent flap fall closed.

Simon reached for it, but Dylan stayed his hand. "That's enough. We've given everyone here a lot to think about. We'll come back later when we can talk to Metwater."

"What about the truck?" Simon asked as they retraced their steps to the car.

"You heard them—it hasn't run in months."

"They might take off in it and try to run."

"They won't get far."

Simon unlocked the Cruiser and they climbed in. "Do you think Metwater was feeling the heat and skipped town? Maybe with Andi Matheson?"

Dylan fastened his seat belt. "Anything's possible, but I don't think so. Maybe it's like she said—he's off speaking somewhere. That's one of the ways he recruits followers."

"I read some of his blog and the stuff on his website." Simon started the engine. "All about family and peace and harmony. I guess that appeals to some people."

Dylan almost laughed. "But not you?"

Simon scowled. "I live in the real world. I don't need a fantasy like that."

"Careful, Simon. You might be turning into a stereotype of a jaded cop."

"Bite me, Holt."

"I'll pass." He settled back in the seat. "We'll check in with Andi and Metwater tomorrow. If they're not around then, we can start a search. Until then, I think all we can do is wait."

Chapter Thirteen

When Kayla emerged from the Montrose Police Station after giving her statement about the previous night's hit-and-run, she was surprised to find a Ranger Brigade Cruiser snugged in beside her Subaru. Her heart beat a little faster and she quickened her pace, faltering when Carmen Redhorse emerged from the driver's seat. Then her elation edged toward panic. "What are you doing here?" she asked. "Is Dylan okay?"

"Dylan's fine." Carmen's smile was warm. "I'm here to give you a ride to Ranger headquarters so you can give us your statement. I know all this paperwork is a pain, but it's important in helping us build a case."

"I can drive myself." She started toward her car, but Carmen stepped in front of her.

"You can, but this is easier. We can swing by your place and you can drop off your car. How are you feeling? That's a nasty bruise on your face."

Kayla touched the bruise she had received two days before in her struggle with the kidnappers. It was only a little tender now. "I'm okay. What is this really about? Did Dylan send you here?" And if he had, why?

"I take my orders from Captain Ellison, not the lieutenant. Considering you've been attacked twice in the past two days, he thought it would be a good idea to keep an eye on you."

"Why?"

Carmen wasn't smiling anymore—she looked pained. "I don't want to frighten you, but you might be in danger."

Kayla wanted to scoff at the idea, but the full meaning of Carmen's words was beginning to sink in. "Wait a minute. Do you—or the captain—think *I* was the target last night? I thought whoever hit us was going after the Cruiser. Did you find the driver? Did he tell you he was after me?"

"We don't know anything yet. We're just being careful."

"I can be careful at home." She started for her car again and this time Carmen let her open the door and slide into the driver's seat.

But when she tried to shut the door, the other woman put a hand out to stop her. "We need you to make a statement, anyway, so you might as well hang out with me for a few hours," she said.

"And then what?" Kayla asked.

The smile returned. "And then I think the captain is assigning Dylan to the night shift."

The words sent a tickle of pleasure up her spine. "I get the idea I don't really have a choice in the matter."

"We're not forcing you, but everyone would feel better if you'd come with us."

Kayla blew out a breath. If she did go home, she'd only sit there and stew. At least at Ranger headquarters she might find out more about what was going on. "All right. You can follow me to my place."

She left her car in the driveway, then joined Carmen in her Cruiser. "I really don't need a bodyguard," she said as she slid into the passenger seat.

Carmen shifted into gear and backed into the street. "Hey, I'm a tough cop and even I think it would be nice sometime to have a good-looking man worried about me," she said.

"You don't have a boyfriend?" Kayla asked, then immediately wished she could take the words back. She hated when people asked her that kind of question. "Sorry, none of my business."

"That's okay. It's a natural question. Let's just say the badge gets in the way of relationships for a lot of men. And even though I'm around men all day, it's not a good idea to get involved with anyone on the job. So that leaves, what—suspects? A few witnesses?" She shook her head. "I'm young. Someone will come along."

"I like being single," Kayla said. "I like making my own decisions and looking after myself."

"Oh, I agree," Carmen said. "It's lonely sometimes, though."

Yes, it was lonely sometimes. She hadn't often felt that way, but since she had let Dylan into her life, his absence left a space she hadn't noticed being empty before.

Ranger Brigade headquarters was a bustle of activity, though Dylan was nowhere in sight. Carmen led Kayla to her desk, where she coached her through her statement about the previous day's activities, beginning with that morning's encounters with Andi Matheson and Daniel Metwater, up to the moment of the crash. "I don't know how much good any of that will be for you," Kayla said when they were done. "I only had an impression of a fairly large vehicle, and that the driver didn't slow down, but hit us deliberately, then sped away."

"It's all part of the record," Carmen said. "Another piece in the puzzle."

The door opened and Simon entered, followed by Dylan. He spotted her right away and nodded, before turning to address Captain Ellison. "We found the truck," he said. "Can we get a warrant to impound it?"

"We can try," Ellison said. "Where is it?"

"At the camp. The two guys who were with it, Abelard Phillips and Zach Crenshaw, say it hasn't run in weeks, but I found fresh mud in the tire treads, and the color and profile fit what we're looking for. Simon got some paint samples."

"I'll get started on the warrant request," Simon said, and headed for his desk.

Dylan joined the two women. "How are you doing?" he asked Kayla. He brushed the tips of his fingers lightly over her bruised cheek.

"I'm fine." She tried to ignore the tremor of awareness his touch sent through her. "I don't need babysitting."

"Maybe not. But it will make me feel better."

She was trying to come up with a snappy retort when the door to headquarters burst open and two young men in dirty shorts and T-shirts, their faces sunburned, their hair windblown, burst in. "We want to confess," the taller of the two said. "And then we need your help."

ZACH AND ABE looked more pitiful than dangerous as Dylan and Ethan patted them down and led them to separate desks to give their statements. Dylan ended up with Abe, who limped to the chair Dylan offered and dropped into it with a groan. "We had to walk most of the way from camp before somebody gave us a ride," he said. "I think my blisters have blisters."

"Why didn't you drive your truck?" Dylan asked, taking his own seat behind the desk.

"That's why we need your help," Abe said. "The Prophet stole it. He can't do that, right? It's my truck. My name's on the title and everything, but he says it belongs to the Family now—along with everything else we brought with us, except what we could carry out with us."

"You talked to Daniel Metwater?" Dylan asked. "I thought he was out of town."

"He came back right after you left. Him and Asteria. I guess they only went up to Grand Junction or something. Anyway, Starfall must have blabbed that you were there and why, and he kicked us out. Told us to get whatever we could carry—but nothing else—and hit the road." He leaned toward Dylan. "That's stealing, right? We can file charges, can't we?"

"Why don't we start at the beginning," Dylan said. "You said you wanted to confess to something?"

Abe sank back in his chair. "Yeah, that." He

glanced around nervously. "Promise you're not going to beat me up or anything?"

"Just tell me what happened." Dylan had no intention of hurting the kid, but a little fear might persuade him to be more cooperative.

"After you interrupted the ceremony last night we were really ticked off that you kept hassling everybody. We're just out here trying to live in peace and you keep poking your nose where it doesn't belong."

"So you decided to teach us a lesson."

"Well..." He looked away.

"Did Daniel Metwater know what you intended?"

"We told him someone needed to do something, and he agreed."

"Did he tell you to follow us?"

"No. But we thought he approved. We thought it would be a good way to impress him." Abe looked glum. "I guess we should have known better."

"What happened?"

"Zach and I got in my truck and followed you out onto the highway. Then we rammed you and sent you into the ditch. We just wanted to shake you up and make you think twice about hassling us. We didn't mean to hurt anyone or anything."

"Why did you shoot at us?"

Abe flushed. "I was trying to shoot out the tires, but I guess I'm not a very good shot."

"You told me before that you didn't have a gun. That the Prophet didn't allow it."

"Yeah, well, last time we went into town I bought one, anyway. He's got a gun, and I was tired of eating so much tofu and vegetables. Not when the place is crawling with rabbits."

"Where is the gun now?"

"The Prophet made me hand it over to him. I mean, we were trying to help him and he raked us over the coals."

"You said he kicked you out?"

"Yeah. He said we were troublemakers. First with that guy who died, then this."

"What about the guy who died? Why did Metwater blame you for what happened to him?"

"Not for what happened to him, but for bringing him into camp. He said it caused bad juju and that was the reason the cops were around all the time. But we couldn't have just left him in the desert for the buzzards. That's just cold."

"What was Metwater doing this afternoon, while he was away from the camp?" Dylan asked.

"I don't know. Only those in his inner circle—his favorites—ever know what he's up to." Abe gave a snorting laugh. "We don't have the right chromosomes for that, if you know what I mean."

"You're not women."

"Right. He needs guys around for security and heavy lifting, but it's really the chicks he likes. We thought when we joined up we'd have access to all these hot women, but the Prophet keeps them all for himself."

"You say he was with Andi Matheson this afternoon?"

"Who?"

"Asteria."

"Oh, yeah. They were all cozy and laughing. She's definitely one of the inner circle. So can you help us get our stuff back? I mean, he can't just take it, can he?"

Dylan gave him a hard look. "You're confessing to attacking a law enforcement officer and you expect us to help you get your stuff back?"

He squirmed. "Well, yeah. We're pleading guilty in exchange for a deal."

"What kind of deal?"

He leaned forward again and lowered his voice. "We know a lot of dirt on the Prophet. We tell you what we know in exchange for…what do you call it—like a flu shot?"

"Immunity?"

"Right, immunity."

"What do you know about the Prophet?"

"Good stuff, I promise. The guy might look snowy white outside, but he's definitely not."

"You're going to have to be more specific than that if you want to avoid going to jail."

Abe went pale under his sunburn at the word *jail*. "Well, like, everybody who joins the Family has to sign a contract that says all the property you have belongs to the group, but what it really means is that it belongs to the Prophet. But that can't be legal, right?"

"If you signed the contract willingly, it might."

"People only sign it because he promises all this stuff—eternal riches and joy and peace, things like that. And then you end up living in the middle of nowhere on tofu, sleeping in tents, and the hot girls won't even give you the time of day."

"I'm going to need more than that if I'm going to persuade the district attorney to cut you a deal," Dylan said.

"Aww, man! We don't have to get attorneys involved, do we?"

Dylan remained silent, arms crossed over his chest.

Abe sighed. "All right. How about this? His name isn't even Daniel Metwater."

"No?" Dylan raised one eyebrow.

"No. I was in his RV one time and I saw a bunch of papers and his driver's license, in a folder on his desk. They all said *David* Metwater. Not Daniel, see? Maybe if you run that name through your computers, you'll find out he has a criminal record or something."

"He had a twin brother named David. The brother died. It wouldn't be that unusual for him to have kept his brother's papers."

Abe looked crestfallen.

"Where was Metwater the morning you and Zach found that man's body?" Dylan asked.

"He was in the camp."

"You saw him?"

"Yeah. Right before we went hunting. He was eating breakfast with Asteria and Starfall and a bunch of others."

"What was he doing before that?"

Zach scowled. "We all had to get up early for this sunrise ceremony. He's big into that kind of thing. I mean, the middle of the night, practically, he expects us all to get up and dance around and chant, and then he delivers a 'message.' After a while it's just the same stuff over and over."

"Sounds like you were getting pretty disillusioned by the whole experience," Dylan said.

"Well, yeah. I mean, I like some of his ideas, and I really don't mind the camping out and stuff, but I thought it would be more fun. And that there would be more women—or at least women who would give me the time of day."

Dylan slid back his chair and rose. "I'll see what I can do, Abe, but I'm not making any promises."

He left to confer with Graham, but on his way he stopped by Carmen's desk to speak with Kayla. "Anything interesting?" she asked, nodding toward Abe.

"I think he found out being part of Metwater's 'family' isn't the laid-back paradise he was picturing when he signed up. He gives Metwater a solid alibi for the morning Asher was killed, though. Apparently he was in plain sight of most of the Family members from sunrise on." Dylan leaned over, one hand on the back of her chair. "I need to stay and interview him and Zach some more, and talk with some other people. I'll find someone to take you home and stay with you at your place."

"I don't need anyone to stay with me," she said. "I mean, you have the guys who hit us in custody now."

"They weren't specifically after you, anyway," he said. "Just dumb and ticked off, trying to scare us a little."

"They succeeded there." She stood and he walked with her to the door. "Do you think they'll give you any useful information?"

"I don't know. But we have to try." He squeezed her shoulder. "You're sure you'll be okay alone?"

"I can look after myself. I've been doing it a long time."

"I'll probably be here late, and in the morning I have to go to Denver. It may be a while before I see you again."

A hint of a smile touched the corners of her mouth. "I can wait."

Maybe she only meant the words politely, but he took them as a promise of more. A promise he intended to collect on when he returned.

Chapter Fourteen

Midnight had come and gone by the time Dylan and the other Rangers sent Abe and Zach to cool their heels overnight in the Montrose County Jail. Ethan and Simon were going to continue the interviews the next morning in hopes of getting something more useful out of them, but beyond a hint at some questionable financial practices, the two had so far produced no evidence of a serious crime.

Dylan sent Kayla a text before he left town. Have a good day and be careful, he typed.

You, too.

As romantic words went, they weren't much, but she wasn't resisting him the way she once had, so he took that as a good sign. He checked out a new Cruiser from the Ranger Brigade fleet and made the drive to Denver in a good mood despite a short night's sleep, and a little after noon he found the house in the Denver suburb of Highlands Ranch the Ashers called home.

Veronica Asher was a tall, curvy woman with dark skin who wore her black hair in dozens of long braids that hung past her shoulder blades. She answered the door of the stone-and-cedar home with a toddler on one hip and two other children peeking from around her legs. "Yes?" She eyed Dylan skeptically.

"Mrs. Asher? Dylan Holt, Colorado State Patrol." He held up his credentials. "I'm sorry to bother you, but I'm investigating your husband's death and I need to ask you some questions."

She held the door open wider, then shifted the baby. "Frankie, you take your sisters to the kitchen and tell MeMaw I said you could have ice cream."

"Okay, Mama." The boy eyed Dylan warily, but took the baby from his mother and left the room.

Mrs. Asher watched them go, then turned back to Dylan. "The FBI has already been to see me," she said.

"They may be conducting their own investigation, but I'm part of a task force charged with dealing with crimes on public land. Since your husband was killed in the Curecanti Wilderness Area, a federal preserve, we're looking into his murder."

She sat on the sofa and smoothed her skirt across her knees. Her beautiful face bore the marks of grief in her haunted eyes and drawn expression. "I'll tell you the same thing I told the Feds," she said. "I don't have any idea what Frank was doing out there in the middle of nowhere. He told me he had to work on a case—for his job. But the FBI tells me he was on personal leave."

"So he lied to you," Dylan said.

"It wasn't the first time."

He studied her—a beautiful, weary woman who had been betrayed by the man who had promised to love and care for her. Was that enough for her to have left those children and driven five hours across the state to murder him? "Mrs. Asher, you say you don't know what your husband was doing out there in the wilderness area, but do you have an idea? Any suspicions?"

"Maybe he went to see that girl he was sneaking around with."

"What girl?"

"I don't think you made it to lieutenant without being a better investigator than that," she said.

"What girl, Mrs. Asher?"

She looked away, her body rigid, as if it took everything in her to hold back the rage—or the tears. "Frank was having an affair with a girl young enough to be his daughter. Senator Pete Matheson's daughter, Andi."

"So you think Frank arranged to meet Andi in the wilderness area?"

"No, I think he arranged to meet her in a hotel. That's what he usually did. I have no idea how he ended up in the desert with his head blown off. Maybe he had another side dish I didn't know about and she had a jealous husband or boyfriend who followed Frank out there and did him in." She looked at him again. "If you find out who did it, be sure and let me know so I can shake his hand."

"Mrs. Asher, where were you on August 14?"

"I was right here. I took my older children to school and my baby to the pediatrician. I had lunch with my mother and bought groceries in the afternoon, and after the children went to bed I drank half a bottle of wine and cried myself to sleep, trying to decide whether it was worth putting my children through losing their father in order to divorce my cheating husband. What I was not doing was driving halfway across the state to shoot him."

"I have to ask," Dylan said.

"I know. But while you're at it, you ought to ask Andi Matheson what she was up to on August 14."

"I've already spoken to Ms. Matheson. Why do you think she could have killed your husband?"

"Maybe he cheated on her, too. Maybe she got tired of his lies."

"Did your husband lie to you about other things—things besides other women?"

"Haven't you been paying attention? The man worked for the FBI. His whole job was telling lies—deceiving people and pretending to be someone he wasn't in order to gather information. Too bad it got to be a habit he couldn't break."

"Do you know anyone else who might have disliked Frank enough to murder him?" Dylan asked.

"I imagine Frank made plenty of enemies, but I can't tell you who they are."

"Have you scheduled any kind of funeral service for your husband?"

"Why? Do you think all his enemies will want to come and gloat?" She looked away again. "I'm sorry. That was uncalled for. The service is Thursday. Grace Memorial Chapel, 6:00 p.m."

An older woman appeared in the archway between the living room where they sat and the hall. "It's time for Kendra's nap," she said, ignoring Dylan. "You know she always goes down better for you."

"It would be better if you left now." Veronica stood.

"If we learn any more about your husband's death,

we'll pass the information along to you," Dylan said. "I'm sorry for your loss."

"Oh, yeah, we're all real sorry." She ushered him to the door. "If you find out who did this, send me a report. I don't promise to read it, but I can at least save it for the children. I'm sure they'll have questions one day. Maybe it would be good to have some answers."

Dylan sat in the Ranger Cruiser in the Ashers' driveway and studied the neat suburban home. He couldn't understand what would compel a man like Frank to betray his family the way he had. Dylan's own father would have cut off his arm rather than hurt his wife and children. Dylan intended to live his life the same way.

He pulled out his phone and scrolled to Kayla's number. "Hi," he said when she answered. "How's your day going?"

"Okay." She sounded suspicious as always. He wanted to remind her that she could trust him, but trust wasn't something you could persuade people to do with words. Kayla would have to learn to trust him in her own time. "Are you in Denver?" she asked.

"Yes. I just talked to Frank Asher's widow."

"And?"

He glanced toward the house and thought he saw a curtain twitch. Mrs. Asher and her mother were probably wondering when he was going to leave. "I don't think she killed her husband," he said. "We'll check her alibi, but I'm betting it holds."

"Which leaves who—one of Daniel Metwater's disciples?"

"Or Andi Matheson."

"I'm not buying it," Kayla said. "You know it could

be some other person we haven't even zeroed in on yet."

"It could be. But what were they doing out in the desert that morning, so near Metwater's camp?"

"I guess if you can figure that out, you'll know who did it."

"There's a memorial service for Frank Asher Thursday. Want to come with me and see if anyone interesting shows up?"

"Is this your idea of a hot date?"

Was she flirting with him? That was a good sign, wasn't it? "If you agree to come with me, I'm sure I could make it worth your while."

"Are you expecting Frank's killer?" she said. "I think criminals watch enough TV these days not to fall for that trap."

"You never can tell. Do you want to come?"

"Sorry, I can't."

"What if I throw in dinner and a movie after the services?"

"You're really tempting me, but I have somewhere else I have to be."

"Somewhere more important than the funeral of a man you didn't know?"

She laughed. "It's just a meeting of the Western Slope private investigators, but I have to go."

"They can't have the meeting without you? Are you on the board? The guest speaker?"

"You're going to make me tell you, aren't you?"

"I'm very persistent."

She sighed. "I'm getting an award."

"Congratulations. What award?"

"It's stupid. Western Slope Private Investigator of

the Year. I'm sure it will just be some cheesy certificate or something."

"It sounds like a big deal to me. I can't believe you didn't want to tell me."

"Honestly, I don't even want to go. I'd rather attend Frank's funeral. But I don't think I can get out of it without causing a fuss."

"Go. Get your honor and celebrate. Congratulations."

"Think of me while you're at Frank's service," she said. "And let me know if anyone mysterious shows up."

He ended the call and left the Asher house. He couldn't believe Kayla had won this honor and hadn't even told him. She probably hadn't told anyone. She acted almost embarrassed at the thought of anyone making a fuss over her. Maybe her family hadn't been one to celebrate accomplishments the way his had. His mom had even baked a cake to celebrate Dylan's first touchdown on the high school football team.

His phone rang and he punched the button on the steering wheel to answer it. "Dylan, it's Carmen." The voice of his fellow Ranger sounded clear over the speaker. "Did you get anything from Frank Asher's widow?"

"We'll need to check her alibi, but it sounds like she was busy here all day with the family. As much as she feels betrayed by Frank, I don't think she would have killed her children's father."

"Are you on your way back to Montrose?"

"I am."

"Good. We've had a new development. Andi

Matheson showed up here a few minutes ago. She's pretty distraught. She says her father's dead."

"LARIMER INVESTIGATIONS. HOW may I help you?"

"This is Simon Woolridge with the Ranger Brigade."

The familiar clipped voice set Kayla's heart to pounding. She gripped the phone more tightly. "Is something wrong?" she asked.

"Andi Matheson is here at Ranger headquarters and she's asking for you. I tried to tell her you're a private detective, not law enforcement, but she's emotional. Can you get over here and see if you can calm her down?"

"I'm on my way." She shut down her computer and gathered her purse and car keys. Andi must be really upset if Snooty Simon had resorted to calling her. Had something happened at the camp? Or to her baby?

When she arrived at Ranger Brigade headquarters, she found Simon and a handsome BLM agent, who introduced himself as Michael Dance, clustered around a wailing Andi Matheson, who sat slumped in a chair. "Kayla!" she screamed when she saw her enter the room.

Kayla rushed to the young woman and bent to wrap her arms around her. "Andi, what's wrong?"

Michael brought Kayla a chair and she slid into it. Andi clung to her, her whole body shaking with sobs. "She's been this way for the last half hour," Michael said softly. "Ever since she got here."

"Andi, honey, calm down." Kayla pushed damp hair away from the young woman's tear-swollen eyes. "It's not good for the baby for you to be so upset. Tell me what's wrong and I'll do everything I can to help you."

"It's Daddy. He's dead!"

Kayla looked at Simon. He shook his head. "We don't know any more than you do," he said.

"Daddy's dead!" Andi wailed.

"Andi, look at me." Kayla grasped the woman's chin and turned it toward her. "How do you know your father is dead? Have you seen him?"

"Daniel told me he's dead. Daniel would never lie to me." A fresh wave of sobs engulfed her.

"Somebody get her some water, please," Kayla said.

Simon filled a paper cup at the watercooler by the door and brought it to her. "Drink this," Kayla ordered, and held it to the young woman's lips.

Andi obediently took a sip. "I can't stand it," she whispered. "I always thought I'd have time to see him again. I said such awful things the last time we were together." She rested her head on Kayla's shoulder and sobbed.

Kayla shook her gently. "Pull yourself together, Andi. Tell me exactly what Daniel said to you that has you so upset."

Andi sniffed and sat up a little straighter, wiping at her eyes with the back of her hand.

"Here, ma'am." Simon handed her several tissues from a box that sat near the cooler.

"Thank you." Andi blew her nose, then took a deep breath and turned to Kayla. "Daniel called me into his RV this afternoon and told me he had some sad news for me, but that I needed to be strong for the baby's sake."

"You are strong, Andi." Kayla squeezed her arm. "Strong enough to tell me everything that happened." She noticed Simon had grabbed a notebook from a nearby desk and was prepared to write everything down. "What did Daniel say?"

"He told me my father was dead. That I shouldn't be sad because he was in a better place now."

"Did Metwater say how he knew this?" Simon asked.

Kayla glared at him, but Andi didn't seem to notice. "He said he saw Daddy's body in a dream," she said, her voice choked with tears. "He said there was blood all over him, and that he knew that meant he was dead."

"Think very carefully," Kayla said. "This is really important. Did Daniel say he saw your father in a dream, or just that he saw your father?"

"He said he saw him in a dream." She looked at Kayla, her blue eyes as wide and innocent as a child's. "He's a prophet. He knows these things. If he saw Daddy dead, it must be true."

Kayla held her close, trying to comfort her. Someone needed to strangle Daniel Metwater and tell him to keep his phony prophecies to himself. What had he hoped to accomplish by upsetting Andi this way?

At last Andi's sobs subsided. She sat up and pushed her hair out of her eyes. "I have to get back to camp," she said. "It's almost time for dinner and I have to help cook." She squeezed Kayla's hand. "I just wanted someone else to know. A friend."

Kayla's eyes stung, she was so touched by these words. "I'm glad you came to me," she said.

"We'll drive you back," Simon said. "And while we're there we can have a word with Daniel."

"How did you get here?" Kayla asked.

"I hiked to the road and hitched a ride with a tourist," Andi said. She stood and Kayla rose also.

"I'll ride with you to the camp," Kayla said.

"That won't be necessary," Simon said.

"Please let Kayla come with me." Andi grabbed her hand and squeezed so hard she winced.

Simon scowled at her, then turned away. "Come on, then."

Chapter Fifteen

Andi remained subdued on the ride back to the camp. She stared out the window in the backseat of Simon's Cruiser. Kayla thought she might even have fallen asleep for a little while.

Up front, Simon and Michael didn't speak, either. Kayla knew Simon resented her presence, but she didn't care. Andi wanted her company, so she would do what she could to comfort her. Besides, she wasn't going to miss the chance to see what Daniel Metwater had to say for himself. Had he really seen Peter Matheson in a dream, or did he know the senator was dead because he'd killed him?

They arrived at the parking area for the camp and Andi opened her door before the Cruiser had come to a full stop. "Thanks for the ride," she said. "I have to hurry and help with dinner."

Simon reached to pull her back, but Kayla grabbed his arm. "Let her go," she said. "You'll have better luck with Metwater without her there, getting worked up again."

He pulled his arm away. "Don't tell me how to do my job."

"She's right," Michael said. "Metwater might be

more candid without one of his pretty followers to impress."

Simon said nothing, but turned and led the way up the path to the camp, Michael and Kayla walking single file behind him. The camp seemed busier than usual, with at least a dozen people moving about among the collection of tents and trailers. An older woman supervised two men who were unloading supplies from a battered blue Volkswagen bus. A trio of children played with a black dog, throwing a stick and laughing as he retrieved it. Other women milled around the cooking fire in the center of the camp, while a group of men and women worked to construct a kind of brush arbor in front of one of the trailers.

Several of the campers stopped to stare as the trio made their way across the compound, the utility belts of the two officers rattling with each step. They climbed the steps to Metwater's RV and Simon knocked.

No answer. Simon pounded harder. "Maybe he's not in," Kayla said.

Simon looked around. "Where's Metwater?" he called to a passing woman.

She stared at him, then shook her head and fled.

Simon beat on the door again. "Metwater, if you don't open up in three I'm going to break the door down."

"Can he do that?" Kayla whispered to Michael.

"He's concerned for the occupant's welfare," Michael said, stone-faced.

"One. Two."

The door opened and Daniel Metwater, in jeans and a loose shirt, glared at them. "You have no right to intrude on my home," he said.

Simon shouldered past him and the others followed. "If you prefer we can take you back to headquarters for questioning," Simon said. "Your choice." He turned to the young woman who sat on the black leather sectional that filled most of the RV's living room. "You can leave now, miss."

She hurried away, not even pausing to say goodbye to Metwater. After the door had closed behind her, Simon addressed Metwater again. "Do you want to come with us, or answer our questions here?"

"I don't have anything to say to you." He flopped onto the couch, one arm stretched along the back, the casualness of the pose a sharp contrast to Simon's rigid posture.

Kayla sat on the other end of the sectional. Metwater's eyes followed her, but he said nothing. "Andi came to see me and she was very upset by some things you had told her," she said.

"There was no need for that," Metwater said. "She would have found all the comfort she needed here, with her brothers and sisters."

"She said you told her her father, Senator Matheson, was dead." Simon, still standing, moved between Kayla and Metwater. "How did you know that?"

"I have prophetic dreams," Metwater said. "I don't expect you to understand."

"Then you must have known as soon as we heard about this particular prophecy we'd be here to question you," Simon said.

"Prophecy doesn't work that way. I only receive the messages my higher power wants me to have."

"So your higher power told you the senator was dead."

Simon's snide tone probably wasn't helping the situation any, but Kayla kept quiet, shifting to the right so she could watch Daniel as he spoke. "I saw Senator Matheson's body in a dream," he said. "He was covered in blood. Too much blood to be alive."

"Or maybe you saw his body in real life," Simon said. "When you killed him."

"I didn't kill the senator." Metwater's expression remained indifferent. "I've never even met him."

"How did he die?" Michael, who had remained standing near the door, spoke for the first time.

"I don't know," Metwater said.

"Where is he now?" Michael asked.

"I don't know that, either. All I saw was his body in a dream."

"And that was enough for you to decide to upset Ms. Matheson by telling her her father was dead?" Simon demanded. Kayla thought she detected real anger in his expression.

"What is upsetting for her now will be better for her in the long run."

"And who are you to decide that?" Simon loomed over him. "The poor woman was devastated. Did you enjoy that? Did you enjoy deliberately causing her pain?"

Metwater straightened. "Now she can grieve and get on with her life. She can finally cut her last ties with her old life and move into a brighter future."

"Was that your plan all along?" Simon asked. "Get rid of her lover, Frank Asher. Then get rid of her father. What about the child? Do you plan to do away with it, too?"

Metwater shoved himself to his feet, so that he was nose to nose with him. “Get out!”

“I could arrest you,” Simon said.

“For what? For having a dream?”

The two men stared at each other for a long, tense moment. Kayla glanced at Michael and saw that he had moved closer, his right hand hovering over the gun at his side, ready to defend his fellow officer if Metwater attacked.

Simon took a step back. “If I find out what you saw was more than a dream, I’ll be back,” he said. He strode out of the RV and the others followed.

“Kayla.” Metwater stopped her at the door.

Startled, she turned. “Yes?”

“Is Asteria—Andi—going to be all right?” he asked. “I thought knowing her father was at peace would be better than the uncertainty of not knowing what had happened to him. Then she left here, so upset, and I heard she had left the camp altogether. I sent people after her, but they couldn’t find her. I didn’t think she would go to the Rangers.”

His concern seemed genuine. “Have you ever lost someone you were close to?” Kayla asked.

His expression darkened. “My father and I were not close. I was always a disappointment to him.”

“What about your brother? Didn’t I read he died last year?”

“Yes.” He looked away. “Yes, David and I were close.”

“Then you know a little of what Andi is going through right now. If her father really is dead—and she can’t be sure until the body is found—it will take her time to process what has happened and heal. You can help by letting her take things at her own pace. Be there for her, but don't press her to behave any certain way."

"I'll keep that in mind. And thank you—for being a friend to Asteria, and for not judging me so harshly."

Simon and Michael were waiting at the bottom of the steps when Kayla emerged from Metwater's trailer. They said nothing on the walk back to the Cruiser, but once they were all buckled in, Simon turned to her. "What did Metwater have to say to you after we left?" he asked.

"He wanted to know if I thought Andi would be all right."

Simon grunted and started the car. The ride back to Ranger headquarters was as silent as the journey there had been, until they turned onto the highway. "What's your impression of Metwater?" Simon asked.

Kayla looked up and met his eyes in the rearview mirror. "I'm surprised my opinion matters to you," she said.

"Dylan said you were a good observer, and a good judge of character."

This information pleased her more than she cared to admit. She considered her impression of Metwater. "I think a man would have to be arrogant beyond belief to kill a man, then describe seeing the body and try to pass it off as a dream," she said.

"Metwater is pretty arrogant," Michael pointed out.

"Yes, but he's also very smart," she said.

"So you're saying you think he really had a dream where he saw Pete Matheson's body covered in blood?" Simon asked.

"Maybe. I mean, it doesn't sound logical, but I

guess stranger things have happened." Her father liked to claim he had prophetic dreams, too—usually as a way of providing "evidence" to support whatever decision he had already made. But a few times his dreams had been eerily prescient. Kayla had always dismissed this as coincidence, but still…

"Peter Matheson is missing," she said. "When someone goes missing, death is always a possibility, so Metwater may be manipulating that possibility to make himself look good."

"How so?" Michael turned to look over the seat at her.

"He says he saw the senator dead. If we find a body, he can say he foretold it, and show how powerful he is. He impresses his current followers and makes them even more loyal, and maybe he recruits a few new ones. If the senator turns up all right, Matheson can say what he saw in his dream was the senator injured—either physically or psychically—and he merely misinterpreted the image. He'll manage to talk his followers into seeing this as another example of how tuned in he is with a higher power."

"You've given a lot of thought to this," Simon said. "I'm impressed. And I agree—Metwater is up to something. And we're going to find out what."

THE SUN WAS setting by the time Dylan pulled into Ranger Brigade headquarters, and his shoulders ached from so many hours behind the wheel. Michael Dance looked up from his desk when Dylan entered. "How was Denver?" he asked.

"It's a big city with too much traffic." He glanced

around the empty office. "What happened with Andi Metwater? Did they really find the senator?"

"Pull up a chair and I'll fill you in."

A half hour later Dylan sat back and shook his head. "And Peter Matheson still hasn't turned up—dead or alive?"

"We checked and there's been no sign of him, nor any indication of foul play. The Feds checked out his house and his office. He's vanished. But Metwater sure convinced Andi that her father is dead."

"And we don't have any proof Metwater killed him."

"None." Michael drummed on his desk with a pencil. "And why admit knowledge of the crime if he did do it? He had to know it would focus all our attention on him as suspect number one."

"What about Zach and Abe? Did you get anything more out of them?"

"Not really. The district attorney agreed to a lesser charge of leaving the scene of an accident and reckless driving. They both have clean records, so they'll probably get off with a fine and probation. And they've agreed to remain available if we have any more questions."

"They're lucky to get off so lightly."

"Except they're still crying about Metwater taking their stuff. We told them that was a civil matter they needed to take up with a lawyer. After all, they did voluntarily sign everything over to the Prophet."

"I'm beginning to think that whole bunch over there are crazy," Dylan said.

"Crazy like a fox," Michael said. "Kayla thinks Metwater is using this so-called prophecy to manipulate his followers to think he has special powers. If the senator really is dead, he predicted it. If Matheson turns up safe and sound he can offer a different interpretation of his dream and still make himself look right."

Dylan nodded. "I guess it makes sense in a twisted way."

"She's pretty smart—Kayla, I mean." Michael gave him a long look.

"What?" Dylan asked.

"Are you two, you know, together?"

"I'm not sleeping with her, if that's what you're asking."

"No, that's not what I was asking. Relax. I just thought you seemed interested in her. And you've been spending a lot of time together."

Dylan shoved himself out of his chair. "Yeah, I'm interested in her. But I'm not sure she feels the same way about me."

"Has she told you to back off?"

"No."

"Then she's interested." Michael grinned.

"Who made you an expert?" Dylan asked. "They told me you were still a newlywed."

"Yep. And I met my wife while working on a case. She found a body in the wilderness, too. And she wasn't that crazy about me the first time we met, but I won her over." He stood also. "I'm calling it a night."

"Yeah, me, too." They left together, headed in the same direction out of the parking lot. But when Michael turned off toward the duplex he and his wife, Abbie, rented near the park, Dylan continued into town.

It was almost eight o'clock when he parked in front

of Kayla's house. Light glowed from the front windows and he caught the scent of jasmine from the vine that wound up the porch post. Maybe it was too late to drop in. He sat in the Cruiser, debating, until the front door opened. "Do you want to come in, or are you staking out the place?" Kayla called.

He climbed out of the car and went to her. He didn't even wait for her to say anything, but pulled her close and kissed her—long and hard, not holding back how much he wanted her. She went very still at first, then melted against him, her arms around his back, letting him take what he wanted.

When at last he released her, she took a step back, her cheeks flushed. "What was that for?" she asked, searching his face.

"I had a hard day and I needed to kiss you." He walked past her into the house.

She closed the door and followed him into the kitchen, where he was leaning into the open refrigerator. "I'm starved," he said. "I could use a sandwich, and a beer."

She grabbed his arm and tugged him away from the fridge. "Sit down. I'll fix you something to eat. Tell me about your day."

"You first," he said, settling into a chair. "I want to know about Andi Matheson. I hear she showed up at the office, distraught."

"Did you also hear why? That Daniel Metwater had a dream about her father?"

"Yeah. Ethan filled me in. Is she going to be okay?"

"I think so." Kayla took a bottle of beer from the refrigerator, opened it and handed it to him. "In a way, her faith in Metwater, or in whatever he represents for her, will help her in her grief, though I wanted to shake him for being an idiot."

Dylan took a long pull of the beer and felt more of the day's tension drain away. "Ethan said you thought Metwater cooked the whole thing up to make himself look good," he said.

"Probably." She pulled out bread, meat and cheese and began assembling a sandwich.

He watched her work, smooth and competent, her brow creased in thought. "Did your father do that kind of thing?" he asked. "Make predictions to manipulate people?"

"Oh, yes. He was a master at it. Even I believed him, when I was too young to know better." She turned to face Dylan. "When I was seven, more than anything I wanted this particular doll that was popular at the time. One of those dolls that come with a storybook and matching outfits and furniture and everything. My father told me that if I prayed and had enough faith, I would get the doll for Christmas. I spent hours on my knees that November and December. By the time Christmas came I was absolutely certain that doll would be mine."

"And you didn't get it." He could read the pain in her eyes, a wound that lingered even after all these years.

"No. I was heartbroken. When I started crying, my father told me it was my own fault, because I didn't have enough faith." She turned back to the sandwich. "I think that was when I stopped believing at all."

Dylan's fingers tightened around his beer. What kind of person treated a child that way? "Where was your mother?" he asked.

"Oh, she always went along with whatever my father said. She was an obedient servant, like we were all supposed to be. But I couldn't do it. I couldn't be good and follow orders only on his say-so. I had to see a reason behind his commands, and too often there wasn't any logic, just what he had decided he wanted, or what would make the best impressions on others."

"I wish I had known you then," Dylan said. "I would have told you you were better and smarter than any of them."

She set the sandwich in front of him. "Don't fret over it. I don't. Or not usually."

"That's right," he said. "After all, you're the private investigator of the year."

"On the Western Slope of Colorado. There aren't that many of us." She took another beer from the refrigerator, opened it and sat across from him. "There are also awards for rookie of the year for a brand-new PI, awards for senior investigators and heroism on the job and who knows what else. Apparently, when the current president took over, she was determined to wring as much publicity as possible out of what had been a fairly sedate dinner."

"So have you picked out a new dress to wear, and practiced your acceptance speech?" he asked.

She rolled her eyes. "I don't even want to think about it." She sipped from her beer. "Tell me about your day. You saw Frank Asher's widow. What else?"

"That was enough." He took a bite of sandwich, chewed and swallowed. "It isn't the violence of this job that gets to me," he said. "I expected that. And the danger—well, most cops will admit that can be a rush. But what grinds me down sometimes is all the ways people can be mean to each other. I sat there with Veronica Asher and all I saw was a beautiful woman, a devoted mother and daughter, who was worn out with grief and hurt. Her husband made a promise to be there for her and then he broke it. And Andi Matheson was hurt, too—by Frank Asher's lies and by Daniel Metwater's manipulation. You were hurt by your parents, and hearing about it makes me want to do something to make it right, but I know there's nothing I can do—for any of you."

She stood and came around the table and put her hand on his shoulder. "Move your chair back."

He scooted it back and she sat in his lap. "Being with you makes me feel better," she said. "Isn't that enough?" She kissed his cheek, then his lips.

He wrapped his arms around her and pulled her closer still, her breasts soft against his chest, her mouth warm and fervent, her tongue tangling with his, tasting of ale and promising a hundred ways to make him forget pain and worry and stress.

He caressed her thigh and moved from her mouth to feather kisses along her jaw. "If you're trying to distract me, it's working."

"Don't mind me." She began to unbutton his khaki uniform shirt. "Finish your sandwich."

"What sandwich?" He slid his hand beneath her T-shirt, the flesh of her torso soft and cool beneath his fingers. He skimmed over her bra, dragging his thumb across her pebbled nipple, and smiled at the way her breath caught. She squirmed, and it was his turn to gasp as she rubbed against his growing erection. She had most of the buttons on his shirt undone now, and bent to trace her tongue along his breastbone.

He nudged his thumb beneath her chin until she raised her head and met his gaze. "Not that this isn't fun, but where are we going with it?" he asked.

"I was thinking eventually we could go into the bedroom," she said. "Though I have a nice sofa, too, if that's more your speed. I wouldn't recommend the kitchen table, though."

"The bedroom sounds good." He rose, and she slid from his lap, though he steadied her with his arm. "You lead the way."

She glanced back at the table. "Are you sure you don't want to finish your sandwich?"

"Later." He nudged her bottom.

Kayla's bedroom turned out to be down a short hall, a small, comfortable room decorated in shades of blue, with a faded flowered quilt on the bed. The air smelled like her—soft and faintly floral. Fresh. In the doorway, she drew him to her once more and undid the final button on his shirt.

He went to work on the zipper of her jeans. "This is the nicest surprise I've had all day," he said.

"Why is it a surprise?" she asked. "You must have known I was attracted to you."

"I hoped, but you weren't sending the clearest signals. Or maybe I just wasn't good at interpreting them."

She shoved the shirt off his shoulders. "Is this a clear enough signal for you?"

"Oh, yeah." He slid out of the shirt, then pushed up the hem of hers. "Loud and clear."

He liked that she wasn't shy about undressing. And she didn't seem to mind that he waited until she was naked before he finished shedding his own clothes.

She had a slim, athletic body, with small breasts and rounded hips. Her skin was so soft, and touching her sent a thrill of desire through him. He cupped her breast and she arched to him, and when he bent to take her nipple in his mouth, she let out a long sigh that pierced him.

She urged him toward the bed, paused to fold back the covers, then pulled him on top of her. When her lips found his he closed his eyes and lost himself in her embrace, forgetting time and place and everything but the feel of her body beneath his roaming hands and lips. She responded with a fervor to match his own, kissing and caressing until he was half-mad with wanting her.

"Tell me you have a condom somewhere in this house," he murmured into the side of her neck.

"Bedside table."

He shoved himself up, reached for the drawer on the little table and pulled out a gold box. "These aren't even open," he said, frowning at the plastic wrapping.

"I bought a new box just for you." She laughed and snatched the package from him. "Go back to what you were doing. I wouldn't want to slow you dow—" The last word died on her lips as he slid down the length of her body to the juncture of her thighs.

"Don't let me slow you down," he said, his attention focused on her sex.

"Don't you dare stop," she said, and he heard the plastic on the box rip.

He slid his hands up to caress her hips, and lost himself in pleasuring her. Her soft moans and breathy gasps encouraged him, as he worked to bring her close to the edge, but not over. She let out a cry of frustration when he slid back up her body to lie beside her. "There's more where that came from," he said.

"Promise?" She pushed him onto his back and climbed on top of him, then took the unwrapped condom from the bedside table. "Ready to get dressed?" she asked.

"Ready."

Kayla kept her gaze focused on Dylan's face as she rolled on the condom. She'd fantasized about being with him, but the reality was so much better. He approached lovemaking with the perfect combination of humor and seriousness that kept her from feeling awkward, and his obvious eagerness for her bolstered her confidence and fueled her own desire.

His eyes lost focus as she squeezed his shaft, and she felt a sharpened pull of desire deep within her. Maybe she had wanted a man this much before, but she didn't think so. With Dylan she felt less wary, freer to be herself, than with any other man, and that freedom was a powerful aphrodisiac. He grasped her hips and guided her over him, and she let out a long sigh as he filled her. Yes, this was definitely one of the best decisions she had made in a while.

She set the pace, rocking slowly, then sliding up and down the length of him, enjoying the sensation, drawing out the pleasure, until he thrust up more firmly and dragged her down to press his lips to hers. The mood shifted to one of greater urgency, and she let herself ride the sensation, closing her eyes as he reached down to stroke her, building the tension, coiling tighter and tighter until her vision blurred and she lost her breath, a voice that didn't even sound like hers calling out his name.

His fingers raked her back as he increased the tempo, and then his own climax overtook him and he crushed her to him, pumping hard, leaving her breathless and exhilarated. He held her tightly for a long moment, his breath harsh in her ears, then rolled to his side, taking her with him, his arms securely around her.

"How's your day now?" she asked, when she had caught her breath. She traced one finger down his cheek, enjoying the roughness of his unshaved face.

"The best." He laid his head on her shoulder and closed his eyes. "The best."

"DYLAN, WAKE UP. Your phone is ringing."

Dylan opened his eyes and stared into Kayla's worried face. Still half asleep, he smiled and reached for her, but she pushed him away. "Your phone," she said. "Whoever it is has called back twice. You'd better answer it."

He struggled to sit, and wiped his hand over his eyes. He'd been deeply asleep, after an evening that had included the sandwich, a shower and another bout of lovemaking with Kayla before surrendering to slumber.

"Answer the phone." She nudged him.

He followed the sound of his ringtone to his trousers, which were on the floor atop his shirt and shoes. "Hello?" he croaked, then cleared his throat and tried again. "Hello?"

"There's been a development in the Matheson disappearance," Graham Ellison said. "Grand Junction Police found his car half submerged in an abandoned gravel pit. There was a bundle of bloody clothes shoved under the front seat. It looks like Daniel Metwater's prophecy might be true, after all."

Chapter Sixteen

Dylan met Graham and Simon at the Grand Junction impoundment yard a little after four in the morning. A forensics team was already at work on Matheson's car. Floodlights on tall stands illuminated the area around the vehicle, where technicians in white paper coveralls and booties combed the interior for hair and fibers, fingerprints, blood and any other evidence. Another man worked on the exterior, examining the body for recent dents and scratches, and collecting samples of soil from the tire treads.

"No good prints but a few of Matheson's own," Simon reported, after consulting with one of the techs. "They're sending the clothing to be tested to determine if the blood is Matheson's or someone else's."

"A dive team will search the gravel pit as soon as it's light," Graham said. "A second search team with cadaver dogs will comb the area around the pit."

"Any theories on what happened?" Dylan asked.

Graham shook his head. "A couple of kids apparently drove out here to make out and noticed the top of the car in the moonlight," he said. "The girl mentioned it to her older sister when she got home, the sister told the dad and the dad called the police. They got a wrecker out here to haul it out of the water and when they ran the plate they knew they had something big."

"I think we should bring Metwater in for questioning," Simon said. "Maybe with this new development we can sweat a confession out of him."

"He's not going to break that easy," Dylan said. "And we don't have enough evidence to hold him. Until we have Matheson's body, we can't even charge him with murder. And he'll have a dozen followers who will swear he hasn't been anywhere near Grand Junction in months."

"Except Abe and Zach said they thought that's where he was for a big chunk of yesterday," Simon said.

"Which I'll admit makes him suspicious," Dylan said. "Except he supposedly had Andi Matheson with him, and considering her reaction to news that her father was dead, I can't imagine her conspiring with Metwater to kill the senator."

"Stranger things have happened," Simon said. "And if we don't detain him he's liable to disappear."

"We'll wait until we have a body," Graham said. "By then we may have enough evidence to make something stick. In the meantime, Michael and Marco are watching the camp. There's only one way into that canyon. The Prophet won't leave without our knowing it."

Simon pressed his lips together. Dylan knew he wasn't happy with this decision, but he wouldn't argue with their captain. Dylan sympathized with Simon's point of view. "Have you come up with anything in Metwater's background that we can use?" he asked. "I tried doing a little digging on my own, but you're better at background forensics than I am."

Simon shook his head. "We've got nothing. He's

the blue blood heir to his family's manufacturing fortune. His dad died last year—apparently he'd had a heart condition for years and died on the operating table, so we can't blame that on the son. Metwater inherited equally with his twin brother, David, who was apparently the family screwup. He embezzled money from the family firm, got crosswise with some Mafia types and ended up dead. His body was found dumped in a river. He'd been shot in the head. A month later, Daniel declares he's had a spiritual revelation, sells the family business and takes his evangelical show on the road, recruiting followers to join his Family. And a few weeks ago they end up in our jurisdiction." He made a face. "Aren't we lucky?"

"So, no ties to the brother's death?"

"The local cops say he's clean. And it was pretty common knowledge that the brother was in over his head with organized crime."

"Maybe Daniel's religious conversion had more to do with fear the mob would come after him than a spiritual revelation," Graham said.

Simon shrugged. "If it did, he's taking it to extremes. If I had the fortune he has, I wouldn't be living in an RV in the middle of nowhere, without running water and electricity."

"When does their camping permit expire?" Dylan asked.

"Next week," Graham said. "But they can move to another spot in the wilderness area and renew the permit. For now, I would just as soon they stay put, where we can keep an eye on them."

They split up, Dylan and Simon in separate vehicles to head back to the Ranger Brigade offices,

Graham to a meeting with FBI agents in the Bureau's Western Slope division. Dylan turned down his radio and contemplated the barren hills and red dirt washes that filled the landscape between Grand Junction and Montrose. He debated calling Kayla, to hear her voice and see how she was doing. Was she having any second thoughts about spending the night with him? Could he say anything to make her feel more comfortable with the decision?

Better to hold off on calling her. Right now it would be too easy for him to betray his own feelings and frighten her off. The truth was, he was falling in love with Kayla. Yes, it was happening fast, but he was as sure of his feelings as he had ever been sure of anything. He wouldn't take things too fast or try to push her, but he would find a way to gain her trust—to show her he was nothing like her father and the others who had let her down before.

He was almost to Montrose when his phone rang. "Lieutenant Holt?" a woman's voice asked hesitantly.

"Yes? Who is this?"

"This is Veronica Asher."

Dylan signaled and pulled to the side of the road. "How can I help you, Mrs. Asher?"

"I received something very strange in the mail this morning. I should probably call the Bureau, but frankly, I feel more comfortable talking to you."

"What did you receive?" he asked.

"It was a plain white envelope, addressed to Mrs. Frank Asher, with no return address, though the postmark is Grand Junction. Inside were a bunch of money cards—you know, the credit card things you can put a cash balance on. I called the number on the back of the cards and each one of them is worth twenty-five hundred dollars. Twenty-five thousand dollars in all."

"Twenty-five thousand dollars?" Dylan repeated. "Does that amount have any significance for you?"

"No. Except it's a crazy amount of money to get in the mail."

"Was there anything else in the envelope? A note?"

"There was a sympathy card, the kind you could buy in any store. No signature or anything."

"Do you know anyone in Grand Junction who might have sent you the money?" Dylan asked. "Maybe a charity or an organization that thought you needed the funds?"

"I don't know anyone in Grand Junction," she said. "And whatever his other faults, Frank left us well provided for. I don't know what to think about this except…" Her voice trailed away.

"Except what?"

"Do you think the money might be from Frank's killer? A kind of guilt payment or something?"

"That's definitely worth looking into. What have you done with the money cards?"

"Nothing. They're right here in the envelope they came in. But I wasn't being very careful at first. They'll have my fingerprints on them."

"Leave them there and call Frank's supervisor at the Bureau. They'll have the best resources to investigate this. Or I can contact them for you if you like."

"Would you? Every time I have to deal with them, all I can think is that they knew what Frank was up to and none of them bothered to tell me. That may be an unfair assessment, but it's how I feel."

"I'll call them and ask them to send over an agent—maybe someone who didn't work with Frank."

"Thank you."

She ended the call and Dylan mulled over the information she had given him. Daniel Metwater had a fortune at his disposal. It would have been easy enough for him to send one of his followers to one or more locations around Grand Junction to purchase the money cards with cash. He and Andi might even have purchased the cards themselves when they came to town yesterday. Even if Metwater hadn't personally pulled the trigger to kill Asher, he might have ordered one of his followers to do so. Maybe he had decided to alleviate some of his guilt by paying off Asher's widow.

Dylan put the Cruiser into gear and pulled back onto the highway. He would do as he had promised and notify the FBI of this latest development. But he would tell Graham first, and the Rangers would conduct an investigation of their own, one focused on Daniel Metwater and his followers.

KAYLA DRIFTED IN and out of sleep after Dylan left, her slumber disturbed by replays of their time together. While he had been with her, she had been sure a relationship with him was the best decision she had made in years. But away from his magnetic presence she felt less certain. She had been honest with him when she told him she didn't do relationships. She didn't have the emotional tools to be comfortable relying on someone else, and she had managed fine alone for years. He, on the other hand, was close to his family and more than comfortable with the idea of settling down with a wife and kids and the whole storybook setting. She didn't know how she would fit into that kind of life. Trying to make things work when they were so different was probably setting them both up for disappointment.

At seven she rose and made coffee, then switched on the television to the local morning program. "Very early today Grand Junction police recovered a vehicle belonging to missing senator Peter Matheson from an area gravel pit," the news anchor announced. "Divers are scheduled to search the pit for the body of the senator, who has been missing since last Friday." Video footage showed a late-model sedan being pulled from the water, the scene lit by floodlights. Superimposed on these images was a still photo of Senator Matheson, one Kayla recognized from his campaign posters.

Though Dylan had shared the news of the discovery before he had left for Ranger headquarters, seeing the footage on television somehow made it more real, Kayla found. She switched off the TV and returned to her bedroom to dress. She should have known news of the discovery of the senator's car would spread quickly. It was probably the top story on every channel. Even cut off from communication the way they were, Andi and the other Family members were bound to hear about this sooner rather than later. Dylan hadn't said, but Kayla suspected he or someone else from the Ranger Brigade would show up at the camp to question Daniel Metwater once more. Andi would be upset all over again. Kayla needed to be there for her.

She was on her way out the door when her phone

rang. Hoping it was Dylan, she hurried to answer it, not even bothering to look at the screen.

"Hello, is this Kayla Larimer?"

"Yes." Kayla checked her phone. *Caller Unknown.* Had someone from the press gotten hold of her number?

"This is Madeline Zimeski, with the Colorado Private Investigators Society. I noticed we hadn't received your confirmation for the awards banquet this Thursday."

"I've been a little busy."

"So I can put down that you're coming? And how many guests?"

"Just me." She shifted her water bottle, digging in her purse for her car keys.

"You don't have someone you'd like to invite to see you receive your award?"

She thought of Dylan, then pushed the idea away. Why would he want to sit through a boring awards banquet? Besides, he had to attend Frank Asher's funeral. "Just me," she repeated. "And I really have to go now."

"I'll put you down for one then. Let me know if you change your mind about bringing a guest. I look forward to seeing you there. And congrat—"

Kayla ended the call and headed out the door to her car. With luck she could make it to the camp before either Dylan or someone who had seen the television reports got there. She could break the news of this latest development to Andi gently and avoid sending the girl into tears yet again.

Traffic was light and she pushed the speed limit on her way out of town. She had just cleared the city limits when her phone rang again. A check of the screen showed an unknown number once more. If Madeline Zimeski had called back about that stupid awards banquet, she was going to get an earful.

Kayla was tempted not to answer, but what if it was Andi, calling from a pay phone? With one eye on the road, she took the call. "Hello?"

"Kayla? It's Pete Matheson. I need your help."

Chapter Seventeen

Kayla's car swerved and she almost dropped her phone. Heart pounding, she pulled over to the side of the road, leaving the engine idling. "Senator? Are you all right? Where are you? Are you hurt?"

"I'm not physically injured, but I need your help."

"Of course. Do you want me to call someone for you? Do you need money or someone to come get you?"

"Promise me you won't go to the authorities. Promise me now or I'll hang up and you'll never hear from me again."

"Of course. I promise. Don't hang up." Was someone there with him, telling him to say that? Did he have a gun to his head? What were the chances of Dylan and his team tracing this call?

"How is my daughter?"

The question was so conversational and unexpected that for a moment Kayla couldn't find the words to answer.

"You've seen her, haven't you?" the senator asked. "You told me you were going to see her."

"Uh, yes, I've seen her. She's well. Though she's very worried about you."

"Is she? I thought she might be glad to be rid of me."

"No! That isn't true. She was beside herself when she thought you were hurt. She loves you very much." The truth of those words made Kayla's chest hurt. Andi did love her father, no matter their differences.

He was silent for so long she thought he might have ended the call. "Senator? Are you still there?"

"I'm still here." He cleared his throat, and when he spoke his voice was rough with emotion. "I never meant to hurt her. You must believe that. Nothing I have is worth as much to me as my child."

"I believe Andi knows that. All she wants is for you to be safe."

"I need you to help me."

"To help you do what?"

"Can you take me to see Andi? Without anyone else knowing?"

"Why don't you want anyone else to know?" she asked. "So many people have been looking for you."

"No." His voice was sharp. "It's too dangerous at this point. When the time comes, I will notify the police. But not yet. Not until I've spoken with Andi."

"All right. I can do that." He wasn't really giving her a choice.

"I have an address for you, where you can pick me up. If you show up with any law enforcement, I'll go away and you won't hear from me again."

"I'll come alone, I promise," she said. "And I won't tell anyone where I'm going."

"Then get something to write this down. It will take you a while to get here, but I'll be waiting."

DYLAN TRIED TO reach Kayla, but her phone went straight to voice mail. Was she deliberately avoiding his calls? "Hey, Kayla, it's Dylan. I'm going to be out of touch for a while, on a stakeout. I'll call you when I'm back in cell range and maybe we can get together for dinner or something. Take care." He wanted to add something else—I miss you? I love you? But maybe it was too soon for that. He didn't want to scare her off. He settled for a simple "Bye" and stowed the phone once more.

Veronica Asher had scanned the money cards she had received and emailed the file to Simon, who was back at Ranger headquarters, combing through the identification numbers on the cards, trying to determine where they had originated from. Graham had made some calls to the FBI and the Bureau had promised to send a sympathetic agent to collect the cards from Mrs. Asher. They had agreed to work with the Rangers on canvassing Grand Junction area gas stations, convenience stores and grocery stores with pictures of as many of the Family members as they could obtain, in hopes of getting a positive ID on the purchaser of the cards. Once they had nailed that individual, they could use him or her to get to Daniel Metwater, or whoever had sent the cards.

The Rangers were also trying to get a warrant to access Metwater's bank records. A withdrawal in the amount of the payment to Mrs. Asher would be another strong indication of guilt. He might say he was only doing an anonymous good deed for the widow of the man who had been killed near his camp, but a prosecutor was likely to see things differently.

For now, Dylan was taking his shift watching the camp for any suspicious activity. He parked his Cruiser out of sight about a mile from Dead Horse

Canyon and hiked to the rocky overlook DEA Agent Marco Cruz had selected as the best vantage point to survey the action in the compound without being seen.

"Anything going on?" Dylan asked Marco after the two had exchanged greetings.

"That big RV is Metwater's, right?" He handed over the high-powered binoculars he'd been using to surveil the camp. "He's had a lot of people going in and out of there—mostly women, but a few men. But I haven't seen him come out."

"How do we know he's still in there?" Dylan asked.

"No vehicles have left the camp, and Randall is watching the road. If Metwater tried to climb out over the rocks we'd see."

Dylan settled more comfortably among the boulders and raised the binoculars. "Any sign of Andi Matheson?"

"She visited Metwater about an hour ago. When she came out it looked like she'd been crying. Any news on the senator?"

"Nothing yet. The FBI is canvassing the neighborhood near where they found the car, hoping to find a witness who saw something."

"It will be interesting to see whose blood is on those clothes," Marco said.

Dylan lowered the binoculars. "You don't think it's the senator's?"

Marco shrugged. "Who knows? It will just be interesting. One more piece of the puzzle." He stood and picked up his backpack. "I'm outta here."

"Hot date?"

He grinned. "You know it. Lauren is flying in from filming a documentary in Texas."

Dylan had forgotten that Cruz was married to television newscaster Lauren Starling. The two had met when she'd been kidnapped last summer and he'd been involved in her rescue. "I'm looking forward to meeting her soon," Dylan said. "Tell her I'm a fan."

"When I see her again, you are going to be the last thing on my mind."

Marco left, moving soundlessly down the rocks, and Dylan settled back to watch. The summer days were growing shorter and here in the canyon the sun set quickly, plunging the area into darkness. As the air cooled and stars began to appear, activity increased in the camp. Dylan trained the binoculars on the center area, where two men were building a bonfire while a third man swept the dirt around the fire pit. About eight o'clock Metwater emerged from his trailer and walked over to supervise the preparations. Even at this distance, Dylan had a sense that something important was about to happen down there. Were they initiating another new member? Celebrating some religious rite he wasn't aware of? Throwing a birthday party?

He had a hard time picturing Metwater involved in something as innocent as a birthday party, but that was the kind of thing families did, wasn't it?

Metwater must have heard the news about Peter Matheson by now. Had Andi's tears when she left his trailer been because he had told her her father's car had been found in the quarry? Could whatever ceremony the group was preparing for have anything to do with the senator?

Carefully, Dylan moved a few feet farther down the slope, hoping for a better view of the action. He had no way of calling headquarters or summoning help without leaving his observation post and traveling back to the road. Better to see if he could figure out what was going on before he did that.

ANDI DROVE SLOWLY in the fading light, craning her head to read the addresses on the ramshackle buildings she passed. Her shoulders ached with tension, and her gun lay on the console beside her, loaded and ready. Everything about this setup felt like a trap to her. She wished now she had disobeyed the senator's orders and had at least let Dylan know where she was. He had tried to reach her shortly after she pulled onto the highway after talking with the senator, and she had let the call go to voice mail, knowing if she spoke to him directly she would give in to the temptation to share the news that Senator Matheson was alive and here in Montrose.

She hit the brakes as she spotted the address she wanted. She double-checked the number against the notes she had made, but this was the place. A faded sign identified the collection of boarded up buildings as the Shady Rest Motel. Judging by the prices on the gas pumps out front, this place hadn't been in business for at least a decade. Was someone holding the senator hostage here? She picked up the gun and climbed out of the car. "Senator Matheson!" she called, keeping her voice low.

"Hush. I'm right here."

She turned and saw him climbing into the passenger seat of her car. She might not have recognized him if she had passed him on the street. Instead of his usual tailored suit and tie, he wore a faded Hawaiian shirt and baggy khaki pants with a rip in the knee. He was unshaven and his hair needed combing. He looked more like a homeless person than a United States senator.

"Don't just stand there. Get in the car," he ordered.

The voice was the same at least, and the imperious tone. She slid back into the driver's seat, but kept her weapon at her side. "Senator, what happened to you?" she asked. "Are you all right?"

"I'm fine," he snapped, and fastened his seat belt.

"Do you need something to eat? Some water? Medical care?" She should have thought to bring him some food. She had a bottle of water and a first-aid kit, but if he needed more…

"I told you, I'm fine."

"The police found your car last night," she said.

"I heard on the news. I was hoping they wouldn't discover it for a while yet—that I'd have more time. Does Andi know?"

"I imagine she does by now." Surely someone would have reached the camp with the news.

"You said she was upset before. I imagine this won't calm her fears any."

"Daniel Metwater told her you were dead. He said he had a dream in which he saw your body covered in blood."

Matheson snorted. "Maybe he really is a prophet, after all." He leaned closer, studying her more intently. "What happened to your face?"

The bruises from her kidnappers' attack had faded to a sickly yellow-purple and most of the swelling had subsided, though she still wouldn't win any beauty contests. "I was attacked while working a case," she said. Not exactly a lie.

"What case? Who hit you?"

She started to tell him that was none of his business, but she wanted to keep him talking. Eventually, she would work the conversation around to where he'd been and what he had been doing. "Two men attacked me outside Frank Asher's hotel room," she said. "They tried to kidnap me, but law enforcement intervened. One of the kidnappers was killed and the other one is in the hospital." Memory of the senator's connection with the event surfaced and it was her turn to scrutinize him. "Oddly enough, they were driving a van that was registered to you," she said. "A vehicle you used in your last campaign."

"None of that was supposed to happen," he said. "They were supposed to grab the laptop and any papers and leave. They weren't supposed to interfere with anyone or anything else."

She blinked, letting his words sink in. "Senator, are you saying those men were working for you? Under your orders?"

"I should have known better than to hire two petty criminals," he said. "I'm sorry you were injured. That should never have happened."

"Why did you hire them to steal Agent Asher's things?" she asked.

"I take protecting my daughter very seriously. I had to insure he didn't have anything incriminating in his possession."

"But, Senator—"

"Start the car." He motioned to the ignition. "We need to get out of here."

She turned the key. "Where are we going?"

"I want to see my daughter. I want you to take me to her."

"Do you want to stop and get something to eat first? Maybe a change of clothes?" Seeing her father like this was going to be a shock for Andi.

"No. I know what I look like. Now get going. We don't have any time to lose."

THE FAINT SCRAPE of a boot on the rocks above alerted Dylan that he wasn't alone. He turned to see Ethan Reynolds making his way toward him. "I came to relieve you," Ethan said. "Anything happening down there?" He jutted his chin toward the camp.

"They're building up the bonfire," Dylan said. "They're into rituals. I think they're getting ready for something like that."

"Cults use ritual to bond the members together," Ethan said. "They can also be useful in reinforcing the leader's message, applying peer pressure, even brainwashing."

"I forgot you were the cult expert."

Ethan settled more comfortably onto the rocks. "I'm not sure this group qualifies as a full-fledged cult. The members seem to have autonomy, and the freedom to come and go."

"Yet none of them are leaving," Dylan said.

"Some of them may have nowhere else to go," Ethan said. "Groups like this tend to attract the disenfranchised."

"Andi Matheson has somewhere else to go, yet she's staying."

"She's found something she's looking for here."

"So what's your opinion of Metwater—twisted murderer or charismatic creep?"

Ethan shrugged. "Maybe neither. Maybe he's a sincere spiritual follower who rubs you the wrong way."

"Is that really what you think?"

"No. I'm voting for charismatic creep. He's slippery and manipulative and I think he's probably hiding something, but I can't see him pulling a trigger and blowing Agent Asher's head off. That's too emotional and visceral for him. He's a plotter, not a hothead."

"What about the money someone sent Asher's widow?"

"Maybe the money came from somewhere else."

"Where?"

"Maybe someone who read about the murder in the paper and felt sorry for the widow and three kids. Someone who wanted to remain anonymous."

"For the sake of our case, I hope it's not something that innocent."

"What about Andi Matheson?" Ethan asked. "Maybe she killed Asher because he left her high and dry with a baby."

"Maybe. But she seems even less likely than Metwater to kill a man in cold blood."

The fire below blazed up and Dylan shifted to look through the binoculars again. "Something happening?" Ethan asked.

A group of people had gathered around the fire, men and women in various stages of undress, their bodies painted, colored ribbons in their hair. As the flames leaped higher, they began to chant, the sound drifting up with the scent of piñon smoke in the clear night air.

"What are they saying?" Dylan asked. "I can't make it out."

"I think it's Latin," Ethan said.

Dylan lowered the binoculars. "You know Latin?"

He grinned. "I was a Catholic altar boy—but I've forgotten pretty much everything." He listened a moment. "I think it's something about sin. And maybe redemption or penance." He nodded. "Definitely penance in there."

Dylan raised the binoculars again. The door to the RV opened and Metwater emerged, dressed in the loincloth again, symbols traced in red and black and white paint on his chest and arms—circles and stars and arrows. They looked, Dylan decided, like a poor attempt at Native American imagery.

"Is that a dagger in that sheath at his waist?" Ethan had pulled out a second pair of binoculars and was focused on the scene below.

"It looks like the one I saw him with before," Dylan said.

"Maybe he's going to finish the ceremony you and Kayla interrupted the other night," Ethan said.

"Maybe." Or was he up to something more sinister?

Metwater clapped his hands over his head and the chanting ended midsyllable. When all eyes were on him he spoke, his voice loud and clear enough that Dylan could make out most of what he was saying. "We are assembled tonight to address the sin in our midst. We must break the chains of iniquity that bind us and purify our souls going forward."

"I'm not liking the sound of this," Dylan muttered. He could still picture the dark-haired girl with the blade to her throat, her eyes wide and terrified. Metwater could talk all he wanted about symbolic sacrifices, but it had all looked pretty real to Dylan.

Metwater motioned two men forward. They carried shovels and at his direction began shoveling coals from the fire and spreading them out in a wide path that led from the fire to Metwater's feet, some three yards away. Someone began drumming, a deep, steady rhythm like a heartbeat. Metwater addressed the crowd again, but the drumming made it impossible for Dylan to make out his words.

"I think he's telling them they're going to walk on the hot coals," Ethan said.

Dylan lowered the glasses once more to stare at him. "Seriously?"

"Fire walking has been practiced for thousands of years as a religious rite and a team-building exercise."

Dylan looked back to the camp. Metwater was motioning to the coals, while two women set basins of water at either end of the glowing path. "Now I know they're crazy," he said.

Ethan moved in beside him. "I've heard of this, but I've never seen it done before," he said. "Supposedly, the risk of injury is fairly minor, because the cool bottom of the foot does a good job of spreading out the heat, and the embers themselves actually don't conduct that much heat."

"That still doesn't make me want to walk barefoot over a bunch of hot coals," Dylan said.

"Who will be the first?" Metwater asked, his voice raised to carry over the drumming.

The silence from the group gathered around the fire was almost eerie.

"Asteria!" Metwater called. "Asteria, you shall be the first, to show us the way."

Andi stumbled forward, as if she had been pushed from behind. Dylan tensed. "What does he think he's doing?" he asked. "She's pregnant."

Smiling, Metwater took Andi's hand and led her to the start of the fiery path, the coals glowing red against the darkness. "Don't do it," Dylan muttered.

Metwater knelt beside Andi and began to tie up her long skirts. She was trembling, the vibrations visible through Dylan's binoculars. He swore and stood. "I'm not going to let this happen," he said, and prepared to climb down the rocks. All he had to do was get within firing range.

With a loud cry, Andi whirled and fled into the darkness, leaving Metwater—and Dylan—staring after her.

Chapter Eighteen

Kayla let out the breath she'd been holding as Andi fled the fire-walking scene. Some of the tension went out of the senator's shoulders, too. "Thank God she hasn't lost all her senses," Matheson said. He turned away. "Come on, let's go find her. Now will be a good chance to talk to her without the others around."

He led the way around the camp. "You act as if you've been here before," Kayla said as she followed him.

"Only once. But I've got a good memory for details. Comes in handy in my job. Now if we keep traveling in this direction, we should be able to come up on the back of the camp. I'm guessing Andi would have fled to her quarters."

He sounded so sane and competent. A businessman with a job to do—such a contrast to his downtrodden appearance. On the drive over he had refused to answer Kayla's questions about what had happened to him and what he had been doing. He wouldn't deny or confirm that he had been kidnapped, and refused to discuss anything about his car or the clothes that had been found in it. "None of that is my concern right now," he said, in answer to all Kayla's queries.

As he had promised, the path they navigated led to the back of the camp. They could still hear chanting and shouts from the bonfire, but the noise was muffled by distance. Kayla wondered if anyone had taken Metwater up on his invitation to walk on hot coals. She noticed the Prophet hadn't volunteered to demonstrate how it was done.

"You'll have to show me which shelter is hers," Matheson said.

"The big tent, next to Metwater's RV." Kayla pointed to it. A lantern hung by the door, and a fainter glow emanated from within.

Matheson paused to draw himself up to his full height. "I'm ready," he said.

Before Kayla had time to react, he left the shadows where they had been hiding and strode the short distance to the tent. He entered without knocking or otherwise announcing himself. Kayla hurried after him and ducked inside in time to see Andi turn toward them, one hand to her throat. The young woman stared, mouth open, face ghostly pale.

Kayla hurried forward, afraid Andi would faint. "It's okay," she said, helping her to a low stool. "Your father wanted to see you."

"Daniel told me you were dead," Andi said, her gaze fixed on her father.

"Daniel was wrong." Matheson pulled another stool alongside his daughter. "I had to make sure you were okay," he said.

"I'm okay." She clutched his hands. "Better now that you're here. What happened, Daddy? I don't understand. Daniel said you were dead, and then we heard the police found your car, with bloody clothes inside."

"I had to go away for a while. And I will have to go away again soon." Matheson smoothed the hair back from her face. "I'm sorry I hurt you. The last thing I wanted to do was hurt you."

"You didn't hurt me," she said. "I'm okay, really."

"Frank Asher hurt you." Matheson grimaced. "I'm sorry I ever hired the man."

"Frank's gone now, Daddy. He's dead." Andi's lip trembled, but she regained her composure. "It doesn't matter. All that matters is that you're okay. I'm sorry. I'm sorry for all those terrible things I said to you. I just…I needed to live life my way, not your way."

"I know, honey, but you need to leave this place." He patted her hand. "That man—Daniel Metwater—he isn't good for you. What kind of man expects a pregnant woman to walk over hot coals? What is he trying to prove?"

"He wanted to free me from myself," Andi said. "He told me walking over the coals would burn away all my guilt and pain. But I wasn't brave enough. I didn't have enough faith."

It's not about faith, Kayla wanted to say. *It's about control*. But she bit back the words, not wanting to interrupt this moment between father and daughter.

"Come back home, Andi," Matheson said. "You'll be safe there. You can have your baby there and you'll never lack for anything. I have plenty of money put aside to make sure of that."

"My baby." She cradled her belly and her voice took on a crooning quality. "Poor baby. Her daddy's dead."

"Frank can't hurt you anymore," Matheson said. "I made sure of that."

Kayla started and moved closer. Andi stared at her father. "What do you mean?" she asked. "Someone killed Frank."

"I killed him," the senator said. "He told me he was coming here to see you again, to ask you not to make trouble for him over the baby. He wanted you to pretend he wasn't the father. He thought the affair would be bad for his career."

"You killed Frank?" Andi asked.

"I only intended to warn him off—to tell him to leave you alone. But he wouldn't listen. He was determined to see you. He'd already hurt you so much. I couldn't stand the thought of him hurting you again. I only meant to threaten him with the gun, but he wouldn't back down. I had to show him that I wouldn't back down, either. I had to protect you."

Kayla gasped. She hadn't even realized she'd made the noise until Matheson turned on her. "You weren't supposed to hear that," he said. "I was having a private conversation with my daughter."

"We all heard you, Senator." The tent flap lifted and Dylan stepped inside, followed by Ethan Reynolds. "Put your hands up and stand slowly," Dylan said. "Peter Matheson, I'm arresting you for the murder of Frank Asher."

"No." Matheson stood and backed up, until he bumped into Kayla. She was groping for her weapon when he grabbed her, his grip surprisingly strong. He wrenched the gun from her grasp and held it to her throat. "Don't come any closer or I'll kill her," he said. "You know I'll do it. I don't have anything to lose."

THE SIGHT OF that gun at Kayla's throat turned Dylan's blood to ice. He met her gaze, and the courage he saw behind her fear strengthened him. He holstered his weapon and took a step back, his hands out at his sides. "Take it easy," he told Matheson. "No one wants any trouble."

Ethan already had Andi and was ushering her out of the tent. Dylan trusted he would go for backup. Meanwhile, he had to find a way to deal with Matheson and save Kayla.

"You need to leave, too," Matheson said, one arm across Kayla's chest, the barrel of the gun pressed to her throat. "We're going to go away and you'll never see me again."

"You can go," Dylan said. "But leave Kayla behind. She hasn't done anything to hurt you."

"I'll let her go when I'm safely away from here."

"Where are you going to go?" Dylan asked. "You know if you leave, every cop in the country will be looking for you. If you give yourself up now, the courts will go easy on you. Any jury would understand a father wanting to protect his daughter."

"That's right. All I wanted to do was protect her. Asher laughed at me when I told him he didn't deserve her. Laughed!"

"He *didn't* deserve her," Dylan agreed. "And Kayla doesn't deserve to be involved in this. Let her go, Senator."

"I'm not a bad person," Matheson said. "I sent money to Asher's wife and kids, to try to make up for their loss. They're better off without him, too, I think."

"We know you're not a bad person," Dylan said. "Prove it by letting Kayla go."

"I won't hurt her," Matheson said. "I don't want to hurt anyone."

"I know you don't. Let her go."

Matheson no longer looked like the confident, determined man who had walked into the camp. He looked old and confused. Lost. "Where is Andi?" he asked. "Where's my girl?"

"She's safe, Senator," Dylan said. "But she's worried about you. She needs to know that you're safe, too. Haven't you put her through enough?"

"I only wanted to protect her." The barrel of the gun slid down, no longer pointed at Kayla's throat, though a shot at that close range would still be lethal. Kayla stiffened, and Dylan read the determination in her eyes.

Matheson seemed to gather himself also. "I'm leaving now," he said, some of the fog cleared from his expression. He took a step forward, tugging Kayla after him.

Kayla lunged forward, throwing all her weight into Matheson's back. He lost his balance and stumbled, and the gun went off, the bullet burying itself in the rug at his feet. Dylan pulled Kayla clear and shoved her behind him, then trained his gun on the senator, who lay sprawled on the floor. "Put your hands behind your head and don't move," Dylan ordered.

Matheson groaned, but did as commanded, and Ethan stepped in to cuff him. Once he was secure, Dylan holstered his weapon and turned to Kayla. "Are you all right?" he asked.

"I'm fine." She was pale and her voice shook, but her eyes were clear and steady. "You showed up just in time."

He pulled her close and cradled her face against his chest, shaky with relief now that the danger was past. "We were doing surveillance on the camp and saw you arrive with Matheson," he said.

"Did you know he had killed Agent Asher?"

"No. But I imagine the lab reports on Matheson's clothes will show the blood is Frank Asher's," Dylan said. "He must have sunk the car himself to hide that evidence."

"When I picked him up this evening he told me he had hoped it would take police longer to find the car—that he'd have more time. Time for what?"

"To figure out how to get out of the country? To prepare to turn himself in?" Dylan shook his head. "Who knows?"

Kayla turned to watch Ethan lead Matheson away. "I feel sorry for him," she said. "I think he blamed Asher for his own estrangement from Andi."

"Killing the man didn't solve anything."

"I know, but love can make people do the wrong thing for the right reasons."

Dylan pulled her more tightly against him. "I think my heart stopped for a second when I saw you with that gun to your throat," he said. "All I could think of was that if I couldn't stop him from hurting you, I wouldn't be able to live with myself."

She looked up at him. "I don't need a man to rescue me. Just one to be there alongside me."

"I'm starting to figure that out."

"Then you're starting to understand me," she said.

"I don't have to understand you," he said. "I just want to be with you."

"That's a good place to start." She slid one hand

to the back of his head and pulled his mouth down to hers. The kiss, more than her words, told him everything was going to be all right between them. They'd found Frank Asher's killer. Kayla was safe. And they would figure out a way to meld her need for independence with his need to protect. Life wasn't a fairy tale, but he still believed in happy endings.

Epilogue

"Do I look all right?" Kayla tugged at the skirt of the dress she had chosen for the awards banquet and frowned at her reflection in the mirror. "I hate this stuff. You know that, don't you?"

Madeline Zimeski, president of the Colorado Private Investigators Society, patted Kayla's back. "You look lovely, dear. I'm only sorry your family couldn't be here to see you receive your award."

"They live out of state," Kayla said. It was easier than explaining the truth—that she didn't have any family who cared enough about her to walk across the street, much less attend an awards banquet.

Madeline checked her cell phone. "It's almost time for the awards," she said. "We'd better get back." Kayla had been hiding in the ladies' room when Madeline had come in search of her. Clearly, the president wasn't going to let even one honoree escape her moment in the spotlight.

Reluctantly, Kayla followed her back to the front table where she had been seated, her back to most of the crowd. She'd managed to choke down a few bites of dinner and make polite small talk with the board members and other honorees at her table, and was counting the minutes until she'd be free to leave.

Madeline strode to the podium and made a show of adjusting the microphone. "Now is the point in the program I know we've all been waiting for," she said. "Our annual awards. Each year we honor those of our members we feel are the finest representatives of our craft." She droned on about the voting process, the history of the organization and some other things Kayla couldn't focus on. She squirmed in her chair and wished she had opted for a drink from the bar.

"And first up, our senior private detective of the year, Malcolm Stack."

A tall man with a shock of white hair walked to the podium to accept the plaque Madeline handed him. Kayla stared at her water glass, mentally rehearsing the brief thank-you she planned to deliver.

"And for our Western Slope PI of the year, Kayla Larimer."

She had expected Madeline to draw out the ceremony more, so the announcement of her name caught her off guard. Awkwardly, she shoved back her chair and stood as a smattering of applause rose around her. As she started toward the podium a chorus of shouts and whistles echoed from the back of the room. Startled, she whirled to see Dylan standing at a table near the back. Beside him, his mother and father stood also, both clapping wildly.

"Kayla?" Madeline prompted from the podium.

Flustered, Kayla made her way to the stage. Madeline shoved the plaque into her hand, and a flash almost blinded her. "Say something," Madeline hissed, and nudged her toward the microphone.

"Umm..." Kayla stared at the plaque. Nervous laughter rose from a few people near the front. She cleared her throat and fought for composure. "Thank you for this honor," she said. She looked out across the room and caught Dylan's eyes. He was grinning like a fool, and gave her a thumbs-up. She couldn't help but smile. "And thank you to all the people who have helped me along the way. And to those who continue to support me now."

She managed to make it down the steps from the dais without tripping, but instead of returning to her chair, she walked the length of the room to join Dylan and his parents.

"Congratulations," Bud Holt said, and pumped her hand.

"We're so proud of you," Nancy added, and patted her arm.

Kayla looked at Dylan. "What are you doing here?" she asked. "Aren't you supposed to be at a funeral?"

"You didn't think I was going to pass up the chance to see you honored like this, did you?" He hugged her to him.

"I guess you don't really need to go to Frank Asher's funeral now that the case is closed," she said.

"Even if it was still open, I wouldn't miss your big night," he said.

She held out the plaque and read the text, which proclaimed her as the Western Slope Private Investigator of the Year. "It's not such a big deal."

"It is to me." He kissed the top of her head. "I'm proud of you," he said. "You deserve this."

She turned to his parents. "I can't believe you came," she said. "Thank you so much."

"You're special to Dylan, so you're special to us, too," Nancy said. "Congratulations." She nudged her husband. "Now, I think we should leave these two alone."

They left and Dylan led Kayla into the hallway. "Senator Matheson agreed to a plea deal today," he said.

"I guess that's for the best," she said. "How much time will he serve?"

"He pleaded involuntary manslaughter. He could be out as soon as eighteen months."

"What about Andi?"

"She wants to stay with Metwater and his bunch. She says she feels at home there."

"I guess Daniel Metwater was innocent, after all."

"Of murder. I still think he's up to something." Dylan pushed open the door to the parking lot. "We'll be keeping a close eye on him, as long as he's in our jurisdiction."

"I plan to stay in touch with Andi, too," Kayla said. "It's funny, when you think about it, how the two of us hit it off."

"Not so strange, really. You both are independent women and felt you didn't fit in with your family's lifestyle."

"I guess that's one way to look at it."

"Were you surprised to see us tonight?" he asked.

"I can't think of when I've been more surprised." She stopped at the edge of the covered walkway that led up to the building and turned to him. "Am I really special to you?"

"You didn't know that already?"

She pressed her palm against his chest. "I guess I did, but I wanted to be sure."

"I love you," he said. "Did you know that?"

"I love you, too. And it scares me. I've never allowed myself to love this much before."

"Don't be afraid." He pulled her to him. "You can count on me, Kayla Larimer. I'm promising here and now that I'm always going to protect you and care for you and do my best for you."

"You know the best thing about all of that?" she asked.

"What?"

"I believe you. And I'm going to do the same for you, Dylan Holt."

"That's what matters most, isn't it?" he said. "Knowing we can count on each other."

"Mmm." She pulled his face down to hers. "Less talking, more kissing."

"Yes, ma—mmm."

* * * * *

THE RANGER BRIGADE: FAMILY SECRETS
series is just getting started.
Don't miss the next book from Cindi Myers when it goes on sale in July 2017.

Look for it wherever
Mills & Boon Intrigue books are sold!

Want more Cindi Myers? Check out
THE MEN OF SEARCH TEAM SEVEN:

COLORADO CRIME SCENE
LAWMAN ON THE HUNT
CHRISTMAS KIDNAPPING
PHD PROTECTOR

Available now from Mills & Boon Intrigue!